WORSHIPPING SMALL GODS

WORSHIPPING SMALL GODS

Richard Parks

PRIME BOOKS

WORSHIPPING SMALL GODS

———

PUBLICATION HISTORY:

"Kallisti" appeared in *Realms of Fantasy,* February 2002, revised for this edition; "The Penultimate Riddle" appeared in *Realms of Fantasy,* August, 2005; "Yamabushi" appeared in *Realms of Fantasy,* December 2003; "Worshiping Small Gods" appeared in *Realms of Fantasy,* August 2003; "The Plum Blossom Lantern" appeared in *Lady Churchill's Rosebud Wristlet* 12, June 2003; "Fox Tails" appeared in *Realms of Fantasy,* June 2005; "A Hint of Jasmine" appeared in *Asimov's SF,* August 2004; "Voices in an Empty Room" first appeared in *Haunted Holidays,* Russell Davis, ed. DAW Books, October 2004; "Hanagan's Kiyomatsu, 1923" is original to this collection; "Diva" is original to this collection; "A Time for Heroes" appeared in *The Shimmering Door,* HarperPrism, Katherine Kerr, ed. 1996; "Death, the Devil, and the Lady in White" appeared in *Realms of Fantasy,* April 2005; "The Right God" appeared in *Realms of Fantasy,* August 2004; and "The Wizard of Wasted Time" is original to this collection.

Prime Books
www.prime-books.com

This book is dedicated with affection and boundless gratitude to Parke Godwin.

TABLE OF CONTENTS

―――――

KALLISTI..9

THE PENULTIMATE RIDDLE...21

YAMABUSHI...29

WORSHIPPING SMALL GODS...40

THE PLUM BLOSSOM LANTERN..46

FOX TAILS...52

A HINT OF JASMINE...75

VOICES IN AN EMPTY ROOM..101

HANAGAN'S KIYOMATSU, 1923..120

DIVA..136

A TIME FOR HEROES..178

DEATH, THE DEVIL, AND THE LADY IN WHITE.....................203

THE RIGHT GOD...219

THE WIZARD OF WASTED TIME...234

KALLISTI

The God of War looked at his sister with open admiration. "You are a marvel, Eris, but what's this about?"

She looked up from her workbench, the sweat of honest toil glistening on her plain face. The object on the bench was beginning to take shape. Ares didn't yet know what it was, but he surely knew what it meant: trouble. Ares liked trouble, and so naturally he adored his younger sister. Eris, Goddess of Discord.

"They didn't invite me!" she said. It was more of a snarl.

"Who didn't invite you? To what?"

"Zeus! Hera! My own mother and father! They didn't invite me to the wedding feast for King Peleus and that slut, Thetis."

Ares shrugged. "Eris, you're my own dear sister but it's reasonable that no one wants Discord at a wedding. Especially this one."

"I know what the oracles said but that doesn't matter," Eris said primly. "What does matter is that I wasn't asked. They *should* have asked, you know."

"Would you go if they did?"

"Of course not! You know I hate parties." She gave him a disturbing look. "You were invited, weren't you?"

Ares nodded. "Weeks ago. I was thinking of not going." He noticed her glare and quickly added, "Out of respect for you, of course." Ares might have liked trouble, but he wasn't a total fool.

Eris turned back to her work, slightly mollified. Being Eris, she was never more than slightly mollified once her anger was in full flower. Strangely enough, Ares, the God of War, was one of the very few who could do it.

Eris smiled then. "Oh, I think you should go, Brother Dear. After all, I am. Invited or not."

There was a hint in her tone that Ares found intriguing. He waited until

9

the object of her attention was finally completed. She held it up, flushed with triumph.

Ares just stared at the thing. He examined it this way and that, read the inscription, stared some more. "It's a golden apple," he said finally.

"Yes," Eris said, as if the fact was self-evident. Which, Ares had to admit, it was. Beyond that he was having a great deal of trouble finding the point. "It's lovely," he said, "but what's it for? A wedding gift?"

Eris glared at him. "Of sorts, but it's not just the apple! It's the apple and the word *together*, otherwise it doesn't work."

"It just says 'Kallisti.'"

" 'To the fairest,' yes," Eris confirmed with more patience than was normal for her.

"I still don't understand," Ares said.

Eris sighed a sigh of pure martyrdom. "Just trust me, Brother—go to the wedding feast. You don't want to miss this."

Paris, Prince of Troy, was a very confused young man. One moment he was watching his flocks like any good shepherd who also happened to be a Prince of Troy. All he had done was find an apple of pure gold lying half-buried and dirty beneath a bush, brushed it off, and read the single word inscribed on it: "Kallisti." The next moment there were three extremely lovely goddesses in front of him. The really strange part was that he was having a hard time being happy about either. The situation was playing a lively game of spin and toss with his sense of reality and yet the sheep on the hillside grazed on, unconcerned with the troubles of gods and mortals. Paris rather envied those sheep just then.

"So let me understand this: by the mere act of finding this golden apple I have been chosen by Zeus himself to judge which of the three of you goddesses is the most beautiful?"

Hera glared. "We said that already. Weren't you listening?"

Paris bowed his head. "It's just that I'm unable to believe my great good fortune."

"Don't lie," Athena said. "It's unwise to lie to a goddess. You're shaking."

"My sister's right for once," Aphrodite said. "So tell the truth and choose me and we can put all this unpleasantness behind us."

Athena snorted. "You? I'm much prettier than you."

"Hah! How can you say so? Around the world, legions of men old and young alike quake in their sleep for desire of me!"

"That doesn't make you pretty, Sister Dear," Athena said. "That makes you a brothel-sign."

"Witch!"

"Roundheels!"

Hera raised a hand in command. "Squabbling before mortals is unseemly. Besides, we all know the apple belongs to *me*. Choose quickly, my good Paris."

Paris was having a rough time all around. Choosing seemed impossible. Hera was rather matronly but that didn't detract a whit from her poise and refined, regal beauty. Athena was tall and dark haired, and to call her statuesque didn't even do her justice. As for Aphrodite, well, Paris' knees wobbled and his reason turned to mist whenever she smiled at him.

Paris finally shook his head. "No."

All three sets of goddess eyebrows raised in anger and Paris saw the fires of Hades burning for him in their eyes.

"No? You have no choice!" they said as one.

"Your pardon, Your Divines, but by your own words I have one choice: who is to get the apple. Whichever one I favor, I make enemies of the other two. Disputes between goddesses and mortals tend to be a bit one-sided, if the stories are true."

"Nonsense," Hera said. "Zeus made us swear to this. We won't hurt you. Will we?" All three shook their heads in emphatic denial.

Paris was not reassured in the least. "It's not particularly unwise for a goddess to lie to a mortal," Paris said, "since there are seldom consequences for *her*. Yet it's seldom to the mortal's advantage when she does so."

All three goddesses merely looked away, whistled or shuffled their feet and tried to look innocent. Paris managed to keep his tone light though the effort cost him. "This is a very important decision, as you no doubt agree. At the least I need time to consider."

"You have until tomorrow," Hera said.

"Early," Athena said.

The Goddess of Love demurred. "Not too early. I need my beauty sleep."

"Yes, you do," Athena said sweetly.

"For immortal goddesses you seem particularly concerned about time," Paris said, but hastily added, "Until tomorrow morning then, Fair Ones."

The goddesses disappeared, and it was only then that Paris put his head in his heads and wailed. "What am I going to do?"

"Not much you can do, really," said someone who hadn't spoken before now. Paris looked up.

Just to the side of where the goddesses had been there was a rather plain young girl leaning against a cedar, a fierce frown on her face. That was just surface appearance; by the glow around her Paris recognized a goddess when he saw one. "Who are you?"

"My name is Eris."

"Not . . . " Paris didn't finish.

The girl nodded, looking a little less fierce and a little more melancholy. "Goddess of Discord. The same. That's my apple, by the way."

"It is? But you weren't with the others . . . "

She sighed. "I didn't say I wanted in that cattle contest, dolt! I said it was *mine*. I made it."

"You made this?" The implication of what the girl—and she did look like a girl, and no goddess—was saying sank in. "This is all your fault!"

"It's my doing. My fault?" She shrugged. "Not in my view. Some few decades ago the gods held a wedding feast for King Peleus and the nymph Thetis. I wasn't invited. Of course I had to do something to get back at them, so I sent that apple rolling in."

Paris held up the apple. "And how, pray, does *this* get back at *them*?"

Eris grinned. "It ruined the party, silly. It was a rather good party before those three started squabbling over my gift. Zeus was terrified it would interfere with the wedding itself. He was whiter than frost."

"Zeus? *Afraid*? Why?"

Eris sighed. "Because the oracles said Thetis was destined to bear a son who would be greater than his father. What if randy Zeus had fathered a child on her before he knew that? Or another god had done so, for that matter? By securing Thetis' marriage to a mere mortal, Zeus kept the child from becoming a threat to his power. And it worked, too. Thetis eventually gave birth to mighty Achilles who, while magnificent, is mortal. The prophecy is fulfilled."

Paris was having a lot of trouble getting his mind to expand enough to grasp the nuances of divine politics and society. All he knew was that, come tomorrow, his life wasn't worth a pile of sheep dung. "Eris, why are you here? Have you come to gloat?"

"I wasn't thinking past the party, to tell the truth," Eris said. "I expected Zeus to give the judgment, and have the other two mad at him. The sly boots wiggled out of it by passing the judgment on to whoever found the apple after he cast it into the world. I've been looking for the apple myself off and on, but you found it first, unfortunately for you." She looked him up and down. "Pity. For a mortal you're not too ugly."

Paris put his head back in his hands. "Too kind. So. If you had known, would it have changed anything?"

"Probably not," Eris said. "I'm a goddess. You're a mortal. Mortals are always getting trampled underfoot as we go about our business, and that's the price of being a mortal. I pay my own for being what I am."

Paris looked up again. "What are you talking about? What could be the disadvantages of being divine?"

Eris nodded. "Spoken with the typical certainty of one who doesn't know what he's talking about. How would you like it if everything you were or wanted to be was out of your hands?"

There was such pain and anger in the girl's voice that, for a little while, Paris forgot his own difficulties. "What do you mean?"

"I mean I'm the Goddess of Discord. Do you think it's because I'm a troublemaker by nature?"

"Meaning no offense . . . aren't you?"

She put her hands on her hips. "I feel very strongly and I act on what I feel. I won't say I'm sorry I ruined Zeus's party since I'm not, but that was as far as I meant to go. Yet because I'm a goddess everything I do is an act of creation and has a life beyond me."

"What about the three who were here earlier?"

Eris shrugged. "It's the same: Hera is queen because she's bossy. In a human that's annoying but in a goddess it's worse. Athena actually is very wise when her pride isn't in the way, but no one who takes her advice really understands it, and often comes to grief. Aphrodite is in love with the idea of love. She can't help it and she can't stop, and you *know* what kind of misery that can cause."

"Not yet I don't," Paris said.

Now Eris blinked. "You've never been in love?"

"No. Nor am I likely to, before the two goddesses who *don't* get the apple do something horrible to me. Have you?"

Eris frowned. "Love? I don't think so." It was clear from her tone that the question had never even occurred to her.

Paris sighed. "I hear it's wonderful and terrible all at once. It's something I'd like to find out."

"Then do it."

Paris laughed. "How? This time tomorrow I'll probably be dead."

Eris shook her head. "None of those three will just kill you outright; they swore to Zeus they would not harm the judge. That won't stop them from seeking revenge, mind, but they'll have to be subtle about it and subtlety takes time. You use that time to fall in love."

"I haven't been able to do so in twenty years of life. I doubt there's that much left to me, even with the delay."

Eris looked thoughtful. "By Zeus's decree the apple sought an honest judge. So tell me the truth: is there one of those three you consider most beautiful?"

Paris shook his head. "That's another problem. It's like trying to choose among three stars in the sky! I can't do it."

"Then don't." Paris opened his mouth to protest but Eris raised her hand. "No, listen to me—in their hearts each of those harpies knows she is the fairest, apple or no. They just want the apple for what it represents. It's the apple that is their goal, not the judgment as such. So don't choose who is the fairest—choose *which one gets the apple*. Let the best offer win."

"They're going to bribe me?"

Eris rolled her eyes. "Of course! You don't think they care for fairness, do you? I got you into this. I cannot get you out, but for what it's worth I say listen to what they offer. You make enemies of two goddesses tomorrow, and you and I both know what that means. As long as you're paying the price, choose the merchandise you like best."

Paris thought about it. "Aphrodite . . . I could choose love?"

Eris smiled sadly. "You can choose whatever you want. Another advantage of being mortal, though for some strange reason you seem to feel it a curse."

Eris slowly faded away.

"Don't . . . " Paris started to say "don't go" to the Goddess of Discord, but felt foolish. Still, hers was the closest thing to a friendly voice Paris had heard all day.

Eris just smiled. "Don't worry, Paris. I am Discord. More than likely you will see me again if you wish to or not."

And Paris knew she was no doubt right.

Whatever Eris' skills as an advisor, it was soon clear she made a good enough prophet. That night in his dreams the three goddesses came to Paris. Hera, being Queen of Heaven, arrived first, splendid and regal. She had forsaken much of what made her appear human to enter the realms of dreams. She was more aspect than woman now, all symbol and dark fire. She took a look around Paris's dreams first, but they were rather innocuous, tentative things that night. If she was looking for his heart's desire she didn't find it.

"I can make you ruler of the world," she said. "Most men would like that."

"If I give you the apple?" Paris said.

Hera glared. "Of course if you give it to me, fool!"

"It is a fine offer," Paris said.

"You won't get a better one," Hera said, and then she left. No haggling, no chance for discussion. Every inch the Queen of Olympus. Paris shrugged and got back to his dreams.

Athena was next. She appeared in full armor and glory blazing, but it was only a dream and Paris was not consumed.

"I offer you great wisdom," she said.

"For the apple?"

"If you can ask that, then you need my gift more than you think," Athena said, and that was all. She vanished.

The dream was calling Paris back. It threatened to turn into something pleasant and vivid, but Paris knew there was no point. He waited for what he knew was to come.

Where the other two simply appeared, Aphrodite made an entrance in a golden chariot pulled by lions. There was one other difference: where the other two told Paris what they would give him, Aphrodite asked a question.

"All right, Mortal. What do you want?"

"I want to fall in love before I die."

The goddess frowned. "Is that all?"

Paris remembered what Eris had told him. "Since I'm likely to die very soon, I consider that a great deal," Paris said. "And neither great wisdom nor great power will do me much good in these circumstances. So I'm asking for what I want."

The Goddess of Love nodded. "For a mortal, you're fairly quick. Yes, it's unlikely those other two harridans will let this go, even though by all right the apple is mine anyway. Very well; I'll grant you your wish if tomorrow morning you give the apple to me."

"How?"

"I'll give you the most beautiful mortal woman on earth as your bride. You'll fall in love then, I wager."

"You mean Helen of Sparta? She's married to Menelaus!"

"You give me the apple and I'll arrange it."

"All right, but it's just a lump of gold," Paris said. He knew there was no point, but thought it needed to be said.

"Nothing is just what it is made of," Aphrodite said, and she drove her chariot right out of his dreams. The next morning Paris gave the apple to Aphrodite and sealed his doom.

Eris had been hearing the prayers for a week or more. It was very much a surprise; no one prayed to Eris. No one wanted to attract her attention. Now someone did. Someone familiar. Eris was too stunned to do much about it for a long time.

Finally she turned to her brother. "Ares, can I ask you something?"

Ares looked up from his new armor. "Hmmm? What is it? I'm busy. Hephaestus has no reason to love me and I just *know* there is a curse on this armor somewhere. I'm going to find it."

"Your armor can wait. I want to know: have you ever regretted something you've done?"

Ares grunted. "I'm a god. Why should I?"

"Don't you regret sleeping with Aphrodite, Hephaestus's wife? You should."

He laughed. "No, I regret getting caught. It was embarrassing. Do I regret sleeping with Aphrodite? No. In fact I'll do it again if I get the chance."

"Knowing that one you probably will," Eris said dryly. "So. Why the new armor? Especially since the Divine Blacksmith is still annoyed at you?"

"Couldn't wait. It's for the *war*, Sister. Haven't you heard? Paris of Troy has kidnapped Menelaus's winsome wife. There's to be a big war about it. I can hardly wait."

Eris didn't breathe for a while. Being a goddess it didn't really hurt her, but Ares apparently noted the changing colors in her face after a bit. "You didn't know? I'm surprised. It was all because of your apple, you know. Aphrodite told me the whole story. You've outdone yourself, Eris."

"Thank you," Eris said quietly. "I worked really hard on that apple." She turned to leave.

"Where are you going?"

"To see the oracles. As a goddess it's my prerogative to take an interest in the world."

The war was going very badly for Troy. Not too surprising, since most of the gods had lined up against Priam's city. Paris watched the battle from a palace window. Much had been made of the fact that he had shirked the fighting before now, but the truth of the matter was he was better suited to shepherding than fighting, and had never shown much interest in the latter before. Yet Hector was dead now, and without him Paris's options were fast diminishing. His armor had been brought, but he dismissed his servants and stood by the window, watching men die.

"I wish I had the choice over again," he said aloud, to no one in particular.

"Who would you have chosen then?"

Paris turned around. It was Eris. He hadn't seen her since the day of the Judgment. "I prayed that you would come."

"And I heard you," Eris said. "Finally. I suppose you have the right to see your Nemesis . . . metaphorically speaking." She came to the window herself, looked out over the carnage below. "I'm the Goddess of Discord. I suppose I should be enjoying this."

"You don't look as if you are."

"It's the lot of goddesses to be defined by their impulses. I wanted revenge, but not this. I didn't know it was all pre-ordained."

"What do you mean, Eris?"

"I mean I've consulted oracles since. If it helps, take comfort that you were fated to choose Aphrodite. A free choice, yet all foretold. Don't try too hard to understand that. It doesn't help."

Paris laughed. "I knew I was doomed. I didn't know just how thoroughly. It's hard to take comfort from that."

Eris shrugged. "How is Helen?"

"Lovely almost beyond mortal comprehension. Also vain, self-centered and with as much wit as a rutting sow. No wonder Aphrodite picked her out."

"I'm sorry."

"Aphrodite betrayed me. She got me Helen at the cost of this war with the Greeks! There must have been another way."

"There wasn't. I told you the war was fated, and even the gods don't muck with destiny."

Paris frowned. "How can you say that? Yes, you sent the apple but didn't this all really start because Zeus was trying to cheat fate?"

Eris smiled then, faintly. "No." Paris just looked at her, uncomprehending, and Eris went on, "As I told you: the oracle said that Thetis was destined to bear a child greater than the father. The oracle did not say, 'Thetis will bear a child who will one day overthrow Zeus.' If she *had*, Zeus would have been as doomed as you are. Yet there was a danger, and he moved to reduce it. He did what he could. That's what we all do, gods and mortals alike."

"I can do nothing."

"You can't do much," Eris corrected, "but that's not nothing. Take your bow and string it."

Puzzled, Paris did as she instructed. Eris selected an arrow from his quiver and daintily licked the barb. She handed the arrow to Paris. "I'm full of poison. That's my nature," she said. It sounded like an apology. "I've envenomed the tip. Shoot Achilles with it."

Paris just stared at the arrow. "What good will that do? Achilles is invulnerable; even Hector couldn't kill him."

"Achilles is mortal, just as you are. And he is fated to die in this war."

"So? Does that mean I'm fated to kill him?"

Eris smiled then, sadly. "You do see the difference. No, the oracle just

18

said that he will die. This part isn't fate, Paris. This part is the thing you can change. It's a small thing, I know, but as I said we all do what we can."

Paris took the arrow. Achilles rampaged through the battlefield below like a force of nature, striking down Trojan warriors left and right. There was a light of battle in his eyes like a beacon, or a funeral pyre, or the flames that were beginning to rise within the city itself. The screams of the wounded and dying reached up to Paris' window.

"If I kill him, will it save my city?" Paris asked.

Eris shook her head. "No. Yet if you do this, perhaps, something of what it was may be spared. Some of your people may live. I don't know for certain. I do know that if Achilles carries this fight before his death no one will be spared."

"Then it's enough." Paris put the nock to the string.

Eris watched him almost shyly. "I almost forgot to ask. Did . . . did you ever find love?"

"Yes, I think so," he said.

"I'm glad about that."

Paris smiled faintly. In fact, Paris didn't think she looked very happy at all, and he understood why. It felt good, understanding one thing the goddess did not.

Eris went on. "It was what you wanted, I mean. You deserved as much, despite Aphrodite's betrayal. At least she fulfilled that part of the bargain."

"No, she didn't."

"But you said . . . "

"That I fell in love. I did. It changes nothing, but it did happen."

Eris looked confused and, after that, just a little afraid. "Mortals die all the time," she said, as if to herself. "With or without our help. One more doesn't matter . . . " Her small hands balled into fists. "Oh, sod that!" Eris looked right at Paris. "I never should have made that damned apple," she said.

"Gods and mortals alike make mistakes, Eris. I should have given the apple to you."

Eris just stared for several moments. "But why?" she finally asked. "Because I made it?"

Paris smiled at her. "Most artisans do not own what they make. No, Eris. Because you never meant to harm me, and never played me false. There's beauty in that, and more than I had sense to realize. I should have given you the apple because it belongs to you by right. Kallisti. The Fairest."

For a moment Eris simply looked at him. "You would give the apple to me, the one responsible for all your misery?"

"Yes," Paris said. "I would."

"Mortals are such fools," she said, but it didn't sound like an insult this time. "Choose."

Paris turned back to the window and let the arrow fly.

THE PENULTIMATE RIDDLE

It is no secret that a sphinx loves riddles and is compelled to ask them at every opportunity. Since it is also a sphinx's nature to devour those who do not answer her riddles, it's likewise well known that sphinxes are the most solitary of creatures. What is not so well known is that sphinxes are very sociable beings at heart, so the circumstances dictated by their fundamental natures seem a cruel irony at best. Doubtless a curse was involved somewhere.

So it was with equal parts excitement and sorrow that the sphinx named Helena watched a young man approach along the stony road that ran past her cave.

"At least he'll have to talk to me before I kill him," she said.

Helena had been sunning herself, as was her custom, on top of the overhang shielding the entrance to her den. She was quite young as sphinxes go, no more than two hundred or thereabout. Her lion's body was sleek and tawny, her forepaws tipped with magnificent claws, and her wings at once more powerful and more lovely than a swan's. As for the womanly portion of her body, well, a man who spied that first could be forgiven for forgetting all about the rest of her, men being as men are.

She wasn't a particularly vain creature despite her beauty, though she did allow herself to wonder what the man would say when he got close enough to see her—reactions varied but were always interesting, usually involving either screams or begging. Yet what actually happened wasn't quite what she expected.

"Oh, there you are," he said, and he smiled at her.

Helena frowned. "Umm, aren't you surprised?"

"Not a bit," he said. "This is a lonely road by a hillside, and clearly the sort of place where a sphinx might live, yes?"

"Well . . . yes. Am I to understand that you were looking for me?"

He shrugged. "You? Well, I would have if I'd known how lovely you

21

were." At that Helena actually blushed, and he continued, "but the truth is I was looking for *a* sphinx. I didn't know that you would be the particular sphinx. That was merely my good fortune. My name is Leontas, by the way."

She blinked. "Pleased to meet you. I'm Helena. I'm also somewhat confused. Good fortune? You do know what a sphinx does, don't you?"

"I have heard," he said. "Yet I also have a suspicion that I wish for you to confirm. Frankly it's a question that's nagged me for much of my life, so much so that I finally decided that it might well be worth risking that life to find the answer."

Helena smiled. "I don't answer questions. For that you want the Oracle at Delphi, though why anyone thinks they can get a useful answer out of that addled creature is beyond me. I mean 'Cross the river and you will destroy a great kingdom'? What was that man thinking?"

"I don't know what King Croesus was thinking, but *I'm* thinking that you won't answer questions, but you'll ask them?"

Helena sighed. "It was rhetorical. You know that."

"Fine, then. You won't answer my question, and I won't answer your riddle. Fair is fair."

"Not answering is the same as failing to answer, and I'll eat you regardless," Helena pointed out.

"Perhaps," Leontas replied, "but is it really as much fun as me getting the riddle wrong? What if I could answer it? Oedipus did."

"The sphinx in that case was placed at Thebes as part of a curse, and frankly she was sick of the whole thing. She must have been, to ask such an easy riddle, and I'm not going to jump off any mountains as she did, win or lose. Still . . . " Helena thought about it. "I haven't had anyone to talk to in such a long time and I'll admit that I'm curious whether you could answer my riddle given a fair chance. Fine, then. Ask your question, and I'll answer. Then it's your turn. Agreed?"

"Agreed," Leontas said. Helena thought that perhaps he agreed a little too quickly for any sane man, which perhaps he wasn't. Not that his state of mind made any difference, but she did wonder. Leontas continued almost without a pause. "My question is this: how many riddles do you know?"

Helena smiled, and couldn't resist preening just the slightest bit. "All of them."

Leontas, for his part, seemed to go mad at her answer. He danced around in a little circle, laughing and shrieking. When he was barely coherent again he shouted, "I knew it! I knew it!"

Helena watched this strange spectacle for a while, then finally sighed. "Well, I hope this was worth your pains, because now it's time for my riddle. Ready?"

"Ready," said Leontas, though it was clearly costing him a great deal of effort to keep from giggling.

The sphinx hesitated. "Are you sure you don't need a few moments?"

Leontas shook his head and managed an expression more befitting the solemnity of the moment. "That's very kind of you, but I'll be fine."

"No, you won't," she said, but there didn't seem to be any point in delaying the inevitable. "All right, here goes: I have many doors in, but no doors out. A bed, but no one sleeps withal. What am I?"

"Well, one could quibble about the part about not sleeping . . . "

"No stalling," she said.

Leontas shrugged. "Obviously you're a tomb."

"Obviously. Go home, Leontas."

"You're showing me mercy. Why?"

"Mercy?" Helena raised up on her forepaws and spread her majestic wings. "Puny human. You answered my riddle and that's enough. Don't insult me or I'll devour you, answered riddle or no."

"I didn't mean to insult you, I just asked why. That was an easy riddle."

"A sphinx? Merciful? Insult enough. And it was only easy because you knew the answer. The outcome could have been very different, you know. Besides," she added, "you've already had your question."

"Suppose I trade you another answer?" he said.

Helena blinked. After a moment she folded her wings and settled back down on the ledge. "You're joking, aren't you?"

"Not a bit. I ask, you answer. You ask, I answer. Just as we did before."

Helena sighed deeply. "I think I finally understand. It's rather rude to use me this way, you know."

"What way is that?"

"The way you'd use a rope or a knife or a precipice. I may be a monster, but I do have feelings."

"You think I'm committing suicide."

"There's no other explanation."

"Then you're not trying hard enough," he said mildly. "I admit, there's a good possibility that I will die today, but, with all due respect, it's not inevitable."

"You're certainly tempting fate."

"A man's fate is sealed from the moment of birth, and the only thing that keeps us interested in life is that we don't know how it ends. No, I'm not tempting the fates, Helena. I'm tempting *you*. Or intriguing you. I'm a riddle, too. One that, despite your boast, you don't know the answer to."

"You're a puny mortal and sooner or later I'm going to eat you. And it was no boast; I do know all the riddles and all the answers. All sphinxes do." Helena wasn't sure if she was more irritated or amused.

"Then why ask them? And don't say 'Because it's my nature.'"

"Is that your question?"

Leontas seemed to consider. "Yes."

Helena sighed. "I do wish you wouldn't waste a question on such a trivial matter. I ask riddles because I enjoy asking riddles."

"Try again," Leontas said.

She frowned. "I beg your pardon? Are you going to repeat the question until you get an answer you like? I never agreed to that."

"No, I'm going to ask the question until I get a proper answer. To say 'you enjoy it' is like saying I eat solely because I love food . . . and I do, by the way, but it's not the whole answer. I eat to live, and so do you. Do you ask riddles to live? Why does a sphinx enjoy asking riddles so?"

Helena, irritated for reasons she couldn't have put into words, forced herself to think about it. After a little while she gave him the only answer she had left. "It's not simply that I enjoy asking riddles, Leontas—asking riddles is the only real joy I have."

Leontas didn't say anything for several long moments. "Well, then," he said at last, his voice gruff, "Ask."

This time, Leontas, I will not go easy on you.

"Find me cold, teach me hot, clean me soft, bear me oft. What am I?"

"Ummm . . . ."

Helena bared her teeth. "No stalling."

"A moment or two to reflect is not stalling," Leontas said. "I allowed as much for you!"

"Fine, fine, but no more than that." Helena licked her lips and was rewarded by a very palpable shudder from Leontas. For a moment his expression went as blank as a block of granite, and Helena was idly debating whether to rip him from the neck down or the groin up when he suddenly returned from wherever far place he'd gone off to.

"G-gold," he said. "You're gold."

"So I am." She looked thoughtful. "You were afraid, for a while. I saw it. Come to that, I could smell it."

"Of course I was afraid! I was very close to death."

"If so, it was only because you were courting death like a lover. The first riddle was my choice but the second was yours. No matter, you're a fortunate mortal and answered the second riddle too. You can go home now."

For a moment, Helena thought she saw panic in Leontas eyes. "I'm not quite ready to leave," he said a bit wistfully. "I have another question."

She frowned. "In that case, so have I."

"A riddle, you mean."

She shrugged. "A riddle is at heart a question. I'll be fair with this one. I won't ask for esoteric knowledge or great cleverness, just a question that only you can answer." She waved a claw in his direction, like a school master wagging a finger. "However, this question is on the same terms as a riddle. Fail to answer me and I'll devour you. Answer mine and I'll answer yours as before. Fair?"

"I suppose . . . " He paused to rub the back of his neck. "Helena, do you mind if I climb up there for a bit? I'm not carrying any weapons, and I'm getting a stiff neck looking up at you."

She shrugged. "As you wish. That way I won't have to chase you as far."

Leontas disappeared for a moment under the overhang then, with a rattle of falling stones, he clambered up to stand on the ledge beside the sphinx. He saw the old bones scattered about and paused to examine them more closely. Some were human but not all. He seemed to be paying as much attention to the animal bones as to the human. Helena watched him as he poked around.

"You haven't killed that many men," he said finally.

"Most have sense enough to avoid this road since I came here," she said. "Besides, I need to eat but seldom."

"I suppose, then, that the poor ox lying here failed to answer your riddle?"

She shrugged. "'Seldom' doesn't mean 'never.' I was hungry, he was meat. You can't always depend on the foolishness of men."

"I'll have to take your word for that," he said, but he was looking off toward the distant hills. "I had two implied questions, which you just answered. Why?"

Helena shook her head in exasperation. "It's impossible to have a decent conversation without sometimes imparting information. That's not important. What matters is what questions you choose to ask, and which you choose to answer."

"I suppose you're right. Very well, then, I'm ready. Ask your riddle . . . er, question."

"Why are you courting death?" Helena asked.

"I told you I'm not . . . all right, I admit that it looks that way. But I swear I'm not, really."

She licked her lips again. "Is that your answer?"

"It is," he said, and Helena was gathering herself to spring when he went on, "but it's not the explanation. Which is what you really want, I think."

Helena subsided for the moment, but her gaze lost none of its intensity. "I'm waiting."

He took a deep breath, let it out. "Life is supposed to be enough."

She frowned. "I don't understand."

"Neither did I, at first. I mean, living things want to live, in general. Certainly, suicides are not uncommon. Sometimes it's confusion, sometimes an obligation. A choice between two bad alternatives, a moment of weakness. All those things. But most of the time life is its own justification. You're alive. You accept the lot that fate deals you, and stay alive as long as possible since we all know mortal men have little to look forward to save being a shade in Hades' realm for eternity. Considering that, is it no wonder we cherish life?"

"A rhetorical question?" Helena asked.

"No more than yours, really. You ask why I'm courting death. What you really want to know is why I'm courting *you*."

She blinked. "Are you? How very odd, but if so you'd do well to surrender that notion immediately. That's not the way for a sphinx, even among our own kind. We're monsters, created by unnatural unions. We do not mate with our kind or any other."

He smiled then, and shook his head. "Maybe 'courting' isn't the right word, but I obviously owe Apollo a sacrifice or two because I can't think of a better one."

Helena sighed. "By Zeus' hairy arse . . . a poet. I should have known."

"A *bad* poet and a worse farmer," Leontas said without a trace of either false modesty or guile. It was the simple truth, and Helena knew it for such. She waited.

"Neither is such a problem, really. I'll get by in life," said Leontas, then added, "Assuming I live past today, that is. Not everyone knows a bad poet when they hear one, and even an inept farmer can grow enough for himself when he has no family or other obligations. Yet sometimes, the idea of 'getting by' in life just isn't enough, no matter how short a span we have to enjoy. Not for a king, or a hero, or even a third-rate poet. Sometimes you have to reach for more, consequences or no."

"I'm not a prize, Leontas. I'm a monster, and I will be your death!"

He smiled at her. "You are all those things. I'm courting you because you are what you are. I'm risking death because, well, sometimes that's the price a mortal pays to be in the presence of something beyond himself. A mystery."

Helena didn't say anything for several long moments and was rewarded with just a touch more fear from Leontas. "Ask your question," she said at last.

He let out the breath he'd been holding, waiting to see if she would accept his answer. "You know all the riddles and all the answers," he said.

"That's not a question."

"You also pointed out earlier that a riddle is at heart a question. So, in essence, sphinxes have the answers to any question a man could ask. That's logic."

"That's also not a question," she said.

"This is: If you know all the answers, why did you have to ask why I'm here?"

Helena was silent for a long time, and Leontas smiled. "No stalling."

"I don't know," she said.

"I think you do," he said, smiling slightly.

27

"I said I don't! Maybe riddles and questions aren't quite the same thing. Maybe I was wrong about that."

"Maybe. So. Now what?"

She frowned. "I don't understand."

"Yes, you do. You didn't answer my question."

She showed her teeth. "You think you're going to devour *me*, Leontas?"

He shook his head. "I may act foolishly at times but I'm not that sort of fool. Still, there should be consequences, don't you think? Fair is fair and, no matter what else we've been to each other, we have been that."

"What sort of consequences did you have in mind?"

He barely hesitated. "I get to kiss you."

She growled low in her throat. "Keeping your life should be quite enough!"

He smiled, even though he was trembling. "Yes, one would think so. Yet, as I already told you, it isn't. Not nearly enough."

Helena stared at him. "I don't pretend to understand what madness drives you, Leontas, poet or no, but there's one thing *you* need to understand—I'm not what you seem to think I am! Some of me looks like a human woman, granted, but it's just appearance and no more. I eat dead meat! My breath is carrion and will likely kill you on its own, even if the scent of you and my own hunger don't overpower my restraint. Say what you will about fairness, but I'm making no promises."

"You're a mystery, Helena. I haven't decided what I think you are, so I can't really be disappointed. As for dying, that's one more chance, isn't it? As with all the other chances, it's mine to take. As for promises . . . well, I didn't ask for any." He approached Helena and she shrank back, almost cowering. Leontas was shaking also, but that didn't stop him.

"I know why I'm afraid," Leontas said. "But why are you?"

"That," she said, "will cost you a riddle."

He smiled at her. "Not today. You can ask me tomorrow."

Helena looked grim. "No I can't. You won't be here."

"One way or another, yes, I will," Leontas said, and kissed the monster.

YAMABUSHI

After the end of the war with the Taira and the death of the child Emperor Antoku, the warrior named Minamoto no Enyo returned to his own province. There he shaved his head, adopted simple, unadorned clothing, and disappeared into the mountains. Naturally those who knew him assumed he had decided to become a monk.

Enyo didn't know what people assumed, nor did he care. His reasons were his own and the mountains, for their part, assumed nothing. The *tengu*, on the other hand, assumed a great deal.

When the tengu looked down his long nose at the human climbing up the mountain trail he was beside himself with joy. Enyo's shaved head and simple garments surely were those of a *yamabushi*, and as all know it is a tengu's nature to tempt and trick holy men from the path of true righteousness. Just as a tiger must roar and a sparrow chirp, so must a mountain goblin mislead, and this one set out to do just that. The tengu adopted its favorite disguise and appeared before Enyo as a fellow yamabushi.

"Good morning," the tengu said, bowing in greeting. "My name is Yoritomo. You look hot, my friend, and tired. If you would listen to me now I can save you some trouble."

"I'm Enyo, and I'm all for avoiding trouble," Enyo said. "I'll listen to anything you have to say."

"I'm sorry to tell you that there is something wrong with these mountains," the tengu said. "Walk their circuit for years as I have done, but you will find no peace here, no enlightenment. This is a very bad place to practice your art; I am leaving them myself for a place further north."

"No doubt the spiritual shortcomings of these mountains is a quite unfortunate matter," Enyo said. "But what I'd really like to know about is the fishing. How is that?"

The tengu was so startled by the question that it told the simple truth.

"Ummm . . . fishing? Quite good, I should think. There are many unspoiled streams and quiet pools along this path."

Enyo smiled. "Excellent." He bid the tengu a pleasant afternoon and resumed his journey. The tengu watched him go, and after a moment it smiled. Clearly this human was going to be a challenge.

The tengu followed Enyo for the next few days, hoping for some clue as to how best to turn him from the path of righteousness, but so far as the tengu could tell, Enyo wasn't on the path of righteousness in the first place. He did not chant the Lotus Sutra daily, or even once. He did not meditate. He did not purify himself in cold mountains streams, though he did bathe regularly. He ate when he was hungry, slept when he was tired, and, once or twice when he came to a promising stream, he fished with a line he kept tied around a wooden dowel in his pack.

This must be a trick, thought the tengu, but for the life of the creature it couldn't tell what the trick might be. The tengu finally wondered if, perhaps, it had been mistaken about Enyo. Only his short robes and his shaved head suggested the yamabushi path; nothing else about him did. Yet the tengu had judged Enyo to be of noble birth; his manner was of one who had both given and taken commands. Why was he here, so far from the comforts of home and obligations of station, if not as one who had renounced the world? A disgraced nobleman, perhaps, one who had gone outlaw and simply adopted a convenient disguise? Possible.

The tengu decided to test that idea. It disguised itself as a pretty young servant, then cast an illusion around a stone to make it appear to be a small golden statue of *Jizo*. The tengu sat down beside the trail in a place where he knew Enyo must pass, set the golden statue on the ground, and began to weep, a splendid tableau of distressed and vulnerable womanhood.

The gold or the girl, one or both will surely tempt him . . .

Actually, it was the tengu's considered opinion that it now appeared so winsome and the gold so inviting that even a man who was neither outlaw nor bandit would be sorely tempted, so it was with quite a bit of anticipation that the creature awaited Enyo's arrival.

"Good afternoon," Enyo said politely, when he finally arrived. "What's troubling you?"

"Oh, sir," the tengu said, "my mistress sent me to make an important offering to the temple at En, and I've become quite lost in these terrible mountains. I've been wandering for days!"

Enyo nodded. "Well, then, be comforted—the very path beside you is the correct one. Just follow it in that direction," he pointed back down the path the way he had come, "and it will lead you to the temple at En directly. I've seen no one on the path save a wandering monk; I'm sure you will have no trouble."

Enyo resumed his journey without another word. The tengu just stared after him in amazement. When Enyo was out of sight the tengu resumed its true form but continued to stare.

As a master of misdirection, the tengu knew feigned disinterest when it saw it. And, for that matter, feigned interest. Indeed, "feigned" anything was as transparent as air to the tengu. And, while the tengu did notice an oddity in the monk's voice and manner when he addressed the servant girl, Enyo had barely glanced at the gold and had shown no inclination to try to possess either. This made no sense to the tengu, hard as it tried to puzzle the matter out. It was one thing if a true yamabushi had shown such restraint; the tengu could respect the man's fortitude and sharpen its plans. Such things raised the level of the contest. Yet for a normal, healthy man to act so was just . . . well, it was just *wrong*, and the tengu resolved to tell him so before it killed him.

When Enyo followed the mountain trail to the crest of a tall ridge, the tengu was there, standing squarely in Enyo's path, waiting for him. The tengu did not bother with a disguise this time. It still wore the clothing of a yamabushi, but the face it wore now was its true face, so far as a tengu had one: long nose, bushy hair and eyebrows, dark red eyes.

"I am the one you knew as Yoritomo," it said. "I am a tengu."

Enyo just nodded. "I wondered. The only other Yoritomo I knew was Minamoto no Yoritomo; it did seem strange to meet another of such a famous name at this remote place. What is it you want of me, tengu?"

The tengu simply raised his sword. "I am going to kill you."

Enyo just shrugged. "May I ask why?"

"I am a creature placed in this world to create confusion, test the holy, and turn men aside from the path of enlightenment! Is that not reason enough? Defend yourself!"

Enyo considered this. "Pointless. Was it not the tengu who taught swordsmanship to the great Minamoto no Yoshitsune himself? I am no match for you; if it is your whim to kill me and my fate to die here at your hand, then so be it. Though I fail to see how this will prevent me from finding enlightenment, since I do not seek it."

The tengu just glared at him for several long moments. He did not lower his sword, but he did not use it either. "I was the servant girl who tempted you in vain; I was the yamabushi who tried to steer you away from these, in fact, quite holy mountains. I failed at both, so I will answer your question if you will answer one of mine: what is it you do seek?"

Enyo shrugged. "Nothing," he said.

The tengu relaxed his two-handed grip long enough to wag a finger disapprovingly at Enyo. "Don't try that trick with me. You shaved your head like a monk and took the habit of a yamabushi, and you came into my mountains!"

"Everyone must be somewhere. Shaving my head just ensured that my own Lord did not come looking for me like some wayward servant. I have not renounced the world—I just don't care about it. If you mean to kill me, then best get on with it. Otherwise I have a ways to go before nightfall."

The tengu smiled. "Aha! That implies a goal, and you said you wanted nothing!"

"I have a direction, not a goal," Enyo said. "I will follow this path until it reaches the villages I know are on the other side of these mountains. There I will either join a temple for a time or find work. When I have supplies enough, I will go back on the trail until I come again to En."

"And then?" the tengu asked, but it had a sinking feeling that it already knew the answer.

"Why, I will do it all again."

The tengu lowered his sword, defeated for the moment. "Frankly, I was going to kill you since I didn't know what else to do. The truth makes my head hurt, but I swear if I kill you now the puzzle of you will wrack my wits for eternity."

"As you wish." Enyo walked past the tengu but the tengu merely fell into step beside him.

"I mean to accompany you until I have sorted you out," the tengu said.

"As you wish," Enyo repeated affably. "It's not as if I could prevent anything you wish to do."

The tengu sighed. "Yet you *have* and you *do*. To trick and distract a pious man is a tengu's highest calling."

"I can't help you, then. I am not a pious man," replied Enyo.

"So you say, yet what is the difference? You are tempted neither by gold nor the flesh. You have no desires to speak of. I've known the most holy of monks who can not say the same."

Enyo shook his head, looking a little sad. "That is not piety. I have not renounced the world—I am merely indifferent to it, and that is not the same thing."

"It *looks* the same," the tengu said. "Is there truly nothing you want?"

Enyo hesitated then. It was a slight hesitation, hardly noticeable, but the tengu noticed it. "Well, I was wrong to say I wanted nothing. There is one thing."

"Is there anything I can do to induce you to tell me? Threaten you? Go away and leave you in peace?"

Enyo smiled then. "To tell the truth, I've had worse company than a tengu in my life, so stay or go as it pleases you. No need for inducement; I don't mind telling you. My problem is that I am indifferent to the world, as I said. I would like very much not to be."

The tengu frowned. "You would like to care again?"

"To care? To feel? Yes, I would. Insofar as I feel anything, I feel like a dead man. I want to engage the world, to feel as a normal man. I think we are not so different in that we both have fairly simple desires. You would like a yamabushi to tempt and bedevil, yes?"

The tengu sighed. "Such have been rather rare in these mountains of late. It's a vexing thing for a tengu."

Enyo nodded. "Then perhaps we can help one another. If you can bring me fully back to the world, I will renounce that world and become a yamabushi in truth as well as appearance. Then you may bedevil and play tricks on me to your heart's content."

The tengu just stared at him for a few moments. "But . . . how am I to do that? And why would you want to re-engage the world of desire and *karma* only to leave it again?"

"As to the first, I have no idea. For the second, to pay the debt I would owe to you, and it makes perfect sense. I consider the pain of loss a small price to pay to be able to feel pain again. Or to feel anything, come to that."

The tengu had thought at first meeting that this man was going to be a challenge. The creature was finally beginning to understand just how right that was.

Enyo was now on his second trip through the mountains. He had reached Togakushi on the far side of the range without further incident, spent the winter in the temple there, and in the spring resumed his journey back the way he had come.

Enyo didn't see the tengu again until he left the path to do some fishing in a slow-moving stream he had found the year before. There, bathing in a small quiet pool, was an exquisite woman with pale skin and long black hair. Enyo was, frankly, a little disappointed.

"Is that the best you can do?"

The tengu didn't even pretend to be surprised that Enyo recognized him. He seemed to expect it. "You think I should be even more beautiful?" the tengu asked. "I'm not sure I can manage. Still, greed may be something of a breakthrough for you."

Enyo shook his head. "That's not what I meant! Didn't you try this before with the serving woman? I expected something different."

"This *is* different," the tengu said. "For a start, I am naked." He stood up in the water for Enyo to see. Enyo was forced to agree that creating a more beautiful face and form would be difficult indeed.

Enyo sighed. "You are quite fetching, but you must have known I'd expect something of the sort. In any case, you must know that a beautiful woman bathing alone in a mountain stream is, well, uncommon?"

"An illusion intended to be seen through. A trick, in other words. Tengu like tricks. Didn't I mention that?" The tengu rose dripping from the pool and walked toward him. Enyo stepped back but the tengu merely walked past him to the willow tree and dried itself with a square of cloth before putting on the kimono. Dressed, it was even more beautiful.

Enyo didn't look at the creature. "If the trick is over, you needn't keep that appearance."

"It is a tengu's nature to take different forms depending on their mood," it said, "nor am I obliged to conform to your expectations. Does my form bother you?"

"I said I'm no priest," Enyo admitted. "Flesh calls to flesh. I have an impulse to make love to you, and yet I still feel nothing. I would make love as a corpse, or an animal, with no savoring of the moment; I could not bear that. More, I would know that it was *you* in there and no woman at all."

The tengu nodded. "Good. The fact that you can be unsettled means that perhaps there is still a human soul in there."

Enyo didn't answer. He just baited his hook and dropped it into the water, then sat with his back against the tree.

"You're not looking at me," the tengu said after a bit.

"Of course not. I'm fishing."

"No, I mean you're deliberately avoiding looking at me. You look ahead, to the right, up, down. You do not look at me."

"Flesh calls to flesh, as I said."

The tengu dismissed that. "There's something to do with women that troubles you, right enough, but it's not desire in your eyes. It is great sadness. I saw the same thing when you looked at the servant girl before, though I didn't recognize it at the time."

"I don't feel sad. I don't feel anything."

"Call it a ghost of sadness then. A memory. What happened, Enyo-san? Were you unhappy in love?"

"I was never in love. Even before—" He stopped, looking a little bewildered and, the tengu thought, fearful.

"Before what?"

Enyo didn't answer, and after a while the tengu sighed. "You do realize, you know, that the best way to find something missing is to remember where you had it last."

"My emotions aren't a pair of chopsticks, tengu."

The tengu ignored that. "Did you lose your soul in the war?"

Now Enyo did look at the tengu again. "How did you know about the war?"

"While you were relaxing at the temple in Togakushi I adopted this form and went to your home village. Amazing how free men are with their conversation when a pretty girl is involved. They're still talking about you. They say you were present at the final destruction of the Taira clan at Dan-no-Ura. That you were a high-ranking warrior, greatly in favor among the Genji, who forsook it all to become a wandering monk. "

"I was there," Enyo said, and that was all.

"That was a privilege many would envy," the tengu said. "To deliver the final stroke against the enemies of your clan? That must have been glorious."

"Glorious," Enyo repeated dully. "Now be silent. You're scaring the fish."

The tengu smiled. "It didn't happen like that, did it? Not glorious at all, was it?"

"Think what you want," Enyo said. He started to wind in his line.

"You didn't catch anything."

"How could I, with you chattering on? You are really the most annoying creature."

"Thank you. It's what a tengu does best in the world. I was glad I could spoil your meditation."

"I wasn't meditating. I was fishing," Enyo said, frowning.

"Don't think you can fool me, Enyo-san. There's more than one path to contemplation."

There was a sudden pull on Enyo's line. When he finally pulled it in there was a nice fat fish clinging to his hook.

"So I guess you eat after all," the tengu said and then vanished.

Enyo did not see the tengu again for the remainder of that journey. Nor did he see the creature on the return crossing. Enyo thought he did, at one point, but the wandering monk turned out to be an actual wandering monk, on a journey of his own to the temple at Togakushi, a monk who thought Enyo was quite mad for trying to pull his nose and see through a disguise that wasn't there. After that small misunderstanding was cleared up, they traveled together for a time, but the monk kept stopping at various mountain streams to meditate, which mostly involved standing under freezing cold waterfalls and shivering a lot and scaring away the fish Enyo hoped to catch for supper. When the path came to one of its few branchings, they finally took separate roads, both with some relief.

Where has that silly tengu got to? Has he forgotten our agreement?

Enyo was, to his own surprise, somewhat disappointed at that. Was he actually missing the tengu's company? It seemed so, but Enyo knew of nothing else to do save what he was already doing. It was only when he returned from Togakushi the following year that Enyo saw the tengu again. He knew it was the tengu. There was no other way to explain why a mature woman with a large sword would challenge him to a duel.

"Tengu, what is the meaning of this?"

"Do you not recognize me?"

"I do. You are the tengu."

"I am the Emperor Antoku's grandmother."

Enyo took a deep slow breath. "The Emperor's grandmother is dead. She died off the coast at Dan-No-Ura, along with the child himself and most of the rest of the Taira."

"True," said the tengu.

"Then why this deception?"

"Can you call it a deception if there was no chance you would believe it? I was giving you something real—or as real as I could manage—to fight."

Enyo just stared at the creature. "Now I see why you have been missing these last two years. You have gone mad."

The tengu laughed. "Not a bit. I left these mountains, disguised myself as a Minamoto retainer and moved among them. That's why I was gone so long; this took time."

"For me? Why do such a thing?"

"To discover why you shaved your silly head, of course. You were being stubborn about the details. I chose the grandmother of the Emperor because I believe she is the root cause of your problem."

"You don't know that. You don't know anything."

"It's not the fact that she died. This was war, and people other than warriors tend to die as well. You knew that. Plus, in her machinations she could hardly be said to be uninvolved. She was a warrior too. Just of a different sort. I know what happened, Enyo-san. Shall I hear it from you, or shall we fight now?"

"I have no reason to fight you. I would have no reason to fight the Nun of the Second Rank if she really were alive. Her clan is finished."

"Yes. That's the frustrating thing, I imagine. That's why the presence of women disturbs you. You see it in them, don't you? Every time."

"See what, tengu?"

"You see the Nun of the Second Rank clutching the child Emperor on the deck of their ship and jumping into the water off Dan-No-Ura, at that time when all hope for the Taira was lost. You see her attendants and the women of her household following in proper order behind her. Going to their deaths as to a wedding."

"People die in war. You said as much yourself."

"And people kill in war. Which part had you forgotten?"

Enyo didn't answer for many long moments. "I forgot the reason I was there," he said softly. "I forgot the men I had killed, and the men who had tried to kill me. I forgot why the Minamoto and the Taira fought each other. I forgot everything, tengu. All I knew was what I saw in front of me, that it had all led to this moment. The women of the Taira clan drowned themselves before my eyes and they took part of me with them."

"And so you forgot yourself as well. A sad story indeed. I'm quite moved to tears," the tengu said. "Now they say the fishermen taking crabs off Dan-no-Ura find faces on the back shells of the creatures, bumps and ridges mocking the appearance of the death-masks of the warriors that drowned there. Will the faces of the women appear as well, do you think? Frozen in the grimace of death as they were when the crabs feasted on their lovely pale flesh?"

Enyo scowled. "If you're not going to help me, you can go away!"

"Help you? What do you think I've been doing for the past three years?" The tengu raised his sword. "Defend yourself."

"I won't. Kill me if you want. I won't fight you."

The tengu changed from the matriarch of the Taira into the appearance of the young woman who had bathed in the river. "Pity. An open and honest enemy is preferable to the demons you've unleashed on yourself. I think you want me to kill you."

"Perhaps. Anything would be better than the half-life I have now!"

The tengu smiled. "You're angry."

Enyo took a deep breath, let it out slowly. "Even a stone Buddha would be annoyed at your nonsense!"

"And why not? You're a yamabushi and I am a tengu. This is what we both do."

"I am not a yamabushi! Haven't you been listening?"

"You were always a yamabushi, Enyo-san. You did fool me for a while, I must admit, but only because you fooled yourself so well. You confused your proper disgust and displacement from the world with a lack of emotion. Yet you were on the yamabushi path once you entered my mountains with the idea of regaining your lost humanity. Every act was a meditation; even fishing. Perhaps especially fishing. Whether you thought so or even intended to be what you've now become is really beside the matter."

"That's not true!"

"Shall we test this? Suppose I take off this kimono now and have a bath in front of you. What do you think would happen?"

"*Nothing*," Enyo said severely.

The tengu smiled. "Yes, and precisely: nothing. But would it be the same sort of nothing? A man truly unaware can trip over enlightenment as well as a root. But don't worry—I'll be there to make sure that doesn't happen. Until next meeting, Enyo-san."

The tengu vanished then, leaving Enyo alone with his fishing. Enyo tried to calm down. Enyo slowly realized that he *needed* to calm down.

Well.

Enyo wondered, just for a moment, if he should learn to meditate properly; it might help his composure when the tengu returned as, Enyo knew, the creature would. Talking more nonsense. Trying to trick him, because the tengu thought Enyo was something he was not.

Let the tengu find me chanting under a cold waterfall. Wouldn't that be a joke?

Enyo thought, perhaps, it was a joke that even a tengu could admire. Not that he wanted to give any real credence to the tengu's delusion that Enyo was a yamabushi. Surely one could not just 'stumble' upon the path to enlightenment by accident, no matter what the silly creature said. Still, the tengu did feel that Enyo owed it a debt and perhaps it was right; Enyo wasn't really sure. Besides, he couldn't fish all the time; he had to find other ways to pass the seasons.

Enyo smiled then. A tengu wasn't the only one who could play tricks.

WORSHIPPING SMALL GODS

Once upon a certain time in a certain ancient land there were gods of all sorts: Large gods, small gods, beautiful gods, ugly gods. Gods of fields and gods of roadways, gods of pestilence and gods of healing, gods of mountains and gods of swamps. Gods who kept pretty much to themselves and accepted no more than the occasional offering, and that mostly to remind themselves that they were, in fact, gods, even if knowing this did little to change either their behavior or personal grooming.

Makoto was one of the latter. His main opinion on being a god was that it was no great thing. In fact, so far as Makoto was concerned the only thing possibly worse was to be either a human or a Saint and, while humans were simply little different from any other animal, Saints were a category of 'unpleasant' all unto themselves.

Saints were something new in that ancient land and Makoto wasn't really sure what to make of them; he had seen a few and could only wonder at what strange creatures they were. Men and yet not just men. Either almost gods or beyond gods. Powerful, capricious, serving some personal view of an "Enlightenment" or "Transcendence," ideas that they didn't really seem to understand and so interpreted as they saw fit.

In short, Saints were trouble.

Knowing this, Makoto perhaps should have been more prepared that fine spring day. He lay on a rock on his mountain, sunning himself as was his custom. The Saint appeared on that faintest of paths that led the occasional human up to make offerings.

Funny thing about Saints. They smelled human. They even *looked* human, though they did tend to dress funny and shave their heads and wear large strings of wooden beads that forever clacked as they walked. Makoto recognized the smell and so thought nothing amiss until the Saint walked right up to Makoto's rock and bound him there. The Saint did it in the Name of an Idea. A very powerful idea, apparently. He called it Shaka.

Makoto looked down at the gleaming golden strands of pure light that shackled him. "Ummm, excuse me? Why have you done this?"

"The buddha Shaka demands a bridge from this mountain peak to the next. You're going to build it."

"Ummm . . . Why would this 'Shaka' want such a thing, and why would I do such a thing?"

"The will of Shaka is not for you or me to question. You will do this because I'll bind you to this rock forever if you don't." The Saint didn't smile. They tended not to, except when they did. It was all very confusing. Makoto longed for the days before the Saints came. Life was simpler for a god, then.

Makoto sighed. "I am a mountain god. I am very strong. This thing you bind me with is an idea. Ideas may be powerful things but they do change over time, in my experience. So do mountains, come to that, but at a much slower pace. Sooner or later this thing that binds me will change in a way that is not a binding, or it will move in such a way that I do not move with it. Either way I will be free. I tell you that I will not build a bridge; I like my mountains as they are. Go away."

The Saint seemed to consider this. "Well, if a relatively mutable thing will not do, then I will take your advice and go for something less changeable. Be a rock."

Makoto was a rock. It happened from one moment to the next, as soon as the Saint said the word rock.

This is very interesting, Makoto thought. Being a god as well as a rock, thinking was not very difficult. And it wasn't exactly a new thing to be of the mountain, since he was, after all, a mountain god.

"I hear your thoughts," the Saint said. "And I know you can hear me. Will you build my bridge now?"

A rock can build nothing. You might, perhaps, make a bridge out of me instead, now that I am a boulder, but I don't think it would reach the next mountain.

"You are a stubborn creature," the Saint said. "but I am patient. I will be back."

The Saint left the mountain then, which Makoto considered a very good thing for him to do. As the days then passed Makoto came to realize that life was not so very different as a stone. He still sunned himself on pleasant days. He did not seek shelter from the wind or storm when the weather was inclement but, being a god, he had never done those things in the first place. In fact, being a stone had much to recommend it. He wanted for nothing, neither food nor water nor company. It was true that company was something he had very seldom wanted, but seldom did not mean never and yet his solitude was assured, even forced, by his very nature. Now his desires matched his nature perfectly and Makoto was, for the first time he could remember, perfectly content rather than merely almost so.

Once a month for a considerable period of time that Makoto, as a stone, barely noticed, the Saint returned to Makoto's mountain. This visit would always coincide with the new moon. The Saint would sit in that funny cross-legged position that the Saints had named after a flower—though in Makoto's opinion it more resembled the legs of a dead beetle—and he would stare at the large stone that was Makoto for a very long time. "Well?" he would finally ask, "are you ready to build the bridge now?"

No, Makoto would think, loud enough to be sure that the Saint could hear him. After a while the Saint would simply rise and walk back down the mountain. On the next new moon he would be back. Makoto did notice a few more wrinkles in the Saint's face as time wore on; he seemed to recall that the Saint had been quite a young man when he'd first appeared.

This went on for some time, yet there finally came a day when the Saint came and there was something a bit different about him. He seemed, well, tired. Yet nothing changed in the first part of his ritual. He sat down in his dead beetle position and he stared at Makoto the Stone.

"Well?" he asked. "are you ready to build my bridge now?"

No, Makoto thought, and waited for the Saint to leave so he could get back to sunning himself in peace as he usually did except during the rainy season. This time the Saint didn't leave.

"We've been doing this for a long time now," the Saint said.

Makoto would have shrugged, if he'd had shoulders. *I suppose.*

"You must realize by now that you cannot escape Shaka's will. You will build his bridge or remain a stone forever!"

I'm sure that's true, was Makoto's cheerful thought, and why not? It seemed an excellent arrangement so far as he was concerned. He only wished he knew what to say to the Saint to make him go away again. He always had before. Yet still the Saint sat there on the rocks and bristly grass, staring at him, and he would not go away.

"I've tried," the Saint said finally. "I've practiced my meditation and I have contemplated this stubborn rock for what seems an eternity, and yet I must confess: I do not understand."

Perhaps I can help, Makoto thought. Anything to get rid of the pesky fellow.

"You can build the bridge," the Saint said. "That would help." He actually looked annoyed. That was new.

Makoto sighed, or at least remembered what it was like to do so. *I won't build your bridge.*

"Why not?"

Because I don't want to build a bridge. I like the mountains the way they are. Wasn't I clear on that point from the start?

The Saint looked unhappy. "It doesn't matter what you or I want! The buddha Shaka was very specific."

Who is this 'Shaka' you're always on about?

The Saint glared at him. "The Enlightened One! He has seen through all the world's falseness, rid himself of his physical desires, become One with the Infinite!"

Makoto considered this. *That's very impressive. So why does he want a bridge? Isn't that a desire, of sorts?*

The Saint just stared at him for a moment. Then, "It's not for me to question!"

Then who is it for?

The Saint frowned deeply and looked as if he were about to say something, then he shook his head and let out a gusting breath. Makoto thought that, perhaps, what the Saint said then was something different from what he had started to say.

"My mission is still clear. I meditated on the Lotus Sutra for seven years, and at the end of those seven years the Buddha came to me in a dream and directed me to come to your mountain and command you to build the bridge I spoke of. He said it would bring me to Enlightenment."

I'm assuming Enlightenment is a place you wish to be?

"It's not a 'place' but, yes, more than anything."

Makoto thought about this for a moment. *Yet another desire, but no mat-*

ter. Shaka never commanded you to build a bridge. He commanded you to tell me to do it. Is that correct?

The Saint hesitated. "Well . . . yes."

They both remained silent for a time. It was Makoto who finally broke that silence.

So, in essence, your buddha commanded you to come to my mountain and endeavor to teach patience to a stone?

For a moment Makoto thought the Saint had been struck by lightning. His breath escaped him in a loud hiss. His eyes grew wide and his mouth fell open, and his lower jaw moved up and down spasmodically, but nothing else came out. For a moment Makoto thought he was going scream, or perhaps cry. What he did do was even more odd—the Saint threw himself the ground at Makoto's feet, or where Makoto's feet would have been if he currently had feet.

"Master!" The Saint's shout was pure joy.

Makoto barely had time to consider this new strangeness before he suddenly had to get used to not being a stone anymore. He stood again on his own two legs, though he was so unused to standing that he decided to sit on a nearby rock instead. The Saint kept his face buried in the dirt all the while.

"Master, I did not recognize the buddha in you. Please forgive your humble and foolish servant," he said finally. He still didn't look up.

"Ummm . . . certainly, if you'll leave this place now."

The Saint did finally look up. His eyes were shining so brightly it was almost painful to look at him. "I will. I will go back into the world now and take the lesson you have taught me."

Makoto didn't say anything to that, not having any idea of what *to* say in the face of evident madness, though the idea of containing this 'buddha' within him was very disturbing. It was only after the Saint was gone for good that Makoto thought of having the Saint change him back into a stone. Makoto had rather liked being a stone. Yet it was probably for the best, Makoto thought, after considering the matter for a while. Who knew what the lunatic might have done if he'd remained? Perhaps turned Makoto into a mist or a frog or whatnot or imposed more of this notion of Makoto containing buddhas, an idea that Makoto resisted with all the god within him. He realized that things were probably better as they were, now that they were finally back to the way they were.

"If only I'd known he was that easy to get rid of," Makoto said aloud.

Still, considering the nonsense that brought him to Makoto's mountain in the first place, there was always the possibility that the Saint would come back. It'd be hard to escape from him then with only that one path up and down the mountain. Makoto eyed the next mountain over, thoughtfully.

Maybe a bridge wasn't such a bad idea.

THE PLUM BLOSSOM LANTERN

Michiko's servant girl Mai carried a pink lantern to light their way through the dark city streets. Mai was dead. Since Michiko was, too, that didn't seem so strange. In fact, very little about the situation struck Michiko as odd or even very different from when she was alive. She did have one regret, however—her feet. Michiko missed having feet.

Specifically, *her* feet. They had been quite lovely feet, she thought. Once, in Michiko's honest estimation, her very best feature, and that in a young woman with many good features: long black hair, a lovely smile, fair and unblemished skin. Now where her feet should have been there was almost nothing; at best a slight vapor, like mist rising on a cold morning or the smoke from a dying fire. She glided along, not quite walking, not quite flying, with Mai leading the way with a paper lantern the color of plum blossoms in spring.

Michiko was going to see her lover. She would come to him in the night and be gone before first light. This was how such things were done. This was proper. A certain amount of discretion was expected from a lady, a delicacy of sensibility and appreciation for the finer points of dress and deportment. While Michiko could no longer change her blue and gold brocade kimono to match the seasons, in all matters in which her current condition did not forestall her, Michiko did what was expected. Now her lover, a handsome, high-born young gentleman, expected her, and she did not intend to disappoint him.

The street was quiet. The gauze veil hanging from Michiko's *boshi* covered her face so that, if anyone had been about, her identity would have been protected, likewise as discretion dictated. Mai's head and face were cowled and hidden as well, but there was no one to see them there. Everyone kept to their houses; the wall gates were all closed, and the lanterns extinguished save for the one Mai carried. Even the dogs were silent.

"Is it so very late, Mai?" Michiko asked, as she looked around.

"The people are hiding, Mistress," Mai answered. "They are afraid."

"Afraid? Of what?"

"Of what they don't understand. Of what they do understand. Of what will happen. Of what might happen." After a few moments Mai repeated what she had said before, in the same dull tone. Michiko sighed delicately. Once Mai had been a lively, mischievous girl, but she was changed now. Sometimes it was like talking to a stone buddha—responses were limited and predictable.

"Never mind," Michiko said. "I would rather think of Hiroi. He seems somewhat unwell lately. Have you noticed?"

"He is very handsome," Mai said. "My mistress is indeed fortunate."

"Yes, but he is pale—"

"He is very handsome," Mai repeated, once, and that was all.

In times like these Michiko imagined herself and Mai in some sort of play, for that is the way her world felt to her then. Only she had the better part, and poor Mai could only speak her brief bit, whatever it might be, more like a wooden *bunraku* puppet than a person. Perhaps this was what being dead meant to Mai. For Michiko's part, it was little different than before. Life went on, as did Death. But she did so miss her feet.

Mai turned off the street and through a garden path that led to Hiroi's home. He was a scholar of good family, sent to the city to study for a time under the monks at the nearby Temple of Thousand-Armed Kannon, goddess of mercy. No monk himself, it had been love at first sight when he saw Mai leading her mistress through a darkened city street. "Plum Blossom Firefly" he had called Michiko, and wrote a poem about the lantern. He never noticed her missing feet.

Michiko found herself captivated from the start, as what young woman of taste and refinement would not? Their becoming lovers had been right, and it had happened as soon as decorously possible. Now it continued. Would continue. This was right, too.

Mai stopped on the path. Michiko, in reverie, almost collided with her. She frowned. "Foolish girl! Why have you stopped?"

Mai said a new thing then, something Michiko could not remember her saying before. "I can not see the way, Mistress."

Michiko sighed. "What nonsense, Mai! Of course you can; this path leads directly to Hiroi's house."

But it was true. There was nothing in front of them now. A solid sort of

RICHARD PARKS

nothing, like the *kuramaku* that concealed those working behind the scene in a kabuki drama. Michiko removed her hat and veil to get a better look. She put out her hand and her long fingers brushed against a wall of darkness, cold and hard, where the path to Hiroi should have been.

"This is very strange, Mai."

Mai said nothing. She merely stood, with the lantern swaying back and forth on the end of its pole. A strong breeze pushed against it, and sent Michiko's long black hair flying around her like a nimbus, but the paper lantern kept the wind at bay and the light did not go out.

I shall be quite a sight to Hiroi, like this, Michiko thought. She wondered if he would laugh to see her thus, but of course she would fix her hair before he did any such thing. Yet there was no time for that just now. She peered at the *nothing* ahead of her and, as the breeze swirled past and through her, she noticed something fluttering ahead of her, like a small caged bird. Before the wind died down she leaned forward and was able to make out small rectangles of paper and, as the breeze pushed and prodded them, the *nothing* ahead also seemed to be pushed and prodded, shifting slightly, now so transparent that she could see the path, now solid again so she could see nothing.

"Someone has written something on these scraps of paper and tied them to the bushes along the path."

"Yes," Mai said, but that was all.

"If the wind was to push hard enough," Michiko said, "perhaps these impertinent scraps might be persuaded to let us pass."

The wind, which had started to die down, obediently picked up again and set the paper rectangles dancing. The barrier shimmered, and writhed, and the wind blew harder and harder. Michiko's hair flowed around her in long streams and little wavelets and curls, like the currents in a glossy black river. One of the wardings tore loose from a bush and fluttered away like a white moth, then another, then another. The black wall collapsed and blew away with them. In a moment the breeze died away.

"I will hold the lantern while you comb my hair, Mai. Do it quickly and let us be gone. Hiroi is waiting."

Someone else was waiting. They found him when they came to the small wooden bridge that arched over a stream crossing the path some little ways from Hiroi's door. He stood in front of the bridge, blocking their way:

48

a young monk with fierce eyes and a staff of rings that jangled when he brought the staff down hard on the path in front of him.

"Stay back, demon!" he said.

Michiko just stared at him for a moment. "I am not a demon. I am Yoshitomo no Michiko and I have come to see Fujiwara no Hiroi at his own invitation. Stand aside, monk."

"Perhaps you were a girl named Michiko, once," he said. "Now you are a night demon come to steal the life from that young man. I shall not permit it. I planted wards covered in scripture from the Lotus Sutra. I don't know how you got past them, but you will not get past me."

Michiko had never been spoken to in such a manner and she was in no mood for it. "Such insolence! Are you going to claim that Fujiwara-san put you up to this?"

The monk looked a little uncomfortable. "Hiroi is not in his right mind, demon. He does not understand what you are, nor can I convince him. Yet I saw what was happening. It was my duty to prevent it."

"To keep me away from my love? How is this duty? What vow does it break, what honor uphold? Hiroi wants to see me. I can feel him calling me. Who are you to say what we should and should not do?"

"This place is for the living. You do not belong here!"

Michiko, being a well-bred young lady, covered her mouth with one dainty hand as she smiled. She stepped closer, fully into the glow of the plum blossom lantern. "Yet I *am* here, little monk. You can touch me if you doubt it."

He drew back. "Don't tempt me, demon. I am stronger than you!"

Michiko sighed. "Of course you are. I am but a frail young woman, and no match for a wise and powerful and pious monk like yourself. So let me ask you one question. If you can answer it, I will go away. I will not trouble Hiroi again, though he pines for me every day and I fear for his health."

"No tricks, demon," the monk said grimly.

"No tricks at all. No riddles, paradoxes, no great obscure pieces of knowledge known only, I am told, to demons of the Ten Hells and the Enlightened. Just a simple question. Agreed?"

The monk frowned. "Well . . . very well. What is your question?"

"First, I want to be clear on your understanding. You say I do not belong

here. You say I was once the girl called Michiko and am now some foul creature that stalks the night and preys upon the innocent. Is this so?"

"It is," the monk said.

"Well, then, tell me: why am I here?"

"Why? To prey—"

"Please do not repeat yourself, monk. Even if I accept that what you say
is true, *what* I do is not the same as *why*. Surely you understand the difference? I am here. Why? I did die; I do not dispute that. I remember a sickness
that claimed half the city, and myself and my dear little Mai besides. And
yet I remain. She remains, too. Sometimes I think she's here merely as a
shadow of me, or of herself, but I remember for us both, and we remain. The
Ten Hells did not open their gates to me, nor did Paradise, nor the River of
Souls. Why?"

"Perhaps . . . perhaps the funeral rites were not properly performed."

" 'Perhaps' is not an answer, yet I am not so impatient as you think me.
Pray for me now, sir monk, with all your power and piety. Open the way to
where you say I should be and I promise you I will go, and with gratitude."

The monk immediately sat *zazen* on the foot of the bridge, legs crossed
and eyes closed, and he began to chant. He chanted for a long time while
Michiko and Mai stood in the glow of the lantern. When he opened his eyes
many hours later, Michiko and Mai were waiting, and the lantern was still
glowing.

"I belong here, monk," Michiko said gently. "And Hiroi chose me and
he made me love him. We are fated to be together and he is waiting for me
now."

"So it seems." There were tears in the monk's eyes as he stood up and
moved aside. His face showed no anger, no fear, but only a great sadness. "A
man's karma belongs to him alone," the monk said. "I will pray for Hiroi's
soul instead."

Mai led the way over the bridge with the plum blossom lantern, and
Michiko followed serenely. "I would not harm Hiroi for all the world, Mai,
but I have no doubt the silly little monk meant well," she said, but Mai said
nothing.

Hiroi was sleeping a restless sleep but he opened his eyes and smiled
weakly when Michiko glided into the room. He did look pale, and weary,
but he was so glad to see Michiko that soon they both forgot all about that.

Mai found a stand for the lantern and made a discreet exit, and when the time came to leave she carried the lantern before them. There was no sign of the monk.

When Michiko went to Hiroi's home again the house was cold and dark, and Hiroi was nowhere to be found. Michiko sent Mai out to make inquiries. Later, in the empty place where they dwelled, Mai returned and told her mistress about the funeral. Hiroi's family was very sad, as was Michiko. She would never forget the beautiful young man, but she also knew that, in time, there would be another. It seemed that there was always another, sooner or later.

Michiko knew it would be soon.

One particular young man, the right young man, the correct and proper young man, would see her walking at night, her servant carrying the plum blossom lantern. He would call her his plum blossom firefly as Hiroi had done, and write poetry to her that did not seem to be about her at all, and yet always was. She would love him, for how could she not? They would be together then and would love one another and be very happy.

For a while.

"The living world was made for joy and sorrow," Michiko said to Mai. "We are part of that as well."

"Yes, Mistress," Mai said, but that was all she said. Night was coming. As she had done so many times before, Mai lit the plum blossom lantern.

FOX TAILS

———

I was just outside of Kyoto, close on the trail of a fox spirit, when the ghost appeared. It manifested as a giant red lantern with a small mouth and one large eye, and blocked access to a bridge I needed to cross. While it was true that ghosts made the best informants, their sense of timing could be somewhat lacking.

"I have information, Yamada-san," it said.

"I'm not looking for information. I'm looking for a fox," I said and started to brush past it.

"A silver fox with two tails? Sometimes appears as a human female named Kuzunoha?"

The lantern suddenly had my full attention. "I'm listening."

"You're chasing a *youkai* pretending to be Lady Kuzunoha. You really do not want to catch it, if you get my meaning."

I did. As monsters went, *youkai* ran the gamut from "mildly annoying" to "slurp your intestines like hot noodles." By the time you knew which sort you were dealing with, it was usually too late.

"How do I know you're telling me the truth?"

The lantern looked disgusted. "The other *rei* said you were smart, Yamada-san. How? You can follow that illusion until it gets tired of the game and eats you. Or we can reach an agreement. That is up to you." The lantern pretended to look away, unconcerned, but having only the one eye made it very difficult to glance at someone sideways without him knowing it.

"You're saying you know where Lady Kuzunoha is? What do you want in exchange?"

"Two bowls, plus prayers for my soul at the temple of your choice."

"One bowl, and I haven't been inside a temple since I was seven. I'm not going to start on your account."

I knew it would all come down to just how hungry the ghost was, but I wasn't worried—I'd already spotted the drool. It was staining the lantern's paper. The thing grumbled something about miserly bastards, but gave in.

"Very well, but do it properly."

"Always," I said. "Now tell me where I can find Lady Kuzunoha."

The ghost knew I was good for it. Information was the lifeblood of any nobleman's proxy, and only a fool would cheat an informant once a deal was agreed. I wasn't a fool . . . most of the time.

"Lady Kuzunoha is in Shinoda Forest."

I sighed deeply. "I don't appreciate you wasting my time, *rei*. My patron already had the place searched! She's not there."

"If the idiot hadn't sent his army he might have found her. She had more of a romantic rendezvous in mind, ne? If you're really looking for her, that's where she is. Go there yourself if you don't believe me."

"All right, but remember—I may not be intimate with temples but I do have contacts. If you're lying to me, I'll come back with a tinderbox and a priest who specializes. Do you understand me?"

"She's there, I tell you. Now honor our bargain."

I reached inside my robe and pulled out a bag of uncooked rice already measured out. I took a pair of wooden chopsticks and shoved them point first through the opening of the bag and held the offering in the palms of my hands before the lantern.

"For the good of my friend . . . uh, what's your name?"

"Seita."

"—Seita-san."

The bag floated out of my hands and shriveled like a dead leaf in a winter's wind. In a moment the pitiful remnants of the offering drifted to the ground in front of the bridge and the lantern let out a deep sigh of contentment.

"Quality stuff," it said. "I hope we can do business again."

"Maybe, if your story proves true and Lady Kuzunoha doesn't send any more *youkai* after me."

"But Lady Kuzunoha didn't . . . ahh, please forget I said that." For a moment I thought the lantern was just looking for another offering, but that wasn't it. The thing was actually scared, and there aren't many things short of an exorcist that will scare a ghost.

"If she didn't send it, who did?"

Just before it winked out like a snuffed candle, the lantern whispered, "Yamada-san, there isn't that much rice in Kyoto."

The servant who had come to my home the day before claimed to be from Lord Abe no Yasuna. At first I didn't believe him, but I wasn't so prosperous that I could chance turning down work. I also couldn't risk the potential insult to Lord Abe if the servant was telling the truth; even the Emperor would think twice before courting the Abe family's displeasure.

Like most members of the Court, the Abe family's ancestral lands were elsewhere, but they kept a palatial residence within the city to be close to the seat of power. Courtiers and supplicants waited two deep within the walled courtyard, but the servant ushered me right through. I didn't miss the raised eyebrows and muttering that followed in our wake. It didn't bother me; I was used to it.

Technically I was of noble birth since the minor lordling who was my father lowered himself to acknowledge me. Yet I had no inheritance, no regular patron, and no political connections, so the main difference between someone such as myself and your typical peasant farmer was that the farmer knew where his next meal was coming from. Yet, if it hadn't been for that accident of birth, people like Abe no Yasuna wouldn't deal with me in the first place, so I guess I should count my blessings. One of these days I'll get around to it.

I was ushered in to the Abe family reception hall. "Throne room" would have been a better description, and not too far from the truth. The Abe family counted more than a few actual royalty in their family tree, including the occasional emperor. The man himself was there, waiting for me. He was tall and imposing, probably no more than forty. Handsome, I would say. There was a peppering of gray in his black hair, but no more than that. He seemed distracted. Kneeling at a discreet distance was an older lady. At first glance I assumed she was a servant, but then I got a better look at her *kimono*, not to mention her face, and saw the family resemblance. It was unusual for a noblewoman to greet male guests save behind a screen, but perhaps the circumstances were unusual. I suspected they might be.

I bowed low. "You sent for me, lord?"

He studied me intently for several seconds before speaking. "Yamada no Goji. Your reputation for effectiveness . . . and discretion, precedes you. I trust it is deserved."

It was all I could do to keep from smiling. A delicate matter. Good— delicate matters paid the best. "I am at my lord's service."

Lord Abe turned to the kneeling woman. "Mother, I need to speak with Yamada-san alone. Boring business."

"Family business," said the old woman dryly as she rose, "but do as you will. It seems you must, these days."

Mother. Now I understood. I had heard of Abe no Akiko by reputation, as had nearly everyone in Kyoto. She had been a famous beauty in her day and, judging from what I could see of her now, that day was not long past. She also had a reputation for being a fierce advocate of her family's position at court and was rumored to have put more than one rival out of the game permanently. Still, that wasn't an unusual rumor for any courtier who'd lasted more than a few seasons. More to the point, she wasn't the one who had summoned me.

Lord Abe was silent for a few moments, either collecting his thoughts or making sure his mother was out of earshot; I couldn't tell which.

"Have you ever been married, Yamada-san?" he said finally.

"I have not, lord."

"I was, for a while, to a lovely woman named Kuzunoha. I rather enjoyed it, but love and happiness are illusions, as the scriptures say."

I was beginning to get the drift. "Pardon my impertinence, but when did she leave?"

Lord Abe looked grim. "Two days ago."

"And you wish for me to find her?"

Lord Abe hesitated. "The matter is a bit more complicated than that, as I'm sure you've already guessed. Please follow me."

Despite Lord Abe's confidence I hadn't guessed much about the situation at all, beyond the obvious. Wives left husbands for numerous reasons, and vice versa, and this wouldn't be the first time I'd been sent after one or the other. Lord Abe's position was such that he had apparently been able to keep the matter quiet; I'd certainly heard nothing of it. Still, the situation was unfortunate but not a real scandal. I followed as Lord Abe led through a small partition leading to a tiny room behind the dais where Lord Abe had received me. We came to another screen that opened onto yet another courtyard, and beyond that was the roofed wall that surrounded the entire residence complex. There was another gate visible.

Lord Abe stopped at the screen. It took me a few seconds to realize that he wasn't looking beyond it but *at* it. Someone had written a message on the *shoji* screen in flowing script. It was a poem of farewell, but despite the obvious beauty of both the poem and the calligraphy, that was not what got my attention. The poem was Lady Kuzunoha's confession, clearly stated, that she was not a woman at all but a fox spirit Lord Abe had once rescued on the grounds of the Inari Shrine and that she could no longer remain with Lord Abe as his wife. The poem ended: "If you would love me again, find me in Shinoda Forest." The poem was signed "Reluctant Kuzunoha."

"My Lord, are you certain this is your wife's script?"

"Without question. She always had the most beautiful calligraphy. She also could copy any text of the *sutras* exactly, but when writing as herself her own style is distinctive."

That his wife had left him was one thing. That his wife was a fox was quite another. Pretending to be a human woman was a fox spirit's favorite trick, and Lord Abe wouldn't be the first man to be fooled by one. At the least, that could be somewhat embarrassing, and, in the rarified circles of court where favor and banishment were never separated by more than a sword's edge, "somewhat" could be enough to tip the scale.

"She knew I didn't allow servants in here, so none have seen this but my mother and myself. I will destroy the door," Lord Abe said, "for obvious reasons, but I did want you to see it first. I have already sealed the document granting you authority to act on my behalf in this matter." He pulled the scroll out of a fold of his robe and handed it to me.

I took the scroll but couldn't resist the question. "What matter, Lord Abe? Pardon my saying so, but if this confession is true, then you are well rid of her. Fox spirits are dangerous creatures."

That was an understatement if there ever was. One Chinese emperor had barely avoided being murdered by a fox masquerading as a concubine, and one poor farmer spent a hundred years watching a pair of fox-women playing Go for what he thought was an afternoon. They were tricksters at the best of times and often far worse.

"It wasn't like that," Lord Abe said quietly. "Kuzunoha loved me. I do not know what drove her to leave or to make this confession, but I was never in danger from her."

"You want me to find her, then?" I had to ask. There were at least as many fools among the nobility as elsewhere, and there was always someone who thought the rules didn't apply to him. I was more than a little relieved to discover that Lord Abe was not that stupid.

He shook his head. His expression had not changed, but his eyes were moist and glistening. "Lady Kuzunoha is correct that we cannot be together now, but she should not have asked me to give up Doshi as well."

"Doshi?"

"My son, Yamada-san. She took my . . . our son."

I was beginning to see what he meant by "complicated." "I take it you've already searched Shinoda Forest?" That was an easy supposition to make. I already knew what he'd found, otherwise I wouldn't be there.

He sighed. "I should have gone personally, but I did not trust myself to let Kuzunoha go if I ever held her again. My mother suggested we send my personal retainers and in my weakness I agreed. They searched thoroughly, and I lost two good men to an ogre in the process. There was no sign of either Kuzunoha or Doshi." He looked at me. "That is your task, Yamada-san. I want you to find my son and return him to me."

"Again I must ask your pardon, Lord, but is this wise? The boy will be half-fox himself. Isn't there a danger?"

His smile was so faint one might have missed it, but I did not. "There's always a danger, Yamada-san. If we are fortunate we get to decide which ones we choose to face. I want my son back."

"By any means required?"

"Do not harm Lady Kuzunoha. With that one exception, do what you must."

At least my goal was clear enough. I didn't for one moment think it was going to be easy.

Another advantage of being of the noble class was that it entitled you to carry weapons openly, and Shinoda Forest was not a place you wanted to go empty-handed. The place had a deserved reputation for being the haunt of fox spirits and worse; most bandits even avoided the place, and any bandit who didn't was *not* the sort you wanted to meet. Yet here I was, for the

princely sum of five imported Chinese bronze coins and one *kin* of uncooked rice a day, plus reasonable expenses. You can be sure I counted that
payment to the red lantern ghost as "reasonable."

There was a path. Not much of one, but I stuck to it. There was a danger
in keeping to the only known path in a wood full of monsters, not to mention it might make finding Lady Kuzunoha even more difficult, but I kept
to the path anyway. Getting lost in Shinoda Forest would have done neither
me nor my patron much good.

Even so, once you got past the fact that the woods were full of things that
wanted to kill you, it was a very beautiful place. There was a hint of fall in
the air; the maple leaves were beginning to shade into red, contrasting with
the deep green of the rest of the wood. The scent was earthy but not unpleasant. It had been some time since I'd been out of the city and I was enjoying
the scent and sounds of a true forest. Too much so, perhaps, otherwise I
would never have been caught so easily.

I hadn't walked three paces past a large stone when the world went
black. When I woke up, I almost wished I hadn't: my head felt like two
shou of plum wine crammed into a one *shou* cask. For a moment I honestly thought it would explode. After a little while, the pain eased enough
for me to open my eyes. It was early evening, though of which day I had
no idea. I was lying on my side, trussed like a deer on a carrying pole, and
about ten feet from a campfire. Sitting beside that campfire were two of
the biggest, most unpleasant-looking men it had ever been my misfortune
to get ambushed by. They were both built like stone temple guardians,
and their arms were as thick as my legs. Otherwise there wasn't much to
separate them, save one was missing an ear and the other's nose had been
split near the tip. One look at them and my aching brain only had room
for one question:

Why am I still alive?

I must have moaned with the effort of keeping my eyes open, since one
of the bandits glanced in my direction and grunted.

"He's awake. Good. I thought you'd killed him. You know an ogre likes
'em fresh."

There was my answer, though it went without saying that I didn't care for
it. Maybe I could get a better one. "You two gentlemen work for an ogre?"

"Don't be stupid," said Missing Ear. "The ogre is just a bonus. Our employer wants you dead, and, since you're dead either way, we sell you to the ogre that lives in this forest. That's good business."

He clearly wasn't the brightest blade in the rack, but I couldn't fault his mercantile instincts. "So who are you working for?"

"You're dead. What do you care?"

"If I'm going to die, I'd like to know why. Besides, if I'm good as dead it's not like I'll be telling anyone."

"Well, if you must know—oww!" Missing Ear began, but then Split Nose leaned over and rapped him sharply on the back of his skull.

"You know what *she* said about talking too much," he said. "What if she found out? Do you want her angry at you? I'd sooner take my chances with the ogre."

Her. At this point there didn't seem to be much question as to whom they meant.

Missing Ear rubbed his head. He had a sour look on his face, but what his companion had said to him apparently sank in. "No. That would be . . . bad."

"So far we've done everything like she said. The ogre will see our fire soon and come for this fool, and that's that. We can get out of this demon-blighted place."

"You two are making a big mistake. I'm acting as proxy for Lord Abe. An insult to me is an insult to him." It wasn't much, but it was all I had. I was still surprised at the bandits' reaction. They glanced at each other and burst out laughing.

"We know why you're here, *baka*," said Split Nose when he regained his composure. "Now be a well-behaved meal and wait for the ogre."

The bandits obviously knew more about this matter than I did. It was also obvious that they had searched me before they tied me up. I could see my pack near the campfire and my *tachi* leaning against a boulder only a few feet away. It was the only decent material object I owned, a gift from the grateful father of a particularly foolish young man whose good name I was able to salvage. It was a beautiful sword, with sharkskin-covered grip and scabbard both dyed black. The *tsuba* was of black iron and the blade, I had occasion to know, was sharp enough to shave with. If only I could reach it, I could demonstrate that virtue on my captors, but it was impossible. As close as the *tachi* was, it might as well have been in Mongolia for all the good of it.

Try as I might, I could not get free of the ropes. I flashed back on something Lord Abe had said.

"Love and happiness are both illusions."

To which I could add that life was fleeing and illusory itself. I might not have been much for the temple, but the priests had that much right. The best I could hope for now was that the ogre was more hungry than cruel; then at least he would be quick.

There was a very faint rustling in the undergrowth. At first I thought it was the ogre coming for his supper, but then I couldn't quite imagine something that large moving so quietly. A light flared and I assumed someone had lit a torch, but the flame turned blue and then floated over the campsite and disappeared. Then, almost on cue, thirteen additional blue fires kindled in the darkness just beyond the campfire.

Yurrei . . . ? Oh, hell.

Ghosts were just like *youkai* in one important respect—there were ghosts, and then there were ghosts. Some, like the red lantern ghost Seita, were reasonable folk once you got to know them. Some, however, tended to be angry at everything living. Judging from the *onibi* and balefire I was seeing now, all three of us were pretty much stew for the same pot. Split Nose and Missing Ear knew it, too. The pair of them had turned whiter than a funeral kimono, and for a moment they actually hugged each other, though Split Nose managed to compose himself enough to rap Missing Ear's skull again.

"You idiot! You made camp in a graveyard!"

"Wasn't no graveyard here!" Missing Ear protested, but Split Nose was already pointing back toward me.

"What's that, then?"

I was having some trouble moving my head, but I managed to see what they were seeing, not ten feet away on the far side of me. It was a stone grave marker, half-covered in weeds and vines, but still visible enough even in the firelight.

When I looked back at the bandits the ghost was already there, hovering about two feet off the ground. It might have been female; it was wearing a funeral white kimono but the way its kimono was tied was about as feminine as the specter got. Its mouth was three feet wide and full of sharp teeth, its eyes as big as soup bowls and just as bulging. One of its hands was tucked within the kimono, but the other, pointing directly at the cowering bandits, bore talons as long as knives.

YOU HAVE DISTURBED ME. PREPARE TO DIE. The ghost's voice boomed like thunder, and the blue fires showed traces of red.

"Mercy!" cried Split Nose. "It was a mistake!"

YES. NOW PREPARE TO ATONE!

"Mercy!" they both cried again and bowed low.

The revenant seemed to consider. BOW LOWER, DOGS.

They did so. Then came two flashes of silver, and the bandits slumped over into a heap. In an instant the balefires went out, and the ghost floated down to earth, and then she wasn't a ghost at all but a woman carrying a sword.

My sword.

I glanced at the boulder and saw that the *tachi* was missing, though its scabbard still leaned against the stone. The grave stone was gone, but by this time I expected that. Fox spirits were masters of illusion. The woman turned to face me.

I had never seen a more beautiful woman in my life. A master painter could not have rendered a face more perfect, or hair so long and glossy black that it shone like dark fire. She seemed little more than a delicate young woman, but the ease with which she handled my sword and the twitching bodies of the two bandits said otherwise. She walked over to me without a second glance at the carnage behind her.

"Lady Kuzunoha?" I made it sound like a question, but really it wasn't.

"Who are you?" she demanded.

"My name is Yamada no Goji. Lord Abe sent me."

"I've heard of you, Yamada-san. Well, then. Let's get this over with."

She raised the sword again, and I closed my eyes. I would have said a prayer if I could have thought of one. All I could manage was the obvious.

This is my death . . .

I heard the angry whoosh of the blade as it cut through the air. It took me several long seconds to realize that it hadn't cut through *me*. Not only was I still alive, but my hands were free. Another whoosh and my legs were free as well, though both arms and legs were too numb from the ropes to be of much use to me at first. While I struggled to get to my feet, Lady Kuzunoha calmly walked back to the bandits and took a wrapping-cloth from one of their pouches which she used to methodically clean the blade. I had just managed to sit up when she returned the long sword to its scabbard and tossed it at my feet.

"I wouldn't advise staying here too long, Yamada-san," she said. "The ogre will be here soon."

"I'm afraid he's going to be disappointed," I said.

She shook her head, and she smiled. "Oh, no. Those two are still alive. We foxes know much of the nature of the spine and where to break it. They'll die soon enough, but probably not before they're eaten. The fools would have been eaten, in either case, of course. Ogres don't make bargains with meat."

Her words were like cold water. If they couldn't totally negate the effect her beauty was having on me, at least they reminded me that I wasn't dealing with a human being. An important point that I had best remember. I got to my feet a little unsteadily.

"My thanks for saving me, Kuzunoha-sama," I said, "but I'm afraid that I have some business with you yet."

"So I assumed. The path is about fifteen paces ahead of you. Stay on it until you reach the river. You'll be able to hear a waterfall," she said. "I'll be waiting for you there."

Lady Kuzunoha moved quickly away from me. In a moment her image shimmered, and I saw her true form, a silver fox bearing the second tail that betrayed her spirit nature. She ran swiftly and was soon out of sight. I gathered my belongings and hobbled along the way she had gone as best I could.

I wasn't clear on a lot of things, not the least of which was why Lady Kuzunoha had bothered to save my life. After all, if she knew who sent me, then she knew why I had come and, if she'd been willing to surrender the boy in the first place, she could have arranged that easily enough while Lord Abe's men searched the wood. And if she *wasn't* willing to give up the child, why not just kill me? It's not as if I could have done anything to stop her, and if I had any doubts of either her ability or will in that regard, I had the wretched bandits' example to prove otherwise.

A lot of things didn't make sense, and if I wanted any answers I'd have to go much deeper into Shinoda Forest to get them. Part of me wondered if I might be better off taking my chances with the ogre. Then I heard a large crashing noise in the forest back the way I'd come and decided not. I picked up the pace as much as the headache and my tingling limbs allowed.

I'd been careless once and was lucky to be alive. This time as I moved down the path, I had my sword out and ready. I wasn't sure how much good it would do me against what I'd likely face, but the grip felt comforting in my hand.

I came to the place Lady Kuzunoha described and followed the sound of rushing water. A cold water stream rushing down the adjacent hill formed a twelve foot waterfall into the river's rocky shallows. Lady Kuzunoha was in human form again. She stood directly underneath the rushing water, her slim fingers pressed together in an attitude of prayer, her long black hair flowing over her body like a cloak. Her hair was the only thing covering her. For a little while I forgot to breathe.

I knew Lady Kuzunoha's human form was an actual transformation and not simply illusion, else she would never have been able to bear a human child, but I also knew it was not her true form. Knowing this did not help me at all. The only thing that did was the sharp and clear memory of what she had done to those two hapless bandits; that was *my* cold waterfall. That left the question of why Lady Kuzunoha needed one.

When I finally managed to look away, I noticed Lady Kuzunoha's kimono neatly folded on top of a flat stone nearby. I'm still not sure why I turned away. Maybe it was my common sense, warning me of danger. Or maybe I had come to the reluctant—and relieved—conclusion that this little show was not being staged for my benefit. Lady Kuzunoha was preparing herself for something, but I didn't have clue one as to what that might be.

There was a small clearing nearby; I waited there. Lady Kuzunoha finally emerged, now fully dressed, her hair still wet but combed out and orderly. If anything she appeared more winsome than before. She looked sad but resolute as she approached the center of the clearing. In her sash she had tucked one of those slim daggers that high-born ladies tended to carry both as self-defense and a symbol of rank. She knelt beside me, looking away.

"I'm ready," she said. She drew the dagger and put the naked blade across her thighs.

I frowned. Maybe Seita the ghost was right about me, since what came out of my mouth then wasn't very intelligent. "I don't understand. Ready for what, Lady Kuzunoha?"

It was as if she hadn't even heard me. "I would send my love a poem but words are useless now. You may take back whatever proofs your master requires. Now stand ready to assist me."

The light dawned. The waterfall was a purification rite, which would explain the prayer but not much else. "You think I'm here to kill you!"

Lady Kuzunoha looked up at me. "Do not mock me, Yamada-san. I saved your life, and I think I'm due the courtesy of the truth. Did Lord Abe send you or not?"

"I have his writ and seal if you doubt me. But I am no assassin, whatever you may have heard of me."

Now Lady Kuzunoha looked confused. "But . . . what else? I cannot return. He knows that."

If Lady Kuzunoha was confused, I was doubly so, but at least I had the presence of mind to reach down and take the knife away from her. "First of all, assuming I *had* been sent to harm you, will you please explain why you're being so cooperative?"

She frowned. "Did my husband not explain the circumstances of our first meeting?"

"He didn't have to—I saw your message. You said that he rescued you from hunters . . . before he knew that you and the silver fox were one and the same, I mean."

"There was even more to it that he didn't know, Yamada-san. You see, I was already in love with Lord Abe, from the day his procession rode past Shinoda Forest three years ago. I came to the Inari Shrine in the first place because I knew he would be there. He already owned my heart, but from that day forward he owned my life as well. If now he requires that of me, who am I to deny my love what is his by right?"

Now it was starting to make some sense. No one had ever claimed that self-sacrifice was a fox trait, but I knew love made people do silly things, and it was clear even to a lout like me that Lady Kuzunoha, fox spirit or no, was still deeply in love with her husband. I had suspected that Lord Abe was deluding himself on that point, but now I knew better.

"If Lord Abe didn't know you were a fox, why did you leave him?"

"I didn't want to," Lady Kuzunoha said, sadly. "I tried so hard . . . You know what I am, Yamada-san. The body I wear now is real, but it is a sort of mask. Sometimes the mask slips; that's unavoidable. Yet it was happening to me more and more. In my foolishness I thought I would be spared this, but the burden of pretending to be something I am not became too much, even for his sake. It was only a matter of time before my true nature would be revealed and my husband and his family shamed. I could no longer take that risk. I am a fraud, but I was honest with my husband about why I had to leave. He did not come himself, so I assume he hates me now."

"He doesn't hate you, Lady Kuzunoha. He understands your reasons and accepts them, though he is very sad as you might imagine."

Lady Kuzunoha rose to her feet with one smooth motion. "Then why did my lord not come himself? Why did he send his warriors? Why did he send *you*?"

"My patron said he did not trust himself to let you go if he ever held you again. I can not fault him in this."

She actually blushed slightly at the compliment, but pressed on. "You didn't answer my other question."

"He sent his retainers and me for the same reason: we were looking for Doshi."

"My son? But why?"

"To bring him home, Lady. Lord Abe lost you. He didn't want to lose his son too. Maybe that's selfish of him, but I think you can understand how he feels."

"But I do *not* understand," Lady Kuzunoha said, and now the gentle, sad expression she had worn since leaving the waterfall was nowhere to be seen. She looked into my eyes and my knees shook. "Yamada-san, are you telling me that my son is missing?"

I fought the urge to back away. "But . . . you didn't take him?"

"I . . . ? Of course not! Doshi's blood may be mostly fox, but in Shinoda Forest that's not enough. He could never have made a home in my world! Doshi belongs with his father."

I took a deep breath. "If that's the case, then yes, Lady Kuzunoha—I'm telling you that your son is missing."

I'm not sure what I expected, but Lady Kuzunoha merely held out her hand. "Please return my dagger, Yamada-san. I promise not to use it on myself . . . or you."

I gave the knife back, carefully. "Do you have someone else in mind?"

Her smile was the stuff of nightmares. "That remains to be seen."

I had more questions, but Lady Kuzunoha was in no mood to answer them, and I knew better than to test my luck. She was kind enough to see me safely out of the forest before she disappeared, but it was clear she had other matters on her mind besides my well-being. I, on the other hand, could think of little else.

The bandit was right to call you a fool. You had no idea of how big a mess you were in.

The *youkai* that Seita had warned me about should have been my first clue. Still, if Lord Abe had sent me chasing wild foxfire, there still might be time to get on the right trail. I didn't like where I thought it was going to lead, but I had given my word, and that was the only thing worth more to me than my sword. I just hoped it didn't have to mean more than my life.

When I got back into Kyoto, the first thing I did was track down Kenji. It wasn't that hard. He was at one of his favorite drinking establishments near the Demon Gate. Technically it was the Northeast Gate, but since that was the direction from which demons and evil spirits were supposed to enter, the name stuck. Naturally someone like Kenji would keep close to such a place. He said it was good for business.

Business looked a little slow. For one thing, Kenji was drinking very cheap saké. For another, he was in great need of a barber; his head looked like three days' growth of beard. I found a cushion on the opposite side of his table and made myself comfortable. Kenji looked at me blearily. He had one of those in-between faces, neither old nor young, though I happened to know he was pushing fifty. He finally recognized me.

"Yamada-san! How is my least favorite person?"

"Terrible, you'll be pleased to know. I need a favor."

He smiled like a little drunken buddha. "Enlightenment is free but in this world all favors have a price. What do you want?"

"I need to seal the powers of a fox spirit, at least temporarily. Is this possible?"

He whistled low. "When all is illusion all things are possible. Still, you're wading in a dangerous current, Yamada-san."

"This I know. Can you help me or not?"

Kenji seemed to pause in thought and then rummaged around inside his robe, which, like him, was in need of a bath. He pulled out a slip of paper that was surprisingly clean considering from where it had come. He glanced at it, then nodded. "This will do what you want, but the effect is temporary. Just how temporary depends on the spiritual powers of the animal. Plus you'll have to place it on the fox directly."

"How many bowls?"

"Rice? For this? Yamada-san, I'll accept three good bronze, but only because it's you."

Reluctantly I counted out the coins. "Done, but this better not be one of your worthless fakes for travelers and the gullible."

He sat up a little straighter. "Direct copy from the Diamond Sutra, Yamada-san. I was even sober when I did it."

"I hope so, since if this doesn't work and somehow I survive, I'll be back to discuss it. If it does work, I owe you a drink."

He just smiled a ragged smile. "Either way, you know where to find me."

I did. Whatever Kenji's numerous faults as a priest and a man, at least he was consistent. I carefully stashed the paper seal and headed for Lord Abe's estate. I wasn't sure how much time I had left, but I didn't think there was a lot.

There was less than I knew.

Before I even reached the gate at the Abe estate, I saw a lady traveling alone. She was veiled, of course. Her wide-brimmed *boshi* was ringed with pale white mesh that hung down like a curtain, obscuring her features. I couldn't tell who it was but her bearing, her clothes, even the way she moved betrayed her as a noble. A woman of that class traveling unescorted was unusual in itself, but more unusual was the fact that no one seemed to notice. She passed a gang of rough-looking workmen who didn't even give her a second glance.

Once the density of the crowd forced her to brush against a serving girl who looked startled for a moment as she looked around, then continued her errand, frowning. The woman, for her part, kept up her pace.

They can't see her.

At that point I realized it was too late to keep watch at the Abe estate. I kept to the shadows and alleyways as best I could, and I followed. I could move quietly at need and I was as careful as I could be without losing sight of her; if she spotted me, she'd know that fact long before I did. I kept with her as the buildings thinned out and she moved up the road leading out of the city.

She's going to the Inari Shrine.

Mount Inari was clearly visible in the distance, and the woman kept up her pace without flagging until she had reached the grounds of the shrine. Its numerous red *torii* were like beacons, but she took little notice of the shrine buildings themselves and immediately passed on to the path leading up to the mountain.

Hundreds of bright red gates donated by the faithful over the years arched over the pathway, giving it a rather tunnel-like appearance. I didn't dare follow directly behind her now; one backward glance would have betrayed me. I moved off the path and kept to the edge of the wood that began immediately behind the shrine buildings. It was easy now to see why hunters might frequent the area; the woods went on for miles around the mountainside. There were fox statues as well, since foxes were the messengers of the God of Rice; they were depicted here in stone with message scrolls clamped in their powerful jaws. The wooden torii themselves resembled gates, and I knew that's what they were, symbolic gates marking the transition from the world of men to the world of the spirits, and this was the true destination of my veiled Lady. I didn't want to follow her further but I knew there was no real choice now; to turn back meant failure or worse. Going on might mean the same, if I was wrong about what was about to happen.

The woman left the path where the woods parted briefly to create a small meadow. I hid behind a tree, but it was a useless gesture.

"You've followed me for quite some time, Yamada-san. Please do me the courtesy of not skulking about any longer."

I recognized the voice. Not that there was any question in my mind by then, but there was no point in further concealment. I stepped into the clearing. "Greetings, Lady Akiko."

Lady Abe no Akiko untied her veil and removed her boshi. She was showing her age just a little more in the clear light of day, though she was still very handsome. "Following me was very rude, Yamada-san. My son will hear of it."

"Perhaps there is a way we can avoid that unpleasantness, Lady, if not all unpleasantness. You're here about your grandson, aren't you?"

She covered her mouth with her fan to indicate that she was smiling. "Of course. Family matters have always been my special concern."

Someone else entered the clearing. Another woman, dressed and veiled in a manner very similar to Akiko. "You said you'd come alone," the newcomer said. It sounded like an accusation.

"It was not my doing that he is here," Lady Akiko said. "And it will make no difference. Surely you can see that?"

"Perhaps." The newcomer removed her *boshi*, but her voice had already announced her. Lady Kuzunoha. She glared at me as she approached. Now she and Lady Akiko were barely a few paces apart.

"Yamada-san, this no longer concerns you," Lady Kuzunoha said.

"I respectfully disagree. My responsibility ends only when Lord Abe's son is found."

Lady Akiko glared at her former daughter-in-law. "And this . . . this *vixen* who betrayed my son knows where he is! Do you deny it?"

"Of course not," Lady Kuzunoha said haughtily. "I know exactly where my son is. As do you."

Lady Akiko practically spat out the words. "Yes! With the person who took him!"

"Yes," Lady Kuzunoha said grimly. She drew her dagger. "Let us settle this!"

"Pitiful fool!"

It turned out that Lady Akiko already had her dagger unsheathed, concealed in the sleeve of her kimono. She lashed out and Lady Kuzunoha gasped in pain. She clutched her hand as her dagger fell uselessly into the grass. In a moment Akiko had Kuzunoha's arms pinned at her sides and her dagger at the young woman's throat.

"One doesn't survive so long at court without learning a few tricks. Or, for that matter, giving your enemies a sporting chance. Now prove the truth of my words, worthless vixen! Tell me before this witness where Lord Abe's son is, and do not try any of your fox tricks else I'll kill you where you stand!"

"You will not taste my blood that easily, Old Woman."

The fight was far from over. Lady Kuzunoha's power was gathering around her like a storm; the air fairly crackled with it. Lady Akiko held her ground, but the hand holding the knife was shaking, and I knew it took her a great effort to keep the blade pointed at Lady Kuzunoha's throat.

"Tell Yamada-san where Doshi is if you want to live!" Lady Akiko said. "And no lies!"

"Why would he believe anything I say," Lady Kuzunoha said calmly, "if he does not believe what I have told him before now?"

I knew that, in a few seconds, anything I did would be too late. I stepped forward quickly, pulling out Kenji's seal as I did so. Both women watched me intently as I approached. "Lady Kuzunoha, do you know what this is?" She nodded, her face expressionless.

Lady Akiko wasn't expressionless at all. Her look was pure triumph. "Yamada-san, you are more resourceful than I thought. I will recommend to my son that he double your fee."

I gave her a slight bow. "I am in Lord Abe's service." I concentrated then on Lady Kuzunoha. "If you know what this is, then you know what it can do to you. Do you truly know where your son is?"

She looked resigned. "I do."

"That's all I need. Please prepare yourself."

Lady Kuzunoha went perfectly still in Lady Akiko's grip but before either of them could move again, I darted forward and slapped the seal on Lady Akiko's forehead.

"Yamada sarrrrrr!!!"

My name ended in a snarl of rage, but Lady Akiko had time to do nothing else before the transformation was complete. In Lady Akiko's place was an old red fox vixen with three tails. Lady Kuzunoha stood frozen, blinking in surprise.

There was no more time to consider. My sword was in my hands just as the fox gathered itself to spring at Lady Kuzunoha's throat. My shout startled it, and it sprang at me instead. My first slash caught it across the chest, and it yipped in pain. My second stroke severed the fox's head from its body. The fox that had been Abe no Akiko fell in a bloody heap, twitching.

I had seen Lady Kuzunoha butcher two men with barely a thought, but she looked away from the remains of her former mother-in-law with a delicacy that surprised me. "I-I still had some hope that it would not come to this. That was foolish of me."

"She didn't leave me much choice."

Lady Kuzunoha shook her head. "No, your life was already worthless to her. Doubly so since you knew her secret. Speaking of that, how *did* you know?"

I started to clean my sword. "Lady Kuzunoha, I have just been forced to take a rather drastic step in the course of my duties. I'll answer your questions if you will answer mine. Agreed?"

She forced herself to look at Lady Akiko's body. "There is no reason to keep her secrets now."

"Very well. There were two things in particular. Someone put me on the trail of a *youkai* that was pretending to be you. Once I knew that you didn't send either it or those bandits, that left the question of who did. More to the point, you told me that Doshi was *mostly* fox, remember?"

She actually blushed. "Careless of me. I did not intend . . . "

I smiled grimly. "I know, and at first I thought you'd simply mis-spoken. But, assuming you had not, for Doshi to be more than merely half fox meant his father was at least part fox himself. How could this be? The simplest reasonable answer was Lady Akiko. Did Lord Abe know about his mother? Or himself?"

"No to both. Fortunately his fox blood was never dominant. Lady Akiko and I knew about each other all along, of course. She opposed the marriage but couldn't reveal me without revealing herself. We kept each other's secret out of necessity until . . . "

"Until Doshi was born?"

She nodded, looking unhappy. "I knew by then I couldn't stay, but I thought my son's position was secure. I was in error. There was too much fox in him, and Lady Akiko was afraid his fox nature would reveal itself, and disgrace the family. The position of the Abe family was always her chief concern."

"If the boy was such a danger, why didn't she just smother him in his sleep?"

Lady Kuzunoha looked genuinely shocked. "Murder her own grandson? Really, Yamada-san . . . Beside, it's easy enough to dedicate an unwanted child to some distant temple with no questions about his origin. In preparation, Lady Akiko had him hidden within the shrine complex; the Abe family is their foremost patron, so it was easy to arrange. Once I

knew my son was missing it took me a while to follow his trail and to arrange a meeting."

"Duel, you mean."

She looked away. "Just so. While I may have hoped otherwise, it was
destined that either I or Lady Akiko would not leave this clearing alive. Her
solution to the problem of Doshi was quite elegant, but you were an obstacle
to that solution and, once you found me, so was I."

"Which explains why she went to so much trouble trying to prevent me
from finding you in the first place. Was she correct then? Won't Doshi be a
danger to the family now?"

"Yes," said Lady Kuzunoha frankly. "Yet my husband already knows
that. Perhaps not how *great* a risk, I concede, but I don't think that would
deter him. Do you?"

I finished cleaning my sword and slid it back into its scabbard. "No, but
as grateful as he's going to be at the return of his son, Lord Abe is going to
be considerably less so when I explain what happened to his mother, proxy
or no."

Lady Kuzunoha covered her mouth as she smiled. "Yamada-san, perhaps there is an 'elegant solution' to this as well. For now, kindly produce
my lord's proxy seal and we'll go fetch my son."

That proved easily done. The presence of both the seal and Lady Kuzunoha herself was more than enough to send one of the shrine priests scur-
rying ahead of us to a small outbuilding near a *koi* pond. There we found
Doshi in the care of a rather frightened wet nurse. Lady Kuzunoha paid off
the poor woman generously, thanked her for her solicitude, and sent her on
her way. The baby looked up, lifting its little arms and gurgling happily, as
Lady Kuzunoha smiled down at him.

"Probably time you were weaned, my son." She turned to me. "Please
take him, Yamada-san. You'll need to get him back to his father quickly;
he'll have to make his own arrangements for Doshi's care. I will give you
some writing to take to my husband before you leave."

I hesitated. "Don't . . . don't you wish to hold your son? This may well be
your last chance."

She smiled a sad smile. "Thank you for that offer, but I can only echo the
words of my lord in this, Yamada-san: If I held him again, what makes you
think I could let him go?"

I had no answer to that, but I did have one last question. "One thing still bothers me: you were unable to maintain the deception of being human, but Lady Akiko had been in the family much longer than you. How did she manage?"

Lady Kuzunoha laughed softly. "Yamada-san, as I told you before: the mask will slip, and we cannot control when or how. For me, my right hand would turn into a paw without warning. For Lady Akiko, it was her scent."

I blinked. "Scent?"

She nodded. "Her true scent, as a fox. But the human nose is a poor tool at best. Those close to her would either miss the scent entirely or at worst mistake it for . . . something else," she finished, delicately. "Lady Akiko was simply luckier than I was."

That may have been so, but Lady Akiko's luck had finally run out. I was afraid that mine was about to do the same.

Lord Abe received me in his private chambers after I placed his infant son back in the care of his servants.

"Yamada-san, I am in your debt," he said. "I-I trust Lady Kuzunoha was not . . . difficult?"

From my kneeling position, I touched my forehead to the floor. "That relates to a matter I need to speak of. Lady Kuzunoha was quite reluctant, as you can imagine, but I was impertinent enough to acquire the assistance of Lady Akiko in this. They spoke, mother to mother, and Lady Akiko persuaded her."

"I see."

I could tell that he didn't see at all, but the die was already cast. I produced the scroll Lady Kuzunoha had supplied. "Lady Akiko told me of the . . . differences, between your wife and herself. That her intense desire to protect the family's name had perhaps blinded her to Lady Kuzunoha's virtues. To atone for this—and other burdens—she has decided to renounce the world and join a temple as a nun. She also sent a personal message to you."

Lord Abe was a Gentleman of the Court, whatever else he might be. He concealed his shock and surprise very well. He took the scroll I offered and unrolled it in silence. He remained intent on what was written there for several moments longer than would have been required to actually read the words. I tried not to hold my breath.

"My mother's script," he said, almost to himself, "Perfect." He looked down at me, his expression unreadable. "I don't suppose my mother revealed to you which temple she had chosen to join?"

I bowed again. "She did not so confide in me, my lord, though I had the impression it was quite far from here. She seemed to feel that was for the best. She hoped you would understand."

He grunted. "Perhaps she is right about both. Well, then, Yamada-san. I've lost both my wife and my mother, but I have not yet lost all. It seems I must be content with that."

I breathed a little easier once I'd been paid and was safely off the grounds. I wasn't sure how much of my story Lord Abe really believed, but if he didn't realize full well that Lady Kuzunoha had written that message, I'm no judge of men. Perhaps that was another choice he made. As for myself, I chose to be elsewhere for a good long time. Hokkaido sounded best; I'd heard that it's very sparsely populated and only a little frozen at this time of the year. But first I went to meet Kenji by the Demon Gate, since I'd given my word and now I owed him a drink.

I owed myself several more.

A HINT OF JASMINE

———

Water Oaks Plantation was ten miles north of Canemill on Route 501. Eli kept the sensic in its case, even after he'd turned down the long tree-lined driveway leading to the house.

The ghosts at Water Oaks should be easy enough to find.

Eli had requested all the general data he could, on both the Stockard family and the plantation, but the plantation's history during the War of Secession was a little sketchy.

Especially around the time of the Water Oaks Massacre.

As for the Massacre itself, Eli knew only what everyone else who had grown up near Canemill knew: the few slaves remaining at Water Oaks near war's end staged a revolt. The master of the plantation, Captain John Stockard, was a prisoner of war after the siege of Vicksburg and absent. Stockard's wife Elizabeth, aided by a single loyal servant and a pair of her husband's pistols, reputedly ended the revolt by the simple expedient of killing every single one of the remaining slaves. Captain Stockard returned home to find only his wife, his infant son, and the one servant. There was one marked grave for his daughter Margaret, killed in the revolt. All the slaves were buried somewhere on the grounds in a single pit.

Details were also sketchy as to how many slaves were in that pit. Estimates ran from five to fifty, though no one seriously believed the latter. There had been talk of an exhumation, inquests, but in the confusion after the war and in light of Elizabeth Stockard's deteriorating mental state, it had never happened. Even the location of the grave was lost. After that the legends grew: books, stories, songs. No one celebrated but everyone remembered, in Canemill, almost as a personal memory, passed along like all others of those times by people who were not there, and could not know, but would forever believe in their hearts that they did know.

There was a gravel parking lot with a few other cars. Guests at the B&B

that Water Oaks now was, Eli assumed. He parked his rental and got his first good look at Water Oaks in nearly thirty years.

The house wasn't a grand Greek Revival town home like Stanton Hall or Rosalie in Natchez; it was the center of a working plantation and was built in the French plantation style. Smaller, by comparison, and a little more practical, but still big enough. Eli crossed the lot to the front porch, carrying the sensic in its case hanging from a strap around his shoulder.

The stout oak boards barely creaked as he walked across the porch. The ceiling of the porch was painted blue in the old belief that it discouraged wasps and spiders. Perhaps it worked, for Eli didn't notice either. In fact, the house was in much better shape in all details than Eli remembered: the white paint was clearly fresh, a rotting finial over the doorway had been replaced with an exact copy of the original. The grounds were immaculate.

Elizabeth's put some money into this.

Eli frowned. The Bed and Breakfast market around Canemill might be steady, but it wasn't such to support this kind of investment. Eli wondered what that meant, if anything, other than his old classmate Elizabeth was clearly doing well for herself. She must have been, to be able to repurchase the ancestral home in the first place. The Stockards, like so many planter families, had been completely ruined in the war and lost Water Oaks for land taxes soon after war's end. When Eli knew them those remnants of the old aristocracy were living in a modest old Victorian home not too far from Eli's own house.

The entranceway was grand; one thing this plantation home had in common with the Greek Revival style houses was the central hallway, running from one end of the house to the other, connecting the front door and the rear door. The staircase leading to the second floor was off to the side so as not to block the flow of air through the house; there was no air conditioning in those days and the homes were built to maximize what air flow there was.

Eli stepped just inside the doorway, hesitated.

"One," he said softly.

"One what?"

A young woman sat at a massive desk just beside the stairway. Eli recognized her, though he'd never seen her before. Elizabeth's daughter, Mary. The resemblance was uncanny.

Eli hesitated. "Just counting chandeliers. How many are there?"

The woman smiled. "Seven. And no you weren't. You just walked through the little girl, didn't you?"

Eli just stared at the woman for a moment or two, but there was really no doubt in his mind. She knew. "I'm Eli Mothersbaugh from the Bureau of Bio-Remnant Reconciliation," he said finally. "I believe you're expecting me."

The young woman was, as Eli had surmised, Elizabeth's daughter. The resemblance was indeed striking—the same jet black hair, brown eyes. The same tall, graceful elegance. Eli suddenly felt very, very old.

He asked the logical question as she showed him to his room upstairs. "How long have you known about the ghosts?"

She smiled. Eli remembered that smile. "Since the day Mother and I moved into Water Oaks. The little girl was just the first."

Eli considered this. "Do you see her?"

Mary shook her head. "No . . . it's a feeling, really. I've heard it described as a 'cold spot' but it's not really cold. It's tingly like cold, and a bit hazy when you're standing there as if you're looking at everything through a mist."

Eli knew the feeling. In fact, he was feeling it at that exact moment. "Two," he said.

"That would be Ruth Benning," Mary said.

"The original Elizabeth Stockard's servant," Eli said. "Who was with her at the time Massacre by all accounts."

Mary stopped at the upstairs landing, and turned to look at him. "You've done your homework."

"Of course. Not that I really had to except for the finer details. When I was growing up people talked about the Stockards of Water Oaks like it all happened yesterday."

"They still do," Mary said.

"Now let me ask you a question: if you can't see them, how do you know who they are?"

Mary sighed. "I don't know for certain. It's what I feel . . . rather like being in the same room with someone you know. I can't explain any better than that. Oh, I know it's all very unscientific compared to what you're used to."

Eli shook his head. "The remnant signatures are very individual and someone who can sense them at all can usually tell at least a little about them. Would you like to see if you're right?"

Mary's eyes widened slightly. "Yes, I would. How?"

Eli unzipped the sensic case. "It may not work if the remnant is too mobile. Still, I gather she tends to hang about the stairway?"

"She's not *always* here," Mary confirmed. "But most of the time."

The sensic's display came up. Eli pointed the sensor and changed the display from charting to mapping. The lines of numbers reformed themselves into an image. It was a little faint, blurred like an old-fashioned photographic negative slightly out of focus, but clear enough. A small black woman stood about mid-way up the staircase, looking straight down the stairwell to the floor below. She wore a plain gingham dress, and her head was covered in a white *tignon*, the cloth wrapped and secured just so. Her age was hard to tell, but she was clearly ancient. Eli turned the display so that Mary could see.

"That's Ruth Benning, no doubt," she said. "I've seen the pictures. Wait . . . if this is just some sort of energy field, why are there clothes?"

"Good question. No one's really answered it yet, though there are theories." Eli started to expound on a couple of them, but a glance at Mary told him that her mind was elsewhere.

"Can . . . can you show me the others?" she asked.

Eli didn't ask what Mary meant about the others. He assumed there were more than two, and in any case preferred to do his own count. "Probably."

Mary looked pensive. "Does Ruth know we're here?"

Eli switched the display back to charting, looked closely at the numbers. "Hard to say . . . " He looked up, saw Mary watching him intently. *She wants the truth*, he thought. He had no way of knowing this for sure, unlike his first impression of a remnant, which was almost always verifiable with the sensic. The living were always harder to read.

"No, I don't think so," he said finally. "Here, look . . . " He switched the display back. "See these numbers? She's just repeating a particular series of actions: the hesitation . . . the look down the stairwell. Then it starts again. She's what we call a repeater."

"Repeater?"

"A remnant caught in some sort of traumatic or deeply significant sequence of events. Now she's not much more than a recording, like a tape loop that just runs."

"Until when?"

"Indefinitely. Or until whatever's holding her here goes away."

Mary nodded. "I think that's where you come in."

"Is she why you called the Bureau? It was you, wasn't it?"

Mary nodded again. "I discussed it with mother first, of course. She wasn't too happy about it, but finally gave in."

"Have the guests been complaining?"

Mary laughed. "Most don't even notice; and the ones that do rather enjoy it, I think. Adds atmosphere to the place . . . not that it really needs any."

"Then what's the problem?"

"Three days ago *something* tried to push my mother down the stairs."

Eli frowned. "Who saw this?"

"I did. I was standing beside Mother when it happened. I heard something hit her, like a slap and she almost went down head first. If I hadn't been there to catch her . . . well, I'm afraid of what might have happened. Before you ask, no, I didn't sense anything besides Ruth."

Eli made a mental note. "Neither of you saw anything?"

"I didn't say that, Mr. Mothersbaugh," Mary demurred, "I don't know what my mother saw."

Eli thought there was something furtive about her expression that wasn't there before. He also noticed that she hadn't really answered his question, but before he could say anything Mary continued: "Mother's looking forward to seeing you again."

Eli resisted the urge to smile. *A bit transparent, Mary. Your mother knew I was alive, but that was about all.*

Eli shut down the sensic. He didn't count himself the sharpest tack in the box, but he knew when he was being distracted. But from what? "I'm looking forward to it, too. It's been a long time. Well then, if you'll finish showing me where I'm staying I can get started."

Mary led the way and Eli followed. He didn't think too much of it at the time, but in the warm air there was the faintest scent of jasmine.

Supper was in the dining hall, and the management of Water Oaks had gone all out: fine bone china, crystal, silverware. Other legacy items abounded:

A shoo-fly fan hung over the table with its cord leading to an empty corner, as if waiting for the young slave who operated it in the old days. There was an authentic flytrap on the sideboard, a contraption that looked like an inverted glass bowl with honey in a dish at the base and small holes for the flies to get in but not quite figure their way out, assuming they didn't drown in the honey. Eli looked at the abundance of forks and felt a little trapped himself.

The guests were a motley lot. Three older couples from Pennsylvania apparently traveling together, a pair of painfully young newlyweds, a small group of Civil War re-enactors from Jackson, and one well-dressed portly man with immaculate hair. It took Eli a moment, but there was no mistaking the man: Malachi Hollingsworth, senior Senator for the State of Mississippi, Minority Whip and major reactionary, even by local standards.

Water Oaks is definitely attracting some interesting clients.

Hollingsworth gave Eli an icy smile that made Eli wonder if he had inadvertently offended the man. Eli looked for his own place and found himself at a position of honor near the head of the table. Mary appeared and sat opposite to Eli. Soon after that Elizabeth Dunstan nee Stockard finally arrived.

'Arrived' was actually a bit off the mark. It was closer to the truth to say that Elizabeth made an *entrance*. She wasn't so impractical as to wear a full hoopskirt in proper belle fashion, but the dress was full and red and would have looked more appropriate for a night at the opera in 1920's than a modern dinner gathering. Still, Eli had to admit that as a bit of showmanship it was very effective; there was even a burst of applause which Eli joined in.

In her mid-forties, Elizabeth Dunstan still rated a round of applause in Eli's view. She had aged extremely well, though whether that was due to good genes, good gerontology, or just good makeup, Eli wasn't sure. He did know her smile was every bit as dazzling as he remembered. Almost as one, all men in the room rose from their chairs. Even, looking a bit mystified, the gentlemen from Pennsylvania.

"I see proper manners haven't entirely deserted this new millennium," Elizabeth said.

In a very short time Eli was little short of amazed. Elizabeth greeted each of her guests by name, set them at ease, turned on the Southern charm and fired up conversation to such a degree that Eli was having trouble remembering that they were simply having supper at a bed and breakfast, and not attending a dinner party at Water Oaks at the height of its glory. Eli studied the other guests and was certain they were in a similar state. Easy enough for the Civil War buffs; that was part of the appeal, but the rest seemed just as enamored.

The years since high school hadn't bought Eli the detachment he'd hoped for, but he found himself wondering about Elizabeth's obvious glamour and presence in more analytical terms. Was it some sort of energy field, related to the bio-remnant signatures that remained after death? Perhaps it could be measured . . .

"Hello, Eli."

Eli blinked. For a moment he didn't realize who had spoken to him. Later he would realize that he hadn't wanted to know. He'd both looked forward to and dreaded this moment. Elizabeth was smiling at him. Eli, to his chagrin, felt a little giddy.

"Hello, Elizabeth."

She smiled at him. "Is that all you have to say?"

Off balance from the beginning, and Eli didn't like it. His annoyance went a great way toward relieving his giddiness. "Nice to see you?" he offered.

Elizabeth laughed softly then, hiding her mouth with her hand. "You haven't changed. Not two words for anyone if one would do." She leaned closer and lowered her voice. "I gather Mary has briefed you on our problem?

"Somewhat, but I wanted to ask you a few questions."

"Of course."

"Was the stairwell incident the first time you were attacked?"

Elizabeth hesitated. "No."

Mary frowned. "Mother, you didn't tell me about this."

"I didn't want to worry you. Assuming you would."

Mary just glared at her. Eli glanced down the table but, so far as he could tell, all of the other guests were deep in their own conversations and taking little notice of them. The one exception was Hollingsworth, who gave the impression he wanted to hear them, whether he could or not. After a moment Elizabeth went on. "There were two prior incidents. Nothing severe.

More like a stinging slap than a blow. Once in my office, once when I was in the kitchen. Frankly, until the stairwell I thought my mind was playing tricks on me. Apparently not."

"Do you think Ruth Benning is responsible?" Mary asked Eli.

"She's not even aware of us, as I said. It couldn't have been her."

"Then who?" Elizabeth asked.

"I don't know," Eli said, "but I promise you that I *will* find out."

Later, after the guests had repaired to the ballroom for coffee and more conversation, Eli took a discretionary retreat to the second floor verandah. His last sight of the guests as he went up the stairs was Senator Hollingsworth in earnest and intent conversation with Elizabeth Stockard Dunstan. To Eli he looked a little like a love-smitten boar hog courting a doe.

There was a warm breeze out on the verandah, but there was a cool edge to it that Eli appreciated. Frogs were singing from a small pond in back of the mansion near the old kitchen building. The moon was rising, and the mythical bats were soaring and swooping at the moths attracted to a pole light near the parking lot.

"There it is again." Mary stood just outside the French doors that led to the verandah. She walked out and stood beside him at the railing. Eli started to tell her to call him Eli instead of 'Mr. Mothersbaugh,' but he didn't. Eli felt better with a little reserve and distance from Elizabeth and her daughter both.

Eli nodded. "Jasmine. I smelled it earlier. Curious . . . So. Why aren't you with the rest of your guests?"

Mary looked grim. "Mother's guests, not mine."

"I gather you and your mother don't always get along."

Mary laughed. "Rather like saying General Sherman didn't get on with General Lee. After my father died I ran away from home on three separate occasions, Mr. Mothersbaugh. I assume all this is in your files."

"Most of it," Eli admitted. "In most of these situations, the human element is as important as the spectral."

"Nice to know the living still count. . . . I noticed you watching the Senator and my mother. I'm afraid we banished him from his customary seat at table so Mother and I could talk to you."

"That explains the 'hurry up and die' look I got from him."

"Simple jealousy. He's in love with my mother, you know. That's why he's a regular here."

Eli nodded. "I assumed as much." He also didn't miss the hint of bitterness in Mary's voice when she spoke of her mother.

Mary sighed. "You knew? Well, I suppose it's pretty obvious, even to a man." She turned to look at Eli intently. "Were . . . were you in love with her, too?"

Eli considered. The look on Mary's face spoke volumes: mild interest on the surface and something raging just below. Jealousy? Envy? Perhaps all those things, or something just trying to be itself, separate from Elizabeth Stockard Dunstan. *It must have been very hard for Mary.*

Eli looked out over the woodlands surrounding the house. "The truth? Every male in town with a pulse was in love with your mother, in those days," he said, simply. "I'm afraid I was no different."

"What about now?" Mary asked softly. "I realize you don't have to tell me anything, but I would like to know."

Eli thought about it. "In anything like a real relationship, people fall out of love all the time. They really get to know each other—not always a good thing. They change, they grow apart. When only *one* of you is in love, then you don't get those chances. The ideal remains. Love fades, but it never really goes away. It has no reason to."

"Like a ghost?" Mary asked, looking mischievous.

Eli nodded, and sighed. "Sometimes. Yes. Just like that."

"My mother and I have a relationship too, Eli. Always have. Yet it's . . . complicated. I do love my mother, whatever your files say. Part of the reason I agreed to come to Water Oaks and work for her was I thought there might be a chance to resolve our differences."

Eli nodded. He had the distinct feeling that this wasn't the only reason she'd agreed to come, but he let it go. "I hope you can."

"I appreciate that, and I hope you'll pardon me for asking this: how do you propose to banish the ghosts of Water Oaks Plantation if you can't even rid yourself of the ghost of an old flame?"

Eli laughed. "Fair question. The answer is: I don't know. I'm not an exorcist, whatever you might have heard, and it's not always the ghosts who have the problem. Right now I have no idea what needs to be done, and that's really what I do, Ms. Dunstan, and what I'm looking for. Not ghosts as such, though I'll probably need to find those first."

"I can show you where the ghosts are . . . well, some of them, anyway, if that will help. I'd like to help."

Eli had the feeling that Mary wanted to lead him toward something now, just as when they'd first met she had turned him away from something else. He did want to do his own count, but he wanted Mary around while he did it. Perhaps she could answer some questions. Perhaps, whatever she intended, she could help him see what questions needed to be asked.

"It might be of help, at that," he said. "No time like the present. Too early for bed, so it's either hunt ghosts or rejoin the party, and frankly I'd rather not rejoin the party."

"You needn't worry about my mother and the Senator, in case you were. He has his uses, but frankly she detests the man."

Eli wasn't worried at all. In fact, at that moment he felt more than a little sympathy for the blowhard senator. The man was out of his depth with Elizabeth, just as Eli was.

"Lead on," was all Eli said, though he had to wonder just where and why Mary was leading him at all, and what she wanted him to find there.

Eli wanted to take some proper readings on the entity near the entrance, but the area was clearly visible from the open doors to the parlor, too close to Elizabeth's social gathering and Eli wasn't inclined to trigger a lot of questions. He let Mary lead him out the rear doors. The sun was well down now; the trees behind the Mansion grounds were one long dark shadow to the north and east.

Eli took out the sensic and brought up the files he'd stored on Water Oaks, including graphics of the layout. Mary moved closer so that she could see.

"Is everything in that computer of yours?"

"Sensic," Eli corrected, "though it's a computer as well, I guess you could say. And no, not everything. Since Water Oaks was never burned a good deal of the original records survived, such as they are. I haven't downloaded everything, but most of it's on file at the Department of Archives and History."

"Bear in mind I'm new to this, Mr. Mothersbaugh. Up until six months ago I lived in an apartment in Atlanta. The ancestral home hasn't been back in the family very long . . . Say, what's that?"

Mary pointed to a group of building outlines on the display that, as they both could clearly see, no longer existed. Eli tapped a few keys. "The slave quarters. Usually they were a bit farther away from the main house, but Water Oaks was a small plantation as they went."

"Oh." Mary looked at the other outline, and the building it referenced. "The kitchen's still here."

Kitchens in the larger homes were detached in those days, partly because no one wanted to bring that much heat into the living areas, partly due to the threat of fire. A regular kitchen had long since been retrofitted into the house proper; since the old carriage house was long gone as well, the original kitchen building had been converted to a garage long since. It had been freshly painted, but the doors were padlocked. Just beyond that was the pond where the frogs were still in chorus. Eli switched the display back to the sensic proper and made a slow sweep of the area.

"What do you see?" Mary asked.

Eli studied the display. He kept it in charting mode deliberately so Mary couldn't decipher it so easily. "What should I see? I assume you brought me out here for a reason."

"I just assumed you'd need to cover the entire grounds."

Eli smiled inwardly. Mary, bless her heart, wasn't the actress her mother was. Eli wondered idly why Elizabeth had never sought out a career on stage. "There's a ghost here, no question. Or was."

"Was? What do you mean?"

"I mean what I'm seeing is a residual trace, not the entity itself. Rather like a footprint. Bio-emanations tend to coalesce slightly if an entity stays long enough in one spot. This one apparently likes to walk between the old kitchen and house. That's all I can tell at the moment . . . wait." Eli studied the display. "Strike that. It's back."

"Can I see her?"

Her. The slip told Eli what he already knew; Mary was aware of remnant activity here. But how aware, beyond the simple fact? Eli hesitated, but there was no reason not to show Mary what the sensic had found. Besides, he very much wanted to see the entity for himself. He switched the display.

"Oooh."

Mary's sudden intake of breath was understandable. As with the ghost of Ruth on the stairwell, the image was like an old-fashioned photographic negative, but still striking. They were looking at a tall woman in a simple smock dress; she wore a plain headscarf, in contrast to Ruth Benning's elaborate *tignon*. The woman's age was hard to tell but there was a definite impression of youth. There was nothing in the image proper to tell what color her skin might have been, but Eli let the facial profile algorithms take their best guess against the databases and they gave the woman a flesh tone the warm light brown of cinnamon.

"She's beautiful," Mary said finally.

Eli just nodded, not looking up from the sensic for a few moments as he looked at the numbers again. He made a link to the State Department of Archives and History and made a request for additional data. It took him a moment to realize that Mary wasn't standing beside him now. He looked up and found her, hand outstretched, reaching for the spot where the ghost was standing.

"Mary, stop!"

Surprised, she drew her hand back. "What's wrong?"

"I'm taking readings here. Most ghosts aren't self-aware, but this one might be. If she is, she may realize she's not alone. That could interfere with the data I'm gathering."

"Is that all she is? Data?"

Eli looked up, a little surprised at the intensity of Mary's reaction. "Do you know who she is?"

Mary shook her head, and Eli was pretty sure she was telling the truth, but there was an expression on Mary's face that Eli found a little disturbing. He wasn't sure what it meant but it almost seemed as if Mary expected something from the entity or, more precisely, wanted something.

"There's something you're not telling me. Are you sure you don't who she is?"

Mary shook her head again. "No . . . Well, I was hoping she was someone I should know, but there's no way to tell, is there?"

"What are you talking about, Mary? Who do you think she might be?"

"My four times great grandmother."

———

"All right, Mary. Out with it."

They sat at a small breakfast table in a room just of the kitchen hallway. The window panes showed only darkness, though an occasional moth bumped itself against the window trying to reach the light. Mary poured coffee from an old stained enameled pot. "My mother was attacked; I was there and it happened just as I said. But it's true I had an ulterior motive in bringing you here."

Eli wasn't exactly surprised. "Me specifically?"

Mary shrugged. "Mother mentioned you now and then. I knew who you were, what you did. So when I contacted the Bureau I used your name as well as the Senator's. I used everything I thought would help."

"Your mother mentioned me? Why?"

Mary smiled then. "Well, well. You *do* have a normal male ego, Mr. Mothersbaugh. I was beginning to wonder."

Eli smiled faintly. "Just trying to get the context straight. An offhand, casual mention, yes? No more than that?"

"Well . . . yes. Though it happened more than once."

"So. What's the ulterior motive? Anything to do with your suspicions about that ghost we saw?"

Mary didn't say anything for a few moments. She finally sighed and said, "Look at me, Mr. Mothersbaugh. Look at my mother. Contrast that to the portraits of the original Elizabeth Stockard. Don't you think perhaps there's something about the two of us that speaks more of certain segments of New Orleans than, say, Atlanta?"

Eli got her implication. It was hard to miss. "You suspect that Elizabeth Stockard is not your direct ancestor?"

"You do put it delicately, but it's more than that. If I'm right, then Elizabeth Stockard not only wasn't my direct ancestor, she murdered my direct ancestor!"

Eli considered this. "The Water Oaks Massacre? Aren't there a few things you're forgetting?"

"Such as?"

"The fact that the only survivors of the incident were the infant Joshua Stockard, Elizabeth Stockard, and Ruth Benning, and Ruth was an old woman well past child-bearing. So even assuming John Stockard had fathered a child on one of the other slaves or servants, none survived. How could the ghost we saw possibly be your ancestor?"

Mary shrugged. "I know all that, including the fact that Ruth Benning died soon after and Elizabeth Stockard was so traumatized that she spent her last years in an asylum. There has to be something we're missing."

Eli sighed. "Records are incomplete; doubtless there's a lot we're missing. However, Mary, you may have to accept the fact that you're *wrong*. I'm going to trust that you can do that."

Mary sipped her coffee. "I just want the truth, Mr. Mothersbaugh. What-ever it might be."

"I'll keep that in mind. You do the same."

Eli glanced back at the sensic, noted a blinking green light. The new data he'd requested was coming in. He pushed a button. Eli turned the display so that Mary could see, and she leaned close.

It wasn't a photograph. Some of those had come in, too, specifically one of Captain John Stockard and his wife Elizabeth, but this was different: it was a digital scan of a painted portrait. Mary's eyes got wide. "That's her! The woman we saw out by the kitchens!"

Eli nodded as he took a closer look at the portrait. "Not much doubt. The sensic was very close in its reconstruction, though it appears her skin color was even lighter than we thought. Her name was Jasmine Devereaux, and according to this the portrait was commissioned by Captain John Stockard himself."

"But . . . why would John Stockard commission a portrait of a slave?"

Eli called up the rest of the data. "She wasn't a slave. She was 'a free wom-an of color' as they said in those days. A young creole originally from New Orleans. She was hired by the Stockards to help supervise the household and care for the Stockard's children. Why Stockard commissioned the por-trait . . . well, that's a good question. Why someone like Jasmine Devereaux would take part in a slave revolt is another." Eli scrolled through the accom-panying text and noticed something he hadn't before. "Strange. There was apparently an outbreak of some sort of fever around the time of the Mas-sacre. Locals thought it might have been malaria but that's not certain."

"Do you think there's a connection? Or just coincidence?"

Eli shrugged. "At the moment I have no idea."

Mary turned her attention back to the portrait. "Jasmine was very beautiful," she said.

"Yes," Eli said. "And so is your mother and so are you. Other than that, what makes you think she's your ancestor, when all the evidence so far is against it?"

Mary blushed, then took a deep breath, let it out. "I admit it's a feeling. Call it a matter of faith, if you want. That's all. I was hoping you could help me prove it, if you let me talk to her. I've read up on the techniques for direct communication with the bio-remnant personality; I know it's possible."

"Not in this case."

"But . . . why? You should talk to her anyway. For all we know, she's the one who attacked my mother!"

Eli shook his head. "Probably the only thing I *do* know for certain at this point is that the ghost of Jasmine Devereaux did not attack your mother. She couldn't have."

Mary's face fell as Eli's words sank in. "You mean . . . ?"

Eli nodded. "I'm sorry, Mary, but I've checked and rechecked the data and there's no doubt about it—Jasmine Devereaux is a repeater."

Eli skipped breakfast, mainly to skip the company. It was mid-morning before Mary found him, making sensic sweeps of the area around the vanished slave quarters and the old kitchens. It was good timing. He was just about to go look for her.

"Why are you still looking here? I thought Jasmine Devereaux was a dead end, so to speak."

Eli grunted. "I said we couldn't talk to her. That doesn't mean she doesn't have anything to say."

"A little less cryptic, please. What do you mean?"

"I mean a repeater is basically a recording. Bio-remnant energy, yes, but with little or no trace remaining of the original personality. You can't talk to a recording, but you can listen. Ruth Benning stares down the stairwell. Jasmine Devereaux hangs out near the old kitchen. In both cases: why? What's so interesting down that stairwell? Why does Jasmine walk out here? She wasn't the cook; Ruth was. So. I've looked at the stairwell. Now I want to see the old kitchen. Do you have a key to that padlock?"

Eli pointed to a large rusty lock hanging from a chain around the retro-fitted garage doors on the old kitchen building.

"Sure . . . just a minute." Mary pulled out an old-fashioned keyring with several black iron keys hanging from it. "I'm not sure which one it is . . . and that lock looks like it needs oil. No one's been in there since we bought the place—"

"Mary!"

They looked back toward the house. Elizabeth stood on the second floor verandah, waving. "Can you come here for a few minutes? I need you to explain something about the property taxes."

"All right," Mary shouted back, then whispered. "Great. I've been trying to get her to look at the taxes for weeks. *Now* she gets busy." She handed the ring to Eli. "One of these should do it. I think mother bought some machine oil for her sewing machine last week; if you need it come find us."

Eli took the keys and Mary hurried off toward the house. There were seven keys. Eli made a quick judgment based on size and narrowed it down to three. The first wouldn't fit at all. The second fit but wouldn't turn, and Eli was beginning to think he might need that machine oil after all. Just for the sake of argument, he tried the third.

The lock clicked open immediately. Eli frowned, then leaned forward and quickly sniffed the keyhole.

Interesting.

He pulled the chains out of the door handles and pulled the rightmost door. The hinges groaned, but turned. Eli went in, looked around. It was obvious that the building hadn't been used as a garage or anything else in some time; there were the remnants of a carriage, badly in need of restoration, but little else except cobwebs and a fine layer of dust. On the far wall was the old brick oven from the building's kitchen days. Its iron chimney had long since been removed and the ceiling patched over, but the oven was more or less intact. Eli wasn't especially surprised; even when need had prompted the kitchen building to be converted back in the 1930's there was great interest in matters of 'heritage.' Any true relic of Antebellum times would be preserved if possible, and the oven certainly qualified.

Jasmine comes in here. Where does she go?

Eli pulled out his sensic. The bio-remnant traces were very faint, but Eli didn't need them; he'd had enough time to make a very good estimate of the remnant's cycle. Eli just waited a few moments and Jasmine Devereaux herself appeared on the sensic's screen. Eli looked up, saw nothing. He sighed. Sensitive as he was to the physical presence of a bio-remnant signature, he seldom could see them without the aid of his sensic. There were others in the Bureau who barely needed a sensic at all, at least for visual confirmation; however, they tended to be almost blind when it came to sensing a ghost directly and learning anything useful. Eli wouldn't have traded abilities, but now and then he did envy the convenience of it.

Jasmine walked slowly past, Eli tracking every step on the sensic's screen. He couldn't resist stepping into the ghost's path, since he was sure she was not and could not be aware of him. The familiar sensation spread over him: not cold, exactly, but rather numbing. For a moment Eli looked at the world through a haze. Eli wondered if this was the way ghosts saw their world, at least those with enough of a mind to truly 'see' anything. Then Jasmine swept past and, as quickly as it had come, the feeling ebbed. The scent remained, however: jasmine, just like her name. Had she worn the scent in life? There was no way to know. Eli stayed behind and kept tracking her. Inside the door, across the floor. A look left and right. Searching for someone? Or making sure no one was about? There seemed to be a furtiveness to her now that Eli had not noticed before.

Jasmine Devereaux, what are you hiding?

The question turned out to be more literal than Eli had first thought. The image knelt for a moment by the base of the oven, and then it disappeared. Eli checked the sensic carefully, but that was a formality. Eli was certain he'd watched the end of the loop of all that Jasmine Devereaux was now. Somewhere in Water Oaks was the beginning; Eli wasn't sure where that was and he wasn't even sure if it mattered, though he remembered the scent from the verandah the night before and had a pretty good idea. That wasn't what concerned him just then. There was more to it, as the sensic had just told him.

Eli knelt down at the place where Jasmine had knelt and looked closer at the oven. It took him a few moments to spot the loose brick on the corner, even with the energy signatures as a guide. He pulled the brick out and found a crevice going deeper into the oven; apparently a few of the bricks inside had been chipped away to make a hole sufficient for what had been placed inside. Eli reached in and pulled out a small unlocked tin box. It was rusted, of course, but well sealed. Inside was a diary. The handwriting on the cover was faded and the cover itself spotted and brittle with age, but the script was clear and bold and still very readable. Eli read the name written on the cover.

"Jasmine Devereaux."

Eli looked at the hole again, then put the brick back in place and looked at that more closely, too. He finally nodded, satisfied, and turned his attention back to the diary.

Well, Eli. Looks like you have some reading to do.

Two hours later, Mary found him sitting on the bottom step in the grand staircase, his sensic pointed at a patch of nothing beside the entranceway. Two of the guests walked by, stared for a moment, then wandered on, but Eli paid them no heed. Neither did Mary.

"You're looking for the little girl now," Mary said.

Eli just nodded. He adjusted the sensic to its finest setting. "I walked through her first thing after I arrived, as you'll recall. I'm used to ghosts, Mary. Sometimes I don't pay them the attention they deserve."

Mary looked at him intently. "You've found something, haven't you? What is it?"

Eli picked up the diary from the step beside him and handed it to her. "I've found a couple of things. This, for one. You might want to let the experts at the Department of Archives and History look it over when you're done, but I'm certain it's just what it appears to be: Jasmine Devereaux's journal. It was hidden in the old brick oven in the kitchen building."

"You've read it? What does it say?"

Eli smiled then. "Slow down. I haven't read all of it; Jasmine was quite the diarist and there's a lot there. I read from just before she arrived at Water Oaks. Read it yourself, but start with the entry for January 10th, 1865. That's the part that concerns you right now."

Mary sat down beside him and read in silence for several moments while Eli tuned his sensic and waited. Mary finally looked up, and her eyes were shining. "She and John Stockard were having an affair! Jasmine was pregnant with his child . . . " Mary clutched the book to her breast; she was almost bouncing with excitement. "This is the proof I need!"

"No, it isn't."

Mary glared at him. "What do you mean? Are you saying Jasmine was lying?"

"No, I'm saying it doesn't prove anything one way or another. Even if we assume that Jasmine was telling the truth—and I have no doubt of it, frankly—that doesn't explain how Jasmine Devereaux's child became the Stockard heir. There's still the little matter of Elizabeth's son. Remember him? Joshua Stockard. You'll note that the entry for April 20th is the last."

Mary nodded, solemnly. "Just before the Water Oaks Insurrection. The Massacre."

"The last entry," Eli corrected. "And if you'll read more carefully you'll see what I mean. There was no massacre."

Mary just stared at him for a moment. Then she swore softly and flipped several pages until she found the entry Eli mentioned. She read for several minutes while Eli waited, patient as a stone.

"Jasmine just talks about how hard things had been for her and Ruth in the past few weeks. What with the Master still gone, her so far along and sick, and no help . . . " She stopped. "Oh."

Eli nodded. "Exactly. *No help.* The women were alone, except for the child Margaret and the infant Joshua, and it doesn't take a crystal ball to know why. The field hands and the few remaining house slaves had either been released or ran away. There was no massacre because there was no one left *to* massacre."

"But then what really happened?"

"I think I know. If you'll sit quietly for a few minutes we might have a chance to prove it."

The readings on Eli's sensic changed. He nodded. Right on time. The ghost was periodic, as he suspected. Most were. But was she a repeater? Eli didn't think so, and in a moment the numbers told him the same. There was someone there, and he was almost certain he knew who that someone was. He changed the display from charting to mapping to see if he was right.

The image resolved into a little girl about five years old. Eli adjusted the image data to the finest granularity that did not compromise the raw data, then let the sensic make reasoned guesses about the rest, just as he had with Jasmine Devereaux's image. When he was done the little girl had turned

93

into a remarkably good match to the only picture surviving.

"Margaret Stockard," Mary said, looking over his shoulder. "But what is that she's holding? A doll?"

"If you'll be quiet as I asked you to we might find out. I'm going to try and talk to her."

Eli used the sensic's projection capability to create an image of himself using the same type of energy field that was all that remained of Margaret Stockard. It covered him in a rough outline and gave him a rather sketchy appearance, but it was more than enough. Eli looked straight at the little girl, and the confusion in her eyes told him that she did, indeed, see him, or at least his projection. Eli spoke carefully.

"Hello, Margaret."

She had no voice, strictly speaking. The sensic simply ran the image's lip movements through a pattern-matching algorithm and read them as a deaf person might. The speaker crackled to life. It was a synthesized voice, but it was Margaret Stockard, shyly speaking to the living again after nearly two hundred years. "Hullo."

"You've been sick, I understand. You should be in bed."

"Are you the dok'ur?"

"Doctor. That's right." It wasn't completely a lie, Eli told himself. He had his PhD. But it still made him feel uncomfortable.

"I feel good now. You're tardy," Margaret said. The synthetic voice was expressionless but there was mischief in her eyes. Margaret's was a child's face; every emotion was clearly readable.

Tardy? Poor thing, you don't know the half of it.

It remained to be seen how much she did know. Eli took a deep breath and asked the question. "Is that your doll?"

Margaret held up the bundle she was carrying, and Eli could plainly see that it was not a doll. But then, he already knew it wasn't a doll. He waited for Margaret Stockard to tell him just what it was.

"My baby brother," she said proudly. "His name's Jos'ua."

It wasn't very long before Margaret Stockard and her brother faded away. That didn't matter; Eli had learned what he needed to learn.

"Well, there's your smoking gun," Eli said. He started to pack up the sensic.

Mary just stared at the place the ghost children had been. "I don't follow," Mary said.

"You heard what Margaret said. She picked up her baby brother because he was crying. Then she went downstairs to find her mother. She's still looking for her mother, still carrying her baby brother. And Ruth Benning is still looking down the stairwell in shock and loss. Think about that for a moment."

Mary obviously did. "The poor child . . . she fell! She fell down the stairs and died . . . along with Joshua Stockard. The original Joshua Stockard, anyway. He was replaced!"

Eli nodded. "It fits."

"Then Elizabeth Stockard murdered Jasmine Devereaux and took Jasmine's baby as her own!"

Eli considered. "Possible."

"Possible? Mr. Mothersbaugh, if you'll pardon my quoting you, 'It fits.'"

"Up to a point. You're forgetting two things: Ruth Benning and the fever. We know from her diary that Jasmine Devereaux was already ill and weak with fever and overwork as her confinement approached. Now, we also know that she and Ruth Benning were friends, and that Jasmine asked her to take care of the baby if anything happened. Perhaps it was a premonition, or maybe she was just being realistic. Childbirth is always dangerous and was more so then." Eli shrugged. "I think it equally likely that Jasmine died in childbirth or soon after and Ruth simply took advantage of the situation."

"Took advantage? How?"

"By seeing that her friend's child was provided for, of course. How better than as Master of Water Oaks? Jasmine was light-skinned to start with and her child probably more so. Captain Stockard was away and had never seen his son; Elizabeth Stockard wasn't in her right mind. In any case I don't doubt that the child's resemblance to his father was unmistakable. Perhaps Ruth thought she could bring Elizabeth back to her senses if she could convince her mistress that Joshua had survived. Perhaps Elizabeth mistook the child for Joshua in her dementia and Ruth was too tender-hearted to correct her. Pick the truth you want, Mary. We'll probably never know for certain."

"Then why the Massacre story? Wouldn't it have made more sense to say that Jasmine and her child had both died? John Stockard would have had to believe any story they told him.'"

"True, but was Elizabeth in any condition to stick to a consistent account? Personally, I think the whole 'massacre' business was concocted out of her fevered brain to explain why she and Ruth were all alone. The only one who could contradict her story was Ruth, who would have had her own reasons for keeping quiet."

Mary looked at the diary wistfully. "It's a good story, Mr. Mothersbaugh. Except for the part about picking the truth you want. I wanted to know *the* truth. I believe Jasmine Devereaux is my ancestor. Maybe you believe it too, but you're right that proving that the 'real' Joshua Stockard died in 1865 doesn't prove that Jasmine Devereaux's bastard child carried the Stockard name. I'm no better off than I was!"

"Not quite. You have living descendants in the direct line from Jasmine's parents; I've already checked and, strangely enough, there are likely candidates living in the area. A simple genetic test can determine if you're related. With what we already have that's more than enough proof."

Mary looked stunned. "You must think I'm an idiot," she said. "Well, I'm not . . . most of the time. I'm not thinking clearly about this and that's simple truth. Those descendants . . . whoever they are, they're strangers. Why would they help me?"

Eli grinned. "For a chance to prove that one of the finest First Families of the Confederacy is actually descended from Jasmine Devereaux? I don't think you'll have any trouble there." Eli finished packing up his sensic. He snapped the case shut and Mary blinked, apparently only now realizing what he was doing.

"You're leaving?"

Eli nodded. "I'd like to find a way to free Margaret and her brother and I'm going to work on that when I can. But strictly within the guidelines of my responsibility, it's not necessary. They're no threat to your mother or anyone else."

"They're not? But they're the only ghosts I know of besides Ruth and Jasmine, and you've already said they weren't the ones!"

"And they aren't. You haven't met the ghost who attacked your mother. You probably never will. It's rather hard to detect."

"I have a right to know, Mr. Mothersbaugh. My mother and I have had our differences, but if she's still in danger—"

Eli shook his head. "She isn't in any danger. You'll have to trust me on that because, actually, it's your mother who has the right to know this part of the story, and I'm going to go tell her right now. After that, I think you should talk to her."

Mary looked down at the diary in her hands, and she smiled grimly. "Believe me, Mr. Mothersbaugh—I intend to."

Eli made his way up the creaking stairs. He paused for a moment at the spot where Ruth Benning kept her painful vigil on the second floor landing, then kept walking.

It's not always the ghost who has the problem.

Elizabeth, the namesake of the long dead Elizabeth Stockard, was waiting for him in her study. Eli had rather imagined more of a parlor, suitable for receiving gentlemen callers—if the senator qualified—and having tea. Instead, he found a library, ledgers, and a large, workman-like desk. Elizabeth sat behind it dressed in jeans and a comfortable old shirt, reading glasses perched on her nose. Eli could see the years on her a little clearer now, but in his eyes she was still the most beautiful woman he had ever seen.

Despite which, at the moment, Eli didn't like her very much.

"Mrs. Dunstan, in a little while your daughter is going to march in here and confront you with Jasmine Devereaux's diary. Please do her the courtesy of acting surprised."

Elizabeth didn't say anything for a few moments. Then she shook her head slowly. "You needn't take that tone with me, Eli—I will play my part. It'd be silly to do otherwise at this point."

Eli sighed. "I wondered if you'd deny it."

"Why should I? Though I'll admit that I'm curious as to how you figured it out," she said.

"For a start, nearly all incidents took place when you were alone. The one time you had a witness, Mary didn't really see anything; she heard a slapping sound and turned just in time to help catch you, though I imagine you'd have used the railing if she wasn't quick enough. She said you'd been pushed because that's what you told her. You'd already mentioned me, oh so casually, and by the time she called the Bureau Mary probably believed it was her idea in the first place."

Elizabeth smiled at him. "That's it?"

Eli shook his head. "Then there was the diary and its hiding place in the old kitchen. The lock had been oiled recently, although supposedly no one had been in the building in months. My instruments showed a distinctive and much too strong bio-remnant signature. The sort left by someone still living. Plus the cobwebs and dust had clearly been disturbed, and the tin had been opened recently. I considered Mary but, frankly, she's a poor liar and a poorer manipulator. She doesn't have your raw talent for either, I'm afraid."

Elizabeth's smile didn't waver. "I imagine that felt good, Eli. Get a bit of your own back for having the bad judgment to lust after me like every other horny dog at school? Feeling righteous and superior now, are we?"

Eli took a deep breath. "I just want to know why," he said. "That's all."

"Is it really? Then I'll tell you: For Mary," Elizabeth said simply. "For my daughter."

"I don't understand," Eli said.

"Then let me help: I grew up with a famous name and no money. 'Genteel poverty'? Isn't that what they call it when the old families hit hard times? Well, there isn't a damn thing gentle about it. Half the people around you thinking ain't it a shame and the other half thinking 'serves them *right*?' We may have lived in the same town but you had no idea what it was like to be a Stockard, Eli. Not one damn clue."

Eli knew it was true. They'd gone to the same school, the same church, but they may as well have been living on different planets. "What does that have to do with Mary?"

"Everything, Eli. Early on I decided that if I had to be a Stockard, then I damn well would *be* a Stockard. I used my looks for all they were worth. I married a well-to-do man, a sweet fool with some money but when he died his estate was worth a thousand times more, mostly my doing. I worked for the day I would take back Water Oaks, as all the other generations of Stockards since the war had failed to do. I used all the tools I had and didn't pay too much attention to those that couldn't help me."

"One of those being Mary?"

Elizabeth's smile wavered then and went out like a guttering candle. "Yes, Eli. Mary. She feels I owe her for the mess I made of her childhood and what I put her father through. You know something? She's right."

"You found Jasmine's diary first." It wasn't a question.

"Of course I did. Aren't you going to ask me how?"

Eli shook his head. "Remember the old Carson place, when a bunch of us walked past every day on the way to school? You used to say you saw Noemi Carson sitting on the porch every day, and she had been dead ten years or more by then. It was only much later that I realized you weren't joking. You can see ghosts, can't you? Even I can't do that most of the time without a sensic."

"Not always," Elizabeth confirmed. "But often enough."

"You had the diary. You also saw Margaret and her baby brother."

The smile returned. "It took a while to realize what the poor child was carrying but, yes, it was easy enough to put together after that. Another descendant of the Devereaux family lives just up the road, an old friend from school, it turned out. It was easy to get the test. Friends help out friends in Canemill, Eli. Maybe you've forgotten that."

"Friends ask. That's all you really had to do, Elizabeth," he said. Elizabeth, stung, said nothing and in a moment Eli continued. "So. Now that you've done all this, what have you done?"

Elizabeth shook her head in exasperation. "Weren't you paying attention? I've just given Mary the one thing she's wanted for years: power! The upper hand. Even, if she's so inclined, revenge. She's going to march herself in here and announce that my carefully tended image of myself as a latter-day Scarlett O'Hara is all a sham."

"Then what?"

"Then we'll *talk*, Eli," she said slowly, as if explaining to a child. "Really talk, for the first time in a while. And fight. Probably cry, and almost certainly negotiate, with Mary holding all the cards. Or so she'll believe which, for my purposes, is the same thing. Mary's looked forward to this day for a long time and I'm going to give it to her. Afterwards . . . well, one way or another our relationship changes. Maybe for the better. I hope so, but it's a risk. I've taken them before."

"What makes you think I won't tell her myself?"

"Are you really so angry with me that you'd take this chance away from her?"

Eli thought about it for a moment, but not too long. "I'm not angry, Elizabeth, and what happens between you and Mary is a family matter and none of my concern. I have to ask though: after all that you've done to regain Water Oaks, are you saying you really don't care that you're not a Stockard?"

Elizabeth smiled grimly. "Oh, but I am, Eli. A true blood daughter of Captain John Stockard, CSA. Nothing that you've found changes a thing."

"Not even in Canemill?" Eli felt a little ashamed of himself, but only a little.

Elizabeth smiled a rueful smile. "You needn't shuffle around the woodpile, Eli. Yes, there are those for whom it will matter. On the other hand, for my guests it will make an even better story than the one I have now. Good for business."

"What about Senator Hollingsworth? What do you think he'll do?"

Elizabeth's grin was as wicked as anything Eli had ever seen on a living soul. " 'Shit a brick or grow a dick,' " she said. "Frankly, I can't wait to find out which."

Eli smiled despite himself. "I almost hate to miss that. Goodbye, Elizabeth." He hesitated, and added, "Thank you."

Elizabeth frowned, but she didn't ask why Eli had thanked her and Eli didn't explain. There was no need; Elizabeth already had what mattered to her. As he left Eli realized that, oddly enough, so did he. Eli felt as if an old and painful burden had been lifted from his shoulders. What had passed between himself and Elizabeth wasn't anything like the sort of relationship he'd mentioned to Mary, or had once dreamed about, but it was honest enough, and intimate enough, and real enough for the brief time it lasted.

Despite Eli's best efforts, he had released none of the ghosts of Water Oaks Plantation. He did, finally, let go of one of his own.

VOICES IN AN EMPTY ROOM

Eli checked his sensic as the seconds ticked down. His latest projected time was displayed in the upper left corner of the screen. The dented and blackened pocket watch propped up on his table between the salt and pepper shakers wasn't much help—its spring was broken and its gears and hands frozen.

Until, all on their own, they began to move.

As soon as the second hand ticked off one discrete, impossible second, Eli checked the time index. 9:27:42 AM.

Damn. I'm still three seconds off . . .

"Mr. Mothersbaugh? I'm Jessie Nichols."

Eli's first impression was of a rather severe blue suit on a trim female figure, but his attention was elsewhere. "Give me a moment," Eli said. He turned away from the time display to the sensic data but it was already too late; the glow that would have shown an active energy signature was already fading.

Missed again.

It had all been captured digitally, of course, but Eli found there was no substitute for seeing the sensic visuals in real-time; he tended to pick up things that the recorders often missed. Still, no help for it now, he'd review it later. Eli looked up to where Jessie Nichols was not so patiently waiting and took a good look at her. His first impression of form and attire was correct, but the face didn't quite match what he'd expected. Jessie Nichols was a thirty-something redhead; she wore her thick, curly hair pulled back in a simple ponytail and she looked like someone who knew how to smile, even if she wasn't doing so at that moment.

"Imperfect social skills," she said. "I'd heard that about you."

Chagrined, Eli didn't bother to ask from whom. The information could have come from any one of dozens of reliable sources. He rose then and extended his hand, which she accepted. "My apologies, Ms. Nichols. You caught me in the middle of logging a reading."

"You've already started?"

"I was a little early for our appointment. I thought I'd use the time."

Jessie Nichols sat down across from him. Eli's table was on the sidewalk outside La Parisian, the decent if pretentious French café on the ground floor of the Walthor Hotel. It was the oldest of several buildings, mostly offices, surrounding Armfield Park. Eli looked across the large expanse of green where several dozen office workers were juggling comcells and lunch, young mothers pushed strollers, and a group of students from nearby Armfield University sat in a circle under the warm spring sun. Jessie noticed his eyes wandering.

"Lovely day, isn't it? Looking at it now it's hard to imagine such a thing happening here," she said.

Eli didn't have to ask what she was talking about; the bombing of July 4th, 2015, was still fresh on everyone's mind even ten years after the fact. Just over a hundred killed on the grand opening of the new Brian T. Armfield Municipal Park, timed to coincide with the Independence Day celebration. Despite the tensions in the world, no one had expected such a thing in the middle of the crowd at an obscure Fourth of July ceremony in the even more obscure city of Canemill, Mississippi. Not so obscure now, and so to remain as long as the nation lasted.

"Hard to imagine such a thing happening anywhere. Yet, somehow, they manage to happen anyway. Memory is short, Ms. Nichols," Eli said, "History is long."

"You can call me Jessie. I assume you were briefed before you arrived?"

"I'm Eli. A haunting, with apparent ties to the events of July 4th ten years ago?"

She nodded. "So it seems. The phenomena was apparently gradual, so no one picked up on it right away. Yet it's more than noticeable now, and people are talking. Apparitions have been sighted, noises heard where no one is visible, the usual. As deputy mayor, I'd like to get this resolved as soon as possible, yet obviously this is no common situation and must be handled with some delicacy."

"Obviously," Eli said, but that was all.

Jessie looked at him. "Is there something you're not telling me?"

"Jessie, with all due respect I could ask the same of you, but never mind that for the moment. Do you have any idea yet how many victims we're dealing with?"

She met his gaze squarely. "I assume several, considering how many people died."

Eli shook his head. "Nasty as the death-event was, it would be very unusual for more than a handful to manifest postmortem after such an extended period. There would have to be special circumstances."

"You're the expert. Do *you* know how many victims are present?"

"I've detected only one so far," Eli said. "But he's not a victim as such."

Jessie just stared at him for a moment. "But . . . that makes no sense! In ten years no one else has died here! Who else would be haunting Armfield Park?"

"Who else? Think about it, Jessie."

Jessie did think about it and turned a little pale. Eli nodded. "I'm afraid so. Ahmed Ali. The bomber."

Eli spent the most of the rest of that day taking readings at various points around the park. He got a few curious stares but not much more than that. The sensic resembled an old-fashioned laptop closely enough so that most people just assumed he was a retro-hardware fancier. Mostly what Eli saw was life going on, as it usually did among the living.

That afternoon as he was looking over his notes a visitor arrived from the mayor's office. A clean-cut, handsome young man in the standard business suit uniform. "My name is John Black, Jessie Nichols' executive assistant. I was sent to inform you that the mayor's Office has decided that the investigation is unnecessary."

Eli didn't look up from his monitor. "It doesn't work like that."

The young man blinked. "Pardon?"

"Once an investigation is initiated, the Field Operator—that's me—decides when it's closed. I have not so decided. I can be overruled by the director of the Bureau, but he's not so inclined. Ms. Nichols is welcome to try and persuade him, of course."

"You've spoken to your director?"

"Right after my appointment with Ms. Nichols this morning. I suspected she'd try this."

"The mayor strongly feels—"

"Bull. The mayor is in Aruba, has been for the last two weeks, will be until next Friday, and, I'm willing to bet my sensic to your Armani, is *not* thinking about dead terrorists. If anyone has decided anything, it's Ms. Nichols herself. If Ms. Nichols wants the investigation ended, I'm perfectly willing to discuss it; she knows where to find me."

There were times Eli was grateful for his lack of social skills, and he proceeded to ignore the young man. After a very short time John Black went away. Eli barely noticed. He did notice that Jessie didn't attempt to contact him right away. He assumed she was checking the statutes and calling in favors in an attempt to circumvent him. He wondered how long it would take her to find out that, in this special case, there was no back door. It was only after he'd eaten dinner that evening and was resting in his rooms at the Walthor that he got the answer.

The phone rang. It was Jessie Nichols. "Meet me out front in ten minutes."

Eli considered her tone. "Should I bring an escort?"

"Bring the goddam Mississippi National Guard for all I care! Just be there."

Eli sighed and put his shoes back on. In eight minutes he reached the park. Jessie was waiting for him, leaning on the edge of the basin of the central fountain; she was carrying a small notebook. She'd also traded her suit for a pair of jeans and a plain white blouse. "Eli, don't you have anything better to do?" she asked.

"That depends. What's the real reason you want me to quit?"

She stared at him for several long moments. "Aren't you getting ahead of yourself? I haven't given you *any* reason yet!"

Eli sighed. "Did you have to? These aren't ordinary circumstances, as you said yourself. The victims have all been designated 'Martyrs of Freedom' by Presidential fiat, for one thing. I assume the press release was already written, something about the mayor's office seeing that peace was given to some poor victim of July 4th?"

Jessie had the decency to blush then, but she didn't look away. "Only it didn't turn out that way, did it?"

"I'll say. It's not a poor victim at all. It's the guy who created all those 'Martyrs of Freedom' in the first place. Politically, how does it look to do a damn thing for him?"

She sighed. "Isn't that reason enough to forget the whole thing?"

"It's not a reason at all, Jessie. Bureau matters are confidential; it's in the charter. All you have to do is keep quiet, whatever happens. No political fallout at all."

"That's not the point!"

Eli shrugged. "Then what is? What if I do free Ali's tortured soul or whatever the bioremnant energies are? No one's going to know except you and me, and I'm enjoined from talking about it. You say whatever you want to say, including nothing at all. Now, if I leave this unresolved, the incidents continue. People ask questions. People go looking for answers anywhere they can get them. Do you want someone *else* to bring the Bureau in? Someone less concerned with discretion and the politics of the matter?"

"To hell with the politics! It's just not right, doing anything to help that son of a—"

Eli stopped her. "All right, that's a reason I believe, even if I don't agree with it. But you misunderstand—it's not Ahmed Ali I'm trying to help."

"But you said he was the only one here!"

"He is. That's the problem. See this?" Eli held the item up for her inspection.

"It's a beat-up old pocket watch. So?"

"It's Ahmed Ali's watch. It was his great-grandfather's and he always carried it, including the day he died."

Jessie took a closer look at it. "How did you get that?"

"Through legal channels. It goes back in the evidence files when I'm done. So. Notice anything unusual about it?"

She shrugged. "Other than the fact that it survived the blast? No."

"It didn't come through unscathed; the mechanism is pretty much frozen. Except when it runs."

She blinked. "Runs? When?"

"When Ahmed Ali makes his rounds. That's around 9:27 AM, though I haven't got the time index for each phase of his journey yet. That's what I was working on this morning. I should have made our appointment for later."

"So what does this prove? You still haven't explained what you meant. Who are you trying to help?"

"I'm not good at explanations, and, since you've already made up your mind, I don't think you'd believe me. I need to show you. Will you meet me tomorrow morning at, say, 9:15? Here by the fountain would be fine."

"I've wasted enough time on this," she said.

"Waste a little more. Let me show you what I've seen, and if you honestly think there's no point after my demonstration, I'll mark the investigation file 'inconclusive' and leave. Deal?"

Jessie's look was pure suspicion. "You're serious? My sole discretion?"

Eli nodded affably. "Entirely up to you."

"All right, but I'd advise you to pack."

Eli already had the sensic set up on the edge of the fountain and set before Jessie arrived at 9:15 on the dot.

"So what now?" she asked, "We wait?"

"Not for long. 9:27 is when the main event occurred; there will be some preliminaries."

The "preliminaries" didn't take long to start. The sensic was the latest model, with full holo capabilities. Eli had created a miniature version of Armfield park that floated in the air about a foot over the instrument, with all the energy signatures represented in faint glowing miniature. There were Jessie and himself standing by the fountain. Here and there were the benches, and here and again there were people sitting on them. Several students waiting for classes at the university Arts Center adjoining the park. Two fiftyish men in business attire sitting and talking. A few early morning joggers, walkers, and strollers.

A new glow appeared on the far side of the park. It seemed no different from the others, except this one changed every other it came in contact with. Two young mothers chatted on the sidewalk, their baby strollers parked beside them. When the glow passed them, they became suddenly agitated, and in another moment the conversation was over as they stalked off in opposite directions. As it happened in the projection, so it mirrored what was happening out in the park. Eli watched the two women walk away from each other. Jessie did too, frowning, but she said nothing.

"You'll see it again, here."

Eli didn't say what "it" was, but Jessie seemed to understand. The glow approached the two sitting businessmen, passed them. In another moment they became agitated, almost on cue. They didn't walk away as the two women had done. They argued. Loudly. It wasn't until the glow was well past them that the argument tapered off and quieted down, but it didn't end. Eli held up the pocket watch, and in a moment the hands started to move.

"Almost here," Eli said. "Wait for it."

Jessie glared at him, but she didn't move, even as the human-shaped glow headed straight for them, through them, past them.

Eli shivered. "Nasty."

"And what the hell is all this supposed to prove?"

"Why are you shouting?" Eli asked.

"I'm shouting because this is stupid! You're wasting my time!"

"You're angry, Jessie. Why?"

"I just told you . . . " She stopped. "Well, ok. I'm annoyed. I should be annoyed."

Eli smiled. "Perhaps, but you weren't annoyed. You were enraged."

Jessie took a deep breath, let it out. "What just happened?"

"The same thing I noticed yesterday when Ali appeared; the same thing that's only going to get worse the longer this goes on. Whatever you want to call it—hate, rage, madness that Ahmed Ali was carrying that day ten years ago. He's still carrying it. What's more, he's sharing it."

Jessie's voice was much more subdued now. "Oh."

"Oh, indeed. I've seen this a couple of times before: once in Memphis, another in New York, but nothing on this scale. The reason there have been 'incidents' is that the living are picking up this aspect of Ali's energy signature, even those who can't see or otherwise sense him."

"Then why weren't you affected?"

Eli glanced at the sensic display. "Because I know how to shield. You don't. As it was, my blood pressure probably went up a few points. But the show's not over. Watch."

They both watched as the revenant that had been international terrorist Ahmed Ali approached the front of the Walthor Hotel, the epicenter of the blast. Eli forced himself to take slow breaths, mostly so he would remember to breathe. Jessie's eyes were fixed on the display, her face a blank mask.

Ali reached the front of the hotel.

Ali kept going.

Absolutely nothing happened. In another moment the revenant was outside of the sensic's range and disappeared from the display.

Jessie just stared. "That doesn't make any sense!"

Eli switched the display from mapping to charting, then back again. Sometimes there was just no substitute for raw data, but it told him exactly what the holo projection had.

"It must make sense somehow, because it did happen. Ahmed Ali didn't stop. Proves one thing, at least: the manifestation may be periodic, but he's definitely not a repeater."

Jessie laughed harshly. "Hardly. Blowing yourself and a hundred innocent people up is not the sort of thing you can do more than once."

"Not 'repeat offender.' A *repeater*. It's a ghost that simply repeats a past action, endlessly. There's nothing left of the 'self' or the 'soul' or the 'coherent memory construct' or whatever we're calling it this year; it's an energy signature and nothing more. It's like a recording. If Ahmed Ali had been a repeater, he would have walked to the middle of where the crowd had been ten years ago and then winked out at precisely 09:27:45 AM. He didn't. He kept walking."

"I'm still having trouble with the idea that scum *had* a soul."

Eli nodded. "I think that bit of anger is all yours. Ali didn't give it to you."

She didn't look at him. "Oh, yes, he did."

"You're referring to your late husband, yes?"

Jessie took a deep breath. "Well. No one can say you didn't do your homework."

"I find it makes the job easier . . . or rather, possible. For what it's worth, I'm sorry about your husband."

"Me too," she said bitterly. "We were barely back from our honeymoon. I still had a semester to go, but Hugh already had a job on Mayor Hemmings' staff. He was assisting with the ceremony; the police placed him maybe three feet away from Ahmed Ali when the bomb exploded; they never found all the pieces. Yes, Eli, I'm angry. Go back to Washington now, like you promised. Whatever passes for Ahmed Ali's soul can walk the earth for eternity for all I give a shit."

"Do you like feeling that way?" Eli asked quietly.

Jessie stared at him. "What are you talking about?"

"You hate Ahmed Ali. You have reason; I didn't say you shouldn't. I'm asking if you enjoy it."

"What kind of stupid question is that??"

"It's a very simple question, Jessie, and I'm asking because I need to know. Think about what it feels like to hate these last ten years. Think about it being no different for the rest of your life."

"I can't change what happened," Jessie said softly.

"I'm not asking you to. I'm asking you to think about what's going to happen next, and change *that*. You saw the effect Ali's having on everyone here. That's going to continue. It's going to get worse."

Jessie unexpectedly smiled. "Rubbish. I've been doing my homework too, Eli. Ghosts tend to fade over time, not get stronger."

"Usually, yes, though it can take hundreds of years," Eli said, "but these aren't usual circumstances. Whatever Ali was raging against is still there. He's as mad as he ever was. I'll admit two samples aren't enough but there's a very slight differential between them. Today he was slightly stronger. I'm betting if I read him tomorrow it'll show another change for the worse."

"And I say again, it doesn't make sense! He did what he set out to do; it was one of the most spectacularly successful terrorist attacks on U.S. soil since 2001! Not to mention the added symbolic significance of pulling it off on July 4th. The son of a bitch should be thrilled!"

"So why is he still here? Why is he still angry?"

"I don't know! Do you?"

"No. But I think it would be a very good idea to find out."

She smiled grimly. "My decision, remember? That was the deal."

Eli sighed. He hadn't wanted to play his last card, but Jessie wasn't going to back down. If this didn't work, maybe giving Ahmed Ali free run for another ten years might be the only solution, though Eli shuddered to think what might be left of Jessie Nichols' humanity by then. Not to mention anyone regularly in the vicinity of Armfield Park.

"*After* the demonstration was the deal," Eli said. "I'm not quite done yet." Eli bent over the sensic and made a few adjustments, then gave the instrument a voice command. "Replay from time index 09:24:00," he said.

"Eli, we already saw—oh."

Eli nodded. "Right. You didn't see this."

"This" was a series of figures that were not in the original display. They appeared as very faint traces, like wil-o-wisps compared to the bright miniature sun that was Ahmed Ali. And whenever he came close to them, they disappeared entirely, lost in the glow. Most of them were clustered by the entrance to the hotel, and when Ali passed through them, they all went away.

Poof.

Jessie looked a little pale. "If this is a trick . . . "

"I don't do tricks, Jessie. Do I have to tell you who those people are?"

She shook her head, slowly. "No . . . Hugh?"

"As it is, it's impossible to say who's here and who isn't. Ali's energy signature is like a high wind blowing away anything else. They're trying to manifest and they *can't*."

"Why are they trying? What do they want, Eli?"

"Maybe to finish the ceremony or just to enjoy the day. It was supposed to be a *celebration*, Jessie. *These* are the kind of spirits who fade, Jessie, and it doesn't take hundreds of years. Usually because after a while there's no longer any reason to stay. As it is, they'll never get the chance to do what they've come to do. Ali has them trapped."

Jessie sat down hard on the bench by the fountain. She didn't say anything for several long moments. Then, "Why didn't you just show me this to start with?"

"With you within a whisker of sending me packing, not sure how you'd react? I played it close to the vest, Jessie, that's all."

"And whose fault was that?" Jessie demanded. "You didn't have to make the deal in the first place."

Eli smiled. "No, I could try to finish what might be a very long and difficult investigation with the mayor's office in the person of *you* snagging me at every opportunity. I took a chance."

Jessie smiled too, but hers was a weak, tentative thing. "Fair enough. All right, Eli—Ahmed Ali deserves an eternity of rage, but his victims don't. I want this settled. I . . . I want *them* settled. If that means bringing peace to Ahmed Ali's spirit . . . if that's the price, so be it. I'll stay out of your way."

"Thanks, but I may need a little more than that. There are some personnel files that even *I* can't get to without the cooperation of the city. I need to know I can call you when I have a question."

Jessie nodded, looking weary. "Sure, but the mayor will be back next week and I can't guarantee he'll see things the same way. Any idea when you'll need that answer?

"Just as soon as I know what the question is."

When Ahmed Ali's spirit passed through the location where the bomb had exploded and kept right on going, Jessie had drawn the obvious inference: "It doesn't make sense." Eli was reluctantly coming to the same conclusion.

There was so much about the events of July 4th that didn't quite make sense. If Ahmed Ali was really a deeply placed terrorist agent as the FBI had said, why pick an obscure target like Canemill, Mississippi? After the fact, naturally, there had been claims of responsibility by various obscure terrorist organizations, one or two credible, but the investigations had failed to prove a connection to any of them. Still, the U.S. had taken the terrorists at their word and acted accordingly.

After Ali's round the next morning, Eli was no closer to reconciling the revenant's actions to what was known to have happened on Saturday, July 4th, 2015. Ali had crossed the park, past the admittedly lax security, and blown up nearly everyone present: The mayor, Jessie's husband, picnickers, lovers, children waving small red white and blue flags. Those were the facts and the event was history. So why wasn't Ahmed playing his part?

Eli had been standing, sensic primed and ready, when the revenant arrived the next morning, punctual as an atomic clock. Eli followed the energy signature that had been Ahmed Ali as it passed through the middle of what had been the opening ceremonies to Armfield Park and passed through the doors of the Walthor Hotel, up the carpeted stairs—the thing could at least have taken the elevator, Eli thought grimly as he hurried in pursuit—to the third floor. It passed through the door to room 303 at the end of the hall. The door was locked, of course. Eli read the signature's disappearance with his sensic but couldn't actually see what, if anything, had happened in there. After a few moments the signature, surprisingly, reappeared. Yet the readings became a little diffuse at that time, less focused.

As if someone else was there . . .

Before the third day, Eli made arrangements with the front desk and there was a rather grumpy-looking young assistant manager waiting with the keycard when Eli arrived, again on the trail, at the same room the following morning. The manager got the door open quickly and Eli had full view of the inside of room 303 before the signature again vanished and he saw . . . nothing.

It was just an empty hotel room. Eli thanked the manager, who left Eli alone on the condition that he not make a mess for the maid. Eli swept the room with his sensic several times, but there was nothing, no residual traces, no persistent bio-remnant spoor, nothing. The open door had told him no more than the closed door had: Ahmed Ali walked across the park, past the blast's epicenter, into the hotel and into room 303.

But why? Nothing happened here. He never got here—

Eli stopped. And then he smiled.

"Well, Ali, 'ol son," he said aloud, "I *am* quite the idiot, aren't I?"

Eli checked the time index and waited a little longer. When the new ghost appeared, Eli wasn't even surprised. He used the sensic to read the image's lips, but she didn't say more than a word or two, a silent voice in an empty room; then she walked into the bathroom and disappeared.

When Eli came down the stairs and out in the park again, Jessie was already there. She was sitting on a bench by the fountain. There was a PDA in her lap and the same notebook Eli had noticed before beside her, but neither was in use. She just stared back toward the hotel as he approached.

"Is my time running out?" Eli asked mildly.

She sighed. "Not everything is about you, Eli. I come here fairly often."

He sat down on the opposite end of the bench. "Jessie, I hope you don't mind a personal question, but you never remarried, did you?"

Her face was as expressionless as a statue's. "I hope *you* don't mind a personal question, such as 'why are you asking me something I know is already in that database of yours?'"

He smiled ruefully. "Fair enough. I couldn't think a better way to broach the subject."

She shrugged. "Not that it's any of your business, but I'm not living in the past, Eli, if that's what you're getting at. Nor am I playing the bereaved widow of a 'martyr of freedom' for political gain. I'm doing what I do because I believe I can make a difference. Hugh believed the same, and that's why he was here on July 4th. I accept what happened."

"Then why do you come here?"

"It's a nice place to spend a day . . . " Jessie apparently saw the dubious expression on Eli's face and sighed. "Oh, all right. I said I accepted what happened. I didn't say I understood it or could reconcile it with my idea of a sane world. So I still think about what happened to Hugh and the others, and this is the best place to do that."

"What's the notebook for?"

She shrugged. "This? I was in therapy for a while . . . you know, after. It was my therapist's idea: write down what I thought, my anger, my grief. This is the notebook I bought to do that ten years ago."

"So what's in it?"

"Nothing," Jessie said. "Not one damn thing. I keep coming here hoping that maybe one day I'll know what to write."

Eli didn't say anything for a while. Then, "I think I've finally got a question for you. There's some information I need."

"A personnel file?"

"Some of what I'm looking for is public record, but I also need billing records from the Walthor Hotel for two separate dates, and those aren't. It'll require a court order, I'm afraid. Can you help?"

She smiled grimly. "Give me the dates and stand back. Is that all?"

"I wish it was. I've got some more digging to do on my end, but, barring a total misread of the situation, I can finish the investigation tomorrow if you get those records."

"The judge is Hugh's father, Eli; we're still close. That shouldn't be a problem."

"Thanks," Eli said, and that was all.

She hesitated. "Eli, you look worried, and that worries *me*. What do you think you're going to find?"

"The truth," Eli said simply.

She frowned. "Wasn't that the whole point?"

"No, getting enough facts to figure out how to free Ahmed Ali from his endless anger was the point. The truth was something I didn't expect at all."

"Explain that, please," Jessie said.

"It's about what people believe. What we know to be true . . . rather, what we accept as true. Not quite the same as facts. Sometimes the one doesn't affect the other. Sometimes facts change the truth completely. Sometimes that's a good thing and sometimes not, but it's always scary."

Jessie just stared at him. "You'd think a politician would be better at seeing through bullshit, Eli, but I didn't understand one word of that."

Eli shrugged. "Jessie, if you come to the park tomorrow morning, usual time, you'll know as much as I do."

The day was overcast and windy. Eli thought perhaps rain was coming; he could practically smell it on the breeze. He set the corner of the sensic on top of the facsimile edition newspaper he'd brought with him. Jessie arrived a few moments later, glanced at the paper.

"I haven't seen a paper edition in five years," she said. "Where'd you get that?"

"A lovely lady named Mrs. Lee at the Department of Archives and History was kind enough to make a facsimile for me. *Canemill Reporter,* July 9th, 2018. Turn to the obituaries; I've marked the one you're looking for."

" 'Stacy Prentice, aged twenty-six,' " Jessie said and then frowned. "That name sounds familiar."

"I imagine," Eli said. "Read it."

Jessie scanned the neat columns. "Oh . . . "

Eli nodded. "Exactly. Ms. Prentice was Ahmed Ali's wife. His soon to be ex-wife; they had separated and she'd filed for divorce. She was using her maiden name at the time."

"I actually remember a little about this. She committed suicide, poor woman, three years after the attack. Apparently she couldn't live with what Ahmed Ali had done."

"Why?" Eli asked.

Jessie blinked. "I don't understand."

"It's a simple question. Why? She was questioned at the time, but there was nothing to link her to the attack; according to the FBI investigation, she hadn't even been living with Ali during the 'planning phase' and was publicly cleared of any involvement. The mayor's widow was seen hugging her on national television, for pity's sake. So why kill herself?"

"So when is guilt logical? Are you saying she *did* know about the attack?"

"No, I'm saying that there's something she knew that we didn't."

"Clear as day-old mud, Eli. And why bother making a paper copy? Couldn't you just download the text?"

"I needed a physical copy for the sensic to scan and model for the simulation."

Jessie shook her head. "You're right—you don't explain very well."

"Sorry. I tend to get worse when I'm on the trail. All will become clear . . . maybe. Put this on." He handed Jessie a wireless headset with video-enabled lenses. "Nice, huh? Last year I was still using a VR helmet." He settled his own headset into place, and a three dimensional simulation of the park came up. It mapped directly to the physical objects already there; the resolution was so fine that it was difficult to tell one from the other.

"We already have the park, Eli," Jessie said, looking around. "Why simulate it?"

"This isn't just a simulation as you know it, and these aren't avatars of us you're seeing; they are mapped projections using an energy signature congruent with bio-remnant signatures."

"You mean . . . he can see us?"

"That's exactly what I mean. If you'll blink down your menu you'll see the 'hide' function. When Ahmed Ali appears, I want you to vanish. You'll still be able to see what happens."

"Like hell."

Eli blinked. "Pardon?"

"If you think I'm going to pass up the chance to confront the scum that killed Hugh, you're crazy!"

"Do you want this ended or not?"

Jessie didn't say anything for a moment. "There are a lot of things I want ended, Eli, and they all start with Ahmed Ali. You show me this and then ask me to give it up? I can't!" she said, then looked him directly in the eyes. "I won't."

"Look, there's no time to argue—"

"You're right. He's coming," Jessie said.

Eli sighed. No help for it now. He'd just have to see what happened.

What happened was that Ahmed Ali appeared right on time on the far side of the park. This was full scale, not the miniature holo display he'd been looking at earlier. Ahmed Ali was a very large and angry young man striding purposefully across Armfield Park. The dark eyes, the flowing black beard, all were as the news photos had shown; only the faint bluish glow that surrounded him marked him as something no longer human. There was no sign of the explosives he'd hidden under his long coat on that fine summer day.

You'd think someone would have noticed the coat.

Eli stood his ground on the sidewalk, but the ersatz-ghost that was Jessie marched forward with full purpose and anger that could match Ahmed Ali blow for blow.

He's not a repeater. He should be able to see us.

There it was. Hesitation. Puzzlement. The reaction that Eli had expected but not quite. There had already been a hesitation logged; the time index on the sensic from the previous three days of readings showed the same thing.

Is it because of us?

In a moment Eli got his answer; Jessie stood in front of Ahmed Ali, master terrorist, and let him have it with a string of invective that would have blistered chrome and cracked titanium. The few choice words she'd used to Eli before now were nothing compared to this, and for a moment Eli could only watch in awe at a master at work.

The revenant just frowned. The puzzlement was there, stronger, but then the hesitation was gone. He walked past Jessie as if she truly wasn't there.

"You will not ignore me, you worthless piece of shit!!"

But he did, and nothing Jessie said or tried to do made one bit of difference. At one point she even tried to reach out and grab him. Eli wasn't sure what good Jessie thought that might do, but of course it didn't work. Her ghostly fingers closed on nothing, touched nothing. Eli waited. When Ahmed Ali was only a few steps away, Eli held up the paper. Another frown, another hesitation. This one wasn't in the sensic's data.

Eli nodded. "Yes. . . . There's a mind of sorts in there somewhere, isn't there? Use it."

Ahmed looked past Eli, started to walk past just as he'd done to Jessie. Eli moved the newspaper, shoved it right in front of Ali's nose, making him see it. He tapped the image of a column of type. Another hesitation.

"Curiosity. That's right, Ahmed. Look."

Ahmed looked. His right foot, already in motion, stopped. He stood still, and as Eli held the image of a seven-year-old paper in front of him, Ahmed Ali read. By the time Jessie reached them, the ghost was already fading.

"Eli, what have you done?"

"Ended it," Eli said, and in another moment Ahmed Ali was gone. The sensic told the same story.

Jessie looked around her. "He *is* gone," she said. "That's it? It's really over?"

"Not quite," said Eli. "There's something else we need to talk about, but it can wait. For right now just come on, if you don't want to miss this." He reached out, living flesh to living flesh, and took her hand.

"Miss what? Where are we going?"

"To the ribbon-cutting, of course," Eli said. "I think it's finally getting under way. Remember the ghosts who were trying to manifest? Now they will. It's happening."

"You're serious? We can . . . oh. Hugh?"

"If he's there. I have a feeling he might be."

They hurried toward the Walthor Hotel where the long-delayed crowd was finally gathered.

Later they sat on the bench by the fountain. There was a long silence while Eli reviewed his data and Jessie just sat, staring into space.

"I can't believe it. Not a terrorist attack at all," Jessie said finally. "A fucking accident!"

"Not technically," Eli said without looking up from his data. "I believe the law says that there are no accidents in the commission of a crime, and Ahmed Ali definitely intended to commit a crime."

"But a domestic dispute? That's what all this was about?"

Eli shrugged. "There's no hate like a personal hate. Some of this may be conjecture, Jessie, but it all fits: Consensus at the time was that Ahmed Ali was a deep cover terrorist agent, but I believe that's wrong. The FBI didn't find his terrorist connections because there *were* none. He was a thug, not a fanatic. Stacy Prentice was divorcing him for violent abuse and a host of other good reasons. Without the marriage, odds are he would have been deported."

"Why?"

"Turns out he had a record of violence in his own country that family connections managed to quash long enough for him to emigrate. He was wanted for assault and attempted murder, among other things. He blamed Stacy when that all came out during the proceedings."

"I assume that she was the one in room 303."

Eli nodded. "Yes. Ali found out Stacy was staying in the Walthor and decided to make a rather loud and messy statement. We may never know if he intended to die from the start or simply meant to plant the bomb close enough to his wife to do the job. In either case I'm betting he didn't even *know* about the ribbon ceremony until he showed up; that explains the first recorded hesitation."

It was obvious that Jessie believed him, but her common sense had to make one more try. "I admit what you say does fit, and I guess it's possible, but it's all a bit far-fetched, Eli."

"Not as far-fetched as Ali being a terrorist. Ahmed Ali never fit the profile. Consider the bomb itself—an FBI reconstruction showed that the device may have been powerful, but it was also crude and unstable, not the work of a trained terrorist with all the time he needed to pick a target and prepare. All it took was one good jostle from someone in the crowd on his way through and that was that."

When Jessie spoke again, it was almost as if she were talking to herself. "The man was just a violent moron."

"Yes, but I will give him points for focus. With some ghosts you just have to prove to them that they're dead; all Ahmed Ali wanted was proof that his *wife* was dead. Her suicide—three years later in that same room—suggests she knew the attack had been intended for her all along. I think that's what she couldn't live with."

Jessie nodded, looking glum. "If it was me . . . yes, it makes sense. But Hugh, and all those people . . . The really sick thing is that, in some places, Ahmed Ali is a hero—" Jessie sat up then, as something new occurred to her. "Eli, we fought a *war* over this!"

Eli sighed. "I wondered when you'd remember that part. A very brief but nasty one, yes. Maybe it made sense at the time but it's history now. Legend. To this day there are people who believe that Ahmed Ali was a terrorist and people who believe he was a hero. They're both wrong, but that doesn't change what happened."

"We . . . oh, God, what will we do?"

Eli took a deep breath, let it out. "I'm sorry, Jessie, but it's what will *you* do. Bureau investigations are confidential; more to the point, they're *sealed*. That rule isn't always convenient, but it's one I don't break. Ever. I told you that when we first met, and nothing's changed: whether you tell this story or not is entirely up to you."

Jessie just looked at him in disbelief for several long moments. Then she said, "And here I thought Ahmed Ali was a son of a bitch."

"I wasn't joking when I said the truth was scary, Jessie."

She smiled then, wistfully. "Guess I should have been paying more attention. Funny thing though—I never wanted to be the widow of a 'Martyr of Freedom' in the first damn place. Goodbye, Eli."

She got up, started to leave. Eli glanced at the bench. "You left your notebook."

"I don't need it. All I really wanted to do all this time was say goodbye to my husband, and now I've done that. I've got no right to complain about the price."

"You may not believe it, but I am sorry about this, Jessie."

She smiled then. "I'm not."

Eli watched her go. He brought up the sensic one last time to confirm what he already knew. No ghosts in Armfield Park. Not even one. The ribbon-cutting ceremony and July 4th celebration of 2015 was officially over, and only ten years late.

That just left the ghost in Room 303.

Eli sighed. It wasn't part of the original investigation, strictly speaking. Yet there were things he couldn't fix, and then again there were things he could, as the saint used to say. Eli was far from a saint, but the things he understood, he understood very well indeed.

"Ms. Prentice," he said aloud, "I think it's time you and I had a chat."

HANAGAN'S KIYOMATSU, 1923

It was early Thursday afternoon after the last class of the day when the director's cherubic face appeared on the screen on Eli Mothersbaugh's desk. "We have a ghost for you, Eli."

Eli made a point of jamming his syllabus back in its folder and filing it with his class notes. "Matt, this is a bad time."

The director just smiled. "I disagree—this is the perfect time. The Bureau approved your leave of absence on the sole condition that you agree to be available for special assignments during campus downtime. Spring Break is about as down as it gets."

Eli could feel the whine creeping into his voice. He stifled it. "Matt, I'm leaving now. This is the weekend of the Josiah Hanagan estate auction. I've been looking forward to this for months!"

The director's grin widened. "Then you might be interested to know that the complainant is Alexander Bonham, Hanagan's executor and the appraiser of his collection. You do recognize the name, yes?"

Eli grunted. "You know I do—I have all his books. He's probably the greatest living expert on 20th-century Japanese woodblock prints in the world."

"And he's got a ghost. Apparently, one that likes to destroy said precious, irreplaceable prints. But if you've got other plans . . . "

Eli glared. *You bastard.* For a moment he thought he'd said it aloud. Then he wondered if it would matter if he had. "All right. Send me the details, Matt. Then go away."

The director's smile didn't even flicker. "Knew we could count on you, Eli. Your sensic downloaded all the information while we were speaking. Your flight leaves in two hours."

Eli sighed. There was no point in getting angry; it wasn't as if he had a choice.

Eli sent his baggage ahead to the hotel and took a cab straight to Alexander Bonham's apartment. If a Park Avenue suite could be rightly called such. Bonham's rooms filled an entire floor; the man himself answered the door after Eli was buzzed up. Bonham was a tall man about Eli's age, with black hair just starting to go grey. Old money family connections and movie-star looks, according to the dossier, but Eli didn't need his files to know that. Eli recognized the face from the book jackets of dozens of references, all of which he owned.

Bonham held out his hand. "Mr. Mothersbaugh? I'm Alexander Bonham."

"I wish it had been under better circumstances, but it's an honor to meet you, Mr. Bonham. I especially enjoyed your monograph on Benji Asada's Kyoto series."

Bonham raised an eyebrow as he led Eli past the foyer into a rather large sitting area. The walls were decorated with the complete run of Hiroshi Yoshida's 1935 series "Eight Views of Cherry Blossoms," all with the *jizuri* seals that indicated early editions. Eli did his best not to stare, but Bonham just smiled.

"I'm flattered. No one told me you were a collector."

Eli shrugged. " 'Enthusiastic amateur' is closer to the truth. Now then, when did you notice there was a problem? When the print was destroyed?"

"No, there had been some indications for about three nights in a row before the actual attack. Moving shadows, cold spots, mists appearing in what should be climate-controlled rooms, all the classic signs, or so I'm told. I kept everything as I found it; I assumed you'd want to examine the print."

"I hesitate to ask, but which print was it?"

"It was one of the second edition Kiyomatsus, 'Girl with Teacup.'"

Eli felt a pang. "That means there are only two left in the world now."

"Three, actually," Bonham said. "Unless there are more in private collections I haven't heard about."

Eli frowned. "I'd only heard of three second editions accounted for, and it was my understanding that you had all of them."

Bonham smiled. "Not many people know that, but it's true. And I still do."

Eli shook his head. "I'm afraid I don't understand."

Bonham looked uncomfortable. "It's a matter of some delicacy, but as I understand it your investigation is completely confidential?"

"Of course."

Bonham nodded. "Not that this sort of thing can be kept secret forever, you understand, but Ichiro Hanagan has scheduled a press conference for Friday afternoon, and I certainly don't want to compromise that."

"Josiah Hanagan's grandson? But the loss was to your private collection. How is the Hanagan estate involved?"

"Ichiro was present during the attack; we were discussing plans for the auction when it happened. As for how else the estate was involved, come with me and you'll see."

Bonham led Eli down a hallway covered with artwork. Not all were woodblock prints; there were several Chinese *sumi-e* drawings, plus a few original watercolors. Eli noted them with appreciation, but he knew these were all peripheral to the man's real passion. Bonham opened a door near the end of the hall on the left and led Eli into what Eli could only describe as a museum in a maze.

Prints covered the walls, and there were a lot of walls. Partitions had been set up throughout the room, seven feet high in a room with twelve foot ceilings, to increase the wall space. Eli soon determined that the partitions had been organized in a regular pattern, breaking up the large room into smaller spaces that were usually dedicated to either one artist or one particular style. Here was a section full of Koitsus. Here another was filled with more Yoshidas, mostly father Hiroshi and son Toshi, but there were examples of other family members' work as well. Another was packed with the entire known output of Kawase Hasui, including one or two pre-earthquake editions. If there was an important artist of the Japanese "New Prints" movement not represented here, it was one Eli had never heard of. It was all he could do to keep following his host and not stop at any one of a dozen places to stare, enraptured.

"Your collection must be the most complete in existence," Eli said as he followed Bonham through the maze of art.

Bonham smiled ruefully. "Perhaps . . . but not quite complete. Now it probably never will be. I'm afraid Mr. Hanagan has had the last laugh on me."

Eli started to ask what Bonham was talking about, but he had the feeling that he'd have the answer soon enough.

They exited the warren of prints and stood near the opposite wall of the room. The windows had been frosted to cut down on print-fading direct sunlight, but overhead track lighting picked up the slack. There, hanging on the wall in uncrowded splendor, were the core prints of Alexander Bonham's collection, three copies of Ito Kiyomatsu's "Girl with Teacup."

The Shin Hanga or "New Prints" movement of the early and middle 20th century was the beginning of the traditional Japanese woodblock print's revival as an art form. There was a strong vein of nostalgia as the artists found inspiration in a vision of Japan that, even then, had mostly disappeared. Landscapes of shrines and temples were very popular, but "Girl with Teacup" showed its older roots in *ukiyo-e*, those actor and courtesan prints that were the commercial illustration of Japan in the 18th and 19th centuries.

The print was of a young girl in a blue and red kimono, holding a lacquered tray with a steaming cup of tea, similar to the famous tea shop prints of Utamaro more than a century earlier, save that Kiyomatsu's print was much more individualistic and expressive. The girl was more clearly a distinct individual than was sometimes apparent in *ukiyo-e*, perhaps even a portrait of the artist's own daughter. The three copies stood side by side and, even though they were probably from the same edition, they showed subtle differences in color, shading, and tone, mostly due to the fact that each print was made by hand.

Eli took all this in at a glance; his attention was immediately drawn to a fourth print hanging a short distance away from the other three.

It was a faded and ruined mess.

Eli went to stand in front of it for a better look—it appeared as if someone had put a heat lamp a few inches from it; years of sun fading and abuse wouldn't have done the job of destroying it so well. Only the black ink keyblock outline showed that this, too, had been a copy of "Girl with Teacup." Eli took his sensic out and scanned the picture, but just to confirm what he already suspected—the print had, indeed, been destroyed by a concentrated burst of bio-remnant energy.

Which meant, beyond doubt, one very angry ghost.

Eli leaned forward and took a closer look. "Strange."

Bonham peered over his shoulder. "What is? Other than the fact that the print is a total loss with no apparent cause?"

Eli pointed at the bottom left of the ruined print, near the margin. "Just that the damage is very precise. For instance, the artist's seal and signature hasn't been touched, nor have the publisher's seals in the margin."

"They're nice examples of Kiyomatsu's signature and Koson Han's post-earthquake seals, but they don't amount to much in themselves," Bonham said drily. "More to the point—can you guarantee that this won't happen again?"

Eli shook his head. "Not until I know why it happened in the first place, Mr. Bonham. It took a great deal of energy to ruin your print, an amount that most ghosts aren't capable of producing. Only two varieties could, and only one type is likely to."

"What type would that be?"

Eli looked grim. "A revenant. A ghost obsessed with revenge to the exclusion of all else."

Bonham frowned. "Who would want revenge on me?"

"That's a good question, and I hope to answer it. Now I need you to answer a few of mine, and we'll start with the destroyed print. Where and from whom did you acquire it?"

"From Josiah Hanagan's estate just two days ago. I took it in lieu of a fee from the estate, with Ichiro's blessing."

Eli frowned. "So Hanagan had an unknown fourth copy of the second edition? I understood he only had one Kiyomatsu, the 1923 first edition that was coming up for auction this weekend. The only copy known to exist."

Bonham smiled ruefully. "That was what Josiah told everyone, and we had no reason to disbelieve him."

Eli felt a chill. " 'Had'?"

Bonham sighed, and pointed at the ruined print. "Mr. Mothersbaugh, allow me to present Josiah Hanagan's Kiyomatsu."

Eli was stunned. "The first edition . . . ? But . . . that's the later Koson Han seal. It wasn't used before 1925!"

"Exactly, and that's what the press conference this Friday is all about. The much-heralded Hanagan's Kiyomatsu, first edition, does not exist."

Bonham had to leave for a dinner meeting with Ichiro Hanagan on the details of the auction, though it was clear now that the auction itself wasn't going to be quite the event everyone had expected. While Hanagan was primarily an *Ukiyo-e* collector of great repute, the jewel of his collection had always been Kiyomatsu's "Girl with Teacup," simply because it was the only copy of the legendary first printing thought to have survived the great Kanto Earthquake of 1923.

The earthquake and resulting fires had destroyed most of Tokyo and several other cities and, in the process, the complete stock of many print publishers, including the carved wooden blocks from which the prints were made. It was two years before Koson Han, Kiyomatsu's publisher, was back in limited production. The prints of "Girl with Teacup" made after 1923 were done with recarved blocks, and bore a new version of the Koson seal, this time with an outer hatched ring around the original flying crane design.

There had been great speculation ever since Hanagan announced his acquisition back in 2010. Rumors of the print's existence had been flying for years; it was something of a Holy Grail for print collectors, but Hanagan was the first to verify it. Apparently, in error.

Eli stared at the ruined print long after Bonham left, trying to find some fit for what he saw there into his understanding of Josiah Hanagan and his lifelong passion for Japanese woodblock prints. As Eli saw it, there were two options, both equally absurd:

Either Josiah Hanagan honestly believed this was a first edition Kiyomatsu, or he deliberately lied.

Eli let out a gusting sigh. He knew he should be concentrating on the identity of the ghost, and it was very possible that Hanagan's deception had nothing to do with the ghost.

It's also possible that genetically unaltered pigs can fly.

All those prints in the room and the ghost just "happened" to pick this one? No, there had to be a connection, and the logical one was Josiah Hanagan. If he was the ghost, then perhaps Eli was wrong about the spirit being a revenant. Could it be that Hanagan had returned specifically to destroy the print and cover his disgrace? That made a little sense; when news of this got out, as it apparently was about to, Josiah Hanagan's reputation as a collector and expert would be blackened forever.

So why were the seals intact?

More to the point, why bother destroying the print? According to Bonham, both he and Josiah's grandson, Ichiro, had first seen the print in Hanagan's vault, and there were no other Kiyomatsus in the collection at all, never mind a first edition. Their word together would be more than enough to ruin Hanagan's reputation.

The more Eli considered the possibility that the ghost was trying to cover up, the less sense it made, but it made even less sense that Hanagan had done such a thing in the first place. Sooner or later the news of his phony first edition would come out. The only real question was "when," and Hanagan must have known that.

Eli noted the light fading through the frosted glass windows and pulled out his sensic to check the time. According to Bonham, the ghost was active after sunset. Eli made a quick sweep of the room but found nothing except the residual traces of the bio-remnant signature clinging to the destroyed print.

Whoever the ghost is, I'm betting it goes for one of the other Kiyomatsus. I'd better stay close to them.

Not that Eli needed much prompting. The prints were beautiful and it was hard, even in Eli's distracted state, to ignore them. Eli went from one to another, admiring the smooth gradations of color in the sky above the girl, the vivid colors of the cherry tree in blossom to her right, the sharp, clear impressions of the key lines that were the hallmark of an early edition—

The key lines . . .

Eli walked from one Kiyomatsu to the other, frowning, until he had taken a good, close look at all three of the surviving prints. Superficially they were very similar, since they were all printed from the same blocks. Yet there were many subtle differences, which were to be expected. Authentic prints from this period were made by hand by skilled craftsmen, with several different woodblock impressions required to make the final print. It was nearly impossible for any two to be exactly alike, but some basic elements, especially the black keyblock lines that formed the image's outline, were generally the same.

One wasn't the same.

Eli looked back at the leftmost print again, then the second print, then third. There was no doubt. The lines in the first undamaged print did not match the other two. It wasn't just that an image line was partially missing, as sometimes happened when the printer varied the pressure too much from one print to another. Several keyblock lines were *different*, including two on the base of the girl's sandaled feet, another in the pins holding her hair. It would take a real expert to identify the specific edition, which Eli did not claim to be, but he knew enough to be sure that one of Bonham's Kiyomatsus did *not* come from the same edition as the other two. For a moment Eli thought of bringing this to Alexander Bonham's attention, but that was a silly notion.

He's seen these prints hundreds of times, and he wouldn't have bought them without a close examination. He already knows what they are.

Eli was beginning to think that he did, too. He went back to the destroyed print, and took a closer look there. The keyblock lines were obscured, but he had the artist's seal and signature to go by, as well as the publisher's seal. The destroyed print matched the second and third. They were almost certainly from the same edition.

And that makes three . . . plus one that doesn't fit.

Eli checked the time again. He had some calls to make and some information to verify but decided that now was a bad time. Especially when his sensic emitted the first warning tone of a detected bio-remnant energy signature. The ghost, whoever it might be, was on its way and, Eli noted from the intensity of the readings, was royally pissed off.

It was as Eli feared. The readings could indicate a revenant, and that was the last thing Eli—or any sane person—wanted to tangle with. But the idea of any more prints destroyed made Eli feel sick. He had to try; all he could hope was that he'd guessed right about what was happening here. He'd know soon enough.

The first indication was a build-up of bio-remnant energy, but that immediately snapped into focus as if someone had flipped a switch. The energy concentrated and coalesced in the center of the room. Eli felt the hairs on the back of his neck tingle; it was a familiar feeling. He started to head toward the ghost, afraid that he was already too late, but in an instant the signature was moving, with no diminishment of the readings that might indicate an attack had already happened. Eli tracked it on a beeline for the third intact Kiyomatsu.

Eli frantically refined his readings; he knew there was little time, but he was looking for something very specific—a pattern match based on the sensic's mapping functions, and he already had the baseline for comparison. He had the results in a few seconds.

Josiah Hanagan.

To Eli, the sensic's confirmation seemed almost inevitable.

If he truly is a revenant, then he's too far gone and there won't be a damn thing I can do. But if he's not . . .

The ghost stepped through the last of the partitions, heading for the third undamaged Kiyomatsu.

"You don't have to do this," Eli said.

The ghost hesitated. Eli could feel its presence, but he couldn't see it without the sensic. The ghost turned toward him. It was saying something, but of course Eli couldn't hear it; producing audible sounds required a great deal of energy and the ghost was saving his. Eli didn't have to guess for what. The sensic's pattern-matching algorithms translated the ghost's lip movements.

I TRIED . . . NO CHOICE . . . THIEF. THIEF!

If the old cliche about the difference between love and hate being a razor's edge was true, the ghost of Josiah Hanagan was teetering on that edge. Eli was certain that Hanagan's destruction of the first print was a gamble, not revenge. If Eli couldn't convince Hanagan that his gamble had paid off, then the destruction of the second print would be nothing but revenge. Once revenge became the ghost's sole focus he would become a revenant, and there would be no stopping him.

Hanagan had already turned back toward the Kiyomatsu, but he hesitated again. Eli hoped that Josiah Hanagan was not too far gone to be reached, that what he had loved in life, he loved still. "She's beautiful, isn't she? You don't want to do this, do you?"

The ghost looked back at him. WANT . . . ? NO . . . THIEF!

The ghost was being very single-minded. Eli knew that, with a little luck, he could put that focus to good use, but that was up to Josiah Hanagan.

"Mr. Hanagan, I know what you were trying to tell us," Eli said quickly. "I know why you're here. You don't have to do this. I have a better way."

THIEF. . . . BETTER? WHAT?

Eli smiled. "Believe me," he said, "you're going to love it."

Much later, when the ghost was gone, Eli treated himself to a long walking tour of Alexander Bonham's collection before he let himself out.

The next morning, Bonham's relief was almost painful to see. He greeted Eli at the door with a big smile on his face.

"Mr. Mothersbaugh, you did it! Nothing was damaged last evening."

Eli nodded. "I'm happy to say that your prints are safe for the time being, but in order to guarantee their long-term survival, I'll need your co-operation for a bit longer."

Bonham was still smiling. "You have it, of course. But what do you want me to do? Is the ghost going to return?"

"I'm certain that the ghost will indeed come back at least once more. What happens then will tell the story, one way or another. And what I want you to do right now is to wait."

"Wait? For what?"

The doorbell rang. "For whom, I should say. That will be Ichiro Hanagan, Josiah Hanagan's grandson and heir. Let him in, won't you?"

Bonham looked a little ill. "Mr. Mothersbaugh, you assured me that your investigation was confidential!"

"Surely you understand that it's not always possible to conduct an investigation without revealing that an investigation is, indeed, being conducted? Ichiro Hanagan already knew that you were having some difficulty, yes?"

"Well, yes. He was here when the first attack occurred; I told you that."

"Then I haven't told him anything he didn't already know, nor will I reveal anything of a confidential nature to him. Especially not my findings. Believe me—those will be for your ears alone. Now, please let him in."

Ichiro Hanagan had his Japanese grandmother's dark eyes and black hair, but the pug nose and the jawline were clearly from his father's side of the family. He shook Eli's hand as he came in. "I'm not sure what I can do, Mr. Mothersbaugh, but of course anything I can do for Alex. He's been a great help to us in trying times."

"Thank you," Eli said. "I know you have a press conference later, but don't worry—this shouldn't take long."

Ichiro nodded. "I'm not happy about having to hold that press conference, Mr. Mothersbaugh, as you can imagine. I'm still having trouble believing that my grandfather could make such a mistake."

"About the Kiyomatsu? Yes, that is strange, isn't it?" Eli checked the time. "Let's go to the gallery, shall we?"

Alexander Bonham glanced at Eli but said nothing. They walked down the hall to the gallery room and back to where the four Kiyomatsu prints hung. At Eli's request, the ruined Kiyomatsu was still in place.

Eli checked the time again, and Bonham frowned. "Are you expecting the ghost now? I thought he only appeared after dark."

"Many hauntings are of a periodic nature, Mr. Bonham, but circumstances can change that in rare cases. I think this will be one such."

"I still don't understand why I'm here, Mr. Mothersbaugh. I'm not an expert on ghosts," Ichiro said.

"No, but you're an expert on your grandfather."

Ichiro glared. "Are you saying the ghost is my grandfather?! That he could—or would—destroy a Kiyomatsu?"

Eli shook his head. "As I told you earlier, my findings have to remain confidential. Yet my speculations, which are no more than that, I'll share as the investigation requires. So the answer is no, Mr. Hanagan, I'm saying nothing of the sort. Rather I'm counting on you to identify for me whether or not your grandfather is the ghost."

Ichiro looked grim. "I'll be glad to clear this up."

"That's all I ask," Eli said.

"Mr. Mothersbaugh, Mr. Hanagan is a busy man, today especially," Bonham said. "I don't think we should keep him."

Eli glanced at the sensic. "And I don't think we will. The ghost is here."

Right on time.

Bonham didn't say anything else. He just stood to the side, looking around intently as if the ghost were about to jump out of the walls at him. Ichiro's anger seemed to have faded a bit and he looked around with some curiosity.

"Mr. Mothersbaugh, I don't see anything."

"And unless 'second sight' runs in your family you won't . . . at least not until I adjust the sensic."

Eli brought up the sensic's mapping display and turned the screen so Ichiro could see. Ichiro looked stunned.

"That . . . that is my grandfather, I'm sure of it. I don't understand . . . Should I try to talk to him?"

Bonham looked pale. "Josiah? Is he going to attack?"

"You don't have to say anything, Mr. Hanagan; I just needed your confirmation. And no, Mr. Bonham, I don't think he's going to attack."

"But he's going toward the Kiyomatsu!"

Eli nodded. *The unknown Kiyomatsu.* "So I see. And his bio-remnant signature is spiking."

If Bonham looked pale before, now he was positively white. "The Kiyomatsu . . . "

"Is safe, Mr. Bonham. The energy level is still much too low to cause damage, so let's see what he's up to, shall we? Hmmmm . . . according to my sensic, he's concentrating on the publisher's seal. See this? He's raising the temperature by about sixteen degrees farenheit."

Ichiro frowned. "That's all? But . . . that won't do anything."

Eli shook his head. "No, it is definitely doing something. Look!"

They looked. The seal on the Kiyomatsu was changing. The outer ring was slowly fading. In a few moments it was gone, leaving the original 1923 version of the Koson seal.

"The ghost is leaving now," Eli said as the bio-remnant energy signature faded, along with the form of Josiah Hanagan. In another moment the ghost was gone and, as they watched, the seal slowly reverted to the outer-ring 1925 Koson Han version.

Bonham's jaw slowly worked up and down but nothing came out. Ichiro Hanagan just looked from one to another in obvious incomprehension.

"I don't understand, Mr. Mothersbaugh," he said, "What just happened? Why did the seal change?"

"The seal changed because your grandfather raised the temperature on the print. The temperature in here is a constant seventy-four degrees Fahrenheit, as was the temperature in the vault where the print was originally stored, within a few degrees. The outer seal ring was created with a modern thermo-reactive ink, which fades at temperatures greater than ninety, so naturally neither you nor Mr. Bonham noticed that the seal had been altered."

Bonham's voice was barely above a whisper. "Altered . . . You—"

Eli jumped in. "Well, that was quite clever of Josiah Hanagan. Don't you think so, Mr. Bonham?"

Bonham finally understood. He smiled, though obviously the effort cost him. "Quite clever. I admit it—I was completely fooled."

Eli turned to Ichiro. "Your grandfather probably didn't mean to destroy Mr. Bonham's print; as I suspected, he needed to test his technique before he risked it on the first edition print. Clearly, he made a mistake." It was a bit of a white lie, Eli thought, but he didn't pretend to know the full extent of what motivated a ghost, even if he had secured this particular one's co-operation.

Ichiro frowned, then stepped up to take another look at the first Kiyomatsu. "You're saying my grandfather altered the seal? Why would he do that?"

"Obviously, to disguise the print as a second edition and thus hide it in plain sight, even if the vault was compromised. This particular thermal ink should prove easy to remove, so no harm done. You don't need me to tell you that your grandfather was a bit . . . cautious, shall we say, where this print was concerned."

Ichiro smiled faintly. "Even I never saw it until Mr. Bonham and I opened the vault. I guess it doesn't surprise me."

Eli nodded. "No doubt your grandfather planned to tell you what he'd done, but his fatal heart attack rather caught him off guard, and so he manifested to try and prevent the first edition from being lost. He's done what he came to do; I don't think Mr. Bonham will be troubled again."

Ichiro let out a deep gusting breath. "Mr. Mothersbaugh, you have no idea how much this means to me, both personally and to the family. You just stopped me from tarnishing my grandfather's good name. I have to go now, since it's too late to cancel the press conference, but I'll have something much better to announce."

"Glad I could help," Eli said. "I'm sure Mr. Bonham feels the same and of course will be willing to verify everything if necessary."

"Yes . . . of course," Bonham said.

"Alex, I deeply regret the loss of your second edition Kiyomatsu," Ichiro said. "Since my grandfather was responsible, the estate will naturally compensate you for the full value."

Bonham waved a hand. "Not necessary, Ichiro. Insurance will cover the value of the print. I'm just glad we were able to avoid a more serious loss."

Eli waited by the Kiyomatsu prints as a smiling Alexander Bonham showed Ichiro Hanagan out. When Bonham returned, he wasn't smiling at all.

"You son of a bitch," he said, with feeling. "Have you any idea what this is going to do to my reputation?!"

Eli shrugged. "It'll take a hit, no doubt. Yet this will do rather less damage than, say, a fraud conviction."

Bonham's glare didn't diminish one bit, but he didn't say anything. Eli nodded. "You started your appraisals a full week before Ichiro was able to come to his grandfather's home. Comparing a rare edition to a known edition is standard procedure, so you brought one print in to Hanagan's home and you left with one. No one thought anything of it. When you opened the vault—you had access, Ichiro confirmed that—it was the *second* time, not the first, and he saw exactly what you saw: a real second edition Kiyomatsu. The first edition was already in your posession."

"Don't wave 'fraud' at me, Mothersbaugh. You brought Ichiro here just so you could hand him that cock-and-bull story. You violated confidentiality!"

Eli smiled. "Let the record show that I did no such thing: Ichiro already knew there was a ghost. I didn't tell him it was his grandfather—he did that. I also didn't tell him that *you* were the one who altered that seal, not his grandfather."

Bonham swore. "I never should have called the damned Bureau."

Eli nodded. "I was curious about that, since you must have suspected that Hanagan was trying to draw attention to the Kiyomatsu. Now, I know you weren't particularly worried about me—amateur collectors are a dime a thousand—yet surely you knew there was a chance the investigator would be able to communicate with Hanagan?"

Bonham scowled. "Ichiro insisted, and I couldn't think of a plausible reason to refuse him. Besides, I didn't want the rest of my collection destroyed and also didn't think there was a chance in hell an investigator would understand what the ghost was trying to tell him; even I know they're not very articulate, as a rule. How did you figure out that this print was the first edition?"

Eli thought of enlightening Bonham on the numerous times he'd found ghosts that were very articulate, but decided it didn't matter. "I didn't, for certain. I only knew that the keyblock lines in the first print didn't match the other two, which meant it couldn't have been from the same edition. Yet you identified them as all being from the 1925 printing. That's a mistake an amateur like me would make, but Alexander Bonham? Hardly."

"Well then, it seems I underestimated you."

"None of this was about the money, was it? You could have acquired the print at the auction. Come to that, you still can; I don't think Josiah Hanagan will object now."

Bonham laughed. "How typical of him . . . Of course it wasn't about the money! The first edition Kiyomatsu would have completed my collection, but, year after year, Hanagan refused to sell! I offered him three times what it's worth, easily."

Eli looked at him a little sadly. "If you had that print, would you sell it?"

Bonham dismissed the question. "Josiah and I were rivals ever since I started collecting. When I found out he'd appointed me executor, that was the last straw. He knew I couldn't refuse and give up the chance of examining his collection, so I decided to use that access."

"So it wasn't enough to get the print. You had to make Josiah Hanagan pay for making you wait. Hanagan's collection is superb, but much of the public and collector interest in this auction depended on the glamor of the Kiyomatsu; there was no way the absence of the legendary first edition wouldn't be noticed. With Josiah's own grandson making the sad announcement, Hanagan's reputation would have been ruined without you saying a word. Quite clever. By the way, you do know that the Bureau's confidentially clause does not apply to the concealment of criminal acts, don't you?"

Bonham turned a little pale, but he quickly recovered. "And surely *you* know that you can't prove a word of this? I say it happened just as you told Ichiro!"

Eli nodded. "And I say you should continue to do so. The ghost is gone, but that doesn't mean he can't come back . . . if he has a reason to. Call that a threat if you want, but it didn't come from me."

Bonham, startled, glanced at his collection, but all was quiet. After a moment he smiled a rueful smile. He was beaten and they both knew it, but Eli didn't feel very triumphant. He even had some sympathy for Bonham;

people sometimes let their anger and frustration get the better of them, and that was as true for the living as for the dead. Eli knew that. Yet after this episode he wasn't sure if he'd ever be able to look at the beauty of a woodblock print with the same innocent enjoyment he'd once known. He felt robbed.

"I would have told Ichiro about the seal eventually, you know . . . not my part in it, of course, but I would have 'discovered' the thermal ink deception after a decent interval and paid a fair price for the Kiyomatsu. Probably more than I'll have to pay at this auction. Whatever you may think of me, I had no intention of cheating Ichiro out of his inheritance."

Eli couldn't quite keep the disgust out of his voice. "No, you merely intended to ruin his grandfather's good name."

"Don't take that 'holier than thou' tone with me, Mothersbaugh! You do realize that it's impossible for me to either libel or slander a dead man?"

Eli smiled a grim smile. "It is now."

DIVA

Marshall Hall reminded Eli of a Greek Revival antebellum town home, but larger: each of the eight pillars on the portico was at least three feet thick. Visible through the tall windows running the width of the facade was the foyer of the auditorium, large enough that it could and often did serve as a ballroom and reception hall. Beyond that lay the auditorium itself, reached through two pairs of massive oak doors flanking a statue niche.

In that niche stood the ghost.

Well, Eli reminded himself, not literally. What stood in the statue niche was, no surprise, a statue. A fine marble likeness of Madame Justine Violetta Caldwell, nineteenth-century soprano and, by most accounts, the ghost of Marshall Hall. Eli remembered the statue quite well from his own student days. With so many new buildings in evidence, Eli thought it rather pleasant to see an aspect of the campus of Armfield State University that hadn't changed at all.

Eli checked the time, sighed, and kept walking. His appointment was on the second floor of the nearby University Arts Center with the Dean of Student Activities, Abigail Wilson. Dr. Wilson's deputy administrator, a rather harried-looking young woman, waved him through to the dean's office.

Dean Wilson hadn't changed much either.

Oh, she was older, certainly, but you forgot that almost immediately. Eli rather had the feeling that Dr. Wilson considered time an impertinence to be tolerated at best and ignored otherwise. She had been something of a legend, even in Eli's time. Now her once auburn hair was pure white, and there was a slight tremor in the hand she extended to him as she rose from behind her desk, but her eyes had not changed, nor the way she looked at him. Eli remembered that look. He couldn't say he'd missed it very much.

"I'm Eli Mothersbaugh," Eli said. "You probably won't remember, but we have met."

She smiled then. "Elijah Mothersbaugh, class of 2002. You once broke a ceiling board while chasing ghosts in the auditorium attic, among other misdeeds. I guess it's fortunate for me now that we didn't expel you."

Eli almost smiled. No matter how old he was or probably would ever be, Abigail Wilson had the knack for making him feel like a kid who'd just been caught with his hands somewhere they didn't belong. "Dr. Wilson, I know you didn't have the Bureau called in just to remind me of old transgressions."

She sat back down and indicated a chair for Eli. "No, my assistant called the Bureau so that we might put that ghost hunting inclination of yours to some practical use. I want you to get rid of the ghost haunting Marshall Hall."

"I see," Eli said.

Dr. Wilson smiled grimly. "No, I don't think you do."

Eli sighed. "All right, I admit it—I don't see. Why do you want Madame Caldwell gone? She's been there for over one hundred and fifty years."

"Far too long at that. She's a ghost. She's disruptive to the smooth operation of this University, specifically in the area which is my responsibility. There have been . . . incidents, recently, and there's a rather large fundraiser scheduled for next weekend with some very important guests. I don't want any of them frightened out of their wits on my watch. Calling the Bureau seemed imperative."

Eli took a deep breath. "With all due respect, Dr. Wilson, the fact that there's a ghost in Marshall Hall and the story behind it has rather aided fund-raising and publicity over the years. Why is this a problem?"

"That aspect isn't a problem at all. None of that will change."

Eli frowned. "I still don't understand."

She smiled. "Then you're not trying. Bureau matters are confidential and inviolate. Or have I been misinformed?"

"No, that's correct: whatever happens during the course of my investigation is strictly confidential."

"Well, then. You find a way to get rid of the ghost. If anyone realizes what you are and why you're here, I say you're here for a separate haunting or that you failed. You can't say otherwise. We're left with a romantic legend but no troublesome ghost attached to it. Have I left anything out?"

Eli stared at her for a moment. Then he shook his head, "As far as I can see you haven't left out a single thing, Dr. Wilson."

"Then we understand one another. When can you start?"

"Immediately."

The sensic sweep of the foyer didn't reveal anything Eli wasn't expecting. So many of the cases he'd investigated lately were so much within established parameters that it was, frankly, a little boring. Not for the first time Eli considered early retirement.

Ghosts are getting a little too predictable.

When Eli got to the darkened auditorium, he was just a little surprised to discover a second signature, but it wasn't a ghost. Third row, middle seat was occupied by a living woman sitting alone. She looked a little familiar, but Eli couldn't make out her face in the gloom. He walked down the aisle.

"Excuse me—"

"I wish you hadn't come, Mr. Mothersbaugh," she said.

Eli didn't bother to ask how she knew his name, because he recognized both the voice and, now that he was closer, the face. She wasn't quite as young as he'd thought at first, perhaps in her early thirties. Her hair was very black and straight. Eli rather thought it resembled an obsidian waterfall. She was Dr. Wilson's administrative assistant, all right, but her name was eluding him.

"I'm sorry, miss . . . ?"

"Bonnie Simner. We sort of met today—I'm Dean Wilson's assistant. Deputy Director of Student Activities is the title, not that this means much."

Eli nodded. Now he recognized the name, too. "Miss Simner, that seems a bit strange coming from the person who actually placed the call to the Bureau."

She shrugged. "I had to do something, Mr. Mothersbaugh. Dean Wilson was practically rabid! I thought starting an investigation through the Bureau would calm her down just long enough to make the issue moot; she's due to retire in a couple of weeks. I never expected things to move so fast."

"Normally they wouldn't have, but I was in town. I was born here."

Bonnie sighed. "I know. Your reputation precedes you, but I didn't know you were in town. Lucky me."

Eli sat down one row away. "Can you tell me why Dean Wilson is so upset? What did the ghost do to her?"

Bonnie shrugged. "Does it matter? You're here now, and you'll work your electronic vodoun or whatever and make Madame Caldwell go away. End of story."

"I don't know what you think you know about either me or the Bureau, Ms. Simner, but I'm not an exorcist. Whether the ghost stays or goes depends a great deal on why she's here in the first place and why, after all this time, that's suddenly a problem."

"I don't think it *was* sudden," Bonnie said. "As for why it's a problem . . . Mr. Mothersbaugh, picture two divas on the same stage and you get the idea."

Eli blinked. "You mean Dean Wilson is jealous of the attention the ghost gets?"

"Not so simple as that. In a way, I think Dean Wilson sees the ghost as a challenge to her authority, more so now that she's close to retirement. Add to that the fact that Dean Wilson is terrified of ghosts and always has been. Didn't you know that?"

Eli blinked. The thought of Dean Wilson being afraid of anything was hard enough to swallow, but this? "No, I didn't know."

"Well, it's true. All the ghost has been doing, frankly, is showing up. Dean Wilson was always nervous around the auditorium, but lately the ghost started appearing to her and that made it worse."

Eli made a mental note. "Have you seen the ghost yourself?"

"No, I've never seen her. I hear her singing."

"Bits and pieces of songs?"

"No. Complete arias, sometimes."

That got Eli's attention. "I know of no mechanism that would allow that."

Bonnie glared at him. "I'm not a liar, Mr. Mothersbaugh."

Eli spread his hands. "I didn't say you were. Yet ghosts, for all the folklore, can't really vocalize well. No breath, no voice. For a ghost to make an audible sound requires a great deal of energy, which is expended quickly yet only rebuilds slowly. Unless the sound is part of a 'repeater' haunting that's more recording than manifestation, it's very rare to find an entity who can produce more than a few words at a time, or a bit of a song. No roamer-type ghost should be able to produce a complete operatic aria; there's just not enough energy present for that."

"All I know is that Madame Caldwell most certainly does."

"When?"

"Well, right now."

Eli frowned. "I don't hear anything."

Bonnie shrugged. "I do."

Eli brought up the mapping display on his sensic. The ghost was there, no question. Madame Caldwell stood in center stage wearing a grand operatic costume that looked like a 19th-century wardrobe mistress's idea of an 18th-century Italian noblewoman's dress. On a hunch, Eli adjusted the sensic to close in on the ghostly diva's face and translate the pattern of her moving lips. In his student days, Eli had sensed the ghost on several occasions, but the sensic allowed a much more complete examination. With the sensic's help he could even tell what she was singing, though he still heard nothing.

"Where is she?" Eli asked.

"I don't know. I can't see her. On the stage, I assume."

"What is she singing?"

Bonnie grinned. "Oh, I see. You're testing me."

"Yes," Eli said frankly. "Do you mind?"

"Not at all. She's singing the role of Violetta from 'La Traviata.' I've always wondered if that's her signature piece; her middle name is the same as Verdi's heroine, and maybe that drew her to the role."

Eli was astonished. *On the nose. How is this possible?*

"Well," he said, "this is something new. Does she always sing Verdi?"

"Not always, but often. I think she likes Verdi."

"And I think I envy you," Eli said. "You may be the only person still living who can say she's heard Madame Justine Violetta Caldwell in concert."

Eli tuned the sensic from the visual spectrum to scan both ultra low and ultra high sound frequencies. Nothing. "Though I think it's fair to say you're not really hearing it. At least I was right about that part—there's no sound."

Bonnie shrugged. "All I can tell you is what it feels like. Maybe she's singing in my mind."

Eli considered. "When this is all over, I may ask you to let the Bureau run some tests, Ms. Simner. What you're doing and how might be important."

"I'll think about it," Bonnie said. "Though I'm not likely to be in a mood to want to help you by then."

Eli shook his head. "As I said before, I don't know how this is going to sort out, Ms. Simner. It may be that there's nothing I can do."

"Don't take this the wrong way, Mr. Mothersbaugh, but I hope you fall on your face."

Eli smiled. "How could I possibly take that the wrong way?"

Bonnie was late for a meeting, but she still waited until the song was done before she left the hall. Eli remained behind, checking his sensic, feeling more than a little overwhelmed by the wealth of information that was flowing to him from many directions. First there was Bonnie's revelation about "hearing" the ghost. It might be an aspect of ghosts that no one knew about. Or it just might be an aspect of Bonnie Simner and very little to do with Madame Caldwell. Then there was Madame Caldwell herself.

Eli, to the best of his memory, had never met such a co-operative subject.

Ghosts tended to be fleeting or repeating—either hard to detect and pin down, or regular as clockwork, however long or short the period of their manifestations were. Madame Caldwell, on the other hand, was not repeating anything. She seemed to be having a grand old time. It was almost as if she were taking any one of an infinite number of curtain calls: singing, bowing, holding ghostly bouquets of flowers, smiling and waving at row on row of empty seats. She glowed so brightly that sometimes even Eli, who wasn't as visually sensitive as some in the Bureau, could make her out plainly without the sensic.

I don't think I realized how beautiful she was.

Eli wasn't the biggest opera fan in the world. He knew a little bit about the subject and now even more through his research for the assignment, but he'd had a rather stereotypical notion of female opera stars which in no regard seemed to fit Madame Caldwell. She was no aging diva, broad-beamed and severe; she was fairly young, perhaps mid-thirties, tall, statuesque, and had the most mischievous smile Eli had ever seen.

"Madame Caldwell, if I'd been born a hundred and fifty years earlier . . . "

Eli frowned, then checked his sensic. He could have sworn the ghost had just stuck her tongue out at him. After replaying from the earlier time index, Eli was certain. She *had* stuck her tongue out at him. Right around the time of Eli's "born too late" remark.

"Well, well. There's no doubt you're not a repeater, Madame. Will you speak to me?"

Madame Caldwell did not speak to him. She sang.

And Eli heard it.

Son of a . . .

For a moment Eli couldn't believe it was happening. He had the presence of mind to check the high and low frequencies on his sensic again, but that didn't tell him anything he didn't already know—the only ambient sounds were the occasional creak of shifting timbers in the old hall.

"So it wasn't Bonnie at all. Madame Caldwell, how are you doing that?"

She didn't answer him. This was one aspect of the whole thing that Eli didn't find surprising. Some ghosts had no mind at all and merely repeated past actions. Other ghosts, for all anyone could tell, did have minds and personalities that had survived, and they could communicate after a fashion. Still, being dead was not quite the same as being alive, and the personalities of ghosts were . . . peculiar, to say the least. Freeing a ghost was seldom as easy as asking the thing what it wanted, what was keeping it bound to earth, and, with rare exceptions, they weren't known for responding to simple questions with equally simple answers.

All that aside, Madame Justine Violetta Caldwell was proving an exceptional spirit on many levels. Besides the strangeness of her unheard song, her response to Eli showed that she was fully aware of what was going on around her, not trapped in some twilight memory in denial of where and what she was.

Eli tried to figure out the nature of what he was hearing. It "sounded" like singing, even though Eli knew there was no singing. Feeling a little desperate, he briefly considered whether the phenomenon was some form of telepathy, but he had nothing to judge the idea against. Whatever was happening seemed unprecedented, but from what he had learned of the spirit of Madame Caldwell, "unprecedented" might be par for the course.

Eli stopped pondering and just listened to the song for a while. He got the feeling that she was singing for him alone and not for some long dead audience of farmers and townsfolk. Doubtless when Bonnie came here to listen she felt the same way.

No wonder Bonnie is upset with me.

Not that Eli thought she would have much reason to be upset long-term. If there was any kind of compulsion, habit, confusion or unfinished business about this haunting, Eli couldn't see it. For all he could tell, Madame Caldwell haunted Marshall Hall simply because she liked it there, and if that was truly the case, there was no weapon in Eli's arsenal that could convince her to leave.

Well, it does fit the story.

Eli had read several of the more common versions of the incident in preparation, and all such tales acquired the patina of legend over the years, but nothing conflicted with the facts as known: in 1868, Madame Justine Violetta Caldwell embarked on a cross-country tour. Her concert for the war-weary citizens of Camemill, Mississippi, had been an especial success. Before an appreciative audience Madame Caldwell said that she'd be leaving a part of herself behind always and swore she would return at the end of her tour for a special engagement. Three days later she'd been killed on the way to New Orleans when the boiler on the steamboat carrying her exploded. The first sightings of Madame Caldwell back on the stage at Marshall Hall had started almost immediately after that. Eli had confirmed the basic facts of the tragedy from newspaper accounts published at the time. Was there something they didn't know?

Eli smiled to himself. It was a foolish question—there was always something he didn't know or misunderstood or missed; witness the ghost's splendid aria. This simple fact was something Eli tended to forget. It was only at those times that he had forgotten that Eli started thinking of retirement.

Eli had an idea. He powered up the sensic again, this time using the projection capability to put a weak energy field around himself, a rough analogue to the bio-energy signatures of ghosts. Nothing that would interfere with light or sound, but one of its functions was to create a barrier to external bio-remnant signatures. Immediately, the sound was dampened to the point that Eli could barely hear it. He smiled to himself.

"This is something new, Madame, and for that and the song, I thank you. It's a very clever trick, but I guess you've had a lot of time to work on that."

The ghost merely put a finger to her lips without a pause. Eli nodded in apology and turned off the sensic. He knew he had only part of the story. He had a pretty good idea who had the rest, but for the moment, he was content to enjoy the concert. After a time the song ended. Madame Caldwell faded from view and Eli went home.

Night had fallen by the time Eli returned to campus. He checked in with security first; strangers wandering around the campus with strange devices were bound to draw attention Eli didn't want. From there he went straight back to Marshall Hall.

The audience was already arriving.

Eli saw them as subtle changes in the numbers the sensic was showing him at first. He switched back to mapping mode long enough to get a look at a few of them; as expected they were all nineteenth century, judging by the clothes. Eli saw whole families with children in tow all in their Sunday best, single men with military bearing and ragged clothes, Union officers in clean crisp uniforms.

He'd seen the phenomenon once before, but as yet no one knew whether these sort of specters were really independent bio-remnant energies or just some aspect of the main haunting itself. Eli wasn't sure yet whether it mattered in this case, but it was one more question to file away for later study. It wasn't the ghosts he was waiting for; Eli put the sensic away and found a nice dark corner to pass the time in.

It was about 8:15 PM when Dean Wilson came in. "I know you're there," she said. Eli frowned, but after a moment or two it was obvious she wasn't talking to him. Dean Wilson stood with her hands on her hips, staring at the stage.

She was shaking.

Eli deliberately made a noise. Dean Wilson flinched but recovered quickly as Eli moved into the weak moonlight cast through the windows. "I should have known you'd be lurking here," she said cooly.

"Sorry, Dean, but I needed to know."

"Know what, Mr. Mothersbaugh?"

"Whether you were more angry or afraid. You're angry enough, I can tell, but I'd place my bet on 'afraid.'"

"Do you think I'll deny it, that I care what you think of me? This isn't about me, Mr. Mothersbaugh. Don't forget that."

Eli shrugged. "In a way it is. Madame Caldwell doesn't have a problem. You do."

It was the simple truth, and Eli instantly regretted saying it. He'd seen this reaction to ghosts before. Just as Bonnie said, it was pure, primal fear.

Dean Wilson smiled at him. It was not a warm smile. "What problem would that be? That I get uneasy around unnatural creatures? That I don't want some long dead *thing* hanging around my students after I'm gone? A little help, here, Mr. Mothersbaugh—what exactly is my problem?"

"Fear is your problem. She can't hurt you. She doesn't even *want* to hurt you."

Dean Wilson didn't answer him. "I'm beginning to wonder if perhaps another representative of the Bureau might be more appropriate."

Eli met her gaze. "Dean Wilson, as the field operative, I'll decide when the investigation is concluded. After that time, if you're not happy with my actions or conclusions, you're well within your rights to request a new investigation and lodge a complaint against me. I don't think that'll be necessary."

"I'll be the judge of that," she said, cold as ice.

Eli nodded. "No doubt. I do have one more question, though, if you'd be good enough to answer."

"What's that?"

"Why do you come here at night, when you're so afraid?"

"This is *my* school, Mr. Mothersbaugh. *My* campus, *my* auditorium. That thing is not keeping me out of any part of it! Do you understand? Not one place."

"I think I do."

Eli sat down in one of the seats, and Dean Wilson frowned. "What are you doing?"

"Listening. Or are you going to claim that you don't hear her?"

Dean Wilson turned bright red. "Go to hell." She turned and left without another word.

Eli sighed. *You had to push it, didn't you?*

No point worrying about it right then. Eli settled down along with the ghostly audience and listened until the concert ended. It was only then that he pulled out his sensic again and started requesting data through the

Bureau's network. He wasn't sure that what he needed still existed, but after a bit he found out. It was all there: names, dates, places.

Eli smiled. "Madame Caldwell, I've been listening to you with great pleasure. It's now time for you to listen to me."

The ghost frowned. Again Eli was amazed at how aware the spirit was. As hard as it was for the living to see a ghost, some ghosts didn't see or hear the living very well, either. It was as if they carried some sort of "selective reality" field around them, the way a human in deep denial could, and only saw and heard what they expected to see and hear. Not Madame Caldwell. She was very aware of those around her and watched as Eli came up on the stage. She seemed a bit puzzled but curious. Eli held up the screen of the sensic so that she could see what was displayed there.

"You don't have to understand what this device is or how it works, but I do think you understand what I'm showing you."

She did know. After a moment she smiled a bit sadly.

OBLIGATIONS.

Eli nodded. "Obligations."

The next morning he was adjusting his sensic in the auditorium when he heard someone come in. He didn't even look up from his seat in the first row; he recognized the scent that Bonnie Simner wore from the day before.

"Is the Dean coming?" he asked as Bonnie sat down in the seat beside him.

"Probably with a baseball bat, to judge from the mood she's been in all morning. What did you say to her?"

He sighed. "Couldn't resist the sophomore urge to needle her just a bit. You'd think a man would grow out of that after twenty years or so."

"Yes, you would."

Eli glanced over his shoulder. "Good morning, Dean Wilson."

She didn't return the greeting. "I've got a meeting in ten minutes, Mr. Mothersbaugh, and I don't intend to be late."

"This won't take long." He held up the sensic. "Do you know what this is?"

"It's that thing you use to detect the presence of ghosts, isn't it? Did you bring me here for show and tell?"

Eli didn't bat an eye. "In a way, yes. I'm going to use the holographic projector here to create a mini-version of the stage and auditorium. Please come closer."

Dean Wilson let out a deep sigh of martyrdom and peered at the faintly glowing projection. She frowned. "If this is a ghost detector, shouldn't it be showing the ghost?"

"That the point, Dean Wilson. It should be. If the ghost was present, that is. She's not. Madame Caldwell is gone."

Eli heard the faint groan from Bonnie, but he ignored that for the moment. One problem at a time.

"This better not be a joke, Mr. Mothersbaugh. Have you gotten rid of her or not?"

"One doesn't 'get rid' of a ghost, strictly speaking but, as you can see, she's not here."

Dean Wilson didn't say anything for several long moments. Then she said, "Well. I suppose I should thank you." She didn't say anything else, just turned and made her way out of the auditorium.

Bonnie was close to tears. "You did it, didn't you? I mean, I know it's your job and all, but . . . damn."

Eli shut down the sensic. "I told you I'm not an exorcist, Ms. Simner. My real job is to find an accommodation between the past and the present. Sometimes that's not possible," He grinned. "Sometimes it is."

She frowned. "But you just told Dean Wilson—"

"That the ghost was gone. I didn't lie. By the way, I worked out how we were able to hear her sing."

"You heard her too? Well, not that it really mattered to me—how?"

"Obvious, when you think about it. Normal sound waves provoke a response in the ear; she found a way to reproduce that same effect with the bio-remnant field itself. Much more efficient, from her standpoint—instead of expending energy creating real sound waves, she's mimicking the pressure of sound waves on the ear. That explains why we hear it but the recorders don't. This may be the only case on record where a ghost has invented a new method of communication. Or invented anything, come to that. I used to think of death as a permanent lack of new potential. Thanks to Madame Caldwell, I'm going to have to reconsider that notion."

"I'm happy for you," Bonnie said.

Eli didn't miss the sarcasm. "Don't worry, Ms. Simner. Things aren't as bad as all that."

"What are you talking about, Mr. Mothersbaugh? Is she gone or not?"

"She is most definitely gone." Eli reached into his shirt pocket and pulled out a folded piece of paper. He unfolded it and handed it to Bonnie. "Do you know what this is?"

She frowned. "It's just a list of places, times, and days of the month. Looks like an itinerary."

Eli nodded. "That's because it is an itinerary. Specifically, it's the schedule for the rest of Madame Caldwell's concerts through 1868 and the early part of 1869."

Bonnie stared at the list uncomprehendingly for a moment, but Eli smiled. "Madame Caldwell is probably the most self-aware and coherent entity I've yet encountered. She isn't here because of unfinished business. She isn't trapped or confused or angry or any of the normal reasons for haunting. She's here because Marshall Hall is special to her and she likes it here. To get her to leave I had to give her a better reason to be elsewhere, one that made sense to her. I'm afraid Dean Wilson's discomfort with her wasn't enough."

Bonnie's eyes grew wide. "The concerts!"

Eli nodded again. "Madame Caldwell was a woman of her time and station in life, and that toolkit included a sense of obligation and honor. Those concerts have been delayed quite a while."

Bonnie shook her head. "It's a lovely and romantic notion but pure nonsense—if she goes to these places now, there won't be any audiences waiting for her!"

Eli remembered the previous night at Marshall Hall. "Oh, yes there will. You'll have to trust me on that."

Bonnie just looked at him for a moment, then she smiled sadly. "If you say so. Well . . . it'll help me to think of her playing forever to adoring crowds throughout the country. Whether it's true or not."

Eli shrugged. "Oh, it's true enough . . . except for the part about 'forever.' If Madame Caldwell sticks to her travel schedule, she'll finish her engagement in New York on March 1st of next year. Several weeks after Dean Wilson's well-deserved retirement to the Gulf Coast, or so I'm reliably informed."

Eli watched the light of understanding slowly dawning on Bonnie's face, and he tried not to smile but didn't quite succeed.

"Madame Caldwell's coming back!" Bonnie almost shrieked with joy. Then her expression turned to one of mock severity. "One last prank on Dean Wilson? You should be ashamed of yourself!"

Eli shook his head. "Hardly. Dean Wilson may be sour as a cider apple, but I have to respect her. It couldn't have been easy, doing her job day after day for over twenty years and yet afraid all that time."

Bonnie smiled at him. "Gained a little perspective since your college days, have you?"

He shrugged. "Maybe. Even if that wasn't the case, I'm not one to begrudge a frightened old woman a little peace of mind. Granted, these things don't always work out, but this time everyone wins . . . if you'll allow that."

"What do you mean? It's not up to me. And while we're on the subject—aren't you obligated to reveal all the particulars to Dean Wilson? She's the complainant, after all."

Eli grinned a little sheepishly. "Well, yes and no. You called the Bureau, not Dean Wilson. That you called on her behalf doesn't change that fact, so technically I can discharge my obligation by giving the particulars to either you or the Dean. Guess who I'm choosing."

"Oh." Bonnie looked very somber for a few moments, but it didn't last. She giggled. "Madame Caldwell is on tour!"

"Only about a hundred and sixty years late." Eli sighed. "Just do us both a favor—don't tell Dean Wilson."

Bonnie smiled. "Oh, I won't. Count on it."

"Odd thing, though . . . Madame Caldwell said something, just before she vanished. It sounded like 'watch the comb' or something like that. She was using the same trick she uses to sing, so the sensic didn't get it and I may have misunderstood, but it didn't make any sense to me."

Bonnie looked like she wanted to say something, but finally just shrugged. "It's probably nothing. Listen, I've got to go. Are you leaving immediately?"

Eli thought about that for a moment. "I haven't decided yet."

"Stick around if you can. I'd like to ask you some questions about Madame Caldwell."

Eli remained alone in Marshall Hall for some time after Bonnie left.

I honestly didn't think I had anything left to learn.

At least, not about ghosts. Oh, there were individual secrets and puzzles, right enough. Every case was different enough to keep Eli interested in his work long after other field operatives had burned out, retired, changed careers or, worse, moved into management. Yet Madame Caldwell had actually surprised him, and more than once. What else was he missing, coming as he did to each new case as a problem to be solved, and not simply as a mystery to be experienced?

"Maybe," Eli said aloud, "it's time for a change."

Three months later Eli sat in the Student Union cafeteria with the remnants of a cup of hot tea and the ruins of his lesson plan before him on the table, trying to forget about that last departmental meeting. He'd hated meetings at the Bureau and didn't like the academic versions any better. He understood in a theoretical sort of way the social and political purposes they served, but it always seemed like too much time spent on things that deserved none.

Eli was so intent on his reading that it took him several moments to notice the woman standing in front of the table, even after she spoke.

"May I sit down?"

Eli looked up. It was Bonnie Simner, formerly Dean Wilson's assistant, now the acting Director of Student Activities. Eli started to rise almost out of reflex, but Bonnie defeated his gallantry by plopping herself down in the chair opposite him before he was halfway out of his chair. Eli settled back down, feeling a little foolish, but Bonnie smiled at him.

"So. How's your class going? The first few days weren't too much of a shock, I hope?"

Eli grunted. "The only real shock was how many students there were. The field trip logistics are going to be a nightmare! I mean, Dean Enfinger gave me the numbers but I thought she was kidding."

She raised an eyebrow. "A big class. And you're surprised?"

"Well . . . yes."

"Eli, we had to turn people away as it was! Dean Enfinger tells me we've had students transfer from Brown and UCLA, among many others."

Eli blinked. "Why?"

"Why? Because Dr. Elijah Mothersbaugh is currently Visiting Professor of Bio-Remnant Studies at little ol' Armfield University, you nit! You do have some notoriety in the field, you know."

"I guess, in some small way—"

"Bullshit. I know for a fact you have standing offers from a host of top flight schools, *including* UCLA and Brown. Yet when you decided to take sabbatical from the Bureau, you came here. It occurs to me to ask why that is."

Eli looked at her. "You know why," he said.

Bonnie nodded then, looking serious. "It's Madame Caldwell, isn't it?"

"Of course it is. Bonnie, she's the oddest manifestation I've ever come across, and that's saying something. She may even be unique. I want to know everything I can find out about her and I couldn't do that with my Bureau schedule. Taking a teaching sabbatical was the only way, short of early retirement. I considered that too, believe me."

Bonnie just looked at him for several long moments. "If Madame Caldwell was a human woman, I'd say you were smitten."

Eli thought about it. "Maybe I am."

Bonnie looked a little annoyed. "You were supposed to get all huffy and deny it, you know. You're a living human male. She's a ghost. It's ridiculous! Not to mention a little weird."

Eli nodded affably. "No argument, but I think it's fairer to say that she fascinates me, and that I don't pretend to understand everything that implies. It's . . . complicated."

Bonnie shrugged. "Well, ok. When you put it that way, she fascinates me, too."

There was a surprisingly comfortable silence after that. He broke it first. "Have you heard from Dean Wilson?"

Bonnie grinned. "An actual postcard, about a week ago. She says she's working on her tan and enjoying the company."

"I assume that was a joke. It's much too cold this time of year, even on the coast."

"Maybe. I assumed the 'company' part was the joke, since she was never one for socializing unless campus politics or fund-raising forced it on her. Maybe retirement is helping her sense of humor. Now let me ask you a question: where is Madame Caldewell, now? I've gone to the theater every day for a week now and I haven't heard her once."

Eli blinked. "What do you mean, where? She's on tour."

"Earth to Mothersbaugh: according to her schedule, she should have finished seven days ago."

"Yes, but the return trip—"

"Would have been made instantly, not in a spectral horse and buggy. She may be a ghost, but Madame Caldwell knows damn well what century this is and what she is now. She'd have come back immediately. Something's wrong."

"We don't know that, Bonnie," Eli said.

"Then where is she?"

"I don't know . . . All right, I've been to the theater myself. But I didn't bring the sensic. I'm not sure she wasn't there."

"If she was there, you'd know. Dammit, Eli, you sent her away. You lost her, you find her!"

Eli frowned. "I'll do that."

When classes were over for the day Eli headed for Marshall Hall. Eli walked down sidewalks shaded by bare oaks. Occasionally a leaf crunched underfoot but otherwise there was very little sound. The silence felt odd after the frenzy of his first few weeks at Armfield, but Eli rather liked it, knowing that it would not last.

Marshall Hall was empty, echoing, and dark. When Eli turned on the sensic the instrument simply confirmed that the hall remained empty, echoing, and dark.

Eli adjusted the sensic repeatedly, then moved on to the stage itself, varying long and short range sweeps as he moved from the stage to the wings and back again. He continued until he had covered most of the backstage and prop and storage rooms. They all told the same story—darkness, shadows, but nothing else. Madame Violetta Caldwell, the ghost of Marshall Hall, was not there.

"Thought that was you."

Eli was startled but still recognized the voice. Bonnie Simner stood by the rightmost entranceway, frowning. "She's not here, is she?"

Eli shook his head. "She could hide from me if she wished, but the sensic? No. She's not here. You're right—she should be here. She's not."

"Why not?!"

Eli took a slow breath, let it out, then switched off the sensic. "I don't know. But I promise you I'm going to find out."

Two days later Eli walked along the Rue Royale in late afternoon, watching the tourists strolling along the narrow streets of the French Quarter. No one seemed in a hurry, or to have a particular destination in mind. Or, if they did have a destination in mind, all the time in the world to get there. Eli rather envied them their aimlessness; he wondered what it was like to experience a place like the French Quarter just as what it had become—a moment frozen in time.

Yes, now the maglev line stopped at what had been the old railroad terminus by the river, and people drove in for the day in cars of various types rather than wagons, but otherwise the time could have been two hundred years earlier. The French Quarter escaped the very worst of the Great Hurricane of 2005 that had battered and flooded the city almost to death, but it had not emerged unscathed. Still, those structures that had to be rebuilt matched the originals so closely that it was uncanny.

Despite the mingling of old and new there was a settled patience about the place that reminded Eli more of Europe than the Americas. There was also another current in the city, a watchfulness that spoke of what might be lurking in the buildings other than rot and decay and age.Eli couldn't have said what this spirit was, but Eli felt that he and the city had developed an understanding of sorts over the years, dating from the first time he had come to New Orleans as a teenager before the floods and continuing on every visit since: he didn't belong there. Eli knew this and couldn't escape the feeling that, on some level, the city knew it too. Now Eli was no teenager but, even so, the place was and remained—no other word for it—spooky.

Eli paused for a moment to get his bearings. He stood on the corner of Rue Royale and Toulouse; his real goal in the city was one block north, at the corner of Toulouse and Bourbon Street. Yet he had already done his reconoitering for the day and had an appointment to keep. He turned south on Toulouse and followed it through the crowds of tourists until he reached the nexus of Jackson Square. He ignored the hucksters and palm and tarot readers clustered there and continued to Decatur Street, then followed that east to the French Market and the Café du Monde.

The café was crowded, which was the café's natural state in the current century, and doubtless had been for most of the last two centuries. Eli glanced around, then tapped a code into his personal messenger and had an answer in a few seconds.

I'M TEN FEET FROM YOU! HONESTLY . . .

Eli looked. Bonnie had a table under the awning. It bore the white dust remains of several beignets and Bonnie was coming to the end of her café au lait. "Sorry, I needed a snack. I didn't have time for lunch."

Eli sat down. He had to raise his voice slightly to be heard over the din. "How was your trip?"

"Not too bad." Bonnie sipped her coffee and smiled. "I took the maglev. The drive down just hasn't been the same since they closed I-55. So. Have you found anything?"

When Eli had announced his intention, it had never occurred to him that Bonnie would want to come along. It had apparently never occurred to Bonnie that there was any other option. School business had kept her in Canemill for an extra day, but now she was here, and Eli was at once irritated and a little pleased.

"A shop off Jackson Square sells netsuke and Asian figurines. Didn't see anything interesting otherwise."

Bonnie glared at him. "You know perfectly well what I meant. You didn't come here for the shopping and neither did I."

He smiled. "I found the French Opera House. Which is a pretty neat trick, considering it burned down in 1919."

"That was where Madame Caldwell was to have had her first scheduled concert after Canemill?"

Eli nodded. "Uh huh. A special one-night-only performance during the regular opera season. Quite a big deal at the time, or would have been."

"So how can we know that Madame Caldwell's revived tour reached this point?"

Eli sighed. "Well, the obvious and unpleasant answer is that we can't. Assuming Madame Caldwell kept to her timetable, there's not going to be a bio-energy remnant signature after a single event, not after all these weeks. Probably the only thing that's going to prove where Madame Caldwell is would be for us to find her. For everything else, instinct and guesses of varying degrees of education are all we're going to have."

Bonnie sighed. "This is an awfully big city and we don't have a lot of time, Eli."

"True, but even a roamer spirit has strictures; she wouldn't be just *anywhere*. She would always be in an area that had some associations for her with the New Orleans of 1868. For the most part that means the Quarter and part of the Garden District. I've already scoped out the home where she was scheduled to lodge; she wasn't there, so my guess is, if she's still here, she's in the Quarter because it's the vicinity of the old opera house. For instance, she could be having beignets with us right now and we'd never know it."

"She could? Would she see this place, know it was here?"

"The Café du Monde, in one form or another, has been in the French Market area since 1862. Thing is, I can't use my sensic around so many living people; it's like trying to find a candle on the edge of the sun. I might sense her directly, but it would be a long shot."

Bonnie looked at him. "You can sense ghosts?"

"Yes, under normal conditions," Eli said. "A few of my colleagues can even see them, but that only happens to me now and then; mostly I use the sensic when I need visual confirmation."

"I don't get it. Does that mean they're more sensitive than you are? I mean, I'm sorry to ask so many questions, but I'm interested." She stopped, and grinned a little sheepishly. "Obviously, or I wouldn't be here, huh?"

"I don't mind," Eli said. "It's just that most of the people who can see ghosts can't tell anything about the remnant's emotional state, unless the visual cues are really obvious. Whereas I pick that up right away as a rule, and the emotional state is generally the first thing I want to know. So, not less or more. Different."

The sun was getting lower in the sky as Bonnie finished her coffee. "So, what now?"

Eli checked the time. "Now we check out the show, assuming there is one. People should be arriving for the evening concert before too long."

"People?"

Eli shrugged. "Well . . . they used to be."

Eli and Bonnie walked back along Decatur Street. Some of the day trippers who had just come in for the shopping would be leaving now. Others who only came in for the clubs and bars would just be arriving, but the net result was that the number of people wandering the Quarter didn't change much from afternoon to early evening. It was only after the shops were empty and most of the tourists had wandered off to the bars and restaurants that the crowds would thin appreciably. Eli reluctantly left his sensic in its case. They crossed St. Peter to Toulouse, then turned north toward Bourbon Street, walking in comfortable silence for a while. There were other people about but fewer than before, walking in couples and groups along the narrow streets.

Bonnie looked up at the ironwork lining the second story windows as they crossed Chartres. "It looks like it's been here since the beginning."

"Some of it has. Some has just been rebuilt in the original style. You'll see what I mean when we get to Bourbon Street," Eli said.

She looked at him sideways as they walked. "How do you do that?" she asked.

Eli blinked. "Do what?"

"Summon up this information right and left. First you told me how long Café du Monde has been around, then when the French Opera House burned down, now I'm getting briefed on architecture. I knew you collected Japanese prints, but I didn't know you were an expert on the French Quarter."

Eli laughed. "That's because I'm not. Most of this is general tourist information, easily accessible on the net. My Bureau connections get me most of anything else I may need in the way of data before an assignment."

"This isn't a Bureau assignment," Bonnie pointed out.

"No, but the principle is the same. In the case of an older haunting, things like where the original building was, who lived in it . . . The details could be crucial to know, so I do my research. Rather narrow focus, I'll admit. Ask me the attendance figures for Saint Louis Cathedral or who owns the local football team and I couldn't tell you."

She looked a little disappointed. "Is that all it is? Eli, you're going to have to stop revealing your secrets so easily. You're taking away all the mystery."

"You asked. Besides, I'm not the mystery," Eli said, "Madame Caldwell is."

"She's not the only one."

Eli didn't know what to say to that, but Bonnie didn't seem to be expecting an answer. They reached Bourbon Street. To the left was a restaurant and a few clubs before Bourbon crossed Canal three blocks west; most of the jazz clubs and bars were to the east. Across the street was a fine French Quarter hotel with beautiful wrought-iron railings at each level. There was a warm yellow glow from the lobby and they could hear jazz and laughter through the open doorway of a nearby club. Local ordinances kept holographic projections out of sight; the bars and shops made do with old-fashioned neon.

Bonnie glanced down Bourbon Street, wistfully, before turning her attention back to Eli and the hotel. "This is it?"

Eli nodded. "Yes. This is where Madame Caldwell's solo concert was scheduled to occur. The hotel on the site now only dates to 1965 and was heavily remodeled in 2008, but it matches its surroundings very well, don't you think?"

"Very," Bonnie said. Eli pulled out his sensic and handed Bonnie a pair of glasses with dark lenses and a short antenna coming off the earpiece. "What's this?" she asked.

"3D holo display. I thought you might want to see what the French Opera House would have looked like in Madame Caldwell's day."

Eli brought up the image from the sensic and put it on the screen; he heard a faint gasp from Bonnie as the image came up on her thin film polymer lens display. He knew she was seeing what he saw: a massive three-story Greek Revival style building that filled much of the block and, for a moment, took the corner of Bourbon and Toulouse back to 1868. The facade was either grey stone or plaster carved to look like stone. "French Opera House" was lettered over the rounded corner entrance. Bonnie took off her glasses, looked at the modern hotel, then put the glasses back on for a moment.

"There's nothing of it left now, is there?"

Eli shook his head, then frowned. "Well, one thing . . . "

He looked down at the street in front of the hotel for a moment then brightened. "There it is." He pointed to a dent in the brick street.

Bonnie frowned. "There 'what' is, exactly?"

"Supposedly it's the place where carriages used to stop when they unloaded gentlemen and ladies for an evening of opera, just outside the entrance of the opera house. Remember, it wasn't just an opera house—it was used for receptions, balls, debuts . . . it was near the center of New Orleans high society for sixty years. Yet the only thing left to show for it now is a dent in the street." Eli made some adjustments to his sensic.

"Things change, I guess. Even here. But what about Madame Caldwell? Any sign?"

"So far the answer is 'no,' though I can't be certain with all this interference."

The number of living people out and about was much lower than it had been during the day or, rather, most of them were already where they planned to be for the greater part of the evening. Even so, Eli was constantly adjusting and compensating for their much more powerful energy signatures.

Bonnie reached up and touched her display glasses. "They're not exactly the fashion statement I wanted to make."

Eli grunted. "This is New Orleans. Do you really think anyone's going to notice a pair of display specs?"

"Good point. So, what do we do now? Wait?"

"No need. I'm convinced Madame Caldwell isn't here."

Bonnie stared at him. "Are you sure that thing's working? I'd expect there to be something."

Eli adjust the sensic to filter out a young Asian couple walking hand in hand east toward the Bourbon Street clubs. "Look down the street, Bonnie. What do you see?"

"Nothing that I didn't see without them. Bricks, buildings, neon."

"That's just it. The only way I can figure that Madame Caldwell would have stayed here was if she'd gotten trapped in some sort of powerful 're-peater' haunting that already existed on the site, and was overwhelmed by its energy field. Yet if that had happened there would be some sign. There isn't. My logical conclusion is that Madame Caldwell isn't here."

Bonnie didn't look happy. "Well, I won't call it a waste; I haven't been down here in a long time, but . . . damn. We can't even tell if she was here at all. If this keeps up we'll have to cover every single stop on her itinerary."

"Maybe there's another way," Eli said.

Bonnie sighed gustily. "Remember what I said about not revealing your secrets? Forget it. You're being entirely too cryptic. If there is a way to find out if she was here, what is it?"

"We take a ghost tour. There's one leaving in just a few minutes."

She just stared at him. "You mean one of those hokey walking tour things they do for the tourists? Eli, you're an expert. I've taken a couple of these and they were all folklore and supposition with a 'scary story' wrapper. How will this help?"

"This one's different," Eli said. "It's led by a real ghost."

. . . EEP TOGETHER PLE . . . "

The sensic kept losing the voice. Not surprising. Anna was constantly on the move. By all accounts she had been a fireball of energy in life, and death hadn't slowed her down much. The sensic's translation algorithms couldn't read her lips if she wasn't facing Eli and the rest of the tour.

Eli adjusted the sensic, and Anna Kirkpatrick came into sharper focus. She was a plump blonde woman in her late forties at the time of death and had been leading ghost tours in the Quarter for nearly twenty years by then. Apparently after her sudden passing she'd seen no reason to stop. Maybe it was just habit, but Eli wasn't totally convinced of that. Bonnie, for her part, kept looking from Anna and the ghostly tour group to Eli and back again as if she couldn't quite believe what was happening.

"How did you find out about this?" she whispered.

"Stumbled across Anna and her group last year on an assignment," Eli said. "I have to say I found the irony of it more than a little impressive."

"So why didn't you do anything about it before now?" Bonnie asked.

Eli blinked. "Do? Why should I do anything?"

Bonnie put her hands on her hips. "Isn't that your job?"

"If by that you mean getting rid of ghosts, you should know better. Else I'd have tried to do the same to Madame Caldwell."

"Maybe you weren't trying, but you managed anyway," Bonnie asked dryly.

Eli winced. "Point taken. Still, that was different. My real job is to resolve conflicts between the living and the dead. There's no conflict here. Now, if Anna was signing up living, paying customers for her tours, I'm sure the other guides would complain. As it is, no one has."

"You'd think," Bonnie said, "with instruments like the sensic around, the ghost tours would have gone out of fashion. Or at the very least gotten more precise about where to visit."

"You're talking about facts. This is entertainment."

Anna paused, looking puzzled. Eli held up his hand before Bonnie said anything else. Anna wasn't a repeater, despite the fact that any re-curring event was a repeater's natural environment and a ghost tour cer-tainly qualified. She was aware, in her own way, and Bonnie and Eli were disrupting the tour. After a moment Anna went back into her speil. Eli beamed what the sensic could translate with its synthesized voice into his own earplug and the mini-headset built into Bonnie's specs as Anna waved to a gated courtyard near what was now an Irish pub for the next stop on her tour.

. . . COURTYARD WHERE A YOUNG CREOLE WOMAN FELL TO HER DEATH SOMETIME IN THE 1800'S, RUMORED TO HAVE BEEN MURDERED BY HER WHITE LOVER WHEN . . . INCONVENIENT . . .

Eli sighed. Sometimes he wished more ghosts had Madame Caldwell's gift for using bio-remnant signatures to mimic sound waves. He had adapt-ed the sensic to filter and record those patterns since the day he'd figured out how she'd managed the trick and couldn't wait for a chance to try his modifications out. An audio file of a concert given by a woman who'd died before sound recordings were even invented would be something indeed, but right now he'd settle for getting all of Anna's tour patter without all the skips and omissions.

They moved up Toulouse. Eli knew they weren't going to the French Opera House location as such; there were a couple of alleged hauntings on Bourbon Street, but nothing was traditionally associated with the site of the opera house that he knew of. Not that this had anything to do with the fact that his own sensic told him that no ghosts where there; it just wasn't considered a haunted site even in the local folklore, which sometimes did and sometimes did not match up with the facts. Considering the potential of a site like the old French Opera House, this was a little strange until you put the Opera House's history against the rest of the history of the Quarter both real and imagined.

Too much competition, Eli thought, and he smiled.

Still, today there was going to be a detour. Eli whispered to Bonnie. "Don't be alarmed, but you're about to start glowing."

"What?" Bonnie asked, but Eli had already activated a software switch on the sensic. She and Eli both were surrounded by a faint blue glow. "What is this?" she asked.

"A weak field that mimics bio-energy remnants. We've just joined the tour properly."

. . . O STRAGGLING OR WE'LL LEAVE YOU FOR THE GHOSTS, Anna said, frowning at the pair of them in mock severity. Eli just smiled and ushered Bonnie forward. "Yes, ma'am," he said.

"You mean they can see us now?" Bonnie whispered.

"They could see us before. Or it might be better to say, they were aware of us before, but in a rather unfocused way. It's mostly that way for the ghosts, as best we understand it. To them it's the living who are indistinct and ethereal. Some ghosts notice us more than others, but now we look pretty much the way they expect people to look. It's the living who are shadows now."

It wasn't just the living who appeared rather distant and indistinct, though—the other "members" of the tour group were a little ethereal themselves. Eli, Bonnie, and Anna the tour group leader were a level of magnitude more distinct, more "real" looking. Bonnie glanced at the others and then looked at Eli, frowning, but Eli just shook his head. "Later," he mouthed silently. Bonnie shrugged and kept up the pace. Eli let go of her arm.

. . . OSTLY CAT IS SAID TO LURK ON THE WALL AND CRIES WHEN A MEMBER OF THE FAMILY IS ABOUT TO DIE. NEXT . . .

Eli adjusted the sensic and pointed it at the top of the crumbling brickwork. Bonnie leaned close. "Is the cat actually there?"

"Sure." Eli showed her the distinct feline shape curled up under a crown of honeysuckle vine. "Though I couldn't attest to its banshee properties."

Eli used his sensic at each stop of the tour. Sometimes there was a ghost, sometimes not. Yet the percentage that he could verify was, to Eli's way of thinking, fairly high.

Of course.

Eli wondered if it would be possible to verify his theory. He did a quick search and found what he was looking for in a static net database, one that had never been deleted or recycled to other uses because, odds were, all concerned had forgotten it was there: Anna Fitzpatrick's old Ghostly Mystery Tour advertising page. It only covered the highlights of the old tour, but even so, Eli was able to verify several deviations from the old tour. Perhaps Anna had changed her actual walking tour pre-mortem, but why would she do that? When it was all story and showmanship, the facts wouldn't have mattered.

They were approaching Bourbon Street again. Eli used his sensic's projection capabilities to restore the French Opera House to the corner of Toulouse and Bourbon, or at least the appearance of it. Anna stopped her standard patter and just looked at it for a moment. Eli knew the time had come, however the next few minutes worked out, ask for something that wasn't on the tour.

"You changed the tour, didn't you?" he asked.

Anna looked at him. CHANGED?

"You can see the ghosts now, can't you? You know which ones are real and which ones are not. You changed the tour."

THIS IS THE TOUR, Anna said as if she hadn't heard a thing Eli had said. OUR NEXT STOP—

Eli knew better. "There are no ghosts at the French Opera House, are there?"

IT IS NOT ON THE TOUR.

"But you would know if there were?"

I WOULD KNOW.

"You would know if any ghosts had been here, yes? You come by here every evening about this time."

YES.

Two simple questions, two simple and direct answers. Eli was beginning to think this wild hare of his might work after all. Yet the ghost of Anna Kirkpatrick looked worried. Almost . . . frightened.

What is she afraid of?

Eli described Madame Caldwell. "Have you seen this person? This . . . spirit?"

Anna just looked at him. Her lip was actually quivering as if she might burst into tears at any moment. I SEE SO MANY . . .

"Like this? Dressed like that, wearing that same emerald necklace?"

SO MANY . . . Anna repeated. SEEN SO MANY. WHY ARE THERE SO MANY? I DON'T REMEMBER THAT. WHO ARE YOU?

"My name is Eli," he said.

YOU'RE NOT ON THE TOUR. GO AWAY!

"Who is on the tour?"

Anna just looked at him. She pointed at the two other couples, but there was so little substance to them now that even the sensic was having trouble focusing them. Another moment and they were gone, and it was just Eli, Bonnie, and the ghost of Anna Fitzpatrick standing at the corner of Toulouse and Bourbon Street. People walked by, but of course they did not see Anna there. Some carried cups from the last bar they had visited as they worked their way down Bourbon Street. Eli heard the strains of a jazz trumpet from the open door of a club just a ten yards away.

I DON'T REMEMBER, Anna said, then she shook her head sadly. NO, I REMEMBER THE WRONG THINGS. She looked up at them. I'M DEAD. WHY DID YOU MAKE ME REMEMBER?

"We were talking about the ghosts . . ." Eli started to say, but Anna was crying now. The sensic saw them as trails of silver down her face.

I DIDN'T WANT TO BE DEAD. I DIDN'T WANT TO REMEMBER.

"It's all right," Eli said and immediately felt like an utter fool. It wasn't all right. It was most decidedly not all right, but Anna had been managing fine. She didn't really need to know better. Now she did.

SHE'S NOT HERE, Anna said, and then she vanished into nothing. Eli didn't need to know what the sensic told him. Anna Kirkpatrick was gone; the tour was over. He took a deep breath, let it out slowly, and waited.

He didn't wait long.

"Am I safe in assuming," Bonnie said, "that the great Eli Mothersbaugh has just royally fucked up?"

He nodded. "So it appears. Anna's gone."

Bonnie frowned. "You mean gone as in gone for good? Blast it, Eli, what did you do?"

"Many ghosts tend to operate within what I've come to call a 'selective reality field.' It's as if they carry a slice of time around with them. A time where they are what they were, that they are where they should be and doing what they're supposed to do. I'm afraid my pestering brought Anna out of her reality for a moment and into mine. One side effect of that is that the ghost gets a little perspective, can see their situation more clearly. Whether they want to or not. While Madame Caldwell may be quite aware of what she is and when 'now' is, for some ghosts that knowledge is too much to bear."

"So she's gone, just like that? You sent her away?"

"I didn't 'send' her, it doesn't work that way. She left. But, yes, I caused it. It wasn't my intention, but that's what happened."

"So how do you know that Madame Caldwell didn't just disappear the moment she left Marshall Hall?"

"I don't," he said.

"You didn't even consider it?"

"Yes, but I also considered that this is Madame Caldwell we're talking about. Still, I knew it was a risk. It's quite possible that we're wasting our time looking for Madame Caldwell here or anywhere else."

Bonnie just looked at him for a moment. "I'm going to listen to some music now," she said, and she turned her back squarely on Eli and headed down to mingle with the people on Bourbon Street. He watched her go. He considered catching up to her but decided—for better or worse—that this was a very bad idea. He started back down Toulouse alone toward Decatur Street. After a short time he changed his mind.

I think I've been up and down this street enough for one day.

He crossed one block over to St. Peters and continued toward the river. The evening was cool but not as cold as the weather often turned this time of year. Most of the tarot and palm readers and artists around Jackson Square had packed up for the day, but the mule carriages were still going, and tourists were still moving up and down Decatur street to restaurants and the brewery and across to the Riverwalk. Eli had a spot between the two in mind: a small fountain near the old tourist information building.

No place in this part of the Quarter was really isolated; Eli could see people walking along the top of the levee just across the cable car line. There was a sidewalk giving access to the river, and benches near the fountain, but there was no one there now. Eli sat down beside the fountain.

There was a hint of moisture in the breeze from the river, over and above the Quarter's faint scent of mold and slow decay. There was scarcely an interior space this close to the river that didn't show water damage, either from a past flood or simple unrelenting damp. Yet as fast as the place aged and crumbled it was rebuilt, as close to the same as it was that anyone could imagine. Eli fancied that sooner or later nano-technology would take over the job that human contractors and technicians handled now and that New Orleans would remain, slowly decaying and as slowly rebuilt, moldering empty on the river long past the time that humanity itself had gone extinct and the city truly belonged to the ghosts.

Rather morbid turn, old son. Even for you.

Eli was still by the fountain a few hours later when his personal messenger beeped at him.

WHERE THE HELL ARE YOU?

Eli blinked. "Bonnie?"

WHO ELSE? ANSWER THE QUESTION, DAMMIT.

"Just off Decatur Street by the old museum, near the fountain."

THAT'S NOT A FOUNTAIN. THAT'S A VERY WET TRASH PIT.

Eli glanced at the scummy water and noticed a beer bottle floating in the current made by the water jets. "Well, it could be cleaner . . . " he said, then blinked. "How did you know that?"

YOU THINK YOU'RE THE ONLY ONE WHO KNOWS ABOUT THAT SPOT? DON'T YOU DARE MOVE! I'M JUST CROSSING ROYAL.

He waited. After a little while he saw Bonnie strolling briskly but a tad unsteadily across Decatur Street. She almost collided with a group of Japanese schoolgirls, who scattered like giggling birds.

LITTLE DEARS SHOULDN'T BE UP SO LATE ANYWAY . . .

Eli waited while she made her way to his bench and plopped herself down beside him. He raised an eyebrow. "Enjoy yourself?"

"Yes, I did, you prig, and, yes, I've been drinking. I enjoyed that, too, thanks for not asking."

He blinked. "I have the feeling you're angry with me."

"Good call. You do have a knack for noticing some things very well and others not so much. Or at all."

"What sort of things?"

"This isn't Remedial Social Interaction 101, Dr. Mothersbaugh. This is life. Or as close as you seem to get."

He didn't know what to say to that, but Bonnie didn't wait for him to say anything. "I am not mad, actually. I am furious! I was drinking to figure out why I am furious. Oddly enough, looking at the matter stone cold sober wasn't helping. It's not that you did anything wrong. You probably did Anna a favor. Maybe you did Madame Caldwell a favor too. I guess we'll have to find out, if we can. No. I'm furious because today the world is a little less mysterious and marvelous than it was yesterday. You did that."

He shrugged. "What do you want me to say, Bonnie? That I made a mistake? I think we've already established that."

Bonnie shook her head and then apparently regretted it. She clutched his shoulder. "Wait till everything stops spinning . . . " Bonnie let out a deep breath. "It isn't about you, Eli. That's the thing—I realized that I'm not mad at you. I'm mad at me."

"Ummm . . . would that make more sense if I'd been drinking, too?" he asked.

"Damned if I know. See, I don't like a world that's nothing but cause and effect. I need something beyond that. For some people that's religion. For me, it's Madame Caldwell and Anna Fitzpatrick and that nameless kitty that hangs out on the wall of the courtyard along Toulouse. As much as Dean Wilson fears and despises everything they represent, that's how much I want and need them. Just knowing Madame Caldwell was there, and the way she made me feel when she sang to me . . . You can't imagine how hard it was to make the call to the Bureau."

"I know you weren't happy; you didn't exactly keep it a secret," Eli said dryly.

She glared at him a little blearily. "I'm not good at reining in my emotions, and I'm really not good at not saying what I think. Work with it. The point is that you scare me, Eli Mothersbaugh, and, just like Dean Wilson or any other human being, I don't like being scared. It makes me angry."

Eli blinked. "That also makes about as much sense as Dean Wilson being afraid of Madame Caldwell in the first place. She's harmless, I'm harmless."

"Ask the former ghost of Anna Kirkpatrick how harmless you are. Oh, that's right. We can't."

"So we're back to that. Bonnie—"

"Shut up, I'm not done yet. You see a ghost as a problem to be solved. You sent Anna away by accident, but you'd have done it just as quickly and with even less regret if you thought there was a reason."

"That's fair," Eli admitted.

"And," Bonnie continued, "you'd do the same blasted thing to Madame Caldwell! Even if you really do want to talk to her, study her, gaze soulfully into her ethereal eyes or wha'ever, you'd do the same thing. If you thought there was a call to make, a purpose to serve, you'd damn well send her away. Probably wouldn't even give her time to pack her damn comb . . . "

Comb? Why was that familiar? Then Eli remembered Madame Caldwell's parting phrase.

"Madame Caldwell was talking about a comb when she left. Are you saying you know what she meant?"

"I said no such thing and don't change the subject!" Bonnie growled.

Chastened, Eli thought about her question, but not for long. "Yes. I would."

Bonnie's anger seemed to subside like a tire with a slow leak. Now she just looked weary and miserable. She sighed. "Whatever your faults, you're basically an honest guy. Right now that might be your only redeeming feature." She finally let go of Eli's shoulder. "Damn, why did I mix Kahlua with a Hurricane . . . "

"Maybe it just seemed the thing to do at the time. That's why I do what I do, for better or worse."

Bonnie groaned, then looked at him. "Why are you here?"

Eli frowned, puzzled. "In New Orleans?"

"No, I mean *here*," she waved a hand at the fountain and the empty benches around them. "This little eddy by the current, so to speak. They don' even clean the fountain more than once a year, if that of'en."

Eli smiled. "Oh, that. Do you remember credit cards?"

"Yeah. Little scraps of plastic with magnetic strips. What about them?"

"When I was a teenager my folks and I came to New Orleans all the time. I remember coming by this fountain on the way to meet them at Café du Monde. Floating in the water with the other debris was a green credit card with the magnetic strip scratched out. Now, people threw coins into fountains all the time. They still do, but a credit card?"

"Maybe that's all they had. What's your point?"

"The point is that when a person wants to connect with something beyond themselves, they find a way. When the world is all gleaming steel and holographs and the spirits of the dead are measured and catalogued and stored in data files, people still find a way. I come to this fountain to remind myself of the day I learned that."

She looked at him very intently then. "Why?"

"Because it's something I don't want to forget. Because you're not the only one who needs the Madame Caldwells of this world, however her story plays out or what my or your part is in it."

Bonnie leaned back slightly as if she was trying to bring Eli into better focus. "That's almost . . . sweet."

"You asked. So. Why are you here? You knew about the fountain. You come here too, don't you?"

"Uh huh. To pet the kitty."

He frowned. "What kitty? Oh, you mean . . . " Eli reached for his sensic but she laughed. "Not a ghost. There used to be a bronze kitty statue on the rim of this fountain. When I was a kid I used to come to pet it, sort of as a joke. Then one day it was gone. Probably some junkie stole it for scrap. I still come to pet it anyway. Maybe that was my connection to the mysterious." She groaned then. "Eli, I know you're old-fashioned, but are you a gentleman?"

He frowned. "I'd like to think so."

"Good. Tomorrow I'm going home. You follow Madame Caldwell to San Antonio or whatever her next stop was, I don't care. Right now I need you to take me back to the hotel and put me to bed. I don' think I can manage on my own."

"No problem."

She nodded, looking a little melancholy. "Didn't think so. I'd shake my head at you but then the world would start spinning again . . . ooh, too late. For extra points and if you're a real gentleman, you'll hold my hair back."

"Ummm . . . your hair?"

She nodded sweetly. "Uh huh. I'm about to throw up."

Bonnie proceeded to do just that. After the spasms were done Eli partly-escorted, partly-carried Bonnie back to the hotel, but it was nearly midnight before her stomach settled down enough for Eli to get her put to bed properly. When she was finally sleeping peacefully, he went back to his own room. He sat down beside the table near a picture window looking out over the genteel squalor of the Quarter. Eli could see the spires of St. Andrews lit up near Jackson Square when he peeked through the curtains. He was still too keyed up to sleep, and something that Bonnie had said was still nagging at him.

She had said quite a lot, and Eli knew there was much in what she'd said that he probably should think about, but the thing that was sticking in his mind was something that seemed entirely trivial.

A comb?

Why was he even thinking about it? It was just an expression. And the fact that Madame Caldwell had mentioned a comb also was likely just a coincidence.

Wasn't it?

Eli pulled the sensic out of its case and quickly made a connection to the Bureau.

The next morning Eli boarded the maglev instead of going to the airport as he'd originally planned. He walked past Bonnie, who was huddled in a seat near the front of the compartment, looking miserable. She was wearing dark glasses and didn't look up as he passed; he assumed she didn't notice him and thought that just as well. He was in his own seat running diagnostics on the sensic when he noticed her standing there, scowling down at him.

"What do you think you're doing? I thought your next stop was San Antonio!" She had raised her voice and apparently regretted it. She rubbed her forehead gingerly.

Eli kept his voice low. "I changed my mind. I'm going back to Canemill too."

"Meaning you've given up?"

"Meaning I don't think Madame Caldwell is in San Antonio." Bonnie wobbled slightly and he sighed. "Bonnie, go sit back down before you fall down."

She didn't go back to her seat. Instead she sat down in the empty seat next to him. "What have you found? Spill it."

"Remember the comb? Madame Caldwell's comb? The one I wouldn't have given her time to pack if I'd decided to get rid of her? That comb?"

Bonnie grimaced. "Yeah. What about it?"

"According to reports at the time, Madame Caldwell said that she was 'leaving a part of herself behind.' I thought she was just playing to the crowd, but she meant something else, didn't she?"

Bonnie grinned, despite her evident pain. Eli frowned. "What's so funny?"

"You are. Unless those circles under your eyes are lying, that one bit of trivia had you neck deep in that machine of yours for most of the night. You could have just asked me."

"I did ask you," Eli said drily, "You basically told me to get skewered."

"Oh, right. Sorry." Bonnie grinned a little sheepishly and went on, "Anyway, some performers are really superstitious, you know? Madame Caldwell had this ritual—if she particularly liked a venue she'd hide some personal item there. She believed that would draw her back again. She never did this lightly in any case and, since the audience at Marshall Hall really touched her, she left something extra special there. Something she really loved, something that Madame Caldwell knew she would return for."

"How did you know it was a comb?"

Bonnie laughed. "Because I found it, that's why. Once I knew *something* existed, I went looking. Took months even so."

"Where is it now?"

She glared at him. "Right where Madame Caldwell left it! Where did you think?"

Eli nodded. "Just that. When we get back to campus I need you to show it to me."

Bonnie massaged her temples with the tips of her fingers. "Owww . . . Why should I?"

"Do you want Madame Caldwell back or not?"

"You know I do. What's the comb got to do with that?"

"Maybe nothing. But I very sincerely doubt it."

Bonnie had parked her car at the maglev station. They threw their luggage into the trunk and she drove them in silence directly to campus. It wasn't until they stood on the portico to Marshall Hall that she spoke again.

"Before we go any further, I want to know why the comb matters one way or another. Are you saying she only haunted Marshall Hall because the comb was there?"

Eli took a deep breath and let it out. "Listen, Bonnie. I can show you examples of data patterns that separate revenants from repeaters from free-roamers. I can even tell you what the lowest field strength ever recorded for a certified haunting was. What I cannot tell you is why Madame Caldwell does one thing and not another. Past a point I simply do not know."

"So why are you chasing the comb, if you don't know that it matters?"

"I know that it mattered to Madame Caldwell."

Bonnie, without further protest, led Eli to a musty storage room that, apparently, had once been a dressing area. She tapped on the outside wall until the echo rang hollow and then teased a brick loose from the wall. The small crevice behind that loose brick was empty except for some recently-disturbed dust.

Bonnie was close to hysteria. "It was right here! I swear I left it just as I found it. I made sure the brick didn't stand out; there was nothing to call attention to it! No one else knew it was there!"

"Someone did, apparently," Eli said. "Calm down. Tell me what it looked like."

"What does it matter what it looked like? It's gone!"

"Assuming it still exists, I'd like to be able to recognize the comb if I saw it. One comb looks a lot like another."

Bonnie sat down on the edge of a box and shook her head, wearily. "Are you thinking of the sort of plastic comb you run through your hair once or twice on your way out the door?"

Eli blushed. He'd been thinking exactly that.

Bonnie sighed. "You've see pictures of the *mantillas* that Spanish women used to wear in their hair, right? English and American women used to do something similar. This one was quite elaborate, maybe four inches high, made of tortoiseshell. It was shaped like a lyre with a lot of piercework decoration. It was exquisite!"

"All right, to find Madame Caldwell I have to find the comb. Or rather, I have to verify its location."

Bonnie looked disgusted. "Look, Eli, I know you're smart and all, but anyone could have taken that damn comb! What makes you think you know where it is?"

Eli just looked at her. "You mean you don't?"

It took a moment or two, but the expression on Bonnie's face slowly turned to a look of horror. "Oh, damn."

Eli nodded, looking glum. "Exactly."

"All you had to do was destroy it, if you really wanted to get rid of Madame Caldwell."

Eli wasn't quite sure what he'd expected, but Abigail Wilson's family had come from old money; her "retirement home" was the ancestral estate on the Gulf of Mexico just outside Biloxi, rebuilt to its former genteel glory after the same killer hurricane that flooded New Orleans demolished the rest of the coast. Dean Emeritus Wilson served Eli and Bonnie tea on a screened veranda with a great view of the water. A surviving Live oak shadowed them from the afternoon sun. Bonnie had handled most of the conversation at first, but now it was Eli's turn.

Dean Wilson sipped her tea. "Mr. Mothersbaugh, I'm sure I don't know what you're talking about."

"Madame Justine Violetta Caldwell's comb," Eli said. "And yes, you do."

The old woman looked grim. "I should ask you both to leave, you know. I don't like being called a thief."

Eli smiled. "There was no theft involved. The original owner has been dead for a period far exceeding the Statute of Limitations. Finders keepers."

"So why are you here?"

Eli met the old woman's gaze squarely. "I want to understand, that's all. You knew about Madame Caldwell's comb for the same reason Bonnie did, and you'd been searching for it as well. Whether you followed Bonnie or found the comb on your own is beside the point. You sat through my demonstration and said all the expected things, though I'm guessing you'd already figured out that Madame Caldwell's absence was only temporary. When you left, you took the comb with you."

She smiled then. "Thought you were quite clever, didn't you?"

"I seldom think so," Eli said, glancing at Bonnie, "because I'm usually wrong. But you did take the comb. Why?"

"You said it yourself—I knew Madame Caldwell would return to Marshall Hall. I didn't know for certain that taking the comb would prevent that, but your presence tells me I was right."

"Our presence tells you exactly nothing you didn't already know.

172

Madame Caldwell is here, and don't pretend you don't realize that." Eli had turned on the sensic before he'd reached the front door of Dean Wilson's home. Now he activated its holographic projection capacity and there was Madame Caldwell, calmly sitting in the porch swing not five feet from them. She did not sing, nor speak, nor do anything except watch the proceedings with what appeared to be rapt attention.

Bonnie gasped, but Dean Wilson didn't even blink. "You needn't engage your infernal devices, Mr. Mothersbaugh. Of course I know she's here."

"But *why*?" Bonnie demanded. "So you can gloat? What is there to gloat over if you're not rid of her? What have you won? Do you hate her that much?"

"Don't talk rubbish," Dean Wilson said softly. "I don't hate her."

Eli nodded. "I wondered if you realized that. Though by all indications you obviously have won," Eli said. "You wanted Madame Caldwell off your campus and she is. Destroying the comb would probably send her away for good, and I think you realize that, too. So why do you want her here?"

"Gloating isn't a good enough reason?"

Eli smiled again. "Dean Wilson, I will speak bluntly: you're misanthropic, bad-tempered, and your tolerance for dissent is somewhere to the right of Attila the Hun's. You are not, however, either malicious or delusional. In order to gloat you have to abide her presence, and we already know how you feel on that score. If she's here, then there's another reason. A non-spiteful reason."

"I'm almost flattered, though next you'll be telling me that you know what that reason is," said Dean Wilson, then her gaze narrowed. "You think you know, don't you?"

"I do know," Eli said quietly.

Dean Wilson smiled with her teeth alone and set her cup and saucer down on the table. "All right, then, Mr. Mothersbaugh—let's put that to the test: if you're right, then I'll guarantee that Miss Simner, as the University's representative, will get Madame Caldwell's comb back safe and sound when I'm done with it. If you're wrong, you both leave now and consider the matter closed, and what happens to the comb is entirely between me and Madame Caldwell. Do we have an agreement?"

"Don't do it, Eli," Bonnie said. "You might be wrong again."

"Of course I might be wrong," Eli said, "but we don't have much choice."

"I retract my previous sarcasm," Dean Wilson said. "You're at least clever enough to realize that."

Madame Caldwell just watched them all intently as Dean Wilson poured herself a fresh cup of tea. The old woman added milk and sugar as she laid down the rules. "Now then—I will ask you two questions, Mr. Mothersbaugh. Each counts for 50% of your grade. Answer both and you pass. Miss either and you fail, and I am the sole judge of that. Agreed?"

"That's not fair!" Bonnie said, but Eli shook his head.

"On the contrary—I wouldn't have it any other way. What's the first question?"

"How did you know I took the comb?"

Eli sighed. "This is the sop part of the test. I assume you're asking that one out of idle curiosity?"

"My test, my questions, my rules," explained the dean primly. "Answer me now or you fail."

"Madame Caldwell was quite famous in her day, but now the Ghost of Marshall Hall is just an obscure local legend to most people," Eli said. "Who besides me or Bonnie knew and cared enough to discover the comb?"

"Someone might have found it by accident."

"After more than a century and a half? Besides, I checked: most of the backstage section brickwork had been plastered over until recently. It was possible someone would find the comb by accident but very unlikely."

"Purely circumstantial. It's not proof," Dean Wilson said.

Eli grinned. "No, but then you didn't ask for proof. You asked how I knew."

Dean Wilson smiled. It was not a reassuring smile. "I will phrase my final question more carefully: why didn't I destroy the comb? Sorry to be so unfair, Mr. Mothersbaugh, but there's no way you can pass this particular test. You'd have to be a mind reader."

"Or you could give me the answer yourself. You already did, by the way."

Dean Wilson looked grim. "Oh? I can't wait to hear this one."

"You didn't destroy the comb because you wanted to win."

She glared at him. "As you yourself pointed out, Mr. Mothersbaugh—I already won."

Eli shook his head. "I said 'by all indications.' You got Madame Caldwell off your campus, which was your stated goal, but you didn't win. You thought you had. You felt a day or two of relief on Madame Caldwell's departure, but that didn't last, did it?" Eli turned to Bonnie without waiting for an answer. "When was the last time you looked at the comb before Dean Wilson left campus?"

Bonnie, taken off guard, took a few moments to answer. "It was . . . that Thursday. The day before she left."

Eli nodded and turned back to Dean Wilson. "That's when you took the comb. You knew Madame Caldwell would be drawn to it."

"Are you saying I led her to my own home on purpose? Why would I do such a thing if I hate her presence?"

Eli shook his head. "Simple: You'd convinced yourself that Madame Caldwell was the problem, but it was only after she was gone that you realized you were wrong. She was gone, and you were still afraid. You won nothing."

"Why is she here?" Dean Wilson asked again. She sounded as if she hadn't heard a word he'd said. Eli knew better.

"To finish the fight, of course. So you can finally win, once and for all. Only it wasn't Madame Caldwell you were at war with and that's especially true now. You have the comb and you can send her away any time you want; that's something you could never do before. Now the fight is on your terms. That's why you didn't destroy the comb."

Dean Wilson didn't say anything for a little while. Then she just smiled again. "Eli, it's been an interesting visit, but I think you and Ms. Simner need to leave now."

Eli just nodded and rose to his feet without a moment's hesitation. "Miss Abigail, it's been a pleasure."

Bonnie was apparently stunned beyond words, though Eli knew that wouldn't last. He inclined his head briefly to the shade of Madame Justine Violetta Caldwell and led Bonnie carefully but quickly out of the house and down the path. It was only when they were some distance away from the house that Bonnie finally lit into him. "You damn idiot!"

"No doubt," Eli said mildly. "But why this time?"

"Why? You lost her! You should never have agreed to that bet!"

"First of all, we didn't have a choice. Dean Wilson was well within her rights to have just told us to go home regardless, and there wouldn't have been a damn thing we could have done about it. You know that's true."

"Well . . ."

"Second, it wasn't possible to 'lose' Madame Caldwell. You don't own her and neither do I. And third, it wasn't a bet—it was a test. I passed, by the way."

For a moment Bonnie just stared at him. "But she said—"

"She said it was time for us to leave, and doubtless she was right. There was a little more that I could have told her, but she may not be ready to hear it. For one thing, I suspect that Dean Wilson's in love with Madame Caldwell. She doesn't know that either, any more than she knew why she didn't destroy the comb in the first place."

Bonnie just stared at him for several long moments. Eli, for his part, was content to enjoy the ocean breeze as they walked back to their hotel.

"She . . . didn't know? She tested you on a question she didn't know the answer to *herself*?"

Eli nodded. "That was the key. Dean Wilson wasn't hoping I'd fail—she was hoping I *wouldn't*. Why do you think she let us in the door to start with? She wanted my help, though I'm guessing she'd rather have eaten ground glass than admit that. It took Madame Caldwell's temporary absence to make Dean Wilson suspect I was telling her the truth about her fear from the start. All I had to do at that point was spell it out."

"Other than not saying 'I told you so,' did you actually help her?"

"We'll know for sure in a month or so. Two at the outside, I'm guessing."

Bonnie blinked. "We will? What happens then?"

"Dean Wilson returns the comb, of course. Twenty years of defying her fears didn't work. Now she's going to try facing them instead, and Madame Caldwell's there to help her do that. Did you notice Madame Caldwell as we left, by the way? I kept the sensic on as long as I could. She winked at me."

"Maybe she didn't understand what was going on."

Eli grinned. "You know better."

Bonnie just shook her head. "I swear, every time I think I've got a handle on you . . ."

"I'm not a bucket."

"No, but then I have no idea what you are. Maybe that's why I'm still hanging around. I really would like to know."

"You're curious," Eli said. "I'm not used to having someone care enough about me to be curious. I think I like it."

"Just don't get the wrong idea," Bonnie said primly.

"I'll do my best."

They walked in companionable silence for a little while, then Bonnie frowned again. "Dean Wilson called you 'Eli.' Not 'Mr. Mothersbaugh' and not even 'Dr. Mothersbaugh.' Just 'Eli.'"

Eli smiled. "You noticed that? That's when I knew I'd passed. We called each other by name, just like two human beings. I guess she figured it was finally time we both graduated."

A TIME FOR HEROES

———

Timon the Black, demon of a thousand nightmares and master of none, came to a sudden understanding. "It's raining," he said. "And I'm cold."

He sounded surprised.

The dwarf Seb was not surprised. The chilling rain had started the moment they reached the foothills of the White Mountains and continued all afternoon. Seb's long fair hair hung limp about his face, and he peered out at the magician through a tangled mat like a runt wolf eyeing a lamb through a hedge. "At last he deigns to notice . . . I've been cold for hours! At the very least you could have been miserable with me."

"Sorry," Timon said. "You know I have trouble with some things."

Seb nodded. "'Here' and 'now' being two of them." Day-to-day practical matters were really Seb's responsibility, but there was comfort in complaining. In his years with Timon, Seb had learned to take comfort where he could.

Nothing else was said for a time, there being nothing to say. Seb, as usual, was the first to notice the failing light. "It's getting late. We'd better find somewhere dry to camp, if there be such in this wretched place."

It was beginning to look like a very wet night until Seb spotted a large overhang on a nearby ridge. It wasn't a true cave, more a remnant of some long-ago earthquake, but it reached more than forty yards into the hillside and had a high ceiling and dry, level floor. It wasn't the worst place they'd ever slept.

"I'll build a fire," the dwarf said, "if you will promise me not to look at it."

Timon didn't promise, but Seb built the fire anyway after seeing to their mounts and the pack train. He found some almost-dry wood near the entrance and managed to collect enough rainwater for the horses and for a pot of tea. He unpacked the last of their dried beef and biscuit, studied the pitiful leavings and shook his head in disgust. Gold wasn't a problem, but they hadn't dared stop for supplies till well away from the scene of Timon's last escapade, and now what little food they'd had time to pack was almost gone.

Seb scrounged another pot and went to catch some more rain. When he had enough, he added the remnants of beef and started the pot simmering on the fire. The mixture might make a passable broth. If not, at least they could use it to soften the biscuit.

Timon inched closer to the fire, watching Seb out of the corner of his eye. The dwarf pretended not to notice. Timon was soaked and neither of them had any dry clothing. Timon catching cold or worse was the last thing Seb needed. As for the risk, well, when the inevitable happened it would happen and that, as it had been many times before, would be that.

"I never look for trouble, you know that," Timon said. It sounded like an apology.

"I know." Seb handed him a bowl of the broth and a piece of hard biscuit, and that small gesture was as close to an acceptance of the apology as the occasion demanded. They ate in comfortable silence for a while, but as the silence went on and on and the meal didn't, Seb began to feel definitely uncomfortable. He finally surrendered tact and leaned close.

"Bloody hell!"

It was the Long Look. Timon's eyes were glazed, almost like a blind man's. They focused at once on the flames and on nothing. Timon was seeing something far beyond the firelight, something hidden as much in time as distance. And there wasn't a damn thing Seb could do about it. He thought of taking his horse and leaving his friend behind, saving himself. He swore silently that one day he would do just that. He had sworn before, and he meant it no less now. But not this time. Always, not this time.

Seb dozed after a while, walking the edge of a dream of warmth and ease and just about to enter, when the sound of his name brought him back to the cold stone and firelight.

"Seb?"

Timon was back, too, from whatever far place he'd gone, and he was shivering again. Seb poured the last of the tea into Timon's mug. "Well?"

"I've seen something," Timon said. He found a crust of biscuit in his lap and dipped it in his tea. He chewed thoughtfully.

"Timon, is it your habit to inform me that the sun has risen? The obvious I can deal with; I need help with the hidden things."

"So do I," Timon said. "Or at least telling which is which. What do you think is hidden?"

"What you saw. What the Long Look has done to us this time."

Timon rubbed his eyes like the first hour of morning. "Oh, that . . . tragedy, Seb. That's what I saw in the fire. I didn't mean to. I tried not to look."

Seb threw the dregs of his own cup into the fire and it hissed in protest. "I rather doubt it matters. If it wasn't the fire, it would be the pattern of sweat on your horse's back, or the shine of a dewdrop—" The dwarf's scowl suddenly cleared away, and he looked like a scholar who'd just solved a particularly vexing sum. "The Long Look is a curse, isn't it? I should have realized that long ago. What did you do? Cut firewood in a sacred grove? Make water on the wrong patch of flowers? What?" Seb waited but Timon didn't answer. He didn't seem to be listening. Seb shook his head sadly. "I'll wager it was a goddess. Those capable of greatest kindness must also have the power for greatest cruelty. That's balance."

"That's nonsense," said Timon, who was listening after all. "And a Hidden Thing, I see. So let me reveal it to you—there is one difference between the workings of a god and a goddess in our affairs. One only."

"And that is?"

"Us. Being men, we take the disfavor of a female deity more personally." Timon yawned and reached for his saddle and blanket.

Seb seized the reference. "Disfavor. You admit it."

Timon shrugged. "If it gives you pleasure. The Powers know you've had precious little of that lately." He moved his blanket away from a sharp rise in the stone and repositioned his saddle. "Where are we going?"

Seb tended the fire, looking sullen. "Morushe."

"Good. I'm not known there—by sight, anyway."

Seb nodded. "I was counting on that."

"It *will* make things easier . . . "

Seb knew that Timon was now speaking to himself, but he refused to be left out. "I know why we *were* heading toward Morushe—it was far away from Calyt. What business do we have there now?"

"We're going to murder a prince."

Seb closed his eyes. "Pity the fool who asked."

"I never look for trouble. You know that."

"I won't marry him and that's final!"

Princess Ashesa of Morushe spurred the big roan viciously, her long red hair streaming behind her like the wake of a Fury. She was dressed for the hunt and carried a short bow slung across her back, but the only notice she took of the forest was mirrored in a glare clearly meant to wither any tree impertinent enough to block her path.

Lady Margate—less sensibly attired—was having trouble keeping up, though she rode gamely enough. A large buck, frightened by the commotion, broke cover and leaped across their path.

"A buck!" shouted Margy, hopefully.

Ashesa didn't even pause. "I won't marry *him* either," she snapped, "though I daresay if he ruled a big enough kingdom Father would consider it." She grinned. "At least he's a *gentler* beast."

"That's no way to talk about your future husband!" reproved Margy. "Prince Daras is of ancient and noble lineage."

"So's my boar-hound," returned Ashesa sweetly. "We have the documents."

There had been almost no warning. Ashesa had barely time to hide her precious—and expressly forbidden—books away before her father had burst in to tell her the good news. The alliance between Morushe and the coastal realm of Borasur was agreed and signed. By breakfast King Macol had the date and was halfway done with the guest list. Ashesa couldn't decide between smashing dishes or going on her morning hunt. In the end she'd done both. But now half the crockery in her Father's palace was wrecked, and her horse was not much better. Ashesa finally took pity on the poor beast and reigned in at small clearing. Margy straggled up looking reproachful and nearly as spent as Ashesa's mount.

"I just wish that someone had *asked* me. Father could have at least let me know what he was planning, *talked* to me. Was that asking for such a great deal?"

Lady Margate sighed deeply. "In Balanar Town yesterday I saw a girl about your age. She would be even prettier than you are except she's already missing three teeth and part of an ear. She hawks ale and Heaven knows what else at a tavern near the barracks. If I were to tell her that the Princess

Ashesa was going to be married to a handsome, wealthy prince without her permission, do you think that girl would weep for you?"

Ashesa looked sullen. "No need to go 'round the mulberry bush, Margy. I understand you."

"Then understand this—Morushe is a rich kingdom but not a strong one. Wylandia, among others, is all too aware of that. Without powerful friends, your people aren't safe. This marriage will help ensure that we have those friends."

"For someone who claims statecraft is no field for a woman, you certainly have a firm grasp of it," Ashesa said dryly.

"Common sense, Highness. Don't confuse the two." Margy looked around them. "We should not be this far from the palace. Two high-born ladies, unescorted, in the middle of a wild forest . . . "

Ashesa laughed, and felt a little better for it. "Margy, Father's game park is about as 'wild' as your sewing room. Even the wolves get their worming dose every spring."

Lady Margate drew herself up in matronly dignity. "Neverthe . . . " She paused, her round mouth frozen in mid-syllable. She looked puzzled.

"Yes?" Ashesa encouraged, but Lady Margate just sat there, swaying ever so gently in her saddle. Ashesa slid from her mount and ran over to her nurse. "Margy, what is it?"

Ashesa saw the feathered dart sticking out of the woman's neck and whirled, drawing her hunting sword.

Too late.

Another dart hummed out a nearby oak and stung her in the shoulder. Ashesa felt a pinprick of pain and then nothing. Her motion continued and she fell, stiff as a toppled statue, into the wildflowers, her eyes fixed upwards at the guilty tree. Two short legs appeared below the leaves of a low branch, then the rest of a man not quite four feet high followed.

He wore fashionable hunting garb of brown and green immaculately tailored to his small frame, and in his hand was a blowpipe. He carried a small quiver with more darts at his belt.

Elf-shot . . . ? Ashesa's mind was all fuzzy; it was hard to think.

The small man reached the ground and nodded pleasantly in her direction, touched his cap, and whistled. Two normal-sized men in concealing robes appeared at the edge of the clearing and went to work with professional detachment. First they removed Lady Margate from her horse and propped her against the dwarf's oak, closing her eyes and tipping her hat forward to keep the sun off her face. Ashesa, half-mad with anger and worry, struggled against the drug until the veins stood out on her neck, but she could not move. The little man kneeled beside her, looking strangely concerned.

"You'll only injure yourself, Highness. Don't worry about your friend—she'll recover, but not till we're well away." With that he gently plucked the dart from her shoulder and tossed it into the bushes.

"Who are you? Why are you doing this?!"

The shout echoed in her head but nowhere else; she could not speak. The two silent henchmen brought Ashesa's horse as the dwarf pulled a small vial from his belt, popped the cork, and held it to her nose. An acrid odor stung her nostrils and she closed her eyes with no help at all.

Kings Macol and Riegar sat in morose silence in Macol's chambers. At first glance they weren't much alike: Macol was stout and ruddy, Riegar tall and gaunt with thinning gray hair. All this was only surface, for what they shared was obvious even without their crowns. Each man wore his responsibilities like a hair-shirt.

Riegar finally spoke. "It was soon after you broke the news to your daughter, I gather?"

Macol nodded, looking disgusted. "I fooled myself into thinking she knew her duty. Blast, after her outburst this morning I'd almost think she cooked this up herself just to spite me!"

Riegar dismissed that. "We have the note, and the seal is unmistakable—"

The clatter on the stairs startled them both, and then they heard the sentry's challenge. They heard the answer even better—it was both colorful and loud.

"That will be Daras." Riegar sighed.

The Crown Prince of Borasur strode through the door, his handsome face flushed, his blue eyes shining with excitement. "The messenger said there was a note. Where is it?"

"Damn you, Lad, you've barged into a room containing no fewer than two kings, one of whom is your father. Where are your manners?" Riegar asked.

Daras conceded a curt nod, mumbled an apology and snatched the parchment from the table. For all his hurry the message didn't register very quickly. Daras read slowly, mouthing each word as if getting the taste of it. When he was done there was a grimness in his eyes that worried them. "Wylandia is behind this, Majesties. I'm certain!"

Macol and Riegar exchanged glances, then Macol spoke. "Prince, aren't you reading a great deal into a message that says only 'I have Ashesa—Timon the Black'?"

Daras looked surprised. "Who else has a reason to kidnap My Beloved Ashesa? The King of Wylandia would do anything to prevent our alliance." Daras said Ashesa's name with all the passion of a student reciting declensions, but he'd seen his intended only twice in his life and had as little say in the matter as she did.

Macol shook his head. "I know Aldair—he'll fight you with everything he has at the slightest provocation but he won't stab you in the back. And Morushe and Borasur have so many trading ties that it amounts to alliance already. Aldair knows this; his negotiating position for Wylandia's use of our mountain passes is quite reasonable. We are close to agreement."

"If Aldair is not involved then the kidnapping is not for reasons of State. And if not, then why was there no ransom demand? Why taunt us this way?"

Macol looked almost pleased. "A sensible question, Prince. Your father and I wonder about that ourselves. But no doubt this 'Timon' will make his demands clear in time, and I'll meet them if I can. In the meantime—"

"Of course!" Daras fairly glowed. "How long will it take to raise your army? May I lead the assault?"

"There will be no assault." Riegar's tone was pure finality.

"No assault!? Then what are we going to do?"

Macol sighed. "Prince, what can we do? Our best information—mere rumor—puts Timon in an old watchtower just inside the border of Wylandia. Do you honestly think His Majesty Aldair will negotiate tariffs during an invasion?"

"Has it ever been tried?" Daras asked mildly.

Riegar looked to heaven. "Sometimes I pray for a miracle to take a year from your age and add it to Galan's. I might keep what's left of my wits."

"My brother is a *clark*," snapped Daras, reddening. "Divine Providence gave the inheritance to *me*, and when I'm king I'll show Wylandia and all else how a king deals with his enemies!" Daras nodded once and stalked out of the room.

Macol watched him go. "A bit headstrong, if I may say."

"You may." Riegar sighed. "Though it's too kind." He winced suddenly.

"Are you ill?"

"It's nothing . . . indigestion. Comes and goes." Riegar relaxed a bit as the pain eased, then said, "I've been thinking . . . Aldair won't tolerate an army on his border, but if the situation was explained to him he might be willing to send a few men of his own."

"I dare say," Macol considered. "If this magician *is* operating in Aldair's territory without permission, Aldair's pride might even demand it. Yes, I'll have a delegation out tonight! After that, all a father can do is pray."

"As will I. But there is one other thing you can do," Riegar said. "Would you be good enough to post a guard on Prince Daras's quarters tonight?"

"Certainly. But why?"

King Riegar of Borasur, remembering the look in his son's eyes, answered. "Oh, just a whim."

Prince Galan of Borasur strolled down a corridor in Macol's Castle, a thick volume under one arm. He didn't need much in the way of direction, though this was his first visit to Morushe. The fortress was of a common type for the period it was built; he'd made a study in his father's library before the trip. Finding his brother's quarters was easy enough, too. It was the one with the unhappy-looking soldier standing beside the door.

"Is Prince Daras allowed visitors?" he asked, smiling. The guard waved him on wearily, and Galan knocked.

"Enter if you must!"

The muffled bellow sounded close enough to an invitation. Galan went inside and found his brother pacing the stone floor. With both in the same room it was hard to imagine two men more different. Daras was the tall one, strong in the shoulders and arms from years on the tourney fields he loved so well. Galan by contrast had accepted the bare minimum of military training necessary for a Gentleman and no more. He was smaller, darker, with green eyes and a sense of calm. When the brothers were together, it was like a cool forest pool having conversation with a forest fire.

"It's intolerable!" Daras announced.

Galan didn't have to ask what was intolerable. He knew his brother's mind, even if he didn't really understand it. "Macol and Father don't want a war. Can you really fault them for that?"

Daras stopped pacing. He looked a little hurt. "You think I want a war?"

Galan shrugged. "Sometimes."

Daras shook his head. "Remember the heroic tales you used to read to me . . . " He apparently caught the reproach in Galan's eye and so amended, "The ones you still read from time to time? Even among all the nobility and sacrifice, the excitement of combat and rescue, I can see the destruction in my mind's eye. What sane man wants that? No. I blame Father and Macol for nothing except their short-sightedness. By the by, I called you a clark today in front of Father."

"It wouldn't be the first time. And not wholly wrong."

"Even so—I was angry and I'm sorry. Despite your faults I envy you in a lot of ways; you know so many things, whereas I know only one thing in this world for certain—wanted or no, a war with Wylandia is inevitable. I'd rather it be on our terms than Aldair's."

Galan changed the subject. He held up his prize. "Look what I found in Macol's library."

"A book. How odd."

Galan smiled. Sarcasm was another thing his brother knew for certain. "Not just a book. Borelane's TALES OF THE RED KING. I've been trying to find a copy of this for years."

Daras showed a little more interest. "Perhaps . . . " he said, then finished, "perhaps you can read to me later."

"It'll have to be later. I'm for Wylandia tonight. Macol and Father are sending a delegation to Aldair. Father thought it might carry more weight if a Prince of the Blood went along."

"Not me, of course," Daras said bitterly.

"Be reasonable, Brother. You've no patience for diplomacy; action suits you better."

"It suits all men better."

Galan swallowed the casual insult by long habit. He'd long ago given up seeking approval from his older brother. He'd never quite given up wanting it. "We wouldn't want to do anything to endanger Ashesa." Her name brought back a little of the envy he'd always felt for Daras. The first time Galan had ever seen Ashesa was barely a year before, when Morushe's royal family paid a state visit to Borasur. He'd spent a month afterwards writing bad poetry and staring at the moon.

"No," Daras agreed, though his thoughts were elsewhere.

Ashesa awoke in a room fit for a Princess—a near perfect copy of her own. The big four-poster bed and the tapestry of the Quest of the Sunbeast were both in place; she was beginning to think she might have dreamed the whole abduction until she saw what was wrong. There were books, and they were not hidden.

She got up, still a little wobbly, and examined the first of them. They weren't hers, of course. She checked a few pages of each, just enough to know they were real books. She closed the last one and checked the door.

Barred.

Someone's gone to a great deal of trouble to make me feel comfortable was all she could think. Her head still ached and it was easier not to think at all. There was an arched window in the east wall and she looked out.

The room was in a high tower somewhere in the mountains—somewhere, some mountains—and even in the dying light the view was breathtaking. The earth folded like a deflated bagpipe in all directions, and one peak snuggled up to the next with a bare knife edge of a valley between them. The window was barred too, but the glassed shutters worked. She opened them and took a breath of cool, head-clearing air.

Someone knocked on her door.

Odd manners for a kidnapper. And there was another thought. "I'm afraid you'll have to let yourself in," she said.

Nothing happened. Ashesa put her ear to the door and heard a faint creaking like an old oak in a breeze. The knock repeated.

"Come in, damn you!"

She heard a scrape as the bar lifted, then the clink of silverware. The door swung outward and there stood a figure in a black robe and hood, carrying a tray of food and wine. His face and hands were both covered—his face by the hood, his hands by leather gloves. He looked like one of the pair who had helped kidnap her. Ashesa stepped back, and the figure came in and set the tray on a little table by the bed. Ashesa considered trying to slip past him, but two more were in the corridor, steel spears glinting. She turned to the tray bearer, looking regal despite her rumpled condition.

"I demand to know who you are and why you've brought me here." Her jailor only shook his head slowly and turned toward the door. Ashesa stamped her foot and snatched at the hood. "Look at me when I speak to—"

There was no face under the hood. A stump of wood jutted through the neck of the robe, around which a lump of clay had been crudely shaped. A piece of it fell to the floor and shattered with a little puff of yellow dust. Ashesa screamed.

"Normally they don't wear anything, but I didn't want to upset you. I see I've failed."

A slightly chagrined man stood in the doorway. He was just past the full blood of youth, with features as fine and delicate as a girl's. His dark eyes were reddened and weak, as if he spent too many hours reading in poor light. None of these details registered as strongly in Ashesa's mind as her first impression—the man had an air of quiet certainty that she found infuriating.

"Very . . . considerate," Ashesa said, recovering her poise with great effort. "Would you please tell me *what* that is and who you are?"

He patted the simulacrum fondly. "That, Highness, is a stick golem. I learned the technique from a colleague in Nyas; you should see what he can do with stone . . . " He stopped, clearly aware that Ashesa had heard as much as she cared to on the subject. "My apologies, Highness. I am called Timon the Black."

Ashesa almost screamed again. She scrambled to the other side of the bed and snatched up a heavy gilt candlestick from the table. She waved it with all the menace she could scrape together. "Don't come near me, Fiend!"

"My reputation precedes me," the magician sighed. "What is my most recent atrocity?"

Ashesa glared at him. "Do you deny that you sacrificed a virgin girl to raise an army of demons against the Red Company?"

Timon smiled a little ruefully. "To start, they weren't demons and she wasn't a virgin. Nor did I 'sacrifice' her . . . exactly. The Red Company took a geld from half the kingdoms on the mainland, so I don't recall hearing any objections at the time. No matter; it's water down the river. You must be hungry, Highness. Have some supper."

In truth, the aroma from the tray was making Ashesa a little giddy, but she eyed it with suspicion. Timon noticed the look.

"Be reasonable, Highness. Would I go to all this bother just to poison you? And if I *were* in need of a virgin there are certainly others easier to hand than a Princess of the Blood, common knowledge and barracks gossip not withstanding."

"You are a beast," she said.

"Red eyed and howling every full moon. So I've heard."

Ashesa shrugged and sampled a beef pie. It was delicious. She poured herself some wine as Timon dismissed his servant. He found a chair and sat watching her, while she in turn glared at him between mouthfuls.

"Well?" she asked, finally. "Aren't you going to tell me why I'm here?"

"You didn't ask, so I assumed you weren't interested. Pesky things, assumptions," he said. "Let's see what others might be floating about, besides that silly misunderstanding about virginity . . . Ransom? There's a common theme. Will I force your doting father to surrender half his kingdom to save you?"

Ashesa took a sip of wine so he wouldn't see her smile. "No," she said from behind her goblet.

Timon looked genuinely surprised. "Why not?"

"Because we both know you wouldn't get it, break Father's heart though it would. And then there's all this . . . " She waved a capon leg at the room and furnishings. "That tapestry alone is of finer quality than my copy, and I *know* how much that one cost—poor Father nearly had a stroke. You obviously have great resources at your beck, Magician. That rules out any conventional ransom short of greed and that's *one* sin I've never heard spoken of you. So. What do you want?"

There was open admiration in Timon's eyes. "You have an exceptional mind, Highness. It's really unfortunate that Daras will never allow you to use it. From what I've gathered of his philosophy your duties will be to produce heirs and be ornamental at court."

"You seem to know a great deal about matters that don't concern you, Magician, but you still haven't answered my question. I wish you would because frankly I'm baffled. I hope for your sake it's more than a whim. They'll search for me, you know."

"And find you, too, since I was good enough to leave a note. I've also bought supplies openly; my location is common knowledge to half the hill crofters on the border. Diplomacy and protocol will delay your father, but Prince Daras will be along soon."

Ashesa was stunned. "Are you mad? As well to draw a map and have done!"

"No, Highness. I'm not mad, though it often seems so—even to me. But to avoid wearying you I'll speak plainly—I kidnapped you so that Prince Daras will try to rescue you. And he will try. His nature doesn't allow for any other option."

"But why—" Ashesa stopped. She knew. It was there for her to see in Timon's eyes.

"Quite right, Highness. I'm going to kill him."

The man Macol selected to watch Daras was a veteran: solid, trustworthy. A competent guard. Not a competent diplomat. The scope of the orders he had received in King Macol's throne room were quite beyond him.

"I want you to guard my son's quarters tonight," said King Riegar solemnly. "He is not to leave his room."

"But," added King Macol, "Prince Daras is an honored guest, not a prisoner. Treat him with respect."

Riegar nodded. "Certainly. But he may have it in his head to do something foolish. Use whatever force you must, within reason."

"But," again added Macol, "Prince Daras is heir to the throne of Borasur. He must on no account be harmed or you'll answer for it."

"Just keep him there," said Riegar.

"Without hurting or offending him," said Macol. "Now. Is all that clear?"

"Yes, sire," the man lied. Later, as he stood at his post in the corridor, he placidly awaited the inevitable.

"Guard," Prince Daras called out, "lend some assistance in here, there's a good fellow."

The guard smiled and walked right in. The bump on his head was no less than he expected, and he was grateful for it. It seemed the simplest solution to a very complicated problem.

190

Princess Ashesa climbed the long spiral staircase to the top of Timon's fortress. Her hooded escort thumped along behind her like a child on stilts. Ashesa wasn't fooled. She'd stumbled once and the thing had snapped forward, supporting her, faster that she would have believed possible.

They passed several doors along the way. All unlocked, most empty, but Ashesa couldn't resist looking for something that might help her escape. One room was full of echoing voices in a language she didn't understand; another held a dark grey mist and she dared not enter. None of them contained anything useful.

Ashesa ran out of doors and stairs at about the same time. She and her golem escort stood on the parapet that wrapped around the outside off the highest level of the tower. The thin mountain wind whipped the golem's robes tight against its stick frame until it looked like a scarecrow flapping in a field. Ashesa looked over the railing and got a little dizzy.

"Too far to jump," said the wind.

Ashesa jumped anyway, but only a little. She didn't clear the railing.

The dwarf sat before a small canvas on the other side of the platform. He had changed his woodland green for an artist's smock stained with the remnants of an exploded rainbow. He concentrated on the canvas and painted with long smooth strokes, unperturbed by the gusts.

"That depends on your reason for jumping," returned Ashesa grimly.

The dwarf smiled, though he still wouldn't look at her. "A noble gesture, but it wouldn't keep Daras out of Timon's web even if he knew. Revenge has a longer pedigree than rescue."

"He's very certain of himself, your Master."

"About some things," the dwarf agreed sadly. "He can't help it."

Ashesa considered a new tack. "How much is he paying you? Whatever your price, my father will meet it. Just help me escape and warn My Beloved Daras."

The dwarf cleaned one brush and selected another. "Would your father be willing to offer me the lucrative and entirely appropriate position of Court Foole?"

"Certainly!"

"Yes," the dwarf sighed. "I thought he might."

Ashesa frowned, and, even as she spoke the words, she wondered how may times they had passed her lips and her thoughts since the kidnapping. "I don't understand."

"My story is simple, Highness—my father sold me to a troupe of acrobats and thieves when I was seven. By twelve I was the best among them at both skills, but I still wore a cap and bells at every performance. Can you guess why?" He studied the canvas. "And when I couldn't abide that any more I took to the streets on my own, and that's where Timon found me. We understood one another. Now he pays me with a little gold and a lot of hardship and aggravation, but part of the price is respect and an appreciation of my talents that totally ignores my height except when it's actually important. That's coin beyond your means, I'm afraid. Consider—we've been conversing for the better part of two minutes and you haven't even asked my name." He swirled the brush-tip in a puddle of gold.

Ashesa stood in the presence of the man who'd kidnapped her, and yet for a moment she almost felt as if *he* were the injured party. It made her angry. "What is your name?"

He touched his cap and left a speck of gold there. "Seb, at your service," he said, making a quick dab at the canvas. "Up to a point."

"I'd like to know where that point is. Timon won't tell me why he plans to kill My Beloved Daras. Will you?"

"My Beloved . . . that's not what you were calling him during your little ride." Ashesa flushed but said nothing. Seb shrugged. "I know—it's the proper title for the betrothed and you do know your duty, even if you don't like it. So. Why not 'to prevent the marriage'? You suggested it yourself, Timon says."

The princess shook her head. "If he merely wanted that, killing me would have worked as well and been a lot less bother. I don't flatter myself by thinking he'd have hesitated."

"He wouldn't," confirmed Seb. "though it would grieve him bitterly. As it will when Daras is killed."

"But *why*? Why does Daras deserve to die?"

Seb smiled ruefully. "That's the saddest part. He doesn't. At least not in the sense of anything he's done. It's who he *is*, and what he is, and what that combination will make him do when the time comes. It's all here, Highness, if you care to look."

Seb moved to one side so she could see the canvas. Ashesa's mouth fell open in surprise when she recognized the portrait. It was Daras, mounted and armored in an archaic pattern. He held his helmet under one arm, his lance pointed to the sky.

"It's lovely," she said honestly, "but why the old armor?"

"That's the armor of the time of the Lyrsan wars. When the folk of the Western Deserts pushed east against the Seven Kingdoms. That's when Daras should have lived. That was a time for heroes."

"Daras isn't a hero," Ashesa snapped. "That takes more than winning tournaments."

"More even than rescuing one princess," the dwarf agreed. "It's rather a full-time pursuit. It might even take, say, a long bloody war with Wylandia."

Ashesa put her hands on her hips. "Do you really expect me to believe that Daras would start a war just so he can be a hero?"

"He wouldn't be starting it, to his way of thinking. But the seeds are already there: real intrigues, imagined insults . . . mistrust. All waiting to take root in his mind until he firmly believes that Wylandia struck first. You see, Daras is already a hero in many ways. He's seen the soul of it in his brother's stories, and in that he sees himself. And why not? He's brave, strong, skilled in warlike pursuits and in no other. All he lacks to make his destiny complete is the one vital ingredient—need. If the need is not there, he will create it. He has no choice. And neither do we."

Most of the blood had deserted Ashesa's face, and she trembled. "You can't be sure! And even if you were, what right—"

"Timon *is* sure," interrupted Seb calmly. "It's his greatest power, and greatest curse. He knows, and he can't escape the responsibility of knowing. That gives him the right."

"I . . . don't . . . believe . . . you!" Ashesa spat out each word like something foul.

Seb smiled. "Oh, yes, you do. More than you'd like, anyway. Far better to see this tale as history no doubt will—a foul crime done by foul folk. Forgive me, Highness, but I'm not as kind as Timon and see no reason why this should be any easier on you than the rest of us."

Ashesa's hands turned into fists and she took a step toward the dwarf. In an instant the golem was between her and Seb, and the dwarf hadn't even blinked. Ashesa took several deep, calming breaths, and after a moment the golem moved aside. Ashesa groped for some shred of sweet reason to pull her thoughts out of the pit. "But . . . but Daras can't start a war on his own! Only the king can do that! Even if what you say is true, there's still time . . . "

While she spoke Seb made several deft strokes on the canvas, and when she saw what the dwarf had painted there her words sank into nothing.

"Time has run out, Highness. King Riegar—rest him—died in his sleep last night."

In the portrait, Daras wore the plain golden crown of Borasur.

Prince Daras had never been on a quest before and wasn't quite sure what to expect, but at least the scenery felt right—it was wild and strange. The forest that bordered the mountain foothills was very different from the tilting fields and well-groomed game parks he was accustomed to: the grass grew high and razor-edged, brambles clawed at his armored legs, and trees took root and reached for the sunlight wherever the notion took them. Daras stepped his charger through a tortured, twisty path, and when an arrow hummed out of the trees and twanged off his armor, that, too, seemed as it should be.

"Hah! Villains! At you!"

Daras spurred forward along the arrow's course as if his mount was as armored as he was. The second arrow showed that notion in error; Daras barely cleared the stirrups before the poor beast went down kicking. Another instant and he was among them.

'They' were men, of course. Forest bandits with no other skill and without enough sense to avoid a victim armed in proof. None of that mattered once the attack began. They were bodies attached to swords, meat in ragged clothes for the blooding, characters in a play of which Daras was the lead, existing only for their cue to dance a few steps and then die. It wasn't how he thought it would be; it wasn't horrible. Daras never saw their faces, never noticed their pain as he turned clumsy blows and struck sure ones, killing with the mad joy of a new-found sport. When it was over it was as if they had never lived at all.

Rather like a tournament, only they don't get up.

After the last bandit fell, Daras, cat-like, lost interest. He cleaned his sword on a dead man's tunic, had a sip or two of weak wine, then resumed his quest on foot, whistling.

Ashesa didn't know what was different at first that morning. She only knew that *something* was not right. After a few moments she was awake enough to notice what was missing. Her clothes. The mantle and overdress she had laid out on the table the night before weren't there. In their place were two rather ethereal strips of cloth appliqued with crescents and stars and glyphs of a rather suggestive nature.

Timon sat in her chair, looking unhappy.

"Magician, where are my clothes?"

He waved his hand at the table. "There, I'm afraid. It's the traditional sacrificial garb of an obscure fertility cult. You wouldn't have heard of it."

"And you're one of them?" she asked, as calmly as she could manage.

He shuddered delicately. "Certainly not. But as much as the prospect would delight *me*, I don't think Daras expects to burst in and find us discussing literature over a cup of tea. I had to come up with something suitably dreadful for you to be saved from. Think of it as a play, Highness. This is your costume for the final act."

Ashesa eyed the flimsy cloth with distaste. "Uninspired as this may sound—suppose I refuse?"

He shrugged. "I can't *force* you to wear it—it tears too easily—but bear in mind that you stretched out on the altar in all your natural glory would suit the play as well . . . no, better. I considered it, believe me. But clothed or no, you will play your part. You have no choice."

Ashesa, bedclothes wrapped tightly about her, gathered up the scanty garments. "I'm getting terribly weary of that catechism, Master Timon. Pray, is there any esoteric reason why I cannot at least get dressed in private?"

Timon looked even more unhappy. "Unfortunately, no."

Prince Daras hid behind a boulder and studied the gate. It was strongly built with oak posts set into the narrowest point of what was already a knife-slash of a valley. Two robed guards stood outside, halberds crossed. Daras idly pulled at a chafing armor-strap as he pondered a sigil carved into the gate. Just like the one on the kidnapper's note. Timon the Black, no question. Beyond the gate a tower rose on a rocky ridge above the valley.

Careless or arrogant?

The sigil was as good as an announcement; Daras couldn't decide what it meant, so he decided it didn't matter.

The prince sat with his back to the stone and considered. There was no way around the gate, nor could he climb the valley walls without being seen. The two guards at the gate had to be overpowered without raising an alarm, and he might have to scale the wall if neither had a key . . . There was cover—rocks and brush—until about ten yards from the guard post. *If* he could reach it unseen.

And unheard.

Slowly, reluctantly, Prince Daras began removing his armor.

"Ready, Highness?"

Ashesa studied her reflection, trying to arrange the material of her costume as efficiently as possible. The effect was dramatic despite her best efforts. She gave up. "Yes, damn you to hell."

Timon entered the room with two of his golem guards. The magician, damn him again, smiled at her. "Follow us, please."

He took her arm and led her down the corridor to the staircase, then around and down the spiral to ground level and out. They moved single file down a narrow path to the valley floor, golems in front and behind her with Timon bringing up the rear. A single wall cut them off from the rest of the valley, and before that was a very suspicious-looking stone flanked by two upright stones of dark granite. A smaller building of stone blocks sat on the opposite side. Closer, Ashesa's fears were confirmed: the building was a small temple with a narrow oval doorway, the flat stone a massive altar with shackles bolted to the four corners.

Ashesa's mouth was suddenly dry. "You said you weren't a member of the cult."

"Props, Highness. Nothing more."

The golems led her to the altar. There was a stepping block to help her climb, and the top was smooth except for a groove cut for—she supposed— her heart's blood. Ashesa looked at the altar, then the guards. Their weapons gleamed brightly in the morning sun, but one held his a little farther away from his body. Ashesa judged the distance and her chances, but she made the mistake of glancing at Timon. His smile hadn't changed a whit, but there was a new and very clear message in his eyes.

Don't.

Ashesa lay down reluctantly and let the twig-fingered guards shackle her to the cold stone. As the last manacle clicked into place she heard a yelp like a hunting horn cut off in mid-note. Timon wasn't smiling now. There was something like worry on his face, perhaps even a touch of fear. Ashesa couldn't have imagined that a moment before.

"Daras is early . . . I'd better hurry and get into *my* costume, Highness. Won't be a moment."

The magician hurried off into the temple leaving Ashesa alone with the golems. There was a commotion at the gate and Ashesa turned her head to look just as the gate burst open and something very much like brown rag sailed through, cartwheeling end over end to smash against the stones. Prince Daras of Borasur strode through.

His entrance made Ashesa skip a breath; she'd forgotten how handsome he was, but that wasn't all of it—a glory seemed to shine around him, like a saint etched in stained glass. He saw her then and rushed forward, all smooth motion and mad joy.

And this is what Timon wants to destroy.

She heard Timon but could not see him. "Stop him, my Pets!"

The golems set their halberds and charged. Ashesa finally recovered her wits. "Flee, My Beloved! It's a trap!"

Daras, of course, did nothing of the sort. He veered to the right and a golem's headlong rush carried it past. Daras struck a trailing blow without breaking stride and the golem's clay head exploded.

Ashesa watched, horrified but unable to look away. There was a battle-light on Daras's face, and his eyes were bright and wild. Ashesa's breath skipped a second time.

He's enjoying this!

The truth of it was like a cold slap in the face. It wasn't the rescue. It wasn't even herself as anything but an excuse. The prince was consumed with a mad ecstasy born of the clash of weapons and pleasure in his skill. He destroyed golems. He would destroy men with as little thought and the same wild joy. Ashesa tried not to think anymore, but it was a torrent held too long in check and the dams were breaking.

This is what Timon wants to destroy . . .

The second golem thrust past Daras's parry by brute force and the prince twisted his body like an acrobat. The halberd merely sliced a thin red line across the front of Daras's tunic and the prince's return stroke left the golem broken and still.

A voice issued from the temple. It was Timon and it wasn't Timon—it boomed like thunder across the valley. "Now you must die!"

Ashesa strained to turn her head and saw Timon step out of the shadows of the temple. He wore a robe decorated with glyphs like the ones on Ashesa's costume, and in his gloved hands he carried a long curved knife. It glowed with a blue balefire that still could not penetrate the blackness under Timon's hood.

Prince Daras studied the magician's knife, then looked at his own sword. Grinning, he dropped the sword and pulled his own long dagger. Ashesa wanted to scream but nothing came out—it was as if an invisible hand clapped itself over her mouth.

The fool, she thought wildly, *the bloody, senseless fool*!

What happened next was filled with terrible beauty. Daras charged the magician, and this time it was Timon who danced aside to let Daras hurtle past like a maddened bull. Timon's blade flicked out and then there was another line of red on the prince's chest. Daras snarled like a *berserk*, but kept some caution as he stopped himself and slowly circled, looking for an opening. Timon kept just out of reach, reacting with a speed Ashesa wouldn't have expected of him. The glow on Daras's face built to new heights of rapture, as if the magician's surprising skill fanned it like the bellows of a forge.

It was like the sword dance Ashesa had seen performed at her father's court—the flash of steel always averted, always eluded as if it *was* nothing more than a dance for her amusement instead of a fight to the death. Timon's knife traced its path through the air like a lightning flash, and Daras's dagger slashed and hummed in a silvered blur.

Then everything changed.

Timon broke from the fight and sprinted toward the altar. "The sacrifice must be made!"

What?!

The wizard hurtled toward her, his knife burning away the distance to her heart. Ashesa closed her eyes.

Someone screamed and Ashesa opened her eyes again, surprised. She had meant to scream but never really managed. *Who*?

Timon. He lay sprawled at the foot of the altar, Daras's weapon buried almost to the hilt in his back. Bright, impossibly red blood oozed from around the steel. Ashesa felt a little sick, a lot relieved and a bit . . . well, guilty. Guilty for wondering why Timon's trap had failed, and for wondering—just for an instant!—if it should have failed. And why the mad dash to the altar? Unless Timon had lied to her . . .

Prince Daras grinned down at her, his chest heaving like a bellows. "Did—did you see that throw?" he chortled. "Thirty paces, easily . . . " Daras seemed to forget about the throw all at once, as he got his first good look at Ashesa. The grin turned into something else.

Ashesa shivered. "For the love of heaven, stop staring and get me loose! There may be more of them."

"You're in no danger now, My Beloved Ashesa," Daras said, placing a hand on her bare shoulder. "And first thing's first."

"Get me loose." Ashesa repeated, all sweet reason. "We have to get away from here."

Daras nodded. "In time. His lackey today, Aldair himself tomorrow. That's the order of business. Right now there are other matters to attend to."

Ashesa spoke very clearly, very urgently. "You're wrong, Beloved. Wylandia had nothing to do with this. I must tell you—" She stopped. Daras's hand had departed her shoulder for a more southerly location. "What are you doing?!"

He looked a little surprised at her attitude. "That 'other matter' I mentioned. Surely you know that tradition demands a price for your rescue?"

"We're not married yet, Beloved," Ashesa pointed out.

Daras shrugged. "A rescue is a separate matter altogether, with its own traditions and duties. Binding, too. I'm afraid we don't have any choice."

That word.

It wasn't the act that Daras demanded, or even her feelings about Daras himself that mattered in what came next. It was the one word Daras had used. That made all the difference.

Sometimes, in those dark hours between waking and sleeping, when night closes in and the sound of their own heartbeats is much too clear, people have been known to wonder how close to the edge of the abyss they dwelled, and what it would take to push them over. In that moment, strapped to an altar under a warming sun, Ashesa became one of the lucky ones. That question would never trouble her again.

She looked at a soft patch of grass nearby, perfect for paying her debt. Very close to where Timon's dagger had fallen to lie mostly hidden. Yes, it was perfect.

"Free me," she said, "and you'll have your reward."

Ashesa leaned on the altar, trying to clear away a red haze from her mind. She tried not to look at Daras's body, tried not to remember the stunned surprise on his face before all expression ceased. Ashesa pulled herself around the stone until she came to Timon's limp form, then her mouth set in a grim smile and she yanked the robes aside.

The blood came from a punctured animal bladder, and the stick skeleton was dappled with thick, blackening drops.

"Damn you!"

Timon stepped out of the temple again, but this time it was really him. Ashesa glared at him and all the world behind. "No one will believe you," she said, pale as snow and twice as cold.

Timon obviously considered the suggestion in questionable taste. "Did *I* suggest such a thing? No, Highness. But they will believe *you* as you relate—tearfully, I advise—how Daras fell in the rescue, slaying the fiend and freeing you with the strength of his dying breath. Will I spurt green ichor? I should think I would."

"I saw the fight—the real fight—while it lasted. Daras was good but your golem could have killed him easily!" she accused. "But you knew I . . . " she couldn't finish it.

"What a mind," repeated Timon with deeper admiration. "And what you say is partly true, Highness. Once Daras took the bait he was finished, one way or another. For your sake take comfort—you can't kill a dead man. But I was curious about you, I admit it. Not everyone has the talent for knowing what must be done *when* it must be done. No, Highness. I didn't know. Add another sin to my head because I wanted to find out."

Ashesa saw the dwarf Seb coming down the mountain path. He led two horses packed for travel and two more saddled to ride, and he played out a grayish cord behind him from a large spool mounted on a stick.

"A few matters to attend, Highness," Timon said. "The first involves something new in the art of destruction. I think you'll be seeing it again." He nodded and Seb struck a flint to the cord. It sizzled with life and burned its way back to the tower. In a moment there was a dull roar and the earth trembled. The tower swayed on its foundation and then collapsed. Flames licked the exposed beams and flooring and soon the whole thing was burning merrily.

Ashesa stared. *Heavens.*

Timon pulled a vial from his robe and poured an acrid black liquid on the golem. There was an instantaneous, nauseating stench and the cloth, wood, leather and blood all hissed and bubbled and melted into a smoking mass.

Seb stared at the remnants of the tower wistfully. Timon laid a hand on his shoulder. "Sorry, but you knew it was only temporary. My magic would have to die with me. Expectations, you know." He turned back to Ashesa. "As cruel as assumptions in their way. They killed Daras as surely as we did."

"What about me?" Ashesa asked dully.

"Don't worry. If you'll wait here I've no doubt that King Aldair and Prince Galan will follow the beacon of flames right to you, combining against the common foe under the push of a father's love. Have you met young Galan, by the way? A kind, intelligent lad by all report, though given to idle dreaming. Who can say? With a firm hand to guide him he might even make a king."

Seb handed Ashesa a cloak. "Master, we'd best be going."

They mounted and rode out the gate without a backward glance. Ashesa gathered the cloak about her and settled down to wait. As she waited, she thought about Timon, and Daras, and herself. Maybe she would talk to her father about Galan. Maybe. They would still want the alliance, but that didn't matter just then. She would meet Galan again, and she would decide. *She* would decide. Her father, whether he realized it or not, would just go along.

She didn't really understand what was different now, but something was, and it wasn't because of her crime as such. It just came down to choice. Once you knew it existed there was no end to it. And no escape from it either.

Forgive me, Beloved, but Seb was right—this isn't a time for heroes.

Still, the Age that couldn't profit from a clever, determined princess had never dawned.

DEATH, THE DEVIL, AND THE LADY IN WHITE

———

Many years ago, in a land so near the underworld you could hear the Devil's hounds chasing souls at night, a deep forest pond was haunted by a beautiful and terrible spirit. Every year a certain number of men, both the young and foolish and the old and foolish, would dare go too near the pool and in consequence leave their bones to sink into the mud or grow moss in the shallows. Since the creature known far and wide as the Lady in White was believed to be among the most malevolent of all evil spirits, this result was to be expected.

What was not expected was that one particularly foolish young man would fall in love with her.

He was from the nearby village of Tunby, which over the generations had supplied many of the bones now resting quietly in the White Lady's domain. His name was unremarkable, but let it be known: John Alby. He was not a complete fool, even in love—he knew that his passion for the Lady in White was pointless and, above all, potentially lethal. Yet in the quiet summer evenings he would come near—but not too near—and wait for his love to appear.

The first sign of her was a plume of white mist that appeared over the center of the pool. Sometimes the mist hovered there and wavered gently, as if the Lady in White was debating whether to manifest. Sometimes she did not appear at all, and the mist would dissipate after a while. John had mixed emotions then. On the one hand, if his lady appeared from the mist, John at least would get a chance to see her. On the other hand, if she did appear, chances were good that someone was about to die.

John tried to prevent those deaths. He would spot a traveler on the path and go to meet him, quickly before it was too late, and warn them. "You'll die if you go any closer," he would say. If the traveler was merely on the wrong path they would thank him and turn away, but that seldom was the case. Usually they would either simply push past him and say nothing or declare as they did so that they were not afraid, but of course they were. Yet they would not turn back. Sometimes John wondered if he should do more but, if a man is determined to find his destiny, there's really not much point in arguing. Still, John continued to try.

So it was that, on that particular evening when the mist started to form that sweet, familiar shape, John got up from his seat on a fallen log and hurried down to the path to meet the next doomed man. However, in contrast to all the others, this doomed man did not act doomed at all. An older man, tall and bony as if weathered away by life, walked briskly down the path toward the pool, whistling as he went.

John hailed the man courteously. "Excuse me sir, but by your manner it's clear to me that you do not realize that this path leads to the abode of a very dangerous creature, and surely you do not mean to go there."

"Thank you, and you are quite correct," replied the thin old man with equal politeness. "Rather, I was looking for you."

John blinked at that. "Do I know you?"

"We've never met before," the man said.

John took a closer look at the stranger. Second inspection confirmed the first: he was a skinny old man, with flesh stretched tight on his limbs and face, but his eyes were bright and his smile quick and there was a spring in his step that wouldn't have been out of place in the tread of a much younger man. His clothes were of good quality but travel-worn. He wore a dagger and a pouch around his waist, and he bore a short staff that was probably more for protection from robbers than to aid in walking.

He leaned on the staff and continued to smile. "My name is Death," he said. "I wanted to get that out of the way so there would be no misunderstandings later, John Alby."

John was too stunned to wonder how the old man knew his name— the old man was clearly mad, and perhaps dangerous as well. John took a step back, and the old man waved his hand.

"No need to concern yourself, lad—it is not your time. Today I merely want to talk to you."

John hesitated, but the old man seemed harmless enough, if completely addle-pated. "Of course. But what about?"

The old man laughed. "Why, the Lady in White, of course. Your love."

John frowned. "How did you know I loved the Lady in White?"

"I simply knew that *someone* would, and, since you are here, you are the one. No need to ask why, I suppose—she is beautiful, is she not? Close enough to touch and yet totally and forever beyond reach. A certain type of man cannot help but love her."

John wondered if he had been insulted, but there was nothing in the man's manner that even hinted so. If anything, the stranger seemed a little envious.

Death sighed. "John, I know you don't believe I am who I say I am, and that's all right. I propose that you test me. I need to prove that I understand the nature of the Lady in White and can be of service to you in the matter of winning her love. That is your secret dream, is it not?"

John stared at the man for several seconds. The old man, for his part, waited patiently for John to find his voice again. "You're serious?" John said at last.

"In all I do," the man replied, still smiling.

"How can you know my secret dream?"

Death sighed. "How could I not? It is the nature of love to seek consummation; all else is philosophy and denial. Or are you going to claim that you do not wish to win the Lady in White?"

"Of course I want to win her! Yet she is not even human; I may be in love, but I do not deceive myself there. It is impossible."

"Difficult and unlikely? Yes. Not impossible. That is what you must believe, and so, again, why you must believe *me*. I know the one way that your dream can come true. How close are you able to get to the pool?"

John pointed up at the small grove to where his customary log lay on a thick carpet of dead leaves. "On top of that small hill. I dare go no closer."

The old man nodded. "Well, then. Follow me and we will get much closer. You needn't worry so long as you stay behind me. If anything happens, I will be first and pay the price of my mistake. Fair enough?"

John shrugged. "I suppose so. Lead and I will follow."

John followed the old man further down the path, closer and closer to the Lady in White's pool. John couldn't help but feel nervous about getting so close; the fact that he loved the beautiful spirit in no way diminished the fact that he had seen what happened to men who got too close to her, and he did not want the same happening to him. Yet as they made their way through the banks of high reeds by the shore, the figure in the mist did not move, did not react. It was as if she could not see them. John started to ask about this, but almost instantly the form with the mist began to solidify, and the old man held up his hand for silence.

This was John's first good, close look at his love, and his concept of her went from half-glimpsed and mostly imagined to very real. She was, if anything, more beautiful than he had believed. She floated on the mist as if she were made of mist herself. Her hair and gown were the white of snowflakes that had yet to touch earth; her face was paler than the moon and her eyes blacker than night. For a moment or two John could do nothing but stare.

The Lady in White, for her part, looked puzzled. She looked right and left as she hovered there over the black water, looking for something and never quite finding it. John knew his life hung by a frayed thread, but he did not want to leave and the old man did not seem in any particular hurry. In fact, he seemed to be waiting for something. He turned back to John and, though his voice never even raised to a whisper, his lips formed a word.

Wait.

Someone else was coming down the path; they could not see him yet, but they could hear him—the man had a great stomping footfall that made the rushes quiver. Now the Lady was looking neither right nor left but directly down the path. The old man who called himself Death nodded and turned back the way they had come, pushing John before him. They had gone less than thirty paces when they saw the newcomer.

John knew the man. Matthew Sanger was a blacksmith in Tunby, a great black-haired lout with more liking for drink, fighting, and bragging than honest work, but someone John had no wish to see come to harm. John reached out and grabbed the man's arm. "Go back!" he hissed. "She'll kill you!"

Like all the others, Matthew simply kept walking, pulling away from John as if he wasn't even there. John reached for him again, but old man Death was there in front of him, bony hands on John's shoulders, restraining him with surprising strength. "You can't help him. Watch."

John watched as Matthew strode defiantly down to the shore of the pool. He watched as Matthew stood suddenly still when he saw the Lady in White for the first time. In another moment Matthew was walking very quickly into the pool, reaching out overhead to try and grasp the Lady in White but of course he could not. She remained there out of reach, not smiling, not laughing, not changing her expression at all as Matthew slipped under the water.

The apparition paid no further attention to the bubbles rising from the water, and after a few moments they ceased and the ripples began to fade. She was searching the shore again with those beautiful, terrible eyes.

"She can hear us, as you might have guessed by now," the old man said. "Let's go back down the path a bit where we can talk freely."

Defeated, John let himself be steered back to a safe distance. He shook himself free, finally, and walked back up the hill to his log. The old man followed at a respectful distance and waited while John sat on his log and watched the specter until she turned back to mist and drifted away. Then the old man joined him on his log.

"I've seen it before," John said. "And I try to help, and I very seldom can. Why? Why do they do it?"

The old man laughed. "Say rather why you sought to help that man even though you knew there was no point. Or why you sit on this log in the cool of the evening and pine for that lovely expression of imminent mortality. Answer your own question, John Alby."

John sighed. "I can't."

The old man nodded. "Neither could they. So. Do you accept that I am Death?"

John hesitated. "I accept that you are a very unusual man and have the ability to get close to my love safely. She couldn't see us. How did you do that?"

"Your unasked question is more important: How will *you* do it?" The old man reached under his shirt and pulled out a small rock crystal pendant on a leather thong. He held it up for John to see. "With this little trifle. It renders anyone who wears it invisible to creatures of the night such as the Lady in White. Quite a useful thing. If you wear it, you can do alone what we just did together."

John sighed. "I have seen my love's true face. Name your price, for without that pendant there is no hope."

Death nodded. "There's little hope even with the pendant, if things continue as they are. Sooner or later you'll go to her. They all do."

John glared at him. "You claim to know so much of the matter—tell me how I solve this problem."

"For the same price? We hadn't yet settled that."

"What do you want from me, then?"

"Only that you listen to what I have to say and act on it. That is how you will pay me. Do you agree?"

John shrugged. There was no harm in listening. "Certainly," he said.

The old man held out the crystal pendant and John, hardly daring to believe his good fortune, took it.

"As you agreed, you must listen to me and do as I instruct, or else, sooner or later, the Lady in White will claim you as surely as she did Matthew Sanger."

John frowned. "You knew Matthew Sanger?"

"I know everyone," the old man said. When John just stared at him he sighed and went on. "Men come to the Lady's pool for their own reasons, but the nature of her power is that it does not compel a man to embrace her unless she can see him. That's a connection between them that must occur first; so long as you wear that pendant, it will not happen."

John shook his head. "I don't understand. You say I will go to her whether she can see me or not. How do you know that?"

"How can you not know?" the old man asked, unperturbed. "Can you be content just to be near her? Almost close enough to touch and never touching? Speaking to her, perhaps, and yet never letting her see your face? Can your love be satisfied with this and nothing more?"

It was several long moments before John could reply. "No."

"Then be quiet and listen—go down the path to the pool when the mist forms and greet the Lady by her name: Alisandra."

John shook his head again. "You could have learned my name or Matthew's in the village, somehow, but how by all that's holy can you know the name of my love?" John asked.

"As I said—I know everyone. Though it's more accurate to say that Alisandra was once the Lady's name. There is a chance that it has been too long, that she will not remember, and in that case I advise you to simply remove the pendant and end your longing, since then there is truly no hope."

"And if she does remember?"

"If she does, she will hold out her hand to you, even though she cannot see you. Do not take her hand yet, no matter how tempted you may be. Simply talk to her."

"That is all?"

"That is a great deal. Take your leave of her when you may, then return the next evening. Do this for three nights. On the third night, if you really are in love with her, you will hear the Lady in White weep."

"In sorrow for those she has killed?" John asked.

"In sorrow," the old man said, "for herself. She has reason enough. When that happens, the Lady will tell you what you must do to end her suffering, and she will offer her hand again. This time you must take it and, no matter what happens, do not let go. This is very important, mind, *do not let go*. Do you understand?"

John nodded, and the old man got up. He did not offer his hand but simply said, "Good luck to you, John Alby."

John looked thoughtful. "If you are who you say you are, then the Lady in White does much work that should be good in your eyes. Why would you seek to end that?"

"You don't know what I seek, John Alby. All you do need to know is that I have told you the truth in all things. Remember that, should it prove necessary."

The next evening came and, despite his misgivings, John walked past the hill and its log seat and continued down the path toward the haunted pool. Already the mist was gathering, as it always did, though the Lady herself had not appeared. John touched the pendant around his neck though he did not take very much comfort in it.

He offered me hope, and I could not refuse. In a few moments we will know if the old man was really telling the truth.

The proof was quick and sure coming, in that the White Lady did not appear at all. The mist was there, and John was there, his feet bare inches from the water, but the White Lady was not. John took a gusting breath of relief, and in that moment the mist began to coalesce. John saw a pair of dark eyes and a flow of white mist that might have been hair. He almost cried out in his fear, but he remembered what the old man had said, and what had happened the previous night.

She can't see me. She can only hear me.

Still not fully formed, the White Lady was searching the shore around the path, looking but, John was now certain, not seeing. So the old man had told the truth about the pendant. Now John had to find out if he had told the truth about everything else. He kept his voice even and pleasant, though the effort cost him.

"Lady Alisandra. Give you good evening."

The mist contracted suddenly and floated a bit higher over the water. John had never seen that before. If this had not been the White Lady, perhaps something closer to human, or at least closer to having a *memory* of being human, John would have sworn that it was afraid.

"I mean you no harm, Lady Alisandra," John said, and immediately felt foolish, but the words had an effect. The mist lowered slightly, and John could see Alisandra's black eyes again, peering intently at the shore.

"Lady Alisandra, I've come to—"

"Please don't say that name again."

The voice was like a cry of pain, but it filled John with hope. "You remember."

"Yes. Who are you? Why do you torment me?"

"My name is John Alby. I'm sorry if the mention of your name hurts you; that was not my intent."

"Why can't I see you?" she asked.

"I am hidden."

The specter held out her hand, but John remembered and he did not touch her. After a moment she lowered it again, but the image of the lady was clear now. She smiled sadly. "It is good that you are hidden, or you would surely die."

He nodded, forgetting that she couldn't see him. "Why do you do that?" John asked. "Why do you kill the men who come to you?"

"I kill no one. It is my nature that men will seek me out and the nature of my current . . . condition, that I must seek them in turn. I cannot prevent it, yet I know they die because of me."

"Do you enjoy their deaths?"

The sad smile again. "Enjoy? I enjoy nothing, John Alby. I do not ask you to understand, but if there is any human kindness within you, then please either reveal yourself or go away. Do not add to my suffering."

John saw the pain on his love's face and the sight was breaking his heart. "I do not wish you to suffer. I wish to aid you in any way that I can."

She hesitated, then shook her head. "Please go," she said, and started to fade.

"Wait!" John said, but in a moment there was nothing over the pool but mist.

The next evening John found a frightened but determined young man walking down the path.

"Rather young to go to your death," John said.

"I'm not afraid," the boy said. "I'll prove it to them . . . "

John nodded cheerfully. "Ah, a dare. Of course."

John didn't bother trying to reason with the lad; he simply clouted him over the head and left him tied to one of the alders beside the path. John didn't feel particularly noble about taking such a new and drastic step; he knew his good intentions were matched by his desire that the boy not interfere. When he was certain the boy would not be following him, he continued down toward the pool where the Lady in White was waiting.

"The boy will not be coming," he said.

Alisandra shrugged. "I saw him walking, then he stopped, then fell down and dragged himself off and tied himself to a tree. It was a very odd sight, John Alby, but I suppose he has you to thank for his salvation."

John shrugged. "One less death for your conscience to bear."

"One pebble in a landslide is meaningless, John Alby."

"I don't think that's true."

"No?" Again Alisandra held out her hand to him, and again John refused to take it, though he wanted to reach out and comfort her in any way possible.

She sighed, and lowered her hand again. "Why do you torment me? Has someone you cared for come to embrace me? Is this revenge?"

"How am I tormenting you? Is my presence so distasteful?"

"Yes," she said frankly. "You remind me of what I am not. You speak kindly to me. Why do you do this, John Alby? Why do you want to help me?"

"I love you," he said.

"You are a fool," she said.

211

John nodded affably. "No doubt. Yet there is the matter in a nutshell, Lady Alisandra."

She shuddered. "I asked you not to say that name. For pity's sake . . . "

"For pity's sake? Not a bit of it. I *shall* remember that name, even if you do not wish to. I will say it with love so you can hear. I want to shout it from the mountain!"

She shuddered again. "Please don't. Please go away."

"If that is your wish, then I will do so. But I will return tomorrow," he said.

"If you really love me, you will not return," she said.

"I don't believe you mean that," John said.

"Then it seems I must be doubly a captive: of my sorry state and of what you believe. Until tomorrow, John Alby."

Once more she vanished into mist. John went back to the alder tree, threw the cursing boy over his shoulder, and carried him back to his mother.

I have little to offer, but what I have is yours.

John fiddled with the beginnings of a speech, what he would say to Alisandra when the final task was done. He had not totally abandoned sense, but hope was a powerful force and he couldn't help but think of what was to come afterwards. Would she love him? She had not said so. Perhaps she would learn? Perhaps yes, perhaps no. There were possibilities aborning now, and all wanted to be heard, both the good and the bad.

"Not yet," John said aloud as he walked down the path. He would not think of them yet. He would not plan speeches, or children, or what Alisandra would wear to Maying Day or their wedding. So much not to think about; it was very difficult. John almost didn't notice when he'd reached the pond.

Alisandra was already there. Weeping. So far, everything was going as the old man had said.

"P-please, no more. All those things you want me to be, that you believe I am . . . I can't stand it any more, John Alby."

"Give me your hand," he said, relentless. "It's time."

"You know of that? Who told you?"

"An old man I met near the path. He knew much about you."

She stopped crying then, though for a time the tears remained, glistening on her cheeks. "Yes, I suppose he would."

"He called himself Death, but I do not believe that. Do you know him?" John asked. "Is he a friend of yours? An enemy? Does he wish you ill?"

She shook her head. "No more questions now. You have been counseled well, but you have not been told everything. There is more you need to understand."

"I want to," John said.

She smiled then. "Long ago I was a human woman, a sorceress, and my name was indeed Alisandra. Magic was my pride but I was beautiful as well, and that was my undoing. Two powerful lovers courted me, and I could not choose between them, so I fled both. I fled until there was nowhere else to run in all the world."

"What happened then?"

"I fled the world," she said simply. "I used my skills and I opened a way out and escaped . . . or so I thought." John waited, silently, and finally she went on. "Where I am and where I came from both became unbalanced once I crossed over. There is a rift between the worlds over this pond, and nothing of me except my longing can cross it unaided. That is what they call the Lady in White truly is, John Alby. Not a ghost—a memory. Men mistake the longing for something it is not, and they die."

"I do not know what you are or might be," John said. "and I do not care. I only know that I love you."

Her dark eyes glittered. "If that is true, then you can do something no one else can do—match my longing with your own. You can reach across the abyss and bring me home. If you take my hand now and hold tight, I will be able to cross this rift and be mortal again."

"Truly? What about your lovers?"

She smiled a little shyly. "Is that jealousy?"

John blushed. "Well . . . perhaps a little."

"It was long ago, John. Though there is one thing I must warn you about—for a time we will be neither of this world nor your own, but moving between them. Just as I come to meet you, there is something of you that will come to me. At that point we are both vulnerable, do you understand?"

"I don't think so," John said. "Vulnerable to what?"

She looked away. "Many things, but mostly the men who have died here.

213

It is likely that some of them can not rest and they walk between, neither of this world nor no longer of yours. They will be able to reach me then, and they will try to make you let go of me so that they may seek their revenge. I can't promise that you won't be hurt, or that you won't be afraid, but I do promise that, if you hold tight, they cannot stop us. If you let me go one moment before I tell you to, then I am lost."

John licked his lips. "I won't let that happen. I swear it. I will trust you to know when the time is right."

"As I must trust you, John, since it seems there's no escaping you."

John reddened again, but Alisandra smiled as she said it, and he could sense no resentment in her. He hoped he was right; he did not want her to think ill of him and confuse his devotion for something less worthy. "I hope you will have no more reason to grieve on my account, and I swear I will make you happy—"

She lifted a finger to her lips, silencing him. "Swear nothing to me, save that you will be guided by me, and do as I say."

"I swear," he said.

"Well then. Let's have it done."

Alisandra held out her hand again, and this time John took it. He gasped as their fingers touched; she felt as ethereal as mist and yet he could hold her. Her touch was like ice and yet he did not let go. After a moment or two the worst of the cold and the *wrongness* of her touch began to fade. At first he thought she was growing more substantial, and perhaps she was, but he had changed as well. The world around him seemed unreal. He almost believed he could see a pebble on the bank of the pool directly beneath his shoe, but he forgot about both the pebble and the shoe as he gazed at Alisandra.

She had left her position floating over the pond and now stood in front of him on the shore. She was not now the cold and deadly beauty he had seen through rift; she was still beautiful, yes, and her hair just as white, her eyes still as dark. Yet her hand was now warm in his, and John fancied he saw the human woman now and not the specter. She smiled at him, as if sensing his thoughts.

"Yes, John Alby. If you're less real now, I am more so. That's the rift trying to heal itself." She looked away from him, then listened intently. "He's coming."

"Who is?" John asked.

"One of many," Alisandra said. "but probably the most recent."

It was Matthew Sanger.

John saw him drifting through the reeds. He looked by turns as solid as a brick and as fleeting as smoke. He seemed to be sniffing the wind like a blind dog, but he came on unerringly toward them.

"Matthew! Stay back!" John shouted, but Alisandra shook her head.

"He won't hear you. There's little left of him now except a purpose. Hold tight!"

Matthew came on, ignoring John completely. John wasn't even sure if Matthew could see him. The shade of the burly blacksmith grabbed hold of Alisandra's right arm and pulled.

"Mine!"

His voice, for all the fire in his eyes, was nothing more than a whisper of the wind in the reeds. John braced himself against the pull, afraid that Matthew would snatch Alisandra from him as easily as he'd brushed John off on the pool path, but this was not like before. Matthew was only a shadow with a purpose and John, though hovering between worlds, was more his match this time. John grimaced against the strain but held fast. He saw the pain in Alisandra's eyes as Matthew's hand dug into her arm, but John did not let go. Matthew clawed at John's arm, unseeing, like someone trying to free a piece of clothing caught in a snag. John felt Matthew's cold hard nails rake his flesh; he cried out but held firm.

"Mine . . . " The voice was despairing now.

"I won't let go, Matthew," John said, though it was more to reassure Alisandra. Matthew, for his part, did not listen and did not let go but, if it was true that he was no more than a purpose now, that purpose was thwarted and could not be sustained. Matthew began to fade away, and in a moment or two he was gone. John was relieved but did not relinquish his grip on Alisandra's hand. There were others; she had said so, and John knew it must be true—scores of men had gone to their deaths over the years at Alisandra's pool. There would be more.

Alisandra smiled at him. "It won't be long now."

John looked around, but so far as he could see the world he remembered still seemed pale and ghostly. "I can't tell that we've moved any closer to our true world."

"I wasn't talking about that, though what you're referring to will happen soon enough." From the distant shadows John heard the baying of hounds, and Alisandra sighed. "Hurry, my love."

John could not hurry, could not do anything save what he had sworn to do. It was a moment or two before he had the cold, immovable understanding that Alisandra was not talking to him. "Who is coming? The other men who died here?"

She nodded. "Those unhappy souls for certain; I can feel them rushing to find me, but they will not find me before he does. Thank you, John Alby. I am in your debt."

" 'He'? I don't understand."

"You will shortly. You won't forgive me, but then remember that I didn't ask for your love."

"There's nothing coming but hounds!"

"And their master," she said.

The baying was a loud chorus now. John could see the hounds' red eyes as they coursed through the shadows, ever closer. He understood then. A pack of hounds moving between this world and the next could only be one particular pack.

"No wonder the ghosts of the other men who died here are so scattered; they had to flee the hunting pack!"

She nodded. "There are still many, as I said, but not so many as there were. No one evades the hunter forever."

John saw them coming, knew there was no escape. "What shall we do?"

Alisandra didn't answer for a moment, and he thought at first he hadn't heard her. She peered into the darkness and smiled. "Ah. There."

John saw it too: a ghostly rider on a horse darker than night. His eyes were redder than the hounds'. Alisandra turned back to look at John in triumph. "What shall we do? I'll tell you—we shall part, John Alby. Let me go. Now."

"Alisandra . . . " He heard the despair in his own voice and could change nothing.

"Now!"

Alisandra slapped him hard and he did release her, more from shock and surprise than intent. He immediately reached for her again, but it was already too late. The pack parted around her as she ran towards the huntsman. In a moment she was beyond his sight and the pack closed in. Yet as they did, they grew fainter, ghostly. John felt the living world rushing back to him like a strong wind, but the pack was rushing harder. He cried out as spectral jaws opened with teeth white and sharp to rend and tear, but they closed on nothing. The rift healed itself from one moment to the next and soon even the sound of the pack was fading to nothing.

John stood on the bank of the pond, staring off into darkness, but he wasn't alone. John heard footsteps behind him.

"Alisandra . . . ?"

"I'm afraid not."

The old man stood on the path behind him. He put his hands on his hips and stared off into the shadows at something John could not see. "The tale comes to its end, as all things must, so for that at least I am in your debt, for what little that is worth."

"I thought . . . " John stopped, shaking his head. "I'm a fool. She never intended to come back to the living world, did she?" he asked softly.

"Her sanctuary was compromised, so she had to make her long-delayed choice. Which I lost, but I knew the risk. As for you, she used you to reach that place between her world and this where her chosen could find her."

The only thing clear on John's face was his utter confusion. "She used me? *You* lost?"

"I'm not used to it," the old man admitted. "The Devil is seldom cheated, but Death? Never, at least until now. Take some comfort in that, if you can—you are not the only lover spurned this night."

John Alby stared at Alisandra's pool for a very long time and then set his mouth in a hard grim line. He took a step toward the dark, cold water before he realized the old man was still there, watching him.

"Death, if that's who you really are, you will not have long to wait for me."

The old man sighed. "Oh, stop it. You had your place in our little play, but this was never about you. Not really."

When John just stared at him, he sighed again and reached into his belt and pulled out a well-worn ledger, which he flipped open and shoved under John's nose. "I do owe you a favor, and since you seem to be having some difficulty, I'll show you the matter plain: here is the day and the date, duly recorded. As you can see, you're going to live a very long time yet. I suggest you get on with it."

The old man left him there, and, because there was really nothing else for him to do, John did go home to Tunby. He never spoke of what happened that day at the pool but, because of the boy John had saved the day before, people came to associate the disappearance of the Lady in White with John's return and made him into a hero despite his objections. In time he learned to let people think what they would, since there was no help for it. Time healed him to the extent he could be healed, and eventually his fame helped him to marry well and grow fat and prosperous.

The details of John Alby's battle with the evil spirit of the pool changed over the years and grew more thrilling with each new version, though John was never the one doing the telling. Less well known is the true story of his end, many years later, when he simply announced that he had an appointment to keep and walked out of his village forever.

He was last seen making his way down the path to the weed-choked forest pond known to this day as the Pool of the Lady in White.

THE RIGHT GOD

———

Don Lang was not a happy man. His unhappiness wasn't due to the fact that hundreds—perhaps thousands—of new gods were physically manifesting all over the world. Granted, this *was* a very vexing thing, but for the most part people were dealing with this development surprisingly well. No, what was really steaming Don's buns was that a particular god named Rockball had marked Don for a singular honor.

Prophet.

Don did not want to be a prophet, and especially not to a sawed-off little runt of a god named Rockball. Don's opinion on the matter had not been solicited.

"What sort of a name for a god is 'Rockball'?"

"*Mine*, of course," said Rockball.

Rockball was currently manifesting in Don's shaving mirror, which was making shaving that morning somewhat awkward. Don got through it by angling his face forty-five degrees to one side of the mirror or the other, depending on which way Rockball's squat brown visage was turned at the time. Sometimes Don couldn't decide if Rockball's face looked more like a shriveled apple or crudely-carved stone, but either way the god couldn't seem to stand still, there in mirror-land. Don grabbed a square of tissue to staunch a cut and studied the result as best he could. He wondered if, perhaps, his black hair was showing a little more gray today. At his age he expected a few gray hairs, but lately Don thought perhaps he had more of an excuse than usual.

"You've got the wrong man, you know. I'm no prophet."

"Why?" Rockball asked reasonably. "What's wrong with you?"

Don sighed. "I'm forty-three, twice divorced, I live alone . . . well, except for you, and I'm pretty sure that keeping a god in my apartment is a violation of my lease. I'm not even allowed to have an aquarium! That's just for starters, and I'm sure I can think of more."

"Waste of time," said Rockball. "Besides, I'm not a goldfish."

Don still wasn't quite sure what to make of Rockball. He said he was a god and Don had no reason to question that. Gods were everywhere these days. All the talking heads on tv were arguing about what it meant and whether the breakdown of the home/church/social mores or planetary alignment was at fault, but no one had the answer. The government claimed to be working on the problem but, for the most part, everyone just coped as best they could.

Coping, it turned out, was surprisingly easy. Once they got over the initial shock, people learned that dropping a coin or two in a little tin pot by the station helped the trains run on time. And that emptying that tin pot when no one was looking brought a plague of boils and halitosis, and thus they also learned to leave the pot alone. Students who burned sticks of incense before the stone lions at the library found their grades improving. Wives and husbands and boyfriends and girlfriends who prayed before the statue of a green woman that appeared in Central Park found that formerly cheating lovers stayed home. Or left for good, depending on the prayer.

There were, as many people now admitted, advantages to the new situation. There was less uncertainty these days. Once people found the right god, good things could happen. People who had never had plans or direction in their entire lives were suddenly finding purpose. So, while world leaders made soothing promises and experts talked, ordinary people got on with their lives. Don, for his part, wasn't really one of them. He had neither purpose nor direction, just like before.

He did, like it or not, have Rockball.

Don glared. "Just what are you the god of, anyway?"

Rockball glared at him. "I don't know."

Don just stood there in front of the mirror for a moment, blinking, like some small animal caught in a spotlight. "What do you mean 'You don't know'?"

"It's sort of complicated," said Rockball.

Don shook his head. "No it isn't. I don't pretend to understand divine nature, but I *do* know that every god and goddess who's popped up so far has a niche and there's a sort of instinctive understanding of that from all concerned. That's why those impromptu shrines are springing up everywhere. How can I be your prophet if I don't even know what you're about?"

There was an oddly hopeful tone in Rockball's voice. "A real prophet would figure it out."

"Well, there's your answer, because I have no idea," Don said, and Rockball just sighed.

"Exactly. Not that I expected better."

Don wiped the remnants of shaving cream and blood off his face. "I don't have time for this. I have to go to work."

"Later," was all Rockball said, and he disappeared from the mirror.

Don got dressed and caught his bus to work, only to find out that what he had told Rockball was, apparently, in error. He had all the time in the world.

It took a few moments for Don to comprehend what his harried-looking supervisor was telling him. "I'm fired?" Don asked finally.

His supervisor was apologetic but firm. "There's been a budget shortfall and the department had to take a cut. You're the least senior staff member, Don, so there really wasn't any choice."

After that things went very fast. Don had his exit interview and was back on the street in less than an hour. Don knew all the reasons he should be angry. He knew that, at his age, there would be companies reluctant to hire him. He knew that the economy was not in great shape and finding another job in any case was not going to be easy. He even knew that there was a distinct possibility that Rockball had a hand in all this. Yet Don was having a hard time caring about any of that. He knew he should, but that didn't change the fact.

Perhaps it would have been different if he had a family to support, or other obligations, but Don had been on his own for some time, drifting from position to position, never too long at one place despite the fact that his computer skills and experience were first-rate. The position at the accounting firm was the first non-contract job he'd held in years, and he'd rather fallen into that at the time. He wasn't particularly attached to it. He wasn't even totally sure what he'd been doing there anyway; one set of numbers was pretty much like another to him.

It's not like I've spent most of the money I've made as it is. I can coast a few months if I have to, not even counting unemployment.

That still left the problem of what he was going to do about the god in his apartment. Don thought of moving but, if he was the god's prophet, giving his deity the slip couldn't be so simple as that.

Could it?

Since leaving the office Don had just been walking without much thought of a direction. He stopped for a moment to get his bearings and realized he had just crossed Jericho Street, so the Municipal Park was just a block or so away. The morning was nice after the rain of the last few days; someone must have found the right weather god. Don strolled along the sidewalk, taking some time to enjoy the day even as he puzzled over what to do. He found a park bench just under the shade of a massive legacy oak and sat down to think, right after checking the tree to make sure there were no shrines about. Nature spirits had become almost as common as gods, and they tended to get irritable when someone used the bounty of their home without permission. Still, so far as Don could see no one had taken residence in the tree as of yet.

Don looked across the park. There were a few students from the nearby college. A pair of co-eds were lying half-dressed on a blanket catching some sun, another group of students was quietly studying, but there weren't many other people around. The park would get busier around lunchtime as office workers from all over downtown gravitated there to eat and visit, but for now it was quiet.

It didn't stay that way.

"I have come to share the Word of Stonemother."

Don looked up into what he assumed were the eyes of a female street-corner preacher. He hadn't seen one in a long time, female or otherwise. Probably not at all since the early days of the Great Emergence, as the pundits had taken to calling it, before the trappings of the formerly dominant religions had begun to unravel. They survived only as pocket communities and scattered cults now, so far as Don knew.

It took him a moment or two, but exactly what the woman had said finally registered. Stonemother. Who the heck was 'Stonemother'? Don sighed. Not a preacher—a prophet, like he was supposed to be. Don had seen a few of those, too, and much more recently, but this woman didn't quite fit the profile. He looked her more closely up and down. She was a little younger than he was, perhaps mid to late thirties. Dark curly hair, tall, rather pretty from what he could tell through the scowl on her face, but that wasn't what finally drew his attention. It was her eyes. There was no burning fanaticism there, or even conviction. She looked tired. Embarrassed. Angry.

"You're no prophet," Don said. "You don't even want to be here, do you?"

She glared even more. "I do so! I am so! I am the Prophet of Stonemother, come to bring you her Word!"

Don sighed. "And what is this 'word'?"

She just stared at him for a moment. The scowl faded and she slumped a bit, looking defeated. "Well, to tell the truth I'm not entirely sure. I know this doesn't make a lot of sense."

Don found himself smiling. "Try. I'll listen."

"Umm, do you mind if I sit down? I've been walking all over this place trying to get my nerve up. I'm beat."

"Not at all. My name's Don, by the way. Don Lang."

She extended her hand and Don took it, briefly. "Amelia Carson," she said, then smiled. "Not much of a name for a prophet, is it?"

"No worse than 'Don Lang.'"

She turned then, and looked at him intently. "You too? When?"

"This morning." Don told her about Rockball and his decision to make Don his prophet. "Which is really silly, since he doesn't even know what he's the god *of* yet. What kind of a message is that? 'Hear me, o people, and know that I am the Lord of . . . something really important, and you better listen!' I mean, really."

"It's the same with Stonemother," Amelia said, looking glum. "but if I didn't at least try, she said she was going to make something bad happen. I believe her; she's done it before. I lost my job yesterday."

"This morning for me . . . Are you sure it was Stonemother?"

"Pretty darn sure . . . Listen, if she asks, can I say I shared the word with you? I mean, I can deal with unemployment for a little while, but I don't want my apartment building burned down around me. At least I have a place to sleep for the moment, though if Stonemother keeps acting up my roommates are going to toss me out anyway."

"I'd be glad to. Maybe you can do the same for me."

"Deal. Though I have to wonder why our gods are so unhappy; most of the others are fairly easy to relate to. Why are these two so difficult?"

"That's a good question," said Don.

Neither said anything for a while. Don watched someone throw a coin into the park fountain, saw the small hand that snaked up out of the water and accept the offering. He shook his head. "You see it every day, and it doesn't seem so strange anymore. No matter how strange it is."

Amelia sighed. "Don't you ever wonder? I mean, how it happened? Why it happened?"

"I've heard the theories," Don said. "That mankind's beliefs became too fragmented to support a consistent cosmology, that these are some sort of psychic manifestation or shared hallucination . . . "

Amelia snorted in derision. " . . . and you give all that about as much credence as I do. Mankind's beliefs have always been fragmented and there's never been a 'unified cosmology,' whatever that nonsense phrase is supposed to mean. The gods appeared whether we believed in them or not. They're here whether we believe in them or not. They don't seem subject to our beliefs."

"Unlike Christianity?"

"Mostly, but not just them. I mean, what good is faith in the numinous and invisible when deities are popping out of the bushes left and right? About the only people unaffected were some strains of Buddhism and the animists, so far as I can see."

"Whereas everyone else went a little bonkers, at least at first. You've been looking in to this, I see."

Amelia shrugged. "Trying to make some sense of it. There doesn't seem to be a great deal."

Don watched the small arm and hand slowly withdraw back beneath the surface of the fountain. "Maybe it just means that the world never worked the way we thought it did. Either way, that doesn't help us with our problem."

Don said it so easily that it took him a moment to realize just what he *had* said. "Our problem." He thought about it for a moment and shrugged. Why not? Don hadn't really thought of it before, but he realized it felt good to talk to someone else about a shared problem. He couldn't even remember the last time that had happened. Don glanced at Amelia, feeling suddenly self-conscious and shy, but if she took any note of the reference she didn't show it. She was just sitting there, eyes closed. She appeared to be dozing.

"Tired?"

"Hmmm? Oh, I didn't get much sleep last night. Stonemother and I had a huge fight after I was laid-off."

Don made a decision. "Tell you what. Go home and get some rest; I'll vouch for your propheting, if need be."

"Thanks. You're a nice person." She got up, and Don hesitated.

"Before you go . . . listen, are you free tomorrow?"

"Tomorrow and every day," Amelia sighed, "thanks to Stonemother. Why?"

"Well, if you've got nothing better to do, meet me at the park about 11Am. I'll pack a lunch. We can talk some more, if you don't mind. Maybe we can figure out something."

"That would be nice, but I'm not convinced we can."

Don shrugged. "For the record—me neither."

She smiled then, "Also for the record: I don't need to be convinced. I'll settle for hope. Till tomorrow, then."

One problem with packing a lunch every day for more than a few days at a time was getting a good variety. On the third day of what had turned into a standing date between Don and Amelia, it occurred to Don that he should have asked if Amelia was Jewish, or vegan. Even if the old ways were a bit out of favor at the moment, they hadn't gone away entirely and habits like dietary strictures were hard to break. Perhaps she was just being polite before now? He settled for chicken sandwiches, plus fruit and a nice pasta salad just in case. Rockball watched him from his perch on top of the cabinet.

"What are you doing?" asked the god.

"Packing a lunch; I'm meeting someone."

"Again? And what has this to do with being my prophet?"

"Quite a bit. She's the one I've been spreading the word with," Don said. "We talked about you extensively yesterday, and the day before." Which, Don allowed to himself, was no more or less than the truth. He wondered if Amelia was having a similar conversation with Stonemother about now.

Rockball didn't interfere. He seemed oddly thoughtful.

Don kept working. "By the way, I meant to ask—it was you who got me fired, wasn't it?"

"Yes," Rockball said.

Don nodded. "I thought so."

"You don't seem upset," Rockball said, frowning.

"Were you trying to upset me?"

The god frowned. "Not as such. It was purely a show of force to get you to take your obligations toward me seriously."

"Oh, I do. Believe me. That's what these meetings are about," Don said. "We intend to discuss your divine self extensively."

Rockball frowned again. "Well . . . I guess that's all right then."

Don nodded. He intended to make his statement neither more nor less true than it needed to be.

"Rockball, I have a question—can you leave the house?"

"Can I . . . ? You've already been fired, Mortal. Are you trying for 'hit by a bus?'"

Don had the distinct feeling that Rockball was bluffing. Not that he *couldn't* have managed such an event, but Don didn't believe that the godling really wanted to harm him. Don wasn't sure why; he wondered if this feeling was anything like faith.

"I'm not asking you to leave, Rockball. I'm asking if you *can*. Is your manifestation tied to this apartment, this building?"

"Why?"

"My lease is up soon. I'm thinking of renting a house."

Rockball frowned. "I'll go where you go."

"Why? Do you like me that much?"

"You're my prophet. I go where you go," Rockball repeated, as if the fact was obvious. Which, Don thought, perhaps it was.

"That's what I thought," Don said, and he didn't say anything else. He finished packing the lunch basket and went to catch the bus. Later, he sat with Amelia on the same park bench where they had first met.

"You make a really fine chicken sandwich," Amelia said. "I'm starting to feel guilty sponging off of you for the last few days."

"No need, and thanks. I've been eating my own cooking for several years now. It seemed like a good idea to become decent at it."

"Most men wouldn't bother to learn to cook," Amelia said. "or clean, come to that."

"Is that so? Why?"

She shrugged. "No idea. But I've seen enough of it myself and heard my roommate's horror stories. The guys take a girl home expecting a hot time in the middle of what amounts to a pig sty. The guys are always surprised when the lady suddenly isn't too keen. A guy who can both cook and clean is quite a catch. Why is it you're still single, if you don't mind my asking?"

"I wasn't, or haven't always been. I've been married before, it just never worked out."

"Why not?"

"For my first marriage we were both too young, I think. No idea what we wanted, but finally decided it wasn't each other. The second failed, apparently because I'm a bit of an emotional cold fish, or at least that's what Julie told me. She was my second wife."

Amelia was studying him closely. "I don't get that from you at all. I mean, you're not exactly a firecracker—oh, don't look like that. You know it's true. But it's not a personality flaw. Mostly you just look a little . . . lost."

"Maybe I am. So. What about you?" It was a topic Don had meant to raise before now, but it had seemed more important to stick to their shared problem, at least at first.

Amelia didn't say anything for a little while. "This wasn't how I had my life planned, if that's what you mean. I expected to be married, have children, all of those things."

"It didn't happen?" Don asked.

"No. I thought I was in love, a time or two. Either I was wrong or there was just one of us in love and that doesn't work too well. Believe me, I tested the theory very thoroughly. Perhaps even stubbornly so. So now I'm thirty-eight, straight, and still living with two other women who seem stuck in an eternal sorority house state of mind." She smiled grimly. "I think the label you're groping for is 'loser.'"

"You're not a loser," Don said quietly.

She smiled again. "That's sweet, but you don't know."

Amelia finished her sandwich, took a sip of tea from the thermos, and changed the subject. "Any new ideas about our gods? That is why we come here, isn't it?"

"Well . . . not entirely," Don said. "But I *have* been thinking about it for the last few days."

Amelia acted as if she didn't hear the first part of what Don had said, though he was pretty sure she had heard everything. "So what have you thought about?" she asked.

"I'm thinking that perhaps your Stonemother and my Rockball are different from the other gods. Look around; do you notice anything consistent about the others?"

There were three main shrines in the park nearby. One was the fountain, with its scaly hand and arm snatching up offerings. The other was a small tumulous of stones near the edge of the common where the deity called the Black Lady manifested for an appropriate offering. The last one was at an ancient live oak near the park entrance; a nature spirit composed mostly of leaves and twigs haunted the lower branches.

Amelia frowned. "They don't seem to have a lot in common. What am I missing?"

"Place. Each deity manifests at a particular site and no other. It will sometimes move limited distances, maybe a few hundred feet; I've seen that, but it never stays away for long, and it always returns to close proximity to its shrine."

Amelia's mouth fell open. "You're right! Hell, there's even one who hangs out in the turnstile at the bus station, according to the papers. Why didn't I see that?"

Don couldn't help preening a little. "I'm sure you would have, sooner or later. The point is that Rockball doesn't have this problem, and I'm betting your god doesn't either."

"I don't know. I usually see Stonemother in the apartment."

"Because you're there a lot, yes? Same for Rockball. Is that the only place you've seen her?"

"Well . . . no. I do believe I saw her where I used to work . . . right before I got fired. It's several miles from the office."

Don nodded. "The thing that's really different about both of them is that they're not attached to a place. They're attached to *us*. Rockball as much as said so."

Amelia let out a deep sigh. "I think you're right, and how did we get so damn lucky? Good question. A better one would be, what the blue blazes do we do about it?"

"I don't know, but there's something that Rockball said once that keeps bothering me. When I asked him what he was the god *of*, he turned the question back on me, as if he didn't know and I'm supposed to."

"Stonemother is the same way. She's never clear on what message I'm supposed to send, I told you that. And when I ask her, she gets mad! How am I supposed to deal with that?"

Don didn't say anything for a while. Then, "I'm going to rent a house."

Amelia blinked. "Well . . . that's nice. How does this help? Or are you just making conversation?"

"I don't know that it does help. It's certainly not the best time for such a thing. So why am I doing it?"

"You're asking me?"

Don nodded. "Yes. I am."

Amelia laughed then. "You're starting to sound like Stonemother."

"Maybe. My lease is up and I'm going to rent a house. Decided all at once. I've already found it, signed the papers. Unemployed and all, but I'm doing it. I thought Rockball put the notion in my head, but he thought I was trying to ditch him and only noted that it wouldn't work."

Amelia smiled a little wistfully. "Does it have a picket fence?"

Don nodded. "Sure does. And a big oak tree in the back yard. I always wanted a tree like that."

"Sounds wonderful. May . . . may I see it sometime?"

"Why not now? I just picked up the key this morning; it's not too far from here. Shall we go?"

They started to get up, but a rather large young man stepped in front of the bench. He had a small, shiny gun.

"I take, you give," he said, in a disconcertingly cheerful voice. "It's a very simple transaction."

Later Don would wonder just why, but the first thought that popped into his mind was, *Rockball, what did I do this time?*

"No," Amelia said.

Don and the mugger both looked at her. The mugger looked a little confused. "I've made the offerings at the proper shrine and my actions are sanctioned! I've got a gun and, believe me, I *will* shoot you."

"For twenty dollars and a bus token?" Amelia asked.

She was shaking, but she didn't back down.

"Amelia, give him what he wants. It's not worth it."

The mugger nodded, still smiling. "Listen to your boyfriend, Lady."

She glared. "He's *not* my boyfriend! I don't have a boyfriend, I don't have a job, and this week I've given up all I intend to, and I'm not giving up any more! Do you hear me you worthless piece of pond scum?! *No more!*"

"Well, there is one more thing," the mugger said.

Don stood up. Now he was shaking, too, and if he'd have thought about what he was doing, even for a moment, he probably wouldn't have moved. But he knew the mugger was about to shoot Amelia. It was the man's unrelenting cheerfulness that convinced Don of this; the man wasn't just a mugger—he was nuts. Whether the avalanche of gods had anything to do with that or not was beside the point.

The gun turned on Don. "A hero come to play. How cliche." Then he apparently realized that he'd made a rhyme and he giggled.

"Leave her alone," Don said.

"Make me."

Rockball, if anything happens to Amelia because of you—

"You call that a prayer? Besides, I didn't do it," Rockball said from out of nowhere.

"Nothing's going to happen to Amelia while I'm here," said someone else. Don just blinked. Two small figures perched on the shoulders of the mugger like a pair of ugly brown gargoyles. Don recognized Rockball right away, but the other he had not seen before. It was female, but otherwise looked a lot like Rockball. They could have been twins.

"Stonemother . . . ?" Amelia said, looking confused, but no more so than the mugger. Don was the only one of them other than the two gods who was not confused. Things suddenly seemed very, very clear to him.

"This man wants to hurt us," Don said.

"I want your money," the mugger said. "Hurting you was a bonus . . . are these your monkeys? Get them off me!"

Rockball glanced at Stonemother, who nodded. "Count of three?"

"One," said Rockball.

"Two," said Stonemother.

"What?" said the mugger.

"Three," said Rockball and Stonemother together.

The mugger was gone. In his place was a small gray squirrel perched on a pile of empty clothes. The gun lay a few feet away. While it was hard to tell with squirrels, Don was pretty sure that the tree rodent was not smiling.

Rockball and Stonemother towered, relatively speaking, on either side of it.

"Isn't it cute?" Stonemother asked, and she smiled with a lot of very sharp teeth. "Couldn't you just stew it with carrots and eat it up?"

The squirrel apparently read that as a hint and scrambled up the trunk of the oak tree, where it scolded them loudly before launching itself deeper into the branches and out of sight.

"Adjusted rather quickly," said Rockball. "They all do."

"Mortals," said Stonemother, looking disgusted.

The two gods looked at each other, then circled each other warily like two strange dogs at first meeting. After a moment Stonemother yawned and started rummaging through the empty clothes while Rockball transformed the discarded gun into an acorn.

"Are you all right?" Don asked Amelia.

"F-Fine," she said, though she was still shaking. "Thank you." She glanced at the two gods. "I suppose I should thank you, too," she said.

Stonemother just sniffed, and Rockball shrugged. "Don't strain yourself."

"Let's all go see the house," Don said.

Amelia stared, but she wasn't shaking so much. "Now? Shouldn't we call the police?"

"And say what? That we were being mugged, but our mugger is now a squirrel, his gun's an acorn, and here's a description of both? Besides, I think this is the perfect time. We're all together."

"All?" Amelia asked, but Rockball and Stonemother merely glanced at each other and nodded.

"Finally," said Stonemother and Rockball together, but they weren't talking to either Amelia or Don and they didn't say anything else.

Don took Amelia's hand. "I'll explain later, I promise."

Don helped Amelia stand up, and she leaned on his arm a bit as they left the park, the two gods following behind, both couples still a little wary with each other. They passed through the red brick gateway and followed the sidewalk down Leland Street, two blocks to house number 447, a large old Victorian style home.

"It does have a picket fence," Amelia said. "And a turret! It's nice."

"You always wanted one like that, didn't you?"

"I wanted a lot of things," Amelia said.

It took a moment before they realized that Stonemother and Rockball had walked right past them. They seemed to shimmer as they walked, and then they were not walking. They trotted on all fours like a pair of happy pekingnese.

"Fu dogs?" Amelia asked, frowning.

"Guardians," Don corrected. As if to echo his words back, Stonemother and Rockball took positions flanking the front door. Rockball held a ball under his paw, while under her paw Stonemother held a smaller version of herself.

"But I thought they were new sorts of gods," Amelia said. "This is something I've seen before."

"New gods but an old idea; they were always attached to us, we knew that, and this is one way of perceiving their function. That whole 'prophet' thing was just the two of them searching for direction. They didn't know what they were, but then they joined forces to help us and now they do. They're household gods, Amelia."

"Nonsense. I have no family and neither do you!"

Don smiled. "Which is exactly why they've been so all fired *testy*. Their household didn't exist. Yet." He put a slight emphasis on the last word.

Amelia didn't look at him. "I don't understand."

"Sure you do. This is the way they're supposed to be, what they've been waiting for. It's the way we're supposed to be, too."

She glared at him. "Well. Aren't you the romantic bastard."

Don sighed. "I know you're being sarcastic, but it's true—I'm not romantic. I don't know how to make that work, and from what you've told me, neither do you. Maybe you still want romance, but I don't. What I want now is a chance to see if my life can be different. *Better.* I think you could stand some of that yourself."

"You sure know how to sweet talk a girl," Amelia said primly.

"No, I don't, and it gets worse. We're not kids, Amelia. We already know what doesn't work. Don't you think maybe it's past time we looked for something that *does* work?"

"We hardly know each other! What, three days? Frankly, Don, I haven't even made up my mind if I *like* you yet," she said, then added, "though I think I do."

Don nodded. "I think I like you too, but the jury's still out. Happy? But what are gods to anyone except a search for meaning? Maybe that's what these two really are all about and why they came to us. Only time will tell, and I'm not asking for anything else. There are two bedrooms with separate baths. If you like, just think of me as a housemate for now . . . who doesn't leave pantyhose on the shower curtain."

Amelia snorted. "And leaves the toilet seat up, I bet. And . . . and this house is too close to the park! Lousy neighborhood."

"Actually, the mugger notwithstanding, it's a very nice neighborhood. Settled. Quiet. Besides," Don glanced at the two guardians, now settled like stone statues on the porch, "I don't think we have much to worry about on that score."

"Well, that's a plus, but I'll have to think about it," Amelia said. "I know I owe you my life—"

Don nodded toward the porch. "You don't owe me anything. You owe *them* your life. Are you going to be the one to tell them it's time to leave?"

Amelia stared at the pair of guardians for a moment. Rockball bared his teeth. After a moment Amelia smiled a rueful smile. "Oh, all right. But there damn well better be a fireplace or the deal's off."

Don smiled too. "In a house this old? Given."

Don and Amelia crossed the threshold together as Stonemother and Rockball, for as long as needed, shut the rest of the world outside.

THE WIZARD OF WASTED TIME

The raggedy man raised his hands toward heaven. "Great is my power. I shall enfold you with absolute despair! No water quench you, no sunlight touch you!"

Leon Matson considered the situation and let out a sigh. "How much?"

The panhandler didn't even blink. "Five bucks."

"All I've got is one."

The man looked hurt. "You're lying, spud."

Leon looked at the panhandler a little more closely, and it pained Leon a little to think of the man as old—he might have been a year or two younger than Leon's fifty-seven years. "Of course I'm lying, and so are you. You want it or not?"

The 'magician' grumbled but he reached out with one dirty hand and took the bill Leon offered. He wandered off then, mumbling about value and cheap sob's. Leon watched him go. He didn't feel relief. He didn't feel much of anything except the overwhelming numbness that had driven him out of his empty house and into the streets of Canemill in the first place.

The sun was moving toward afternoon when Leon found himself at Battlefield Park. Later in the evening there would be hookers and dealers and muggers and even darker manifestations of the urban economy, but it was still early yet. Leon felt the sun on his skin, watched it filter through the live oak and sycamore trees that still hadn't shed for winter. Soon though, he judged. The leaves were already starting to turn. Leon passed by the painted iron cannons and found an empty bench by the Fountain of Lost Dreams.

That was Leon's name for it. Battlefield Park was dedicated to an incident in the War of Northern Agression. It had cannons arranged in nothing like battle order, and a stone obelisk listing the names of the four men on each side who had died in a skirmish so minor it didn't even have a proper name. The fountain statue was different. It wasn't a soldier, or a cannon. It was a bronze woman, seated, a boy and a girl standing solemnly at her knee as she held the letter saying that her husband would not be marching home.

Leon dug into his pocket and pulled out the first coin he found, a shiny new nickel. He placed it on the top of his fist and snapped it spinning into the air with his thumb. The nickel landed in the fountain's basin with a surprisingly loud splash.

"Why did you do that?"

"For luck," he said, though he knew it was a lie. It took him a moment to realize the voice asking the question wasn't his own. He turned.

She sat on the edge of the fountain basin. A bag lady, with large shopping bags filled, apparently, with everything she owned. Leon thought she was older than he was at first, then younger, then he decided he just wasn't sure. Her blue sweater and dress were shabby; her hair covered with a blue and white kerchief was black with only a little gray, so far as he could see.

"Oh, hello. I didn't see you there," he said.

It occurred to Leon that he damn well *should* have seen her there; she was only a few feet away from his seat on the bench and in plain sight now. She must have been there all along, and he'd just tuned her out the way he and most everyone else tended to view the homeless, for such he took her to be. Part of the scenery, like a bush or fire hydrant.

"You didn't see me because I wasn't here before. Now I am," she said. She looked back at the water. "What makes you think you can buy luck with a nickel?"

"I don't, really. It's just . . . well, it's a fountain. It's what one does."

"Why?"

"I don't know," Leon said, beginning to get a little irritated. "Do you?"

"Of course," she said, not looking at him. "I come here when I feel down."

"That's not an answer."

"You didn't ask another question. You just asked if I knew, and I answered that one. Don't be stupid."

"Now see here, Ma'am—"

"Deborah. If you call me anything, call me by my name. I get so tired of 'bitch' and 'old lady' and 'hey you.'"

"I'm Leon. And I'm not the one who started—"

"School's out, school's out. Ring the bells and lock up the erasers. See me behind the gym, when I was very young and very fine. See me then. Now's no good to anyone." She smiled at him then. "I'm not crazy," she said. "Most of the time."

"I didn't say you were!"

"You're thinking it. Doesn't take a tin foil antenna and brain wave radios to know that."

Leon reddened just a bit. He didn't understand everything she'd said, but she'd called that one right. He started to get up. "I need to get going – "

"Oh, sit down, sirrah. I'm harmless as a fly and only slightly more irritating. I didn't mean to ruin your melancholy."

Leon settled back down. He wasn't sure it was a good idea, but from his years on the bench he knew a challenge when he saw one. "My what?"

"Your *melancholy*," she said with careful patience. "A state of reverie that's almost enjoyable with the right attitude. I thought you had it. That's why I didn't understand about the coin."

"I've never really thought about it. I suppose you think it's a waste of money."

Deborah shook her head. "Paying to shave off a poodle's coat and then buying it a sweater? *That's* a waste of money. Paying the average congressman more than minimum wage? *That's* a waste of money. A coin in the fountain is something else again."

He nodded. "I guess so. Someone who needs it more than I do can pluck it out."

She turned on him. "Do you think I'd steal that lousy nickel? How dare you!"

Leon just stared at her for a second. "I didn't mean . . . " he began, but of course he had. "Well, someone else."

Deborah shook her head. "No one will touch it. The park service cleans it out every so often and spends it. Not the same thing."

"If you say so."

She glared at him. "Give me two quarters," she said.

"Huh? Oh . . . " Leon's hand was in his pocket before it occurred to him to refuse. He brought out the requested coins and held them out to her. She took one in her right hand and one in her left.

"Watch the magic closely, please."

She closed her eyes for a few seconds. Her lips moved but he heard nothing. Finally, without looking, she dropped the coin in her right hand into the fountain. Leon watched the ripple it made, saw it lying shiny on the bottom of the fountain basin beside a small stone. Deborah took the other coin and placed it very carefully on the basin's wide rim.

Leon watched all this in silence. "So when does the magic start?"

"Mine already has. I made a wish. Yours happens when you come back tomorrow," she said, "and see which coin has disappeared."

She gathered up her bag and walked away without another word, and without looking at him. Leon did look at her, and he continued doing so until she was hidden by trees and distance.

Leon remained by the fountain for a while, eyeing the two coins, wondering if there was meaning to his encounter with Deborah or if it was just so much randomness.

"Either everything is random or nothing is. Those are your choices. Pick one." Leon smiled at the memory. Mary had been a great one for faith, and had done nothing, so far as Leon could remember, by half measures. It had made life with her interesting for as long as it had lasted. Which, he realized with a little surprise, was exactly ten years before to the day. Maybe there had been a reason he'd come to the fountain after all.

Leon thought about it a little too long. Evening came before he realized it and caught him there, like an unmoored jon boat floated off by a hard rain upriver. Leon didn't want to go home but he knew better than to stay in Battlefield Park after dark. The pleasantly cool breeze of the afternoon was turning chilly. He zipped up his coat and started back toward home.

"Well, hello, Judge! Remember me?"

The man came out of the trees or out of nowhere; Leon was never sure. He was just there, suddenly, in Leon's path, grinning a grin of pure malice. "Remember me?" he repeated, as his fist snaked out and struck Leon hard in the stomach. Leon bent over, trying to retch but could do nothing, nothing at all as the fist came down again, hard, on the side of his head and sent him spinning toward the sidewalk. He saw nothing, felt everything and everything was pain. He was vaguely aware of being kicked, hard, but after a moment even the blows and pain faded leaving nothing but the question, repeated: Remember?

Remember?

I won't.

Leon walked in the park. He moved slowly—his ribs were still healing—but his pace was steady.

The wizard was there. "Fear me, mortal! I can summon spirits from the vasty deep!"

Head down, avoid eye contact. Leon knew all the rules of paranoia. He didn't apply them now, any more than he ever had. "Summon spirits? 'Why, so can I. So can any man. But will they come when I call?'" Leon was a little pleased with himself for remembering his Shakespeare. He reached into his front pocket and pulled out a five, but the wizard refused it.

"You know the secret," he said. "We are brothers in art." He walked away, pointed at a more likely pair of pedestrians back on the sidewalk. Leon shrugged and put the money away. He kept walking.

Leon went to the fountain. That had been his goal all along. Through his time in the hospital, and the depositions, and two weeks of physical therapy, he never stopped wondering what he would see when he came to the fountain, whenever that would be.

The park service has probably emptied it by now.

But they hadn't. His quarter, not so shiny now, lay exactly where Deborah had dropped it almost a month to the day before. The one on the rim of the fountain, however, was gone. There had been a sense of inevitability about that which Leon now experienced to the fullest.

"I took that one myself," Deborah said. "After you left. With what I already had it was just enough for a cup of coffee."

Leon had heard her approach this time. It was little more than a faint rustle of leaves, like a breeze, but he knew she was coming. "I rather suspected that. So what was your point?"

"You get the living shit kicked out of you, and you still care about that little bit of business? And they call me crazy."

"He didn't kill me," Leon said. "So I still have to decide which event was more important, don't I? Life hurts; that's a given."

"Life is pain, then you die," she said, and that's all she said for a long time. "We all heard what happened. Did they catch the guy?"

"Hmmm? Oh, sure. Greg Matthew Coltman. Petty thief, sometime crack dealer I put away a few years ago. He knew he'd be caught." Leon shrugged.

"He also knows most of what he does on a daily basis will get him killed, sooner or later. He just doesn't care."

Deborah nodded, not looking up from the water. "You're a lot like him."

Leon stiffened. "How do you figure that?"

"You're not angry. You're not sad. You're just . . . not. I'm surprised you came back."

"I always visit the park in the afternoon."

"That's not what I meant. Not what you meant, either."

As he walked home, Leon wondered just how close had he come to dying during the attack. Close enough, the doctors said. He wasn't a young man, and an older body can't take the abuse a younger one could. Still, there was no question in Leon's mind that Coltman hadn't meant to kill him. Just hurt him, and let Leon know who had done it, consequences be damned. Coltman was already in custody. He'd be tried and convicted, and put away for a year or two. Five, if the judge had any leeway at all. It wouldn't make a lot of difference to Coltman one way or the other.

"You're a lot like him."

It was crazy. She was crazy. Leon told himself he'd already thought about both Deborah and what she said far too much. He wasn't a vicious thug like Coltman.

She didn't say vicious.

That was a technicality. Leon knew about those. Problem was, sometimes those ticky distinctions were important. Part of his job on the bench had been to decide when they were, but he was retired now.

Leon left the park and found the sidewalk that led up Morgan Street. There were almost as many trees along the street and sidewalk as there were in Battlefield Park. It was a genteel neighborhood, quite upscale at one time but turning shabby now as the city center declined. Maybe there would be one of the periodic rebuildings of downtown and the neighborhood's cachet would increase again, but just as probably not. It didn't matter. Mary hadn't wanted to move, and now he didn't either. Maybe it was just force of habit. He turned up his own sidewalk almost without knowing what he did. He unlocked the front door and went inside.

Mary was everywhere he looked.

Their wedding portrait hung on the wall; other pictures covered almost every surface: the mantel, the table, built-in bookcases. Leon stopped in front of the wedding portrait. He tried to reconcile the nervous young man in the portrait with the man he was now, and failed. He had a little better luck with Mary. No matter how much she changed over the years, he had always been able to see that same smiling nineteen-year-old girl looking back at him. Even after the dementia started, he could still see her there.

She'd forgotten who he was, had to be reminded every day, but that wasn't the worst. That happened the day he'd found her standing in the hallway, staring up at their wedding portrait with a look of pained concentration. After a while she'd shaken her head and looked at him, tears starting at the corners of her reddened eyes.

"Who is she?"

Leon took an early retirement; for three years he'd remembered for both of them, until the pain was just too much. She died two weeks to the day after he signed the commitment papers.

I couldn't last two more lousy weeks...

Instead he had left her with strangers, and she had died with them because Leon had been too slow to answer. The doctors said her system had just failed. Leon knew it was because there had been no one there to remember her, and when everyone forgets you—including yourself—what else is there?

Leon went and poured himself a Glenfiddich, neat. When he ran out of scotch he started on the bourbon.

"You look like hell," Deborah said.

Leon closed his eyes against the glare. "Nice to see you, too."

"I can summon spirits... Oh. Hello."

Leon opened his eyes, though the effort cost him. The imposter Glendower stood there by the fountain, his arms half-raised for the threatened incantation. He now lowered his arms, then sat down on the rim of the fountain. "Lovely day," he said.

"Hi, Bill," Deborah said. "How's the wizarding business?"

"It stinks," the crazed man said, though he sounded considerably less crazed than Leon remembered. "When you've only got one act for the groundlings it always plays thin. So. How's it hanging, spud?"

Leon smiled. He couldn't help it. "I've been better."

"No shit." Bill pulled a mostly empty bottle of Rebel Yell out of his coat pocket, offered it to Leon. "Hair of the dog," he said, "though in your case it might be more like 'scale of the leviathan.' How much did you drink, anyway?"

"All of it." Leon knew all the reasons he shouldn't have taken the bottle from Bill the homeless loon but he did it anyway. Leon took a polite swig and gave it back. He didn't feel much urge to drink now, but he wondered how long that would last.

Deborah refused the offer. "Thanks, Bill. My brain is in quite enough of a whirl as it is." She turned to Leon. "I suppose you expect us to feel sorry for you?"

Leon shook his head. "No. By your lights I've got pretty high-class worries, I suppose."

"Got it in one, Spud," Bill said. "Not that we're *happy* about what happened to you, mind, but when one of us gets beat up or worse it's not exactly news."

Deborah glared at him. "Save the sermon for Sunday, Billy," she said. "I wasn't talking about that."

Leon frowned. "Then what?"

"You tell me. You didn't drink up your liquor cabinet because you got beat up."

Leon found himself blushing. "Pain sounds like a good enough reason to me."

"Doctors got pills," Deborah said, "which they scatter among patients like a farmer sowing a field, and then they act surprised when the get a crop of junkies. You'll have a medicine chest full of pills, sirrah. You didn't need no booze. You don't have to tell me what the problem is. We all got problems. Bill's problem is he's an alky and won't fix it. My problem is I'm crazy and won't fix it. We share pain here by the fountain because that's a good way to handle pain. It don't mean we feel sorry for each other. That don't help."

" 'Pity is a burden carried by the victim, not the giver,' " Leon said.

"Who said that?" Bill asked.

Leon shrugged. "I dunno. Somebody. Sometime. And what do you mean, 'won't fix it?'"

"'How do you minister to a mind diseased?'" Bill asked.

"Doctors got pills," Deborah repeated. "Some of them even work."

The light dawned. "You're saying you won't take your meds."

"That's it, Spud. She won't. Now me, I take mine every day and twice on Sunday." Bill unscrewed the cap from his bottle and guzzled what was left. He threw it with a surprisingly graceful overhand that landed the bottle in a trash can twenty feet away. "Need more medicine," he said, and wandered away. Leon thought of offering him money, then wondered if that was a good idea, and again, in the end, did nothing as Bill disappeared into the trees. Deborah just looked at the fountain.

"She got on, you know."

"Who?"

Deborah nodded at the statue. "Her. Them."

"How do you know that?"

Deborah looked at him as if he were being deliberately dim. "Because she didn't have any choice. It was either survive or die, and people tend to do what they have to do. I didn't say it was pretty, or nice, but when I look at her, I know. And I don't worry about her. Not one bit."

"Then why come to the fountain at all?"

"To remind myself, Judge Leon, that being crazy isn't the worst thing that can happen to a person, and that person still survive."

"I'm not a judge now."

""Judge not lest ye be judged.' Too late. You do. You are. As are we all."

Leon wasn't sure if that part was supposed to make sense or not, but he was afraid that it did. "I suppose so."

"So why do you come here?" Deborah asked.

"Maybe for the same reason as you."

"We share pain by the fountain; I told you. You don't share anything."

"There's nothing to share."

"Like hell. Who was she?"

Leon blinked. "I don't understand."

"Sure you do. Unless you're into boys, and I rather doubt that. Everyone's got pain. Some more, some less, but it all feels like more to the one who's got it. Yours must feel like an elephant; Bill's an alky and even *he* wouldn't pull the stunt you did with your liquor cabinet. Who you trying to kill yourself for?"

"It was just a bender. I'm over it now."

She nodded. "Sure you are."

"I don't think you believe me."

"So? I'm just a loony on the street, and my name is Legion. Lie or don't lie; suit yourself. Live. Die. There's no pity here; I told you that, too. Weren't you listening?"

"Yes," he said, a little surprised that he did remember that part. "I'm not after pity."

"What, then?"

"I don't know."

Deborah looked pleased. "There's honesty, if ever I saw it. Figure it out, Judge Leon. It's not like you've got anything better to do. Maybe Bill can help."

"Why Bill?"

"Bill's a wizard. I thought you knew that. A master."

"The wizarding bit I heard about, but master? Of what?" Leon asked.

"Wasted time. That's his specialty. He wastes time even better than you do."

She got up and left him there. Leon sat by himself for a while, but this time he didn't stay past sunset. He wasn't even tempted.

I still don't know what I want. But maybe death isn't it.

Leon called in favors. As a municipal court judge he'd tended to accumulate them like used pens, and with about as much thought. Now he decided to see what they were worth, and they were worth quite a bit.

"Deborah Sayer McNaught," he said, when he returned to the fountain.

"Age?" she asked, without missing a beat.

"Umm . . . Forty-seven."

She nodded. "You've been looking in the trash."

Leon started to protest, but then thought about it and realized she was more or less right about that. "Well, all right, I admit it: I'm curious about you."

"You could have asked."

"You might have said no. Or nonsense."

"I might," she said pleasantly. "You'll never know now, will you? Nor, for that matter, will I. That's two of us you've robbed at once, Judge Leon. Coltman seldom did so well."

"I wanted to help you," he said, softly. "I didn't know what or how. I thought maybe more information would let me figure that part out."

"You are an arrogant bastard, you know that? You can't even help *yourself* at the moment, and you think you can rescue bag ladies? Hah. Princesses in the coils of the baddest dragon Grimm ever imagined got *nothing* on us. Rescue from what? The world? Ourselves? It doesn't work that way."

"Then how does it work, Deborah? I really would like to know."

She laughed, but there was nothing harsh or mocking about it. It sounded almost . . . sweet. "Hah. I had that part figured you think I'd be scrounging burger joint trash for breakfast?"

"Well," he said, "at least that's one dragon I might be able to skin. Come on."

Leon took her to a sidewalk cafe near the park. In deference to Deborah's unwashed state and the other patrons, they ate outside. Other than that it was like a thousand lunchtime conversations Leon remembered, and more pleasant than most.

"I don't know how long I'll be with you, if you know what I mean," Deborah said between bites of a smothered steak, "I've been feeling a bit peculiar today."

"You always feel that way before . . . ?" He didn't finish.

"Before I start channeling space aliens?" She winked at him. "I'm always a little off, but yeah, there's usually a warning of some kind. I've learned to pay attention."

"And there are medications for your condition and you won't take them. That's what Bill said."

"Right."

"Why not? I'm asking."

"Only because your snooping didn't give you the answer," she said. "Well, that's as may be. The answer is: none of your damn business. I mean, thanks for the food and all, but that was your idea. I don't owe you anything."

Leon shrugged. "I'm still asking."

"And it's still none of your business."

"Let me ask you something else, then: would you like a bath?"

"I stink, huh?"

"Yes, but that wasn't the question. I'm asking you—would you like a bath?"

"Yes," she said. "I would *love* a bath. So what?"

"Come home with me, Deborah, and you can have one. As hot and as long as you'd like. I'm pretty sure some of my wife's clothes will fit you—"

Leon couldn't tell if there was more shock or disgust showing on her face then. "You've mistaken me, sirrah. I am a bag lady, not a whore."

"You've mistaken *me*," Leon said firmly. "Coltman's left me broken in several places and bruised everywhere else. Doc says I so much as sneeze in the next six weeks I risk coming apart at the joints. I'm no threat to you, Deborah. Sexual or otherwise."

"There are threats and then there are threats." She bit her lip. "Don't matter. Tomorrow I'd just get dirty again. I'm used to dirt, Judge Leon."

"No doubt. Do you prefer it?"

She scowled. "No."

Leon didn't see Deborah take the glass cat. It was only later, after she'd rejected his offers of the spare bedroom with some vague mumble about "open shelter" and left, that he noticed. A very small thing. Something he wouldn't have noticed himself, except he had changed nothing of what his wife had done to the living room decor except to dust now and then. Everything in its place, and the one thing that was not in its place jumped out at him like a panther from a thicket.

Leon was a little surprised; during his years on the bench he'd proven time and again that he was a more than fair judge of character, and he'd have sworn on any number of Bibles that Deborah was not a thief. Yet even more strange than the theft itself was what had been stolen. Deborah had been alone in several parts of the house, at one time or another. His curiosity growing, Leon methodically checked anywhere valuables were kept, including an unlocked box with a substantial sum of cash in it. Nothing had been touched.

Just that little glass cat. Nothing else.

It didn't make sense by any measure he applied to it, but it did raise questions. Another thing Leon's time on the bench had taught him was that knowing all the answers usually wasn't as important as asking the right questions. The next afternoon he came to the park early. He waited for a long time, but Deborah finally showed up.

She looked a little rumpled, after whatever sleeping place she'd found the night before, but Mary's slacks and sweater fit her fairly well. Her hair was red, with only a few strands of gray. Perhaps it was just the fact that it was much cleaner now, but he'd never really noticed her hair before.

"You're always here," she said. It sounded like a complaint.

"I need to talk to you," Leon said.

"Do I need to talk to you? Who are you? Leave me alone!"

Leon looked into her eyes but could read nothing there except confusion and a touch of fear. "I'm Leon."

"Judge."

It was there for a moment: recognition. It was a fragile thing, and Leon reached for it with the only means he had. "It's about the cat, Deborah."

She blinked. "Cat?"

"The carnival glass cat. The one that sat on my mantel for the last twenty years."

"Knick-knack paddywack give a cat a home," Deborah said, brightly. "Maybe it's a stray."

Leon shook his head. *Oh, no you don't. Not with me.* "You're hiding, Deborah. Hiding in your madness. You know very well what I'm talking about."

"Him lost his pretty? Buy another. Him got money."

"It's not about the cat or the money, Deborah. It's about you."

"Me?"

She blinked at him. Shocked, perhaps, out of the madness. Or the mask of it. Leon wasn't sure, but this was no time for hesitation.

"The cat was a cheap knick-knack, like you said. There were many more valuable things you could have taken, Deborah. Why the cat?"

"I didn't take it," she said clearly, but she was just as clearly lying. Leon waited, saying nothing. "All right. Guilty. I plead it. You gon' have me arrested?"

"You can have the damn cat; it's not valuable. I want to know why you took it."

"Maybe as a souvenir of my first hot bath in six months."

" 'Maybe' isn't an answer."

She smiled. "I'll cut you a deal, Judge. Plea bargain. You tell me why you tried to drink yourself to death the other night—the unvarnished truth—and I'll tell you about the damn cat. That's fair."

Deborah sat down on the bench beside him and waited, looking demure and smug. She clearly expected him to refuse. Leon wanted to do just that, but it occurred to him that he didn't have the right. "I killed my wife," he said. "I was trying to forget that."

Deborah frowned. "Your wife died in a hospital," she said, and then it was Leon's turn to be surprised. Deborah grinned wickedly. "I'll put my grapevine up against yours any day of the week, Judge."

"Fine, she died in a hospital. That doesn't mean it wasn't my fault." Leon told her the whole story, leaving nothing, sparing nothing. Especially himself.

"Sad," was Deborah's sole comment. Then, "All right, Judge—a deal's a deal. I took the cat because I used to have one just like it. I guess I missed it. I didn't know that I did until I saw yours. So I took it. I'm sorry."

Ask the right question. Leon took a deep breath. "Why did you lose your cat?"

"Because I lost the house."

"I didn't ask 'how,' Deborah. I asked 'why.' Stop hiding and tell me the truth."

"You want truth? Here it is—my husband left me! I couldn't afford the house on my own, and I didn't have any other skills or family. I wound up here. Sad? Yes. Unusual? Hell, no. Happy now, yer honor?"

Leon shook his head. "Those are the facts. Now I want the truth. They aren't always the same; if I didn't learn anything else from twenty years on the bench, I learned that. So why did your husband leave?"

"Because he didn't want to be married to a loon! Even after . . . " She didn't finish. Leon made his best guess and finished for her.

"Even after you were examined by competent doctors. Even after you both discovered what I already suspected, and called in some favors to find out—there's nothing wrong with you, Deborah. You're a character and a half by anyone's measure, but that's it. You're basically fine."

"Fine?" She seemed to ponder the word. "No. Not fine. He wouldn't have left—"

"Maybe that was just his excuse."

"I wasn't fine! I was crazy. Ask anyone," Deborah looked at Leon with a gaze as heavy as all the weight of the world. "Ask him," she said, finally.

"I'm asking you," Leon said.

"Go to hell," Deborah said, and looked as if she meant it.

"Not an option. We had a deal, remember? My pain for yours, and I don't think I've got my half of the bargain yet. The cat represented something you'd lost, that's all. Something you didn't know you missed. It hurts to remember, doesn't it?"

Deborah pulled the cat out of her tattered purse. She looked at it this way and that. "It's just a knick-knack. Glass. No heart in glass." She opened her hand and the cat tumbled out, dropping for the hard stone of the fountain's edge. Leon darted forward and caught it at the last second, then collapsed on the bench as pain wracked him.

"I-I shouldn't have done that."

Deborah nodded, her eyes wide. "No, you shouldn't. Why did you? You said the cat wasn't important! Were you lying?"

He shook his head, and handed the glass figurine back to Deborah. "I said it wasn't *valuable*. I never ... never said it wasn't important. It is, or you wouldn't have taken it."

"You're a weird one," Deborah said, but she carefully put the carnival cat back in her purse. "Come on, I'll help you home." She helped Leon stand, and offered her shoulder to lean on while he found his balance. "Should I call someone?"

He shook his head. "I just need some aspirin and some rest. I'll be fine."

"Good for you," Deborah said.

He looked at her then. "I'll tell you one thing about your ex-husband, Deborah. I never met the man, but I know this much for fact and truth."

"Yeah?"

"He was a damn fool."

She shook her head and sighed. "Take *lots* of aspirin, Judge," she said. "Pain's got you crazy, too."

At the Fountain of Lost Dreams Leon found Bill the Wizard of Wasted Time trying to turn a pigeon into a rat. He wasn't doing very well. The pigeon simply perched on the head of the statue of the bereaved wife and mother. It eyed the human wreck gesticulating before it with something like disdain.

"Don't you think turning a pigeon into a rat is rather redundant?" Leon asked finally.

"Yeah," Bill said. "That's why I thought it would be easy, even for weak magic. Small difference, and all that. Can't say it's turned out that way, though."

"You really want to work magic, don't you? It's not just an act."

Bill shrugged. "A man needs a purpose. A foolish one will do, as history tells us. So. What's your excuse?"

"You mean Deborah, don't you?"

"None other. Are you in love with her?"

Leon almost took a step back. "Am I what?"

"It was a simple question, Spud. I thought maybe you were. You don't strike me as the user type, but you are interested in her. After all, I don't notice you trying to rescue *me*. There are other people on the street that could benefit from your munificence, you know."

"Maybe. You're not one of them. At least, not until you decide to stop drinking."

Bill smiled, showing the gaps in his teeth. "You're smarter than you look, but wisdom has many forms."

Leon stretched carefully and then sat down on the bench in his usual spot. "Some judges could work a dozen cases at once and keep an army of law clerks busy finding precedents and case studies. Me, I took them one at a time. I don't start reading a new book before I've finished the last one. I'm linear, and unimaginative, but I am also damned thorough. That's my wisdom, such that it is."

Bill inclined his head in something like a bow. "Well, then. So long as we're sharing at the fountain I'll tell you mine—you can't help Deborah, either. Whether you're doing it out of honest concern or to atone before whatever gods there are for what you did to your wife, it don't matter. Prospero's books and Caliban's mother couldn't help her."

Leon shrugged. "You're right. I can't."

"Then why bother?"

"Because I'm trying to get to know someone who can."

"You're avoiding me," Leon said. "You haven't been to the fountain in a week."

Deborah looked up at him from the depths of a sagging refrigerator box. "No solicitors," she said. "Didn't you see the sign?"

"Someone must have stolen it."

They were in an alley behind one of the local appliance superstores, one of an endless "sale every week" and perpetrator of the "jovial commercial host not nearly so appealing as he thinks" variety.

"I can't deal with your pain, Judge. I've decided. Go away."

"Then let's talk about yours. Isn't that what the fountain is about?"

Deborah pointed at a leaking pipe-faucet by the loading dock door. "This look like a fountain to you? What I got is mine. Ain't sharing. Gonna be selfish for a while."

Leon put his hands on his hips. "Occurs to me, Deborah Sayer Mc-Naught, that you've been selfish for a long time already."

"My whole name. Damn. Even my mother didn't do that. What are you babbling about?"

"You. You blame your divorce on your being crazy, and then you try your best to go crazy to prove it. You deprive your ex-husband of his God-given right to be an asshole. That's not selfish?"

"You weave nice words, Judge. Do they keep you warm? Doubt it."

Leon smiled. "You hide well. Does it keep you safe? Doubt that, too."

She sighed. "What do you want from me, Judge? I got nothing anyone needs."

"Liar. You've still got the cat, don't you? And you need that."

"I do not! I'll smash it," she said, looking grim. "I swear I will. You won't be able to catch it this time."

"I don't want to catch it."

She took it out. "It'll break easy."

Leon nodded. "It should. It's delicate. Worth keeping, though. Now that you've found it again. It's all up to you, just like always."

"You're babbling."

"No, I'm leaving. I'm going to the fountain. You do what you want."

"I won't stay away. Not for you."

It was three weeks almost to the day since Leon had found Deborah in that cardboard box. Leon had come to the park every day since, rain or shine. He knew about patience.

"I'm not asking you to."

"Right. Don't ask me anything. I don't want to talk to you at all."

"Fine."

Deborah sat on the fountain. She looked at the statue, as she usually did. "She was ok," she said aloud. "I know she was."

Leon said nothing for several long moments. The silence seemed empty, needing something to fill it. Leon waited.

Deborah sighed. "You do try a girl's patience, Judge . . . I didn't say that *you* couldn't talk."

"But not to you?"

"Not to me, no. Now, then, let's try that once more: She was ok," Deborah said again, slowly, "I *know* she was."

"She wasn't all right at first," Leon said aloud, to no one in particular. "And maybe not for a long time after. But she was stronger than she knew. She survived. Then she got better."

"I can summon spirits from the vasty deep!"

Bill shambled up, reeking of beer and less pleasant things.

"Hi, Bill," Deborah said. "We're talking, but not to each other. Care to join us?"

The Wizard of Wasted Time stared at them for a moment, blearily. "Oh, it's you two again. Kiss kiss. Get a room."

"Bite me," said Deborah.

Instead, Bill sat down and began to conjure spirits from the vasty deep of the fountain. All that rose to the surface was an old label from a Jack Daniels bottle. Still, it did rise. They all saw it.

"Rather puny, as spirits go," Deborah said, mostly to herself.

"I think it's like the coin in the fountain," Leon said aloud and to no one in particular.

" 'Why is an old bottle label like a coin in a fountain' is a riddle. I might ask for the answer," Deborah said. "If I were asking for the answers to riddles. Which I am not."

"If I were answering riddles," Leon said, "I might say that it only means that there comes a time in a person's life when they have to decide how much magic is enough."

Bill just smiled a cryptic smile. No one said anything else for a while, but all agreed—if not to each other—that for right now what little magic they had would have to do.